LAST HUMMINGBIRD WEST OF CHILE
"The writing is pellucid, the sentences beautifully balanced.
Reading is effortless. Nary a bump on the road.

Have you ever read an author whose voice is so potent
that your own voice bends to it, takes on its rhythms and syntax?
And so you proceed through your day hearing events
narrated in the voice of this newly discovered author who has
you under his or her spell? This is what happened to me
reading *Hummingbird*."

—JESSICA GRANT, AUTHOR OF *COME, THOU TORTOISE*

ACCLAIM FOR NICHOLAS RUDDOCK'S SHORT FICTION

"Esther" (winner, 2017 Bridport Prize for Short Fiction)
"It has real humanity to it, and a tremendous cumulative power,
conjuring the lives of its protagonists in a handful of pages,
allowing us to live beside them for years, and ensuring
that the final emotional pay off, played out over a single long
sentence, is utterly devastating." —PETER HOBBS

"Mario Vargas Llosa" (winner, 2015 Carter V. Cooper Prize, *Exile Quarterly*)
"To discover, in an often-lyrical prose, a magical new continent that
are the lives of Latin American immigrants in Toronto, one of
North America's largest, swarming cities, is daring, and took great
imaginative gumption." —GLORIA VANDERBILT

"Squid"
"It inhabits and reflects a charged, liminal state:
between innocence and experience, youth and age, solitude
and community, life and art." —STEPHANIE BOLSTER

"How Eunice Got Her Baby"
"Darker, but also imbued with a charming sing-song voice…
buoyed by the local rhythms of speech and thought,
Ruddock has a refined ear for dia⸻⸻⸻⸻
sense of humour." —D⸻

"Sculpin," "Telescope," and "Burin"
"A remarkable triad of prose-poems, so finely executed that
they seem burnished, compressed and elegant."
— ANNE SIMPSON

"The Housepainters"
"Accomplished, original, witty, and wise…
a wonderful piece of writing." — HELEN HUMPHREYS

"The Steamer"
"Nobody can mistake the ingenuity of Nicholas Ruddock…
terrific read, talent to burn." — MADELEINE THIEN

"Genetic Memory"
"Allows us to simultaneously exist in the past, present, and future."
— CLAUDIA RANKINE

PRAISE FOR NICHOLAS RUDDOCK'S PREVIOUS NOVELS

NIGHT AMBULANCE
"Nicholas Ruddock strips away the politics and policies
that have trapped and defined women for decades and gets
to the heart of the people who live with these decisions.
[He] reveals a world controlled by men….and the women who
navigate this system…Ruddock's tense warning could easily
be a vision of the future in a novel as poignant
as it is painfully hopeful."
— LINDSAY RAINING BIRD, *ATLANTIC BOOKS TODAY*

THE PARABOLIST
"Comic and inventive." – *EDMONTON JOURNAL*

"*The Parabolist* has a strong push that
will keep your heart beating until the end." – *GLOBE AND MAIL*

"Dazzling…an exciting, compelling, and expertly layered mystery."
— ANTHONY DE SA

"Passionate, offhand, deeply charming and deeply original."
— DAMIAN TARNOPOLSKY

LAST HUMMINGBIRD WEST OF CHILE

LAST
HUMMI
WEST OF
☪HILE

NGBIRD

NICHOLAS RUDDOCK

BREAKWATER

BREAKWATER
P.O. Box 2188, St. John's, NL, Canada, A1C 6E6
WWW.BREAKWATERBOOKS.COM

COPYRIGHT © 2021 Nicholas Ruddock
ISBN 978-1-55081-884-0

A CIP catalogue record for this book is available from Library and Archives Canada

We acknowledge the support of the Canada Council for the Arts.
We acknowledge the financial support of the Government of Canada through
the Department of Heritage and the Government of Newfoundland and
Labrador through the Department of Tourism, Culture, Arts and Recreation
for our publishing activities.

PRINTED AND BOUND IN CANADA.

Breakwater Books is committed to choosing papers and materials for our
books that help to protect our environment. To this end, this book is printed
on recycled paper that is certified by the Forest Stewardship Council®.

The fallow deer, the wary fox, the yew, the spider, the servant girl.

1832

CLOVIS OLDHAM, 16

Miss Albertson told me that every baby is born into peril, squeezed earthward by the instinctive contractions of the womb, pushed down into a rigid girdle of bone. The baby's chest cannot expand. The umbilical cord wraps itself as a ligature around the throat. The head might prove too large to pass. "With that in mind, dear girl," she said, "any woman would be wise to measure the circumference of her lover's head before yielding to him, should she wish to live past seventeen."

Such were her cautionary words as she sent me, the youngest of the chambermaids, to the third-floor bedroom of the manor house. There I was to stand motionless, warm blankets in my arms, as Lady Amberley, well advanced in labour, produced her first child.

But those instructions proved impossible to follow. In the first place, the Earl, the father, had been drinking in the library. His excessive laughter filled the stairway, causing visible discomfort to all attending. Secondly, the doctor, on arriving, immediately thrust me front and centre, saying, "Take up the lamp, Clovis— that is your name?—turn the wick up high, stand by my side, shed light upon the vestibule. Do not let your hand shake, no matter the provocation." So there I was, unexpectedly in a position of importance, watching the crowning of the head, the gushing forth of the child's body in a shocking stream of fluid. But then, instead of joy filling the room, desolation ensued. The child was grossly malformed, limp, pale, glistening. Nor did he—I spied the tiny penis—cry out. The Lady, her leg-drapes having slipped to the floor, began to weep as any mother would, after such a fruitless effort.

The doctor then suggested, motioning with his eyes, that I pick up the child, wrap him in a coverlet and whisk him from the room. I was about to comply when in rushed the Earl to find his firstborn, his heir, moribund. He fell to his knees, tore at his hair, called his wife "a barren field." Next he rushed past us in a whiskey-driven wind and we heard, from below, the repetitive sound of glass shattering.

Then the doctor whispered, "By heaven, I can see the crowning of a second head!" We jumped to attention. One chambermaid was dispatched to recall the father and another to fetch the family solicitor, whose presence was mandatory, according to the doctor, at the birth of twins. Why, I did not know. Nor could I speculate upon it, for once again I was Lady of the Lamp, and the doctor was spreading a fresh white sheet— "for modesty," he said, though he was the only man present— over the mother's thighs. Next he confessed, surveying the tip of the new baby's head, that he was out of his depth, that perhaps we should send for the midwife, Mrs. Mason, from the village. An admirable decision, I thought, for I had heard of doctors pretending capability when they had none, with unfortunate results.

A man from the stables was therefore dispatched to the village with four of the finest horses and the finest carriage. Such luxury, I thought, for Mrs. Mason, but she was deserving of it, for her years of service. Then Miss Albertson—raising an eyebrow when she spotted my promotion—ushered in a second team of housemaids to carry away the soiled linen, mop the floor, rush back and forth with fresh towels, carry jugs of warm water. Meanwhile, I stood with my lamp, wondering at the marvel of women's bodies in childbirth, how one indignity after the next was inflicted upon them while men were left to laughter and drinking. Hardly fair, I thought, at the same time joining the others in a coordinated exhortation to our Lady to "push, push, push!"

But her capabilities in that regard had been exhausted. She seemed no longer to grasp her purpose. Fortunately, we then heard a ruckus on the stairs and Mrs. Mason burst into the room. "Whatever is going on here!" she said, and she ripped away the sheet of modesty, casting it to one side. She washed her hands in a basin of soapy water, made several adroit adjustments at the Lady's vestibule, hooked her index finger deep within and pulled with force downward, the muscles of her forearm bunching with strain. Out popped, thirty seconds later, a healthy girl-child caught by the midwife and the doctor together as they battled for primacy, jostling against each other. Several of the chambermaids clapped their hands in jubilation. Then, however, as though he were an Australian boomerang, back came the Earl to lean against the door jamb, slurring his words, saying "A girl? Of no account." So callous were those words that I nearly called out "Sir!" but I was saved from certain dismissal by the appearance of a firm hand on the Earl's right shoulder, pulling him upright, turning him around, shaking him in a friendly but authoritative manner. The family solicitor had arrived, a tall and handsome man, composed, smiling, and to all of us he announced, "I have brought my materials."

From an inner pocket of his jacket he produced a tangle of coloured threads, blue, green, and red, cut no doubt from individual skeins of wool. "Return the first-born," he said, "still-birthed or not," and the little body, wrapped in muslin, was hurried back from the kitchen. To one of the ankles peeping out, the solicitor applied a blue thread, and then, to the living girl's kicking foot, he applied a green thread, in two separate and dignified ceremonies that drew an outcry from the Earl, "What a charade! A thread? To distinguish the living from the dead, a boy from a girl?"

I had to agree with him, but the solicitor then spoke up, explaining that first-born males of noble families inherited the name, the land, the fortune, and although such practice was a lamentable remnant of feudal times, nevertheless it was his mandate, as an officer of the court, to ensure that no babies in his jurisdiction were ever shuffled at birth. "He who arrives first," he said—*he* being the operative word, I noticed—"should never be placed second or third, for if he were, he could be cheated of his inheritance by a dark uncle, a plotting cousin, a mincing priest, as happened recently in Suffolk. With the application of these coloured threads—imagine if there were two lusty boys, one directly on the heels of the other!—I have formally established the birth order of the Amberleys, and, duty done"—he rubbed his hands together—"would the Earl not retire with me downstairs, to settle my account? My own invention, the threads, I should add."

Barely had they left the room, however, when Mrs. Mason said, calmly, that a third child was on the way. Discretion and modesty having been long since cast to the wind, each and every chambermaid came to my side to peer over my shoulder. "Good Lord," they said, or variations thereof. Lady Amberley then gathered strength from some distant well of motherhood. She pushed vigorously, and a perfectly formed little boy popped into our world, lively with crying, quick with movement. The solicitor rushed back upstairs and placed a third string, red, upon the ankle. "How wondrous these twins, such beautiful, lovely creatures!" He then went to the mother's side, bent to her, touched her hand and spoke so softly to her, I could not hear.

His kindness brought tears to my eyes. But then the Earl reappeared at his elbow and became completely unmoored. Pointing a shaky finger at the babies, he claimed that they had deprived his first-born of oxygen and nutrients in the womb. He then rushed silently at them, intending to do them harm, and surely he would have succeeded had the solicitor not jumped into his path, fragments of threads falling to the floor as they sparred and pushed and danced against each other. Two chambermaids, holding little bundles, ran from the room. Mrs. Mason grasped the Earl's shirt from behind and, as he was not a big man, she swung him in a circle until he fell to the floor. There he sat, unabashed, but lacking coordination to continue.

"Horrible man!" I whispered, hating him for his insensitivity at the moment, and even more for what he had done to me personally. Two weeks in his service and already he had taken liberties slipping his hand up my skirt, probing as I reached for a spider on the leaded windows of the library. Timidly I froze, twisting away when it was far too late. I ran to the kitchen, to Miss Albertson. "Clovis," she said, "whatever is the matter, your cheeks are on fire!" "Oh, nothing," I said, "I just need a drink of water." There he now was, helpless on the floor. I felt like stabbing him with the nearby knife, already used to cut the birth cords. Do it, Clovis, do it, I thought, but I stayed my hand. I feared the hangman. As it was, the solicitor intervened, helping the Earl to his feet, ushering him from the room.

Later, in the kitchen, I confessed my murderous impulse to Miss Albertson. I even asked her, casting shyness aside, "Has he ever put his hand up your skirt, does he treat you as a chattel?" She did not actually say yes, but I think that was her answer for she stood up abruptly, said that she was twenty-six years of age, that she had seen enough.

"Who would discover us anyway, Clovis, if we did kill him?"

"No one," I said, "if we are clever." We opened an upper drawer for the two largest knives at hand—those for dismembering pigs—and together in our slippers we set out for the upper reaches of the manor house, where all were fast asleep. We stepped quietly, weightlessly, as women of no account must do.

MISS ALBERTSON, 26

We held our knives reversed in our grips, blades resting against our forearms wrist to elbow, tucked into the sleeves of our nightgowns. Dawn was hours away. The night was moonless, only owls could be peering within. We proceeded cautiously upon the carpeted floor towards the suite of five guest bedrooms, in one of which, we were certain, we would find the Earl. It was his habit to collapse there on nights of inebriation, to flop fully clothed upon one bedspread or another, to snore, to urinate upon himself, to walk out unashamed in the morning.

After opening the third door, we found him lying face-down, fallen to the floor. We knelt to his side. Vapours of sour brandy rose to us like a pestilence. To breathe, we turned our heads aside but then returned to our task, taking our knives from our sleeves in unison, sharing a glance. As the elder, my turn came first. "Exemplar," I whispered, "do your duty." But rather than stab frantically, I pressed the tip of my blade first to his clothing, to feel for the space between his ribs. Then I pushed more firmly, penetrating layers one by one, first linen then wool then linen again. Finally the elastic resistance of flesh announced itself. "Now," I said, and I advanced the tip forcefully with a quick thrust to the hilt, hoping to strike the heart or major vessel. Strangely, he did not move, nor alter his breathing. I withdrew the blade. Clovis then inserted her knife from her side, though more quickly, with the same result. "Abandon caution?" I suggested.

She answered by striking down firmly mid-thorax, and I followed suit until at least a dozen penetrations had been made. Finally he took notice, gasping, trying to rise, spinning like a bug in a quarter-circle on the carpet. It was then that we realized that our victim was not the Earl but the Friar, a man of similar build, portly, who must have been called to the manor, unbeknownst to us, to pray for the stillborn.

Realizing our mistake, yet knowing we must finish, we accelerated our aggression with a sequence of rapid thrusts to the front of his chest. By then he was sitting up, eyes rolling like marbles. "Mercy!" he cried out once, but a hemorrhage rushed from his lips and spilled down his cloak, choking him. Our fingers by then were as slippery as eels. Clovis lost her grip upon her weapon, retrieved it, struck him again, until finally he uttered a wracking sigh and tumbled to his final rest, supine, arms and legs akimbo.

The stink of brandy was even stronger upon us. Clovis said we should open a window. "Yes," I said, "that one, Clovis, for it will provide access for a murderer." "I hope he has not suffered unduly," she said. "Don't worry your pretty head about that," I said, "he is as bad as the Earl. He has fathered four children with his housekeeper, only to deliver them to the orphanage." We wiped the blades of our knives against his garments. We rose to our feet. A spatter of rain lashed against the window frame. One of the babies cried from the distant nursery. We tiptoed downstairs to the kitchen, and there we submerged our weapons in soapy water, dried them, aligned them neatly in their drawer. Then we removed our bloodstained gowns, bundled them, watched them catch fire upon the coals of the stove. Naked, averting our eyes, we scrubbed our hands and arms, thighs and ankles, covered ourselves next with clean tablecloths from the pantry. Pale as ghosts, we swore fealty to each other, promising to tell the same lie. We were fast asleep in our beds, we heard nothing. "Good night, Clovis," I said, clasping her in my arms, feeling her heart beat against mine.

CLOVIS OLDHAM, 16

Early the next morning came the expected drama. The local constable arrived at noon hour, asking that all residents of the manor be brought together at the scene of the crime. The Friar was still there, lying in a pool of blood thickened to the consistency of custard. Several of the staff had already fainted and were being revived by salts. Miss Albertson and I, however, were clear-headed, expressing our amazement, saying, "Heavens!" The constable asked if anyone knew where the Earl was. "Perhaps he is the murderer," I suggested, "absconded." Miss Albertson was about to wholeheartedly agree when the young footman, Emerson Callaghan—with whom, by the way, I had taken several walks on Sunday afternoons, to the verge of the forest— said that he had personally placed the Earl upon a horse shortly after the birth of the third child. He had watched him canter away to the southeast, barely keeping to the saddle. So, a perfect alibi. The investigator then surveyed the room and said confidently that the killer must be present. The window had been open, the drainpipe was sturdy enough to support a grown man, but there were no footprints in the soil below. In his experience, even master criminals could not fly. "He has died of multiple stabbings, and I have found large knives in the kitchen. Could they be the weapons? Miss Albertson?" He looked directly at her and she replied, giving not an inch, "Pig knives, Sir, for disarticulating pigs, and yes, we keep them in the kitchen, in the top drawer." "Bring them to me," he commanded, and Miss Albertson did so, taking no longer than a minute away. He examined each blade with a magnifying glass. Then he bent and inserted, gruesomely, the largest knife into a major wound in the Friar's right side, through the clothing. He inserted a smaller blade into a cut at the base of the throat. I felt warm, vertiginous. Another of the chambermaids fainted. Miss Albertson, however, remained bright as a daisy, and she spoke up to say that a cat-burglar must have gained access to the manor by the front door, come upon the Friar on the stairway, killed him out of fright, dragged him to the bedroom. The investigator, smiling, said that in his experience cat-burglars set out with their own weapons at hand. "And look," he said, "the fit of these pig knives is astoundingly perfect, not only in wound A"—he pointed to it—"but also in wound B, down to the very characteristic whorl on this handle, imprinted on this patch of dried blood, above the clavicle." So what, I thought. Miss Albertson and I had nothing to fear. Unless we broke rank and confessed, he would never know.

He would never know unless walls and floors and the night itself could talk, and only my grandfather believed that possible. "I have heard the trees whispering to each other a thousand times, Clovis," he said, "and never do they sound the same."

1851 NINETEEN YEARS LATER

QUERCUS ALBA, 251

I was a tree, a white oak, one of a countless number in the Adirondack Mountains. We were integral members of the Carolinian forest, stretching as far as we could see. Perhaps, for all we knew, we went on forever. At any rate, there we were, rolling in dark green over the dips and valleys of the earth in all directions, covering the longest hills in undulations unbroken but for the odd cliff face or waterfall. In autumn our green changed to yellow-red, and then we were bare and black in winter, presenting a more sombre, windswept landscape. Pockets of conifers stood out as daub-slashes of blue-green or, if weighted down with snow, they were white. I burst to life, presumably, from a single acorn planted by a squirrel, a morsel of intended food. But, as chance would have it, my squirrel forgot me, as squirrels are prone to do. They are good at planting, but are even better at forgetting.

My taproot took hold. It burrowed into sandy loam and was incubated under layers of bent grass and fallen leaves. I grew three inches in my first year. Then, for two hundred years, I added annually a growth ring to my heartwood and became—speaking modestly—a straight and solid adult member of the forest, a *Quercus alba* of impressive, unmeasurable mass, my height one hundred and twenty feet, my circumference at base sixteen feet. I was surrounded by similar trees, hundreds of us. My squirrel must have had a legion of friends planting and forgetting, planting and forgetting, until there we were, fully grown, majestic, magical, a breathing forest impervious to storms, lightning strikes, hurricanes, drought, the ravages of insects. Our roots locked themselves into earth, intertwined. Raindrops from the canopy nourished us, trickling to the river that glittered in the sun and bent to the southeast, its water as clear as air, its source fifty miles north, a lake known as Tear of the Clouds. Decade after decade, we bore witness to the choral voices of insects, birds, animals, vines, flowers, stones. We heard rustlings and buzzings, woodpeckering, chip-chipping, scuttering. We knew the habits of chipmunks, the canny fox, the jay, the falcon, the skunk, the porcupine, the snake, the toad, the trout, the dragonfly. With humans, we coexisted. They built cooking fires at our feet. They cut smaller trees for longhouses. They identified themselves by various names, such as Haudenosaunee, Abenaki, Mohegan. But for the odd arrow gone awry, or one of our branches falling, we inflicted no injuries on each other.

Then came the English. Self-doubt was not in their nature.

Using firearms and disease, they waged war against the native people. They committed skullduggery too, treaties made and broken until all the land was theirs. Still they were unsatisfied. They turned their eyes to us, calculating our worth in pounds sterling. They sharpened their tools, and one autumnal afternoon, shortly after the first frost, two hundred of them arrived in carts and wagons, built a camp by the river, and set upon us with the same frenzied rapacity as they had upon the Haudenosaunee and the fur-bearing beaver, the marten, the muskrat, the mink.

It was from the English that I learned the name *Quercus alba*, or *white oak*, but Latin nomenclature was no help for any of us against crosscut saw and wedge, against the fires they set to our roots to sap our strength, against the thousand further strikes that transformed us into board-feet of lumber. We shook the earth when we fell, conscious of bedrock shifting beneath us to accommodate our weight, but it too had been torn to pieces, large stones upturned, soil and undergrowth ripped asunder, squirrels on the run, snakes a-slither for their lives. We lay crisscrossed, helpless, night stars that much farther away. Next came the humiliation of our branches being stripped. We were floated downriver as logs. The English—some French—danced with hooks and poles upon us, singing songs about the pleasures of their lives. Then came Albany, and then New York, where a gauntlet of ripping saws reduced us in half an hour to rough-cut planks two feet by twelve, two inches thick. We were piled with others on a pier. The first snow came, bringing a brief familiarity but precious little comfort, and then it was farewell America! We were lifted by heavy cranes and dropped into the hold of a ship of weathered pine, with whom we commiserated. We crossed an interminable body of water, hoping for shipwreck, imagining a long deserted beach where we could find freedom of a sort. But no such luck. Instead we arrived at the town of Bristol, in England, shipwrights pouncing upon us, building with their hammers a man-of-war they christened *Formidable*, a frigate, a ship of the line. By chance of carpentry, I formed the entire stern section of *Formidable* and realized, ironically, that once again I was standing straight, vertical, but my feet were planted in the shifting sea rather than in solid earth.

Thus did we, an entire forest, pass from majesty to servitude. For the next forty years—until 1850—we sailed the sea for England. Rarely were we caught up in battle. More often we rested in harbours or sailed off the coast of France and Spain, flying the flag, firing our cannons for sport at the spouts of whales until finally it occurred to the Admiralty that *Formidable* was old and creaking. I did not feel that way myself, just strait-jacketed, as though my arms had been pinned to my sides forever. The ship was decommissioned and sold for a song to private business, to a man who rechristened us in his own name, *John Roberts*. Those letters were written in cursive script directly on my back. The christening bottle smashed across our bow one Bristol foggy morning, 1851. The owner, fancying himself an orator, stood upon our foredeck before the gathered crew and said that he intended to make a salubrious trade in dry goods to and from Chile, in South America. We would be a force for good on the high seas by virtue of our strength in armaments. The newly hired sailors shouted *hip-hip-hooray*, and some of them threw hats in the air. Who were they, these men, these sailors, I wondered. Many were old, some were barely grown. Either way, the officers would treat them as scum, laying on the lash. In the absence of women, men would lie with men. Rum and blood would be spilled in equal measure.

If *Quercus alba* meant *white oak*, which apparently it did, in Latin, then *homo sapiens alba* would be *white man*. Would that I could remove that alba from my name, disassociate myself from such a selfish race.

MISS ALBERTSON, 45

Nineteen years have passed. Clovis and I have grown closer and closer. She is married, with three children. I am on my own, and will be forever. You would think that we have little in common but in fact, since the Friar, we sit together many evenings over tea. We muse, philosophically, about manor life. Well, *muse* is far too gentle a word. Often we rage.

Last night, for the hundredth time, we dwelt on the continuing maltreatment of the two Amberley children. We could not avoid it, for we had eyes to see and hearts to cry out. Clovis reached far back in time to their birth, reminding me how ludicrous it was that the stillborn child was buried with pomp and circumstance in a closed casket of silk and mahogany while the two living children were ignored completely. Well, they had been given names, Catherine and Andrew. That was it. They rested fair-haired and blue-eyed in bassinets a foot apart in the nursery. And also ludicrous, Clovis said, was the obituary for "Little Harry"—so the misshapen baby was called, by his father—published in all the London and Dorset newspapers. "Little Harry Amberley, sweet and brave, heir to the Amberley fortune," etc., etc. Not a mention of the twins. Two hundred guests came to the funeral, trumpets were played sombrely over a few shovelfuls of grave. Such hypocrisy, and the twins did not see their callous father again at close quarters for eight more years. Eight years! And their mother was of no help. She entirely lost the maternal spark. She withdrew physically and emotionally from marriage, from motherhood, sitting for hours in her darkened salon, novels unopened on her lap. We who came to love the abandoned waifs, as we called them, wondered about their future. Yes, they had been provided for in clothing and in food, but emotionally they had been cast adrift. What would be the repercussions, we wondered.

We sipped our tea and shared a biscuit. We remembered their eighth birthday party, when at last the Earl deigned to see them. They were holding hands, unsure of themselves, abashed. Surely he will warm to them once he knows them better, we thought, for look, they are straight in stature, tall and slim and well-spoken, fair-haired, athletic at play, whereas the Earl is relatively short and dark, verging on obesity, a stumbler at sports. Who should arrive then but the family solicitor, he of the coloured threads. We had not seen him for years. He was holding in his arms a wriggling present for each child, a puppy. "Happy Birthday to the two of you!" he said, and it was then that Clovis and I were struck by the same thunderbolt, so to speak, for the solicitor was tall and handsome and fair-haired, and his eyes were as blue as the children's, and their three noses, in profile, were much the same, even to a slight upturn at the tip. What fools we have been, we thought. The Earl's cold and unforgiving nature made sense at last. The more we watched the children play with their puppies, the more we noticed the solicitor's fond glances, and the Earl's continued glowering. The birthday party, such as it was, petered out, but Clovis and I decided to visit Mrs. Mason on our next shared Sunday off-duty.

She was as feisty as ever but had patience with us as we asked our simplistic questions. "How, Mrs. Mason, do children inherit height and weight and eye colour? Can spermatozoa from two different sources interact with female eggs, thus forming twins or triplets from separate sources?" She laughed knowingly. "Clovis, Beulah," she said, "a fertile woman can take two lovers, five or six for that matter, on the same night, and such a woman can deliver, nine months later, a dark and wizened stillborn from the first union and, close behind, during the same parturition, fair and living twins from the secret dalliance. Children never come stamped with their father's name, but time has its way of revealing, by physiognomy, the truth." She then asked us if we remembered how the solicitor had fought for the two babies at the manor, scattering threads, pushing at the Earl, even throwing a punch that she could only describe as a double-windmill. "Who in the world would do that but a father?" she said.

Shortly after that discovery—which we certainly kept to ourselves—the Earl hired an Italian landscape engineer, a Signor Balestra, from Firenze, to create a maze just to the west of the manor house. I was present in the library during the Italian's introduction, dusting cabinets, and I heard the Earl demand that his maze be the largest in Britain, extending over three acres, featuring abrupt endings and false turnings, and straight runs that would give an illusion of progress. Its obstructions would need to be so thick and heavy and tangled that a mouse could not pass without dewhiskering. Ever the foolish optimist, I found it quite enchanting that the Earl had conceived a lighthearted project until it became clear, two years later, that the ultimate purpose of his maze was to provide a training ground in terror for the solicitor's offspring.

Clovis and I walked the maze upon its completion. We found it built as the Earl had wished, solidly. No glimmer of light penetrated its foliage. In fact, it was another world, divorced from reality, so much so that I turned to Clovis in the privacy of the hedges and kissed her, surprising her. I kissed her directly on the lips. No one could see us but for hawks and jackdaws. To my pleasure and surprise, she responded. She did not pull away, and we might have continued had not footsteps from some other explorer approached. We adjusted our bonnets. We found our way out after another quarter-hour, fully able to testify to the maze's disorienting influence.

It was the next Sunday that we heard the Italian gardener's creation would have its first official event. Innocently, we took a position at an upper window to watch as the Earl took Andrew and Catherine by the hands. He bent to them and spoke. Clovis and I thought we were witnessing a tender rapprochement until he abruptly pushed at them and shouted for them to run. Understandably, they stood puzzled, and did not move. He cracked a whip over their heads and off the twins ran, dutifully, slowly, looking back until they turned the first corner. We could still see them from our vantage point. We could see the Earl too, unleashing his clutch of wolfhounds, setting them out upon the same path but at ten times the speed, scrambling, with a wild baying. The children by then had come to a closed corridor, mid-maze. They were pressing themselves against the hedge, against sharp tips and tangles, and it was there the dogs found them, leaping at them, and we heard such cries that we flew downstairs without touching a step, then outside to the first long stretch of maze. There we were met by the Earl returning, dogs leashed, pulling the children roughly along, faces scratched and bleeding. Clovis reached for Catherine but she was pushed away by the handle of his whip. Laughing, he said, "Look, tender hearts, fools!" Grasping the nearest hound, he pulled back the upper and lower lips. "I have rendered them toothless, at the blacksmith's, they are as harmless as rabbits! These craven snivellers, clean them up!" That evening, in the kitchen, I drew up a roster of servants, all volunteers, resolving never to leave Andrew or Catherine alone with that man again.

Years passed. The children matured. The Earl began to go through the motions of fatherhood by appearing for dinners. Nevertheless we felt storm clouds gathering. Their mother turned to knitting tiny imperfect blankets for dolls, or she sat gazing into the fire, mumbling. The unread novels fell to the floor. Andrew was preternaturally quiet, day after day. Courtiers came for Catherine. They listened as she played the pianoforte, but whom did she eventually choose? The worst of them, a clearly insincere schemer infatuated more by her fortune than by her beauty or character. Scion of a bankrupt family from the north of England, one Gerald Egerton. Had she been properly raised, with even a modicum of attention, she would never have given him a second glance. She would have thrown him out like peelings from the kitchen, like scrap food for a dog.

A comment referencing our kiss, in the maze. Clovis is happily married to Emerson Callaghan, but sometimes we lie together fully clothed, breast to breast, and we kiss. It is our secret, and, to me, more than a comfort.

CATHERINE AMBERLEY, 19

Andrew warned me that he was reaching a breaking point with our father. He hated him entirely. He hated his politics. He hated his sneering sense of entitlement. He hated how he treated us as afterthoughts, how we had even been held back, after the age of fourteen, from formal schooling. When I conquered my brother in chess, as often I did—I applied myself more to books of strategy, leaving him at a disadvantage—he would topple his king quietly to one side, smile, concede, walk to the window and say that his life too was toppling. Not that he was gloomy. "Cheerfully oppressed," he called it. "What do you see in Gerald, by the way," he asked me once, "I would like to know." "A way out," I wanted to say, "and you have to admit he is spirited." Instead I reset the board and offered to play black. "Catherine, he is not your match in any way. He loses his Queen in ten moves, he is incapable of planning." That was as close as we came to sharing our emotional lives, in metaphors of chess. Twins have no need to talk, some say, they are like tuning forks set to A, vibrating at the same frequency since birth.

It was still a shock when the rupture came. We had settled, as a family, into a routine at dinnertime during which we pretended normalcy. It was a détente of sorts that an outsider might consider cowardly, but in our defence—Andrew's and mine— we had learned to suppress spontaneity, just to survive. To question Father was to brook battle royal. He would make his point and, if challenged, he would overturn dishes, leave the room, Mother would whisper "tut-tut, tut-tut," and my fiancé would throw his napkin down and rush away to mollify Father. That meant drinking and playing billiards to all hours. As for the servants, I felt for them, I was embarrassed, but they were trained to carry on under all circumstance. Surely they despised us, plentiful food sitting before us, turning cold.

The night in question. Roast beef, Yorkshire pudding, Father pouring himself a third glass of wine, a danger sign. It loosened his tongue. He started up on the touchiest of subjects, saying, "I have heard from our agent in County Galway, Mr. Burke, and he informs me that our tenants have managed just one-quarter of their rents for the past six months. And, as if that insult were not enough, we have been presented with a bill from the local authorities for the disposal of bodies." "Bodies?" I asked, startled, breaking protocol, hoping Andrew would not speak up. "Why yes, Catherine, bodies. Once dead, they cannot move on their own." I plunged ahead, saying, "Father, I have read that starvation threatens the west of Ireland, from the potato blight." He ignored me. Gerald, attempting wit, said, "Do you mean, Sir, that the Irish authorities have actually managed to send a bill to this address, all the way to England?" Father raised his glass in a toast. "Not only did they manage," he said, "but they peppered it with farcical details. We are being asked to pay for the burial of several individuals from the town itself, with no direct connection to our land other than supplying us with seed and building materials." "An overreach, that," said my fiancé, "but of course they are the great exaggerators, the Irish. They spy one faerie under a toad-stool, there will be a dozen in the retelling." "How true, my boy, how true," Father replied, "but there was also good news. Our cattle are in excellent health, growing fat upon the land.

How could there be a blight in the air if that were true? Anyway, I have drafted my reply. I will not pay for bodies or burial. They can rot in their hovels."

The conversation was taking a predictable turn. Gerald clapped his hands and said, "Good! A formal burial would mean coins for the digging, coins for the priest, coins for the wake." "You have an admirable grasp of Irish economics," Father said. "Thank you," said Gerald, "and is it true, Sir, that they attempt to extort landowners by charging double for a pregnant female, deceased, as though there were two bodies instead of one?" "Remarkably, yes," said Father, "even for those out of wedlock, which is the majority." He slammed his fist on the table for emphasis, making the dishes jump and clatter. Then he poured himself another glass and said that the famine was a wholesale fabrication, that he had instructed Mr. Burke to cast out all tenants be they fat or thin, starving or not, Papists or Protestants, by force if need be. But first Mr. Burke was to collect whatever rent was due by searching pockets and turning over the stones of the field. They were wily bastards when it came to hoarding, they'd been doing it since the Danes.

My brother pushed back his chair. He stood to his feet and announced that he was, from that moment on, renouncing his name, his inheritance, the manor house, the social privilege it carried. He would leave the premises within an hour on one horse and one saddle, taking nothing else. He would make his own way in the world. Father, he added, was no longer a father to him, though he had never been one anyway.

"Bravo," I wanted to say, but my spirit was too weak. Father said, "Well, some gumption at last." Then, with a cold eye and steady voice, he said that Andrew was welcome to leave but he should know that the Amberleys had fed off the fat of Ireland forever, so it was a bit late to deny that privilege. "Good riddance, by the way, should you leave," he said.

My brother did not back down. Passionately he said, "As a family, we should make amends. I pledge to dedicate my life to living justly, not at the expense of others." Gerald suppressed a laugh. At that moment I was prouder of Andrew than I had ever been. Mother, sensing disorder, began to cry. The servants stood aside. Andrew walked from the room, and but for a quick kiss later at the door—"Pawn to King 4," he whispered to me, "wish me luck"—I did not see him again. I heard the stamping of his horse, the galloping away. A deluge of rain came gusting into the hallway. Gerald took my hand and apologized for openly supporting my father, saying that yes, he was currying favour but such behaviour was the prerogative of the future son-in-law. I should not take his remarks seriously. He kissed me, thinking that the answer. He asked to come to see me later, in my bedroom. "No," I said, "my brother's departure has left me distraught." "Catherine," he said, "if that is the case then I will take to horse immediately and set out upon his trail and catch him within the hour. I will talk sense to him, and bring him back."

But I did not want my brother back, I wanted him to fly away. I wanted him to save himself. If only I could have bolted with him, I thought. Yet my fiancé's offer seemed genuine, so I accepted, to give him a higher purpose than drink and billiards. He would never catch him anyway. "Check the seaports," I suggested, "for he often mentioned to me that he would be a sailor, if he ever had the chance to be something other than what he was."

To my surprise, Gerald left within the hour. He was gone for three weeks, returning tired, mud-covered, without success from Plymouth, Falmouth, Bristol, Penzance, St. Ives. "No sign of an Amberley anywhere," he said, despite searching the manifests of a dozen ships, departed and in port. Nor had he heard rumours of a nobleman at loose ends, or travelling inland.

Such was his report to me, and then to Mother. "Tut-tut, tut-tut," Mother said. Clovis Callaghan, helping with my hair, tugging at my knots, said that Andrew would return, that he was far too fond of me to stay away, that anyone who remembered our birth would know that we were forged in the same fire, so to speak, and so were made of steel.

Would that were so, I thought. "You were there, Clovis, weren't you?" I asked. "Yes," she said, tugging harder, "I certainly was."

GERALD EGERTON, 22

I set out on horseback in pursuit of her brother. Catherine was unhappy. I would have to watch my step, but, caught as I was between father and daughter, daughter and brother, it required an acrobat to dance upon the tricky wire that stretched between them. All in all, I had acquitted myself quite well over the roast beef, and what was my reward? To be turned away from her bed, to be sent out into rain as the salutary effects of the wine wore off. Christ, I thought, what was I doing? Why should I discomfort myself? Andrew disliked me openly, mocking me with every glance and gesture. Why should I look for him, when in fact—truth be told—I wished he were gone forever, or even dead.

Down came the deluge more ferociously. I tucked my head into my collar as best I could, but icy rivulets coursed within. I imagined carrying on into the hinterlands like a faithful dog. "Come to your senses," I said. I pulled back on the reins, turned about so the wind was behind me. Then, in much greater comfort, I trotted back to the manor. A few yellow lights still reflected on the watery path, from the study. But her bedroom window was dark.

How long had I been gone? One hour. It was far too early— by a full two or three weeks—to return empty-handed after making such a promise. I stopped. I considered my options. I imagined myself haunting the piers and seawalls of Bristol, St. Ives, Penzance and so forth, clambering over rocks, bending my head into gales, shouting, asking for him. I then imagined myself with my feet up in London, by a roaring fire.

Decision made. I spurred my horse to the east at a gallop and had no regrets, for when I arrived in the city I found that news of my betrothal had preceded me. My gambling debts were forgiven. I had carte blanche at my favourite establishments, even those that had recently spurned me. New ledgers were opened to my name. I only thought of Andrew now and then. What would I do, upon return? Roll about in a puddle or two and say to her, "Dearest, he is gone without a trace."

ANDREW AMBERLEY, 19

I patted Mother on the head, I kissed my sister, I took the reins from Emerson and was off into the night, disbelieving what I had done. I was filled with a turbulence, a near-ecstasy that I recognized as being dangerous, for it was almost, but not quite, irrational. The sleet and rain were nothing, the wind was nothing. Bristol, I thought. I galloped for half an hour in that heady state before slowing. I should, I knew, husband my resources. And so I did, the enormity of my revolt dawning on me at sunrise. I was penniless, homeless, a fledgling cracking his way from an egg, not knowing what to expect.

In Bristol, after finding a stable for my horse, I walked the waterfront. Wishing not to let the heat of my impetuosity pass, I signed aboard the first ship that would have me, the *John Roberts*, using the semi-conjured name Andrew Golliver as mine. I retained Andrew, for I was fond of it, but searching for a surname I thought of Gulliver, the famous traveller. I changed just one vowel and became Andrew Golliver, and no one cared or questioned me. The *John Roberts* was sailing within the hour so I had no time to reconsider. Soon I was standing with a hundred other men on the port side of the ship, gazing at the piers of Bristol as they dropped away, and the captain was ordering the sails to be unfurled.

I looked aloft. Up I went, having no choice, following hard on the heels, literally, of my experienced companions, and although my ineptitude was soon evident, I acquitted myself well enough. I was accepted. The swell of the ocean, the near-rhythmic rolling soon became second nature to me. I thought no more of the manor, concentrating instead on my new situation, my home now being a frigate of one hundred cannon, two hundred men. On our tenth day, our captain summoned us to the deck and announced that we were travelling to the west coast of South America. "There," he said, "we will exert, by virtue of our uncommon power, a moral force for good. In the meantime we will train daily in the discharge of our weapons, keeping sharp to any danger but in no way casting a warlike shadow. The armed man walks in peace." He was gesticulating like a preacher, and next he said, "Hop to the guns, gentlemen."

Weeks passed. Before I knew it, we had crossed the entire Atlantic Ocean and Tierra del Fuego loomed before us. Romantically named, yes, but there were no fires visible. Instead we were overshadowed by pitch-black cliffs rising to more-distant mountains. The sun and the moon struggled equally to reach us. On we sailed regardless, westward, until one mid-afternoon we broke free from land and were on the open ocean again. But this time it was the Pacific, characterized, I thought, by a more golden hue of sunlight shimmering upon it. By then we were two months at sea. We were still without a public agenda or purpose, a puzzle to all of us until one day, at the noon hour, the captain called another meeting of all hands to announce that we were at the latitude of Valparaiso, in Chile, and would soon change course for the Orient.

The Orient? We looked at each other. The more experienced sailors whispered that if that were the case, we had been misled. Obviously, we were bound for the opium trade. What else would we be good for, they wondered, for we were bristling with weaponry and our holds were full of powder and cannonballs. We were eminently unsuitable for the transport of Chinese silk or porcelain, or fish from Kamchatka. "Surely it is the poppy for us," they said, "either guarding it from marauders or stealing it for ourselves." Our captain, sensing the general concern, denied it. "Preposterous," he said, stroking his beard, but whatever the truth was of our mission, we soon altered course for the west. For a week we continued to revel in favourable winds. Luck, however, could only last for so long. One morning we saw our sails empty in a minute, as though all moving air had been sucked from them. A similar torpor infected the sea, becalming it. That listlessness spread quickly to the crew, older sailors spitting overboard to demonstrate our stasis, saying they would never have signed to the *John Roberts* had they known the Doldrums awaited. When I asked for the meaning of the Doldrums, I was told that it was a windless desert from which we would leave changed, and not for the better. I marked that first day of lassitude into my calendar, so I knew that it was three days later, on December 30, 1851, at three in the afternoon, that through the surrounding mist crept a vision we could scarcely believe, a three-masted vessel with rigging in disarray, sheets falling to the water, utterly abandoned by humankind but encrusted, extraordinarily, by thousands of tiny green birds.

Puzzled, galvanized by curiosity, we gathered with telescopes in hand and looked across the intervening sea. Mist rose wraith-like on all sides. Our captain, summoned from his cabin, ventured his opinion that the birds were hummingbirds, exhausted by migratory effort, taking refuge upon that ghostly barque to rest their wings. He had seen them often in the Americas, and how strange it was, he added, for they were very far from their usual passage, and they looked a sorry lot. Next he ordered, for a cheerful pastime, that we shoot our cannon directly at them to assess their vitality.

Our First Officer, Mr. Stevens, suggested, with due respect, that such a proposal smacked of cruelty, that sending the tender across with a crew of six would serve the same purpose. But the captain scoffed, saying they were birds, they lacked complex feelings, to see them jump to the air would be a spectacle well worth the price of a scoop of powder. By then the Second Officer had begun the process of raising the most proximate cannon into battle-ready position. He gave orders to load, and so the sailors did, prodding the explosive deep into the maw of the beast, so to speak, and after the signal for readiness was given, the captain gave his order and the fuse was lit, and ball and grapeshot roared across the intervening water, ruffling the surface by the force of their passing, grazing the bow of the target vessel.

Immediately the birds came to life. They rose, startled, like ornate cloudlets of red and green particles, iridescent, muted somewhat by the haze born of smoke from the cannonade and from a humid sweat rising from the sea itself. The startled swarm flew upwards, causing a wondrous buzzing like a nest of bees. They headed away towards, we thought, the west. "Capital!" our captain shouted, "first-rate!" Then we felt, miraculously, a breeze, as though nature too was frightened by the firing of our cannon, and our captain quickly ordered that we should set the exact same course as the rubythroats, as he called them, for in that direction must be landfall, even though it was not apparent on the maps.

The crew cheered as one, and many admitted, later that evening, as the *John Roberts* pitched in a brisk easterly, that we had been at the end of our tether. The Doldrums was a frightening place, a hideous absence rather than a presence, a hush rather than a cry. Moreover, there was naught to do there but tempt the Devil with idleness. In fact, many of us acknowledged, prior to the cannonade, we were much like the hummingbirds themselves, dispirited, exhausted, at our wits' end.

ZEPHYRAX, 3

By the early nineteenth century we had tacitly accepted the English word *hummingbird* to describe ourselves within the biological world. It captured the hum, and certainly we were birds. Let them call us what they wish, and if we liked it, we would make it ours.

Therefore it was as hummingbirds that we gathered over the beach at Valparaiso, 237,742 of us, counted to the last feather. We were primed for travel, preening ourselves, anticipating the Andes, the Amazon, the Gulf of Mexico, Louisiana, the Rivers Mississippi and Ohio, the Adirondacks and beyond. But it turned out differently, to say the least. Our cadre of leaders had overheard a conversation between an albatross and a storm petrel and, on that flimsy basis, they had decided to venture in a westerly direction for the first time in our species' history. We would leave Chile and set straight out over the Pacific. If we flew for long enough—according to the albatross and the petrel—we would arrive at a Land of Milk and Honey.

But wait, Zephyrax, I thought. Neither milk nor honey was a prime constituent of our diet. And I had long believed, from close observation, that a bird's wingspan was inversely proportional to its intelligence. Therefore I said to my closest friends that caution was indicated. I had no faith in loose-lipped albatrosses or, for that matter, seabirds of any kind. We should stick to our time-tested North American route with its recognizable flowers and nectars, dim-witted insects, and landing opportunities always close at hand.

The matter was put to a vote and I lost. Madness, I thought, but hummingbird ethics demanded that I follow my leaders to hell and gone, so there I was in the midst of the flock, anonymous at one thousand feet as we left the reassuring coast of Chile. We flew non-stop westward for three days and nights, during which we found nothing to eat or drink, nothing to rest upon. We were nearing exhaustion when nature dealt us another blow. The incumbent air became heavy, sodden with moisture. The wind, until then spirited at our backs, vanished entirely, making it more difficult for our wings to carry us. But we pushed on as best we could, pretending to each other that we were as dauntless as ever until word passed through the flock, nervously, that our leaders feared that we had, perhaps, entered the Doldrums.

At that dreadful news, many of the younger birds fell outright to the sea and were lost, causing a brief splintering of our formation. Wry observations came hard and fast from sardonic ones, saying that I, Zephyrax, had been right all along, that it was foolhardy to embark on such an uncharted journey, that we would pay a heavy price for the hell-bent-for-feathers attitude of our squadron captains. Caution and tradition would have served us more expeditiously. But such comments, however welcome they were to me personally, rubbed salt in the wounds of the decision makers. "Pessimists," they cried out, "move to the back of the flock!" No one did. Instead we continued to struggle, pressing through the choking miasma from below until suddenly a young female spun deliriously back to us from a scouting sortie, saying that she had spied a break in the flocculent mist gathered on the ocean below. "A dark speck floating there," she said, "something solid." Hopeful at last, we descended, following her in a still-luminescent cloud of green and ruby-violet, as beautiful in arc and flow as ever, and there, upon the greying sheen of the sea, was a merchant vessel adrift, apparently abandoned, sails collapsed, rigging torn, multiple lines of rope hanging overboard like unkempt tresses of hair.

Our leaders voted for immediate action. They suggested that we land upon the vessel for, despite its rag-tag appearance, we might find sustenance in the form of fruit from which to take a sip, or, at the very least, a source of fresh water and a few hours' rest. Gratefully we completed our descent from the heavens and landed, encrusting the vessel from yardarm to forecastle, bow to stern, a magnificent sight that I expected never to see again.

Imagine our horror when, within a few minutes of our settling into place, another spontaneous rent appeared in the fabric of vaporous heat. A second vessel appeared, also hopelessly adrift, with a worn and dirty flag of England drooping from its tallest mast. Several hundred bearded men were crowded upon its near deck, pointing at us, raising a hue and cry, applying magnifying glasses in our direction with such overt interest that we felt a nakedness—absurd, you might think, but true—and a vulnerability that was soon justified when a roar and flame of fire erupted from their forward cannon. A charge flew towards us, barely missing the bow of our adopted shelter. Little wonder that we rose startled, frightened, that we pirouetted in the air to avoid a second salvo—though a second salvo never came—and we marvelled, as we made our escape, at the overt malice of those human beings who had tried to kill us, men to whom we had actually felt a brief kinship, sharing as we did, temporarily, the tropical nightmare of the Doldrums.

We spun to the higher sky, energized by alarm. Wondrously a breeze was then felt, and the clouds that had clung so persistently to the skin of the ocean cleared, presumably by evaporation. By turning our heads, we could see quite clearly that the English ship was then under full sail, having caught the same gusts of wind. It seemed that their captain was taking his navigational cue from us, for as we dipped and turned they followed in step, raising more and more canvas, as though in hot pursuit.

Of course we knew our followers by their reputation. They were white men from the Old World, the worst of creatures who ever walked or crawled upon the earth. Dominion over all natural species was their goal, so it was understandable that trepidation coursed through our younger birds. More juveniles plummeted from our ranks, presumably from heart-burst. Lamentations were heard from all sides. Our leaders consulted among themselves and said, as we stalled in three columns in the sky, that hummingbirds should never run from naked aggression. "We must exact a price," they said. They advised that we should alter course, thirty degrees to the north, and then fly directly over a mile-wide reef the scouts had spotted in the near distance. It was, they said, "a paragon of mass thrown up from the earth's crust, of flint or granite made, upon which monstrous waves rise and fall endlessly, thunderingly, a cataclysmic shelf to which we can draw these murderous sailors, as though by a pull-string."

Revitalized by the prospect of revenge, we found our second wind. We flew on, the ship in our wake. The sun was turning scarlet, dropping to the horizon, and I have to say that not one of us, however generous of spirit, felt regret at our deadly enterprise.

"How often," our leaders shouted—their words, excited, were dissected by the wind but came back plainly to us in the flock— "how often do hummingbirds have such a chance as this, to redress nature, to take the measure of Man?"

THE REEF, 500,000,000

We saw, approaching from the east, a vast formation of birds. First came a dozen leaders in a pocket vanguard, conversing among themselves, chippering, nattering, plotting, strategizing. All characteristics, we knew, of hummingbirds. It was their unique custom to complain, to never be satisfied, to constantly be on the lookout for advantage. Had we ever seen a hummingbird? Yes, before tectonic plates shifted, before we were subsumed by salt water, before they changed their name from *dinosaur*. They were flying en masse in a formation almost as towering as cumulonimbus, green and gold against the darkening sky. They were difficult to count, being so tiny, individually, darting about like minnows. A buzzing emanated from their wings, as though electric eels had been released to the air. They formed a shifting curtain against the eastern horizon, the waning light playing tricks upon their feathers, green and red changing to gold and silver. By contrast, we were solid rock, our jagged teeth fortified by iron. We were fixed as solidly to the earth as the polar star was to the firmament. But despite that immobility—or because of it—we were open to be thrilled by those feathered acrobats who rose and fell as one, balletic, sweeping our evening sky. Come morning they would be gone, and we would be left with a horizon bleak in all directions, empty but for the usual wind-blown gulls, raucous or silent, resting on the sea.

Then, as though the flight of the coloured birds were not enough, we became aware of a wooden ship running flat out before the gale. There she was, on collision course, five hundred yards distant, three-masted, not a soul on deck. We counted slowly to twenty before she slammed against us, before we felt the familiar soft ripping of wood. The iron of our incisors drove effortlessly thirty, forty, sixty feet into the shuddering hull, into the galley where pots were still a-bubble on the stove, into the sleeping quarters where every man and object drowned in total silence, sailor, master, desk and quill, mandolin, fiddle, lantern, book. Down came the mainmast in a grand finale, and whatever was left of that careless ship was thrown over our shoulder, to the sector of the ocean that we could not see.

ANDREW GOLLIVER, 19

The captain pointed to the hummingbirds, silhouetted against the setting sun. "Follow them," he shouted, "nothing to fear on the charts!" Massive seas flew by, much like stooks of grain in a field of endless proportion. I was out of my depth, a novice to heavy weather. He tied me to the helm, leaving a serrated knife for quick release. "A safety feature," he said, "now I'm going below with the others." Seawater spilled endlessly through open gun ports. I held on as best I could. The sun half-dropped below the jagged horizon, altering the evening light. I rubbed my eyes, at first disbelieving then having to believe, for in the near distance, not half a mile away, an unmistakable line of surf was frothing. White on black, solid, uninterrupted. I cut myself loose, intending to rush and give warning, but I managed only a few steps before the *John Roberts* struck and I was lifted high into the air, thrown forward, and after that I was swimming, gasping, struggling, all three.

QUERCUS ALBA, 251

I was still the stern section but I was no longer attached. I was ripped out of the *John Roberts* in an ecstatic shout of freedom, a watery rebirth, a shaking off of chains, a final accounting to throw in the face of the men who had cut me down, a testament to the durability of one white oak ripped long ago from the earth of the Adirondacks. Englishmen! I thought, How do you feel now?

Then someone clambered aboard me, a survivor, clawing, pulling. "Have a splinter for your trouble," I thought, and I was rewarded with a sharp cry of pain. He slid closer to my centre, a wise decision, for the storm raged on. Yet the sky was surprisingly clear, a three-quarter moon was rising, an evening star. The implacable reef slipped away. The sea calmed. The hummingbirds, a curious lot, returned and hovered over me, appearing like coalescing wisps of smoke, now and then eclipsing the moon.

ZEPHYRAX, 3

We enjoyed the ship's crushing. We circled over the area of the strike, keen to make personal observations of suffering. But it was almost nightfall by then and even from twenty feet, hovering directly over the impact zone, there was nothing to see but a hundred thousand splinters of wood. Our juveniles were deeply disappointed. I explained to them that within the reef structure were pockets of deep water attracting, by gravity, the heavier flotsam of the wreck. Cannons, grapeshot. Such items would never be seen. Nor would the bodies of trapped sailors ever rise to the surface just to please us.

Some of the older birds, those of gentler disposition, suggested that we wheel away into the night. The wind, after all, was propitious. Many agreed—I certainly did—and our leaders were about to render a tactical decision when the young female scout, the prodigy who had spied the ship in the Doldrums, claimed to see an object afloat in the water on the lee side of the reef, well past the point of impact. Cheekily she suggested that the eyes of older birds, "such as those of Zephyrax," were not up to the task of night vision. I let her remark pass. I joined the others and soon we hovered over a half-submerged chunk of wood pitching to the pleasure of the waves. A fragment, I could see, torn from some portion of the hull. In its centre lay a young man dressed only in knee-length trousers of torn cotton, lying as though dead. But Miss Sharp Eyes chattered, "Look! His chest is moving!"

Indeed it was. A debate then ensued, one faction clamouring for immediate departure but a more warrior-like group scoffing, saying that a party of three hundred males should dive down upon the last of the colonialists, drill holes in his head, release his brain matter. Annihilate the last of the Englishmen who had tried to annihilate us.

Bloodthirsty, I thought, but not out of line with other actions we had taken. An urgent vote was proposed, prompting me to speak up. I did not mince words. "We should leave. To dally here is to court danger. He has no chance of surviving. He has no food, no water, no means of propulsion, no navigational aids. The weather forecast is for cloudless, skin-blistering skies. We should not bloody our beaks." Sixty percent of the flock agreed with me, so we flew democratically away, leaving the raft and its occupant to their own devices. "Hasta la vista, English sailor," I said, openly flaunting my language skills.

ANDREW GOLLIVER, 19

I had received, in my right thigh, upon pulling myself aboard, a gash two inches in length, globules of fat poking from it, glistening and white. An effort to stand up caused a sharp increase in my discomfort. Knowing well the dangers of suppuration, I crawled to the raft's edge, where I cupped salt water in my hands and bathed the area as best I could. I tore a long and winding strip of cotton from my dungarees, using my teeth as scissors. I pressed a portion of that dressing on the wound and anchored it with circles around my waist and thigh. Better, I thought, standing again, flexing my hip.

There was no sign of the reef. We must have drifted many leagues overnight, swept away by whatever currents were specific to that latitude. The bleakness of my circumstance was complete. Well, almost so. Beneath my feet were the familiar letters *John Roberts*, etched in watery cursive. I crawled from one side of the raft to the other to pursue a more detailed examination, raising my spirits somewhat for she was constructed, or deconstructed, of solid oak, and was large enough for a platoon of soldiers. All four sides bent in a gentle curvature to the sea, making it unlikely she would capsize.

Next I spotted the probable source of the wound in my thigh, jagged splinters poking from the raft's leading edge. Well, I thought, a small price to pay. Who was I missing from home? Let me think...Catherine, Clovis, Miss Albertson. Who would miss me? Just those three.

Silent lightning strikes on the eastern horizon brought a parade of dark clouds to coalesce and block the sun. By midmorning a heavy rain was falling, quenching my thirst. The rain blew itself out as evening approached, night advanced, the moon set early, stars multiplied. I lifted my hand and reached up to the Milky Way, drawing it down to me, a silvered blanket. I was in serious jeopardy but I was sole master of my vessel. I had no ropes to wind, no sails to mend, the decks swabbed themselves on a regular basis without being asked. What more could any captain ask of his first command.

MISS ALBERTSON, 45

Clovis explained to me, when first we met, that her name was highly unusual, that she might be the only girl named Clovis in all of England. Certainly I had never known anyone named Clovis but for one boy who came from the Jersey Islands. He was of French origin and spoke so differently that the word Clovis, coming from his lips, did not sound like Clovis but more like *Clovee*. So Clovis, my Clovis, was unique, a fact I already knew from her character.

Once we became better acquainted, I admitted that my first name was Beulah, Beulah being a traditional name of Biblical origin that I disliked intensely. But my parents had decided upon it as soon as they noticed I was a girl. *Beulah* meant, apparently, *wife*. "We will call her Beulah," my father and mother said. Both of them had faces like carved stone. Perhaps they were brother and sister, or close cousins, anything was possible. Their plain-spoken intent was to marry me off by the age of fourteen. With that in mind they taught me, as soon as I could toddle, to knit and sew and stoke the fire and milk the goat and set the table and take care of the next six children, who were boys. Also to wash their clothes and hang them upon a line. Clovis thought I was exaggerating—she could hardly imagine a toddler milking a goat—but by then she could see tears forming in my eyes. She did not challenge me. She said that it was incomprehensible that parents could so quickly designate a girl-child to be a burden, rather than find her to be a treasure. She held me close, to comfort me.

I then told Clovis that I knew, even before I came of age, that marriage would not suit me. But I had no means of escape. At thirteen, I, Beulah, was paraded before six old men as though I were a colt for sale, or some other farm animal. Had I not developed an aptitude for secret reading, on Sunday afternoons, I would never have had the imagination or nerve to run for it, but run I did, with bread and cheese wrapped in cloth and nothing else but a scarf and the clothes I wore. By night I picked my way through planted fields and wild meadows and hedges and woodlots until finally I was far enough away to chance a step into the sun. There before me was the Amberley manor. No one knew me, but because of my demonstrable skills I was taken on as chambermaid, and then housekeeper, and then whatever they needed me for. Never, as far as I knew, did my parents set out to find me. All they noticed, I surmised, was that their burden had vanished.

I revealed such intimate details to Clovis because Lady Catherine was soon to marry Mr. Gerald Egerton, a most unsuitable man, and I wished to draw a comparison between her—Lady Catherine—and me. Both of us were, at different points of time, potential brides, but I had run away and she had not. Who would be the happier? Well, we would have to wait and see.

As expected, it fell to me to organize her wedding. Other than partridge shoots for men, no public event had graced the manor since the funeral for Little Harry, nineteen years before. The Earl made it clear that the nuptials were of little interest to him, that it would have to be a small and private affair. In contrast to the hundreds invited for Little Harry, he would tolerate no more than a dozen guests for Catherine. He emphasized, however, that he had found Mr. Egerton to be a vast improvement on Andrew, disappeared three months or more. To simplify matters, he ordered Clovis's husband, Emerson, to pull Little Harry's funeral tent out of storage, and if moths had not been too busy with it, set it up upon the grounds beyond the now-tumbledown maze. I could serve one special meal, and that would be it.

When the day arrived, it was a sunny one. The tent was unnecessary. It flapped audibly in the breeze, however, punctuating the only other music presented, that of bees moving heavily through lavender. The Earl refused involvement, so Catherine chose Clovis to escort her down the grassy path—an extraordinary, class-shattering rebuke to her father—and they were equally beautiful, I thought. Next came the vows, the kiss, Gerald as handsome as always, immaculate, pleased with himself. Did I spy the solicitor riding by slowly on the London road? One lone man on horseback, I could not be sure. "Clovis," I said after the ceremony, "For me, you were the transcendent one. Now stay a moment..." But it was her children's bedtime. Off she rushed with a swaying lantern, and I watched until she turned the corner, until the pool of light followed her into darkness.

1852

ANDREW GOLLIVER, 19

My third day shipwrecked, I could no longer ignore an increased throbbing in my thigh. I unwound the rough dressing I had applied and was dismayed to see, upon the proximate skin, a deep reddening. I touched it with my fingertips. From the depths came an immediate sharper pain and a malodorous stream of yellow pus. Infection had taken hold. I undressed completely, spread my knees apart, and with only fingers as instruments, I pried open the festering wound. Tiny roundlets of fat stared back at me, glistening. With deeper pressure, holding my breath,

I could feel a hardness, an intrusion. A splinter, I feared, from frog-legging my way aboard, embedded. A death sentence for a sailor. I spent the next hour fruitlessly, pain my only reward, trying to extract it, fingers slipping away as the raft rolled and pitched, toppling me a dozen times. Changing tactics, I applied circumferential pressure with my thumbs, and finally a spicule of wood, dark and shiny, raised the tip of its head. I managed to pincer it between thumb and forefinger—yes!— and, pulling it from the depths, I saw an inch-long jagged spike of shattered *John Roberts*. Reflexively, I threw it overboard. The waves swept it away. Within an hour my pain had all but disappeared so I rose to my feet and walked naked from port to starboard, fore and aft. I would live, I thought, but I could hardly ignore my next threat, the cloudless sky, the blazing sun, my raft soon an oven and I a roast upon it.

GERALD EGERTON, 22

In the days after the wedding, much drinking was required. Catherine's father demanded it. I took up the challenge, starting at noon, keeping pace with him. He had an enormous capacity for brandy, in particular. We played billiards together until all the coloured balls looked the same to me, and the pockets had shrunk to quarter-size. Then it was time, according to him, to step out on my rubber legs to the horses, or to the fields. He liked to shoot birds. He slapped me on the shoulder one afternoon and said that neither Catherine nor Andrew ever touched a drop or pulled a trigger. So it was clear to me—it had long been clear to me— that he lacked manly company. To satisfy him in that regard I began to tell him stories from London or Paris— I had never been to Paris but some of my friends had—in order to lighten his mood. I had no end of such anecdotes. I forged ahead, describing, for example, how my friend Perry Anstruther had, in Paris, on rue au Maire, stumbled into a brothel by chance and, by sleight of hand with coins, enjoyed three girls for the price of one. But then he had to run for his life, unclothed, into the River Seine. The pimps of the establishment were after him, but he was able to duck under the surface of the water and hold his breath and then imitate, in the darkness, the profile of a goose, hooting and honking like one. And so on and so on, the more ribald the tale the more the Earl appreciated it, bringing him to his knees with laughter. Together we often collapsed against the walls of the billiard room, sitting down to catch our breath. God knows what he really thought of me, but I thought of him as, primarily, a very rich man. That was enough of a character study for me, at least at first. But later I realized, as days and weeks passed and I became used to my new station, that despite his dissolution, he had the constitution of a much younger man. He rode his horses and trod the fields endlessly, and his handgrip was like iron, and his laughter, though rare, was boisterous. He might live for decades. Already I was imagining myself as Earl, Catherine at my side. And why not? Her brother was gone, her mother was addled, Little Harry was skeletal nineteen years. The Earl's longevity, it occurred to me, was not in my best interest.

Also, some of my duties were becoming tiresome. Listening to Catherine on the pianoforte, for example. *"Brava!"* I had learned to say, and to clap my hands together. At sexual intercourse, she was unschooled and not as lively as some, no matter my altering of tempo, technique, tongue or fingertip. Then along came the Earl to walk me through endless fields in search of deer. My life as lord-in-waiting was not quite what I would like, to be frank. Not only that, I had skeletons in my closet to rattle. I spoke to her one morning as she dressed. Creasing my forehead, I admitted that I had, before we met, racked up debts in the city. Many I had paid off, but not all. "Gerald," she said, "I have heard of such indiscretions, by young men." That gave me hope. "I am ashamed of myself," I said, "and I will never do it again, but even as we speak interest is mounting. If we act promptly, gather a lump sum, settle immediately, in the long term we will be better off. I should travel to London to take care of it. The last thing I want to do, but...perhaps, darling, you could expedite affairs by writing a note to your London solicitor? I cannot remember the exact sum, but with your recommendation..." "Gerald, of course," she said, taking out pen and paper from a drawer in her desk. Soon, I knew, by the laws of marriage, she would have to beg me for every penny we owned. But what exactly did we own? The Earl no doubt still had a grip on it all.

Six days later I arrived in London. I settled at the Cavendish Hotel, on Jermyn Street, and though my intentions were pure, I ended up tossing the dice on my first night, and on the next I was taken to a pleasure house by friends. Resisting temptation was never my strong suit. I leaped into the fray, so to speak, exhausting myself. On the third night I swore abstinence. I sat alone in my room and thought of my wife's father, his irritating health, his rosy-whiskered cheeks.

The next day I ventured into Southwark, hard by the river, to see how difficult it would be to foreshorten a man's mortal span. Speak plainly, Gerald, I thought, you'd like him killed. Yes you would! The first obvious scoundrel I asked took me by my shirtsleeve and, laughing, said it was easier to have a man killed in London than to step in sewage. He suggested that I hire the very best, a Mr. Figby, who could be found in a tavern called the Duck and Spoon, half a mile distant.

Well, I thought, the stars were aligning. Proceed therefore, dear boy, but leave no tracks. I asked my new friend if he would act as an intermediary for me, to this Mr. Figby. "For a fee," he replied, "of course!" "Capital!" I said, "tell Mr. Figby that Lord Amberley of Dorset, much hated in Ireland for his political views, is planning a trip to Galway, and if he were killed over there his death would hardly raise an eyebrow. If Mr. Figby's reach extends that far, to Ireland, he would be well compensated." My friend appeared aggrieved. "Sir, Mr. Figby's reach is unmeasurable. He is the spider at the centre of a vast web of murdering, one that covers the entire civilized world. Plus Ireland," he added, "why, with a twitch of his finger, Mr. Figby can topple a man in Belfast, Bray, or Ballycastle." "Capital!" I said, "Once I know more of the lord's travelling plans, we shall finalize our arrangement." "Your name, Sir?" he asked. "John Smith," I said, not even pretending to tell the truth. "Mr. Smith," he said, "a pleasure to meet you, to be of help in troubled times."

ZEPHYRAX, 3

Thirty-six hours after we peeled away from the raft, we spied an island, our first potential landfall since Chile. Our leaders were ecstatic, quick to praise themselves, saying that the albatross had predicted it, perhaps the critics in the flock would like to eat humble pie. But there was no groundswell of apologies forthcoming. No one wished to bend the knee before the fractious leadership. It was enough that the approaching island was beautiful, covered with greenery and encircled by an orange-tinged coral reef, lazy surf breaking upon it. It resembled an orchid set in azure, I thought, a sanctuary. Inside the reef, as we overflew it, was a quarter-mile of crystalline water, blue-green and of such shallow depth that we could see sharply outlined molluscs of various shapes and sizes, and patches of grass waving to and fro in currents of the tide, and stones large and small scattered haphazardly. Among those stones and shells and grasses dashed fish of many species, and also sharks and eels and rays and fierce barracuda in abundance, and turtles of immense size floating in repose upon the surface, swimming without effort, flippers like wings outstretched. Of course there were shoals of smaller fish too, more like hummingbirds one might say, their spectacular colouring rivalling ours—if that were possible—but even in that paradise, we noticed, some of those smaller fish, isolated by chance or design, were under constant threat, twisting away at the last instant from a predator only to have the chase begin again. As I watched, entranced, a sparkling-yellow fish of modest size was seized, and a frenzy of feeding began, and the water roiled with blood. A lesson there to be learned, Zephyrax, I thought.

Then our leaders called for our attention and nodded to the beach. Several rows of palms bent seaward from it. They suggested that we suspend ourselves in the air, with minimum movement of our wings, taking advantage of the uplift from the silicon-reflexive warmth of sand. We should use the energy saved, they said, to discuss whether we should charge straight ahead and replenish our resources or send out scouting parties to reconnoitre.

Predictably, nattering followed. Some of the younger birds lost interest. They rose out of the flock and shot heavenward upon the wafts of air, and to our horror one was plucked out of the sky by a sharp-taloned hawk or kite. We closed ranks. We attacked, and by sheer weight of numbers put fright to the predator. He flew away, still clutching his bounty. There was nothing more we could do. Paradise seemed more a paradise for those with teeth and claws, I observed, than for those without.

Then our leaders ordered—they would brook no further argument—that an expeditionary force should fly to the peak of the island, where a single mountain, cone-shaped, rose to five hundred feet above sea level. Another troop should encircle the reef in its entirety. Both should return within the hour, and the rest of us would hover where we were. Little dissension was raised. Five scouts took off to the mountain peak and were back in thirty minutes, reporting the presence of bougainvillea, frangipani, roses, orchids in abundance, poinsettia, hibiscus, the mati fruit, mikimiki, cashew, papaya, tamarind, and various overripe melons fallen to the ground. On the negative side, they said, the mountain's cone was volcanic and a stench of sulphur wisped from it. Next returned the other five explorers, who had found an island of many beaches, mangrove swamps rich with birds and tiny fish, but in the middle of the island, well protected from prevailing winds, was a village of human beings housed in forty-one dwellings of thatch and reed, well served by a small river that ran from a spring in the mountainside. On the leeward beach were seventeen small canoes and three larger ones pulled to shore, and seven other vessels as well, each with a single mast and a rudimentary sail dyed to a ruby-red, identical to the colour of our throats.

So, humans. But the scouts added that the local natives had shown no signs of ill will when they were buzzed experimentally. In fact they had opened their eyes in amazement, standing so stock-still that our troop could count exactly their numbers, two hundred and twelve individuals divided equally between the sexes, short and stocky rather than tall and thin, similar to native Chileans in that respect but their clothes, rather than being multicoloured, were dowdy, as uniformly drab as sackcloth. They obviously cared little for fashion or design.

Our leaders, after mulling it over, concluded that if the villagers showed no warlike tendency then we could chance a landing, blend into the surroundings. Orders were given to disperse widely, each bird under his or her own recognizance, and to meet exactly where we were, at dawn two days hence, to resume our westerly flight.

Then, to no one's surprise, there was a breakdown of discipline. Miss Sharp Eyes, giddied by self-importance and the power of the updraught, shot to such a height that she was a dot against the sun. Had she been killed by hawks, no one would have cared. Luck was on her side, however. Unharmed, she dropped like a stone to say, in an excess of excitement, that the same Englishman whose life we had spared was drifting our way on his raft. Almost, she added, spinning in the air, as though he were in love with one of us.

No one laughed. The sun was lowering. We were too tired for frivolity. We flew off to an abundance of nectar and insects, as though we had been magically transported to Trinidad. I had to admit, half an hour later, that my opinion of albatrosses had improved, slightly.

THE ISLAND, 12,000

The arrival of the birds reminded me—I was in a nostalgic mood—that we were all immigrants, that I myself had burst through a crack in the ocean floor, tectonic plates shifting apart, molten lava steaming to the surface, until sixteen hours later I had formed an asymmetrical cone thirty feet above sea level. My open mouth spewed rocks that sizzled into the sea. I rose to four hundred feet, eight hundred feet, as fireworks lightened the sky. Then, months later, I subsided to an atoll with a necklace of hardening stone around me. I was volcanic-black, elemental, sculptural, a fortress mid-ocean. I possessed no living organisms until twelve ants floated to me on a pandanus leaf. "Hello," I said. They were sustained by microscopic kernels of fern and bracken that eventually became the first flush of vegetation, withering annually to become soil. Grains of sand were thrown to my edges by storms. Generations of waves formed beaches, and currents from the east brought coconuts, and generations of coconuts became palm trees, and birds flew over with seeds in their droppings, and so on until several thousand years passed and I was covered in green, softened by green, every crack infiltrated by green. Only my sulphurous breath betrayed my origin.

Then came the next wave, so to speak, the mammals. The flying fox, the bat, the capuchin monkey, wild pigs, and finally humans blown in on a particularly wild storm that lasted weeks. They took shelter, beached their canoes, and why should they leave when everything they wanted or needed was provided, when even monsoons and seasons of drought and wildfire and tsunami, however individually terrible, were forgotten in the midst of abundance. I was a paradise for ten thousand years. My living organisms treated each other with respect, with kindness, with an absence of malice, sharing as we did the only solidity in our watery world.

But then my humans acquired a poisonous substance for their arrow tips. They could kill whatever they wanted more easily, from a distance. They no longer listened to the pleas of trees or birds or animals. More recently, they have begun to pay far too much attention to a flawed man, a single man, a childless man whom they elected to a position called Advisor to the Headman. He carries a slender cane as a whip. He wears various feathers around his neck, plucked from the body of a bird far more clever than he. More to the point, he has forgotten his own history. A thousand years ago his ancestors swam ashore from an overturned canoe, and he was treated generously, given food and shelter and adopted into the village.

ADVISOR TO THE HEADMAN, 32

I was elected by a majority to council. My mandate was to advise the Headman, and by extension the Headwoman, on foreign affairs. Also to lead our warriors into battle. But we were so far from the rest of the world that foreign affairs did not exist, and no battle had been waged since legendary times. Therefore the position of Advisor was viewed as a ceremonial one by most members of the tribe. If they saw me whispering in the Headman's ear, they assumed we spoke pleasantries. In fact I was constantly asking for his support, asking him to reach out to his wife and explain to her that we needed always to be on the alert, to imagine the unimaginable, to fear attacks on our village from all four directions of the wind, lest one day we be found sleeping and overconfident. "Advisor," he would say, "do what you feel is necessary, but leave me out of it, you frighten me with your intensity."

He was joking of course. But, to be in readiness, I regularly dispatched warriors to the heights and to the beaches. They were to observe the horizons day and night, and if they complained of boredom, I doubled their hours, to teach obedience. "The past," I said, "is not the present, and the present can, with little warning, become the future. Keep your eyes peeled!"

My diligent approach was rewarded sooner than I expected. One evening, my most talented lookout felt a distinct tremor transmitted through bedrock. A major cataclysm at sea, he felt, a reef being struck or a subaquatic collapse. I advised increased alertness. I doubled the number of observers. The very next day, at dawn, the same warrior reported subtle pressure changes from the same sector, arriving in a pulsing, languid rhythm, a small craft, powerless, adrift on moderate seas, moving as one with the current. He estimated, using our mathematical tables, that it could land directly upon our shores in seventy-four hours. "Sharpen your weapons," I told my guards.

Later that afternoon we experienced an invasion of avifauna, thousands of extraordinary birds appearing from nowhere to hover over our lagoon. They were of a species we had never seen. They arrived without warning, shadowing the blue-green water, making a unique racket from their wings, a buzzing entirely novel. They suspended themselves first as a low cloud, taking advantage of draughts rising from the sand, shooting skyward without effort, as sparks might rise from a bonfire. It was a sight that invested them superficially with mystery and beauty, but for me they offered proof that I had been correct, that my instincts as Advisor were praiseworthy. Hidden by the jungle's edge, my lookouts and I watched the birds' audacious play for ten minutes. "By their cocky ebullience," I said, "they are laying claim to our island." I dispatched a runner to the village requesting assistance. A dozen warriors answered the call. "Send the hawk to the sky," I said. The raptor was fetched, her blindfolds removed. She took to the air and returned in less than a minute with a tiny prey, pierced through by a talon. We placed it in a small basket, and personally I raced back to the village to rouse the Headman and the Headwoman, to show them our prize, our first captive.

The Headman scratched his head, stumped, but the Headwoman picked up the carcass and tenderly turned it every which way and held it up against the sun. Then she snapped her fingers and said, "Yes! Yes! How remarkable! I have heard of them in legends, and they are called hummingbirds, storm-blown from their usual path. They are no threat to us. They will be gone in the morning, so wish them well." But then she caught herself, realizing that she had overstepped, into my territory, that of foreign affairs.

I thanked her for her traditional knowledge. "But wishing them well," I said, "however warm-hearted that may be, is dangerous. As Advisor, I fear they could be an early manifestation of a more malignant invasion. Already tremors are warning us. We should deliver these visitors a hard lesson in humility." "Really," the Headwoman said, as though she thought me an alarmist. "Yes," I said, undeterred, "we should capture several hundred, openly feast upon them, temper their arrogance, put a stop to any plans they have to stay." Sighing, she and her husband waved me away. It was my prerogative. I summoned my warriors and half the women of the village. We stayed up throughout the night preparing glue sticks, mixing half an ounce of water with juice squeezed from the ginger flower, producing the binding yet fragrant substance usually used for sail-making. We spread it by torchlight upon the closed mouths of trumpet flowers, upon twigs and sticks, and our revenge was sweet for by noon hour the next day we had three hundred and eleven of the birds stuck fast, each one easy to pluck off with our fingers. A mad chorus of *chip-chip-chip* gibberish filled the sky above, from a hundred thousand furious tongues.

I was almost shaking with joy, ridiculous though that may seem. So compact as individuals, they nonetheless constituted a massive cumulative threat. We wasted not one bit of flesh. Each was smothered by the pressure of a fingertip—compassionately, for the Headwoman was watching—and the neck feathers were plucked for amulets, feet severed for earrings, beaks for needles. Their meat, what there was of it, was seared over flames. As tender as young turtle, most agreed. Later we piled the leftover bones upon the beach to form a celebratory cairn. It came only to our knees, so tiny were the skeletons, but we set it afire at high tide and the lagoon licked at the flames and swallowed the ashes while I gave praise to our island, to our sea, our reef, our jungle limpid-green, our volcano dark and slumbering.

My warriors cheered. The birds abandoned their invasion. But danger had not passed us by completely. Subtle wave-pressures still advanced from the east. I stayed that entire night on the mountain and joined in casual conversation with my guards as we scanned the night sky. Some stars move, most do not. We discussed how the horizon seemed to bend away at the edges, like an overturned bowl. Our world's shape was round, we had long suspected, not flat as we experienced it. "But," I said, amusing my warriors, "if our world is round, how fortunate that we are on top of it. If we get pushed to the sides, we might fall." Then all of us felt several firmer tremors, and I vowed to harden myself even more for our next visitor.

QUERCUS ALBA, 251

My sailor was either sleeping deeply or unconscious. He rested on his back for the most part, now and then changing position. The waves swung us to and fro. Although the sea had calmed somewhat, now and then a rogue crest rose high enough to swamp us, sluicing forcefully in its collapse. But the man's arms and legs were outstretched like a spider's, and he was still there two days later, holding on. Then came another morning and afternoon of brilliant sunshine, and I felt him curl to a fixed position on his right side. After that he no longer moved. For all I knew he was dead. All was silent but for the lashings of water around us. Well, I thought, if he were still alive, he was only barely so. And the maddening thing was, with that realization, my heart went out to him. As though I had learned nothing from my difficult life. It was the last thing I expected to feel, empathy for a white man, but there we were, the two of us, bound together by circumstance. There was nothing in sight the rest of the day but water and the curve of sky. Evening approached. I noticed a low-lying cloud or patch of mist settling in the west. I had seen land present like that once or twice, when I was with *Formidable* or the *John Roberts*, but more often than not it turned out to be nothing but a mirage.

ADVISOR TO THE HEADMAN, 32

One of the lookouts arrived from the mountain to say that a raft had been spotted in the distance. I grasped my spear. "Come," I said. We left the village at half-pace, but as soon as we turned the corner to the jungle, we hit racing speed and did not hesitate at the foot of the volcano, leaping up the switchbacks until, short-winded, we arrived at the first ledge. Parrots burst out and beat their wings at us, frightened. We redoubled our efforts, pushing aside vines and hanging leaves to penetrate to the inner pathway, slightly less precipitous. But the vegetation eventually vanished. It could not root itself in shale alone, so after ten minutes of crawling on hands and knees we broke out into near-blinding sunshine on the exposed face of the mountain. Pumice and sharp flint crumbled under our feet. Irregular concretions of black ash clattered to the edges and fell away. The stench of sulphur thickened. We laid down our spears and clawed at the scree with our fingertips until finally we were standing as high as we had ever been before, on a shelf of rock no larger than my hut. A careless step and we would tumble to the smoking heart of the volcano. I shaded my eyes with my hand and looked to the east, and there it was, a raft well advanced. Certainly not of conventional design, I thought, for it appeared to be flat and low to the water, not as buoyant as those we made ourselves, of vines and palm. On it lay an unmoving figure of a man or woman, but at that distance we could not tell which.

So, I thought, here comes the real invader. Then one of my warriors casually said that he had made an interesting observation he wished to share, that the front edge of the oncoming raft appeared first over the edge of the horizon, and it wasn't until an hour later that the fallen figure was visible, proving once again, as we had earlier discussed, that the world was round, like a coconut. "If the world were flat," he continued, "I should have seen the resting figure first." His comment was not irrelevant to our lives generally, but it seemed out of place, considering the immediate crisis. "Later," I said, irritated. Then another of my men spoke up, saying, "Did you ever think, Advisor, if a celestial eye were watching us, right now, we would appear as black ants crawling on the lower lip of the volcano's mouth, rather than what we are, fully grown men?" I grew angry and corrected him, saying that it was no time for chit-chat, that we were in imminent danger, that we should not compare ourselves to ants in the face of a serious threat to everything we held dear.

He apologized and then, as if to mollify me further, he pointed to calculations he had scratched onto the rock surface. He expected the raft to arrive, assuming its present rate of drift, in four hours, give or take a quarter-hour. It might even slip undamaged through the eastern passageway and touch land near the cairn, where we had burned the bones of the hummingbirds.

"A bad omen," I said, "which we shall not allow to happen. Time to act." Down the steepest slope we scrambled, picking up our spears, half-sliding, half-tumbling to the mountain's base, running full-out to the village, to the Headman's hut. Through the shell-bedecked curtain I recommended that he and his wife approve the dispatch of a war party to meet the approaching vessel at sea, beyond the reef. There we could assess the situation at close hand and if necessary kill the interloper rather than risk a landing. We heard whispering from within, and then the voice of the Headwoman said, "Advisor, we are otherwise occupied. Please take charge of the war party yourself. Stand in the bow as commander, in place of the Headman, but restrain yourself, do not be bloodthirsty."

It hit me that she had bestowed a singular honour upon me. No Advisor, even in legendary times, had ever stood in the bow of a canoe. My men looked at me with widened eyes. "Yes, Headwoman," I whispered back through the curtain. Ten minutes later we were striding, sixty of us, to the launching beach, our paddles, lances, clubs, slings and daggers, bows and arrows bristling, a powerful force on land and sea. There would be little danger, I knew, because we were highly trained, focussed and alert, while our enemy appeared to be at best comatose, or already dead.

Therefore we set out fearlessly, joyfully even, with thirty paddlers to a side, pulling our largest and most ornate canoe from the sand to the shallows, leaping to our places, paddling briskly towards the eastern cut, meeting the combers as they crested and collapsed upon us. We were well braced, we broke through easily, we lost no headway entering the swells. Our two young boys bailed. Already we could see the enemy craft rising and descending, rising and descending, its occupant curled centrally, a mile distant. Despite the contrary wind and current, we approached until we closed to within seventy paces, and there we stood off from her, all the while maintaining perfect silence, avoiding even the accidental clamour of wood on wood.

The body aboard was that of a man, his hair yellowed or whitened by the sun to an extraordinary degree. His skin had been burnt to red and black. He was curled on his side, back to us. As for the craft itself, it was a massive, highly polished slice of wood, reflecting sun on its upper surface, torn at one edge as though it had been ripped apart by giant hands. It was well worth the salvage, if only for firewood. I turned to my warriors to speak, intending to relax their vigilance, but suddenly the lifeless body moved, raising itself first to an elbow and then to both knees, and then it stood without purpose, staggering. Yes, a man, shirtless. By then the currents had brought us closer. Some of his skin was hanging in shreds, a classical presentation of sunburn, far advanced. He was not a giant, but he appeared to be taller than any of us by at least three hands. Yellow hair fell tangled to his shoulders. In that vulnerable state, we could easily take a spear to him, I realized, ending the crisis. I raised my arm. We resumed paddling, approaching closer. Still he did not see us, but then a chance wave raised us higher and, descending, our bow bumped slightly against the raft. He fell back to his knees. He began to crawl towards us, no longer quite the simple target. I heard mutterings from behind, saying, "Advisor, we cannot kill a helpless man." Then he was back on his feet and coming towards us, and a wave broke upon him from behind, sending him hurtling towards me, falling at my feet. I jumped away and drew my knife, and I would have killed him had I been alone but already the forward paddlers were bending to him, and the others were thumping their paddles on the gunwales as if to say "Welcome, stranger." Had they already forgotten the birds? Refugees, immigrants, invading forces, chance arrivals, drifters, kill them all, I wanted to say. But I was standing in for the Headman, and he would never be so harsh. I gave the signal to seize the foreign craft and turn for shore.

QUERCUS ALBA, 251

The canoe that approached was far more ornate than the birchbark craft of the Haudenosaunee. It was twice my present length but narrower in beam, with tall prows of intricately carved wood at bow and stern. The gunwales were sleek and low, close to the water. There were twenty-five to thirty warriors on each side lifting paddles to the air, dipping them to the sea with military precision. They held off from us in silence at fifty yards, each holding his paddle high and in parallel to the next so that they reminded me, remarkably, after all those years, of a porcupine with its quills erect, sending a warning to an enemy. As a snake might rattle, or a fox might spit. Clusters of communal spears bristled aboard her too, sprouting at intervals. They were more than well armed, yet I felt a wariness in their gaze. However, they would get no wariness from my sailor, for he had long ago been overcome by the elements. Perhaps our visitors realized the same, for they drifted closer, showing no sign of malice. Perhaps it was their proximity, perhaps they made a sound I could not hear, but suddenly my sailor was on his feet, staggering, lurching about. Waves lifted us, dropped us, slid us sideways until I felt a bump. He had lost his footing. He fell directly into the front of the canoe, at the feet of their foremost warrior, an older man marked by a leather clasp around his neck, a white feather dangling. Forward paddlers bent to his assistance, shielding him from the sun with a carpet of woven grass. It had been fifty years since I had seen such spontaneous generosity. The commander then spoke a few words and four young men jumped onto my deck, embedded four knives in my nearest corner, tied a rope to them, secured it fast to their own stern, and then, waiting for the falling side of a wave, they timed it just so and leapt back to their places. The full complement of paddlers then dug deep to the furrows of the sea, pulling away until the towline tugged and I was swung passively in a half-circle. I heard surf approaching, I felt the seabed rise. I braced for another impact but instead was slung through an opening in pink coral, dropped into a silent, languorous warmth, where the tumult of surf fell away, where schools of fish and single turtles brushed by. Variegated grasses bent to a current. The natives were by then standing in their canoe, knocking their paddles together in a martial catharsis, I thought, a recognition of victory. They beached their vessel on white sand. They lifted my most recent and least troublesome captain to a stretcher of palm leaves, from which his legs extended comically, and, without looking back, they took him away at a fast pace to the forest, leaving me entirely on my own, my tether drifting landward under the influence of the tide. Hawks and kites and gulls flew overhead. Gradually the shadows of the seaside palms grew to cover me, with a cooling effect.

Another hour passed. I wondered if I would see my sailor again, and what our fate would be. Our captors could hardly be worse than Englishmen. Had they been Englishmen, we would already be destroyed. Either way, my singular loneliness at the moment could not be denied.

Then, at dusk, a dozen young men and women appeared. They pulled me partially to the sand. They removed the cluster of embedded knives, rolled up the rope—made of tautly twisted vines—and walked over me respectfully, curiously, marvelling at my lacquer. My spirits rose. One of them traced my letters with her fingertips. Then they left me and swam in the lagoon, phosphorescence turning the shallows to a shimmering green, the mountain's profile a black wedge against early stars. By torchlight they returned and crouched barefoot on my centre. They chipped away at me, at my letter O—the O from the second word of *John Roberts*—using knives and wooden hammers. They undermined it, creating an independent rectangle a quarter-inch thick and a foot square, which they lifted from me. I watched as a girl put it under the crook of her arm. They were preparing to leave, so it was decision time.

Stay where you are or jump to it, Quercus alba, I thought, and although the letter O was but a sliver of myself, a very small portion, I took the chance. I leapt to it. I would follow my sailor. Torch shadows jittered as we passed through a fringe of palms into denser forest. Vines and webs of branches tumbled around us. The young men gathered even closer together and began to run into the deeper darkness, the girls joining with them, closing ranks, elbow to elbow. I heard unfamiliar cries of night birds, the familiar droning of frogs. After ten minutes we arrived at a village of forty to fifty huts, small fires smouldering, dogs poking through ashes, and she, whoever she was, took me to one of the huts and placed me shoulder-high upon a shelf. Then she left, and by the wavering outside light I saw above me a roof of palm leaves interwoven to thatch, walls of reeds hung close together, a doorway for each direction of the compass, curtains of seashells, jangling or still. The floor was of brushed earth, and in the far corner, on a mattress, curled on his side, as he had been when at sea, was my sailor. Whether he and I were guests or prisoners, I could not tell.

ADVISOR TO THE HEADMAN, 32

Upon arising, I was surprised to hear that the young men and women had been swimming at the beach at dusk, and someone had cut out a portion of the captured raft, and Jaimia, my own niece, had personally carried it to the prisoner. I strode immediately to my brother's hut and woke Jaimia from her sleep, kneeling down to her, speaking to her—her beauty disconcerting—saying "Jaimia, whose idea was it to provide comfort to the white man, to strengthen him with a talisman?" She looked to her parents for guidance. Her brain-damaged father was shifting small pieces of dried fish about in a bowl. Her mother, who would never have the courage to speak out against me, was lying sideways on a mattress against the wall, observing us. I repeated my question, taking Jaimia's chin in my hand. Finally she replied, "All the boys and girls wanted to do it, Uncle, and it's a souvenir, not a talisman, and it was the Headwoman who asked me to take it to the guest's hut for his comfort, as a gift of kindness. So I did." She sat up to face me more directly, tucking her shift between her legs. I dropped my hand from her chin and touched my cane to her chest. I traced a path downwards, stopping at her waist. She leaned away, much less sure of herself. "I would like that gift of kindness tossed on the nearest fire," I said. "Uncle," she said, "please, talk to the Headwoman." "I will not forget this, Jaimia," I said, and I left without another word and went straight to the prisoner's hut. A nurse of much experience was in attendance. She reported that she had, overnight, placed the dehydrated guest on his back on a mattress of compressed leaves, that she had applied seawater poultices to his blistered and shredded skin, that she had squeezed diluted lime juice to his lips and tongue.

I said he should be shackled, that he was a prisoner, not a guest. She said that the blisters on his wrists would be irritated by the pressure of restraints. For my benefit she ruptured one of the surface blebs on his shoulder with her fingernail, showing me a clear and sticky substance oozing from it, saying that I should dip my finger in it too, to feel its slipperiness, and if I wished I could taste it, that it reminded her of eucalyptus oil. "That suggestion," I said, "fills me with revulsion." Then I looked about the hut to find the cursed talisman, and there it was high on a shelf, staring down at me with its solitary eye, oval, darkly pigmented. She caught my glance and said it was her hope that the young man would live. I said that it would be far better if he died, if we carried his body back to the lagoon and placed it upon the raft and built a bonfire over his remains, and the cleansed ashes would first litter the beach and then float down through clear water to the rippled sand, or be swept away by the wind, and we would be victorious.

Then I tired of talking to her as an equal. I kicked at his body with my foot and suggested he was a malingerer. I searched the floor and found a thorn and pushed the thorn deeply under one of his long and filthy fingernails, but he did not respond other than local bleeding. She looked at me aghast. "White men are carriers of disease," I said. Hardly were those words out of my mouth when the west curtain parted, rattling its shells, admitting the Headman, and he spotted my thorn and the bleeding fingertip. I explained the time-honoured test I had applied, to distinguish unconsciousness from malingering.

He said, "Advisor, one man's test is another man's torture." For the first time since my appointment, I felt admonished, but then he put his arm around my shoulders and said, "Your niece, I must compliment you, how kind she is. She has just agreed to sit throughout the hours of the night with our guest. It was my thinking, if he were to rouse, he would find a comforting face." I pretended to be pleased, galling though it was. Then he waved his hand, dismissing me, and I brushed through the shells quietly, thinking that the Headman and Headwoman were dreamers, innocents, well-suited to times of peace, to calm water, but not to times like this, to storm surge, tsunami. I walked homeward not knowing what to do with myself. Then I saw Jaimia heading towards the river with laundry on her arm, and I changed direction for a more friendly conversation, to apologize for the cane-touch I had given her. But then she was joined by two friends, so I turned aside and took the path to the beach to clear my head. I realized, watching the endless surf beat down upon our reef, how much I loved my island. Better even than myself. I would do anything to save her, send our visitor to the Puzzle, to the boars, before he destroyed our way of life.

FETU, 8

Our ancestors were pigs. They had no expectations. They wallowed in mud for a year or two and were packed off to market as ribs and bacon, fat and gristle. They would have remained pigs but for an accident, six of them toppling off the stern of a Malay junk, falling into the South China Sea. The crate in which they were imprisoned had been split apart by the cumulative weight of others piled above, so there they were, pigs swimming, or trying to swim, in the vanishing wake of what they called, realistically, their death-ship.

None had experience in water. But they found, joyously, that they were not overmatched. Their snouts were well-suited to the task, held four inches above calm water, while below the surface their hooves churned away with reasonable efficiency until, within an hour or two, they approached a line of surf they had seen and heard, and, no doubt, nervously remarked upon. They were still in fine shape, however, all things considered, until they were swept up on combers before the reef and thrown down upon razor coral. They suffered multiple lacerations as they tumbled landward, but even as they bled they knew that every cut, no matter how deep and painful, was nothing compared to what they had expected at market. Free at last of coral, they found themselves in warmer, calmer water, hearts beating with contentment until shoals of barracuda, attracted by the taint of spilled blood, set upon them in droves and harried them towards shore. Their hooves churned again, their curly tails wiggled uselessly. The predatory fish were by contrast fiendishly well equipped, tail fins and teeth designed for speed and for slashing chunks of raw pork from flanks and shoulders. But the six pigs were large animals. They could afford an incremental loss of mass. They swam through their attackers with snouts and eyes fixed on the beach, stumbling through the shallows, shaking the barracuda off like fleas, still vigorous despite their hemorrhaging, scarcely believing what they had managed to do.

Next they lay on the hot sand, cauterizing their wounds. Wrinkling their noses, they smelled a stench of humans. They stepped quickly away from the beach and found shelter beneath a fringe of palms. They then pushed into denser vegetation and slept their first night curled together in a hollow by a tree. In the morning they resolved as a group, given the miracle of their escape, that they would no longer be food-fodder for more attractive life forms. "We will push the boundaries of piggery," they vowed, and that was exactly what they did over the next fifty years, carving a determined life for themselves from the jungle, renaming themselves as boars, wild boars, their passive softness replaced by quickness afoot, by a mottled darkness of skin, coarse hair bristling like a mane along the spine. Their incisors grew, curling outwards from the lower lip. Their legs lengthened and narrowed for speed, their snouts toughened from digging, their bodies narrowed too, streamlined by exercise.

I was born to one of their offspring, my given name Fetu. I had thirteen siblings. Having grown, I had sex with vigour and frequency, producing boarlets who acted nothing like pigs.

They were violent by first nature, growling before they breathed. We held dominion in the swamp, with carrion and bugs and berries and root and bark and rodents and birds' eggs to satisfy us, and snakes to be pummelled by our hooves. Each of us was fearsome. We frightened each other if we met by accident upon one of the secret paths, if we turned a corner to find two hundred pounds of muscle and malevolence facing us, as though a mirror were being held up by a phantom hand.

But, as it turned out, my generation was born in the wrong era. The natives, who had always left us alone out of fear, acquired a paralyzing substance for the tips of spears and arrows. They became aggressive. They came to the swamp to kill indiscriminately, coordinating their attacks from all sectors, showing no mercy to females or to squealers, shooting them, sticking them, roasting them over burning pits until there were just three of us left in hiding. I was one, moving, forever moving until the final battle royal. A rain of arrows caught us napping and soon we lay paralyzed, barely breathing. Their toddlers stepped up to us, walked on us, poked sticks into our nostrils, laughed as children laugh, thoughtlessly. But the warriors, for some reason, did not kill us. Instead we were revived, the three of us, imprisoned in a fortress of bamboo eight paces by eight by eight. We were fed on vegetable gruel and various mushes and the bitter rinds of fruit, and they even tossed us, in derision, the bones of our dead relatives to gnaw upon. That we refused to do until more time had passed. Eventually, to sharpen our teeth, to harden our gums, we had no choice but to chew on those same bones, not looking at each other as we did so, out of shame. Maybe, we came to think, we were always pigs, our years of ascendancy an illusion.

ZEPHYRAX, 3

Our shaken leaders suggested that, having fled the island of glue sticks, we continue to the west without delay. But thousands of voices objected, saying we should not leave our sisters and brothers, even if there were nothing we could do but circle back to the island and cry out, to show solidarity. Other more practical birds argued differently, saying that such an action would be an emotive response, empty, useless to those on the ground, heart-rendingly difficult for those who had lost a loved one. We were bifurcated in our opinions, and physically too, hovering like the separated wings of a butterfly. In the middle—the thorax of my imagined butterfly—was the largest, undecided group, unable to make up their minds. Sensing danger to our esprit de corps, I thought, Zephyrax, speak up!

And so I did, turning to one of my friends, uttering the one sentence we could all agree on. "Never trust an albatross," I said. Ruefully, sympathetically, my companion turned away and repeated it to another, and so it multiplied and the words *Never trust an albatross* rang through the sky from every faction.

Our leaders hung their heads. I had stung them not by direct criticism, but by a cutting aphorism. And what was the result? They announced an immediate review of our journey's direction and purpose. To facilitate that, we shuffled into adjacent pillars in the sky, and immediately came the revolutionary question, bold as brass—though not from me—"Why have you, our leaders, chosen the albatross route?" "Because," they replied, "hummingbirds historically have a spirit of adventure. We are not shirkers, and there are islands over the horizon set out like a string of pearls, each with a cornucopia of nectars and insects of high nutritional value."

Cries of derision rose from all quarters. "Too many times we have heard the same lies!" "Change the leadership!" "Let there be one leader, to whom each and every one of us can swear allegiance!" And so on and so on, the usual demands of an aggrieved underclass. But our leaders regained their feistiness, asking if the complainants had any one bird in mind, for "If so, we can call that bird Dictator."

That hushed the voices. Not long ago a Dictator had indeed been in charge, suppressing ideas not consistent with her own, gathering a cadre of zealots to enforce rules. Many of us had lived in fear. Laughter, joy, spontaneity, wit, disappeared. Had that Dictator not grown fat and slow on syrups, had she not been assassinated by birds unknown—oh, Zephyrax, be honest, you were centrally involved—we would still be under her iron hand. The Dictator proposal was quickly withdrawn, and those who had raised the possibility were abashed. Off we whirled to the west, obedient again.

But Zephyrax was not born yesterday. We were being led by bravado, not by brains. I said to my same, most trusted friend, "Each species on earth has a fundamental set of skills. For example, the albatross can, with one twitch of a wing, coast a thousand miles. Yet never in a million years could he or she take nectar from a flower. Did you ever wonder, as I have, whether we arrived into this world with that particular skill intact, or did we develop it slowly, over generations? Did we acquire, in other words, in response to particular, demanding needs, our unique expertise?" "An interesting question, Zephyrax," my friend replied, "but personally, I find that beating my wings at four thousand times a minute, remarkable though that may be, is exhausting." "True enough," I said, "almost I would be an albatross at this moment, however horrible that fate might be otherwise." Then we ceased our conversation and I wondered, to myself, whether the world we had left behind still existed. Well, it hardly mattered. You are where you are, Zephyrax, bend your head to the wind.

CLOVIS CALLAGHAN (NÉE OLDHAM), 35

I told Miss Albertson over our usual tea, at the end of a sixteen-hour day, that my husband had been asked to accompany the Earl on a trip to Ireland. His Lordly One wished to reassess the family's holdings there. The exact date was not set. Although they had many servants in Galway, the Earl preferred the company of Englishmen. He had ordered Emerson to arm himself from the shooting closet, saying there were rumours of unrest among the Papists, and if so he would meet force with force. Miss Albertson then said, gazing straight through the walls of the kitchen, that she imagined green fields, tumbling brooks, rock-strewn barrens, dark clouds, rainy skies, waves throwing themselves heedlessly against cliffs. More disturbingly, she also saw ragtag groups of revolutionaries hiding in hollows, planning insurrection. We wondered how much we had heard of Ireland was true, whether Catholics actually sat in confessionals and spoke their sins to a priest. If that were true, we agreed, it made us grateful to be non-believers, never to have to confess to anyone about the Friar, and grateful that we could still wish, without guilt, that the Earl had died instead. "Had we killed him," I said to Miss Albertson, "there would have been no maze, no mal-treatment of the twins, no years of misery, no marriage to Mr. Egerton. In fact, perhaps the solicitor would have soon asked for Lady Amberley's hand, and she would have accepted, and the children would have had a kindly father." A pipe dream, we knew, but pleasant to imagine. Then I asked if she thought Andrew would thrive during his adventures away from home or would suffer for his innocence. The latter, she thought, for he seemed younger than his nineteen years. He was far from worldly. Often we sat for quite a while, until the teapot grew cold, until we could hear the hooting of owls. She asked me how long my husband would be gone, in the company of the Earl. I said that I was unsure of the distance to Galway but there was the Irish Sea to cross, then all of Ireland, plus however long they spent there, plus the return home, so I thought at minimum, two months. That made her happy, I could see, for she blushed and jumped up and made herself busy with the teapot.

JAIMIA, 17

My uncle's so-called success with the hummingbirds had broken an inner dam of restraint. He appeared in our hut while my parents were out, brushing his way through the curtains, holding an abalone shell that he said was for me. He pretended to look about for my father and mother. Not finding them—they were walking to the beach, as he very well knew—he said, "Look Jaimia, a particularly beautiful shell, its whorls, its inner colours! And it is for you!" Then he smiled in a new and disturbing way and gave up his friendly masquerade. He reached for me and touched my breasts through my shift. "Jaimia," he said, "Jaimia," and then he started to apologize as he moved his hand about, saying, "I am sorry, my niece, but it is not taboo if I say it is not, and I say it is not."

I felt nothing but abhorrence. I could not move or speak. He suddenly pulled his hand away and rushed out, but my inaction must have given him licence to return the next day, and the next, and the next. Each time he touched me, I did nothing. I waited for the storm to pass. I also thought to myself, with shame, Jaimia, how can you just stand there? Eventually I was able to mention it to my best friend. We were washing clothes in the river, and she said, "Jaimia, let me tell you, you are lucky that is all he does." I sensed that our conversation was more awkward for her than it was for me. I let it drop. We pounded our laundry more vigorously, both of us raising so many soap bubbles that we had to laugh as they drifted away and burst on the rocks. We forgot, purposefully, what we had been talking about.

So the arrival of the white man coincided with a difficult time in my life. I was part child, part adult, wholly confused. Then the Headwoman altered my life. She asked me to sit with the guest at night, an extraordinary offer. She was recognizing me as an important member of the community. My uncle had strict rules—I was not to be out after dark unless chaperoned, or with a group of ten or more—but the Headwoman had spoken up.

I came of age. I was accepted by the nurses as a full-fledged member of their rotation, despite my lack of experience. I followed their instructions to the letter. For ten nights I did not fall asleep, sponging coconut milk to his lips, bathing his entire body in seawater but for the area covered by his garment, waist to knee. I measured and recorded his rate of breathing. And between those duties I settled into my own routine, sitting on my mattress in the centre of the hut, tapping rhythms with my fingers, singing to myself, walking over to the wooden O, saying hello, watching the silhouettes of the four guards as they crouched or stretched in the doorways. The atmosphere was far from that of a prison, I thought, so it would not have pleased my uncle, had he known how pleasant it was.

But he was not there. I began to feel happiness until one afternoon when I awoke in my hut, my parents gone again, my uncle standing over me. He was touching me with the tip of his cane, poking at my back, saying, "Jaimia, I am hearing good reports of you." "Yes, Uncle," I said. I sat up to face him, keeping my hands firmly in my lap. He crouched down and adjusted the white feather at his neck. He recited for the hundredth time the reasons for which I should be grateful. He had cared for me since my father's accident, he had provided me with food and clothing, not to mention prestige. "Yes, Uncle, we are thankful," I said, wishing that he would just do what he wanted and leave.

Instead he took out, from a leather bag, a tiny ceramic bowl no bigger than a thimble. "Take this to your nursing duties tonight, Jaimia, and rub its contents into an unhealed area of the prisoner's skin, up by his shoulder, where the sun has done the most damage." A fragment of green pandanus leaf tightly covered the little bowl. I lifted its edge and a characteristic odour came to me, like rotting flesh. "But this is the paralyzing substance," I said. "He will die anyway, Jaimia, either naturally or in the Puzzle, so look upon it as providing a kindness." He smoothed the green leaf back down with his finger. I heard my mother's laughter outside so I knew that I was saved, this once, from further humiliation.

ADVISOR TO THE HEADMAN, 32

I left my niece with the poison. Could I trust her? No. I needed a contingency plan. I resolved to speak to the Headman at my next opportunity, to push my case with him, to explain the reasons for my intransigence. I would track him down after my exercises, I thought, but as luck would have it I was only halfway to the beach on my run when there he was, dogtrotting ahead of me.

Within a minute I was by his side. I slowed my pace to match his and wished him the best of that most beautiful day. Then I asked after the Headwoman and was told she was excellent, and then I said, "Forgive me, Headman, but I wish to reiterate, strongly, how important it is for our survival that we strike our guest down before he recovers. He looks harmless, he may be the gentlest white man in the world, but we have received terrible reports, bloodcurdling reports, from those who have experienced contact with his people. Mass slaughters, casual murdering, smoke and fire pouring from the mouths of weapons, seizure of land, rape of women and boys, new diseases that kill outright or bring suffering for months while they themselves, the white men, remain untouched. All who come in contact with them have regretted it. They offer baubles of glass and blankets as gifts, and if those are accepted, three weeks later there is widespread death from a pox."

At that point, breathing heavily but still trotting at my side, the Headman held his hand up. "Advisor," he said "you have made your point. How well-spoken, by the way, you are while running, full sentences pouring forth, unaccompanied by breathlessness. I wish I had paid as much attention to my waistline as you have to yours." Hearing those compliments and pleased by them, I thought to press my advantage, to take my argument to its logical conclusion. I said, "Headman, if this white man survives his exposure to the elements, we should run him through the Puzzle. Let the boars take care of him."

The beach came into view. He suggested we sit with our backs against two palm trees, to think. We did so. Mopping his brow, he said, "As a rule, I would not like to resort to the Puzzle for visitors. It could do harm to our reputation for hospitality." "Well," I said, "with all due respect, Headman, if outsiders knew he was here, that might be true, but as no one does...." I let my voice trail off. "What of the hummingbirds?" he said. "They almost certainly know." "The hummingbirds are doomed," I said. "their knowledge is doomed with them."

We shared a silence for a full ten minutes before he said, weighing the pros and cons, that he was unable to formally commit to the Puzzle but he would keep it at the back of his mind. "Advisor," he said, "time to run back to the village." "Yes, Headman," I said, but once we started I found his pace frustratingly slow. Therefore I invented an important obligation on the mountainside, with my lookouts. I turned on the next suitable path to the right and ran upwards faster, faster, burnishing my reputation with myself, if not with anyone else.

QUERCUS ALBA, 251

Day after day, night after night, he lay motionless on his mattress. He was breathing, so there was hope. Older nurses bathed him by day, but after midnight his care fell to a young girl who was,

I thought, the same who carried me from the beach. I felt close to her because of that—a sentimental flaw, yes, but I was not going to castigate myself—and she did not ignore me. She came to me regularly, tapped me with her finger, pursed her lips almost like a kiss, spoke sentences of gentle musicality. My spirits rose. But at the same time I knew nothing of our future. My sailor and I were metaphorically adrift between life and death.

But on the girl's eleventh night—I kept close count—he moved. His limbs twitched, he turned from what had been his constant position, on his back, to his right side, slipping an inch or two from the mattress as he did so. The girl, whom I could see quite clearly—the light from outside torches filtered through the reeds, dappling the interior—jumped away at his first sign of life. Then she knelt and brushed his long hair from his face and she took, from somewhere in her shift, a container no larger than a snuff-box. She placed it on the ground at her knee and dug a hole with a stick, burying whatever it was deeply, covering it up. Then she stamped her foot a dozen times upon the burial site, so there was no sign of a disturbance. Then she lay down on the floor behind him, on his mattress, and curled up until she had assumed his exact position, tucking her knees behind his, putting her left arm over his waist until she fell asleep. She had never done that before, while on duty. I have felt the warmth of that same arm, I thought, bringing me from the lagoon.

At dawn, at the sound of the first nurse arriving, she peeled herself away from him, stood quickly to her feet, reported what she had seen—pointing to his legs, shaking her hands in imitation of his positional adjustment—and she left the hut, muting the rattle of the shells with both hands.

ANDREW GOLLIVER, 19

I was lying on my side and the stars had disappeared from the sky. I lifted my head to get my bearings. Above me, rather than the arc of heaven, I saw a dark ceiling thatched in palm, a doorway to my left, a doorway to my right. A soft greyness came from outside, and I thought I felt the weight of an arm on my waist before it lifted away, taking a scent of flowers and woodsmoke with it. I heard then the running feet of children, a dog barking, a rooster crowing. Somehow I had come to land. Soft hands turned me onto my back. Fingers opened my mouth, probing at my tongue. I choked and instinctively sat up, and two women with dark hair fell away, alarmed. Four men appeared with spears and fierce expressions. They stared down at me and I must have responded, because the next thing I knew the four of them were opening the curtains and shouting to the world at large. I touched my face to imagine what I looked like. An unruly beard, such as I had never had, such that my own fingers did not recognize my face.

ADVISOR TO THE HEADMAN, 32

Shouts came from the centre of the village. My first thought was that Jaimia had done her duty and the prisoner was dead. But then I heard the words, "He is alive!" and two of the nurses ran by, fluttering their hands in joyous celebration. My niece had defied me. She had done nothing, but I could deal with her later. I strode to the prisoner's hut as though merely curious, and there I found pandemonium, my warriors converging from all sides, daggers drawn, brushing through a shifting throng of villagers. For a moment I wondered if I should not just pick out a hot-head and nod to him, and watch him spring into action. But I could not openly disobey my superiors. Their pacifist views were well known. Therefore I touched my feather and indicated, by a quick motion of my hand, that all knives should be resheathed. How ironic, there I was, ordering my men to do the exact opposite of what I wished. But that was politics, I realized. I was learning how to juggle principle with practicality. And I was proving to be good at it, for even my most aggressive men quickly put away their knives and bowed to me, and we spent the next several minutes forming a human barricade, linking arms to prevent access to the prisoner's hut. "We shall wait," I announced, "for the Headman and Headwoman."

Hardly were those words out of my mouth when the two potentates came into view. They were walking side by side, unhurriedly, he with his hair tied back and his head encased in a helmet of shells extending a foot to the sky, she beside him in a similarly shaped headdress, but adorned even more colourfully with blooms of white and red and yellow flowers. Rarely had we seen our leaders in their full regalia. They cleaved their way through the hushed crowd and motioned for me to join them, and as a unified troop of three we strode to the closest doorway of the hut. The guard opened the curtain. We entered as a slow drum began to beat, coming from near the firepits, lending, I thought, a solemn gravity to our procession. Although I was personally in a turmoil, wary and concerned, the Headman and Headwoman projected nothing but a casual amiability, as though they had done this a thousand times.

The prisoner was sitting knees apart on his mattress, drinking from a halved coconut. His head was tipped back, his beard a mat of tangles. Upon seeing our leaders, however, he put his drink quickly to the floor and tried to get to his feet. But he staggered from the effort—just as he had done on his raft—wobbling uncertainly but not falling. His height, we all perceived, was above that of our Headman, even including the headdress. The prisoner then dropped to one knee as a courtesy, lowering himself. Although the Headman and Headwoman acknowledged him with a smile, I fixed him with my coldest stare, to set myself apart. "Advisor," the Headman said, "you should relax," and then he asked me how I thought we should communicate with the young man.

I was well-prepared. I suggested we step to the centre of the village, where we could draw pictures that even children could understand, on well-beaten earth. "Then out we go," said the Headwoman, and so we did, two guards supporting the wobbler, one on each arm. The villagers raised a low murmur and backed away, as though they were seeing an emaciated ghost, an apparition. The lone drum beat a trifle faster. Then we formed a tight circle at the centre of the village, children and dogs running wildly about our periphery.

Taking the initiative, I raised my arm. The drumbeat stopped. I bent low to the ground with my dagger and drew a rough diagram of a raft in rippling water, with one person lying upon it. My skill was considerable, I thought, so it was no surprise that the young man immediately nodded and pointed to himself. "Yes," I said, and then I drew a semblance of our war canoe, much reduced in length, with only four paddlers per side for expediency, and then I smudged out the figure on the raft with my finger and drew it flying bird-like across the water and falling into our canoe. Then, even more rapidly, more deftly, I drew a likeness of our beach, two palm trees bent to the lagoon. He nodded again. By then the villagers had gathered so closely around that I was almost forced into physical contact with the white man. But I held myself aloof and proceeded to draw a tall man with long legs being carried into a hut, and next I fashioned a reasonable facsimile of the hut's interior, with the same man recumbent, and two women—I drew their breasts, for differentiation—crouched over him. He nodded and smiled. I almost drew his talisman but decided to leave it unacknowledged, and I thought how oral language was much overrated, that speech could introduce subtleties, yes, but many of those subtleties were overrated.

Then the prisoner gestured, weakly, holding out his hand, asking if he could have my dagger to make drawings of his own.

"No," I said, "but fetch him a harmless stick." A mad scramble then ensued among the children and dogs to find one, which they did. I slightly sharpened its tip and, after checking with the Headman and Headwoman for approval, I handed the pointed instrument to him generously, as though I were actually waiting with interest for his self-exculpatory pictures.

ANDREW GOLLIVER, 19

I forced myself to concentrate. It became clear that the man with the feather was, through his drawings, describing my rescue at sea. Murmurs rose from the crowd but I could not judge their significance. There was nothing for me to do, I realized, but explain my presence and express my gratitude. With that in mind I asked for his knife, to initiate my own picture-making. Instead I was given a sharpened stick, with which I scratched a likeness of the *John Roberts*, an ungainly behemoth of a vessel, three masts, square sails and, on its deck, one tiny human figure. "That is me," I said, pointing to my chest. Then I drew monstrous waves overwhelming the ship, turning it on its side, sinking it beneath a wavery line etched in the dirt. "Shipwreck," I said, if only to myself. With the edge of my hand I wiped out what was left of the *John Roberts*. I attempted to duplicate the feathered man's drawing of a lone figure lying on a raft, but I was less skilled as an artist. Nevertheless everyone nodded. They understood. I also wanted to express my gratitude, and my good intentions. How would I do that? I had no idea. Villagers were pressing in closer and closer, touching me, smiling. A black curtain descended, extinguishing my view, and the next thing I knew I was back on my mattress, covered in sweat, and there, on the far wall, looking down at me from a shelf, was the single letter *O*, torn from the heart of my raft.

So far from privilege lay I, but not entirely without a friend.

THE HEADMAN, 41

When the young man fainted, I motioned to the guards to pick him up and carry him inside. Confluent areas of crusting were still present on his shoulders and back, and the sun was so high in the heavens that his underlying condition could only be aggravated. I looked about to assess the mood of the crowd. To my pleasure, I saw only kindliness and genuine interest in his welfare. My wife touched my arm and said that he seemed so young, and wasn't his hair quite remarkable, almost as white as the feathers of a gull. It was not my habit to comment on any man's physical appearance, but I could not deny that he looked both fragile and otherworldly. I mumbled vague words of agreement. Then my Advisor began to broach his favourite subject, that our prisoner—as he called him—was a danger to the island, a malingerer, and so on, an opinion that my wife and I were already too familiar with. To assuage his bloodthirstiness, however, and so as not to undercut his authority before his warriors, I ordered that the young man be kept under constant surveillance, that Jaimia should continue her midnight vigils—they had, after all, been ultimately successful—and the older nurses should continue direct care of his wounds. Then I added, to irritate my Advisor slightly, "Why rush to judgment, for all of us can verify, as of last night, that the moon and fixed stars are still undisturbed in the night sky."

Then the Headwoman and I turned directly to our people. I spoke a few words of reassurance. We asked them to disperse, for the day's excitement was over. We returned in the direction of our hut, watching with amusement the shadows of our head-dresses preceding us, and she mentioned to me that my Advisor was ill-named, that he could just as easily be called Pest to the Headman. "All he does," she said, "is pester us endlessly about that nice-looking young man, who has been through so much." "Oh," I said, teasing her, "then you are much taken by him." She laughed and said, "Yes, almost as much as I am taken with you, my Headman." I reminded her that our Advisor had been chosen by acclamation and would be in that position for the foreseeable future. We had no acceptable means to usurp him, and besides, were we not better served by a zealot such as he than by a laggard such as the last? She replied that in her opinion zealots were far more dangerous, for they insisted on inflicting their views on everyone rather than seeking compromise. I said that it was our mandate to listen to advice, but we need not act upon it. And, I added, did she agree with me that we should offer the young man, with whom she was so much taken, whose hair was as white as the feathers of a gull, four weeks of intensive physical exercises, under my guidance, to allow him to fully recuperate? "Why, yes, Headman," she said, and she agreed that in the morning she would formally make such an announcement.

By then we were climbing the steps to our porch. I said that there was one more thing I should mention. My Advisor had, the other day, raised the possibility of the Puzzle, as a means of solving the crisis. He was leaning towards it, saying that the Puzzle would absolve us of our collective responsibility, that the boars would bear the ultimate blame. "Absolutely not," my wife said, "no Puzzle without a formal vote."

We stopped and looked back at our village, thinking how peaceful it was, how peaceful it had been for so long. We looked at each other too, smiling at our regalia. She put her hand on my paunch—my very slight paunch—and said, "Perhaps, Headman, you should join our guest in his physical exercises." "Oh," I said, "now you too wish to become an Advisor to the Headman." "I already am," she said, "and have been for years." "Perhaps," I replied, "we could take this opportunity, right now, to exercise together. You are most attractive, bedecked as you are with flowers." "Yes, Headman," she said, and so we closed the curtain behind us and proceeded to intimacies. Afterwards

I lay upon our mattress as she slept, and I planned, meticulously, in my mind, without moving a muscle, a complex recovery regimen for the young man.

Those moments allowed me, the next morning, to arrive bright and early at his hut with four men his age, to take him from his nurses and challenge him to run to the beach with his new companions. He nodded. He was game for it, I could see, already looking stronger than the day before. Off they ran, the five of them, slowly, down the path to the lagoon. In an hour they were back, and already he was standing straighter, even taller, and the next day he did two full circuits, and by the third he did five. His natural size and strength were much to his advantage. By the sixth day his escort was hard pressed to keep up to him, and two of them even looked at me plaintively, as though they needed to be relieved. Instead I took a severe page from my Advisor's book and commanded them to climb the mountain to mid-level, and there our guest was to lift heavy stones for fifteen minutes, and the next day for an hour, bending and stooping and carrying sharp rectangles of shale and armfuls of pumice to the cliff edge, there to throw them off to the jungle and listen to them clatter below.

Obediently they ran off. I heard later that he had worked harder than anyone had expected, so much so that his guards had been shamed into helping, pitching rocks to nowhere and feeling quite foolish for it. When the throwing was over, they took him down to the beach for a brief cooling-off spell, a dip in the water. But even there, on the strand, my regimen required him to pick up fallen coconuts and, two hands cupped together, cast each coconut as high as he could, making a dark sphere against the blue of the sky. One hundred times, two hundred. Then he was allowed to return to the village but running, running all the way, his guard-companions looking as prickly as sea urchins with their armoury of spears and knives. He of course had no weapon of any kind, yet he was getting stronger, faster, out in front of the others as though they were chasing a spirit but could never catch it.

He and his guards had, by that time, bonded. They were unified in their purpose. Tight muscles bulged in their shoulders and upper backs. They sang songs together too, nonsensical ones, as they did not share a language. They whistled tunes. The young man shaved his beard with a shell and combed and cut his hair to look the same as the rest, but for his colouring. When there were five days remaining in his four-week prescription, I ordered my last but very precise drill. I demonstrated it myself, to the amusement of the Headwoman and the guards, but I felt it important and did not want to stand on ceremony. I took him to the edge of the jungle and I dove into its verge and rolled and leapt to my feet, and I somersaulted quickly here and there, to the right, to the left, to the left, to the right without establishing a pattern. I gestured to him to do the same, and so he did, but he was much faster, able to complete three dives and four somersaults to one of mine. He was as nimble as a cat, so it occurred to me that if he were to stay with us and become part of our warrior society, he would be a formidable foe to our enemies. But, as I said to the Headwoman, "Really, dearest, we have no enemies." She replied, "How true, my Headman, so why don't we just let him go, give him a serviceable boat, let the boy go. He must have a home somewhere."

GERALD EGERTON, 22

One afternoon, at billiards, the Earl mentioned to me that his long-awaited trip to Ireland would take place in three weeks. "Really," I said, and then I predicted I would knock the yellow ball into the side pocket, which I did easily, despite the brandy. My brain was on fire. Would three weeks give me enough time? I would have to return to London, meet with Mr. Figby, his trigger-man would have to make the trip to Galway. Not a simple matter. The Irish Sea could kick up. The Earl then potted three difficult caroms in a row to jump ahead of me on the chalkboard. Distracted, I missed a simple shot of my own.

"How long, Sir," I asked, "do you expect to spend there?" "As little time as possible," he said, "no more than four weeks. Plus the travelling to and fro." Reassuring, I thought. Then I offered— knowing he would refuse—to accompany him. "No, Gerald," he said, "for the manor needs a man about the house, and with Andrew absconded, you should be that man." "But Sir," I said, "Ireland is a perilous place, and I would be a loyal musket by your side." He scoffed, saying that he had Mr. Burke, and Mr. Burke could shoot the feathers off four-and-twenty blackbirds if he wished, even while the birds were in flight, and they would fall naked into a heated pie crust, for a meal. He had no personal concern for his safety. Plus, he added, he was taking Emerson Callaghan, no slouch at arms either. He would keep his pack of dogs ahead to sniff out rats and cowards.

Inwardly I danced a jig. London, the game is on. Besides, I deserved another break from patting his wolfhounds, watching rain streak down the windows, adjusting logs on the fire. Her mother's knitting needles going *clickety-click-click*, Catherine's thumping on the pianoforte. It had become torture to me, so much so that now and then I would formulate an excuse—once even a cramping in the bowels—and I would rush from the salon and make my way to the stables, there to leap to the first horse and dash about for an hour or two in fresh air, until my composure returned.

But still there was pressure of time. "London is no longer a place I wish to frequent," I said to Catherine, "but a friend is ill!" "Stay with me," she said, pouting as I kissed her and swung her in my arms, circling until we were dizzy, until I was able to squeeze past her. Off I went to arrange her father's killing.

To both our benefits, I might have said—considering their contentious relationship, she might have agreed—but some things in marriages are better not said aloud.

In Southwark, in the narrow streets behind the church, I found my cutthroat friend. He was still as unshaven, still bent at the waist, a caricature of a scoundrel, really, a pantomime of one, which gave me comfort as I handed him my purse. "But how will Mr. Figby engineer our project?" I asked. "Have no fear, he has more tentacles than a giant squid and octopus combined!" "But you referred to him as a spider last time," I said. "He is all three, good Sir, all three." Stealthily I followed him on his mission—I lacked full trust, needless to say—until he pushed open the door to a ramshackle little box of a tavern called, by its sign, the Duck and Spoon. It looked as though it might fall to the Thames at the next rush of tide. I approached with double caution and, peering through a dirt-encrusted window, I saw my intermediary huddle with a large man in a greatcoat, leaning on the bar. My purse changed hands. So, the first part of the deed was done. "Capital!" I said, for I had become a cog within an efficient criminal enterprise, yet remained anonymous. I was John Smith. I walked away from the river whistling and next I found myself singing "he's asleep, asleep, fathoms down in the briny deep," a lyric from my school days. It must have come to me unconsciously, referencing the only other obstacle in my path, her brother, almost certainly somewhere at sea.

MISS ALBERTSON, 45

It was late in the evening, and Clovis and I were preparing corned beef and cabbage for the Earl's trip to Ireland. Finally, having had enough of working our fingers to the bone, we poured tea for ourselves and, gazing straight at me with her oh-so-blue eyes, Clovis said, touching my wrist, "I have a confession to make. I told Emerson, years ago, how we killed the Friar, mistaking him for the Earl." "Clovis!" I said, "how could you, how could you, that was our secret and no one else's!" "Oh Beulah," she said, "Emerson would never tell a soul, and look, the proof is in the pudding. Years have gone by and nothing has happened. Not only that, but now, because of my telling him, quite an opportunity has arisen. Our blunder can be corrected." Baffled, I said, "Clovis, please explain yourself." And so she did. "In bed last night, Emerson whispered in my ear that he had never forgotten how we had murdered the Friar—how could he forget, such a macabre scene!—but now things had come full circle, for he had just received a remarkable offer, at the Bridport market. He had been leaning against the wall by the clock tower waiting for fresh produce to appear. A stranger struck up a conversation, asking if he were not, judging by his livery, a footman in the employ of Lord Amberley. Yes, Emerson replied, he had been a footman of the Earl's for more than twenty years. The stranger then remarked, did he not detect a slight Irish lilt to the footman's speech? And Emerson, blushing, admitted that yes, his parents were from Donegal and had taken work in London, where he was born, to make ends meet. Perhaps he still had a bit of the brogue, inherited. The man said he thought so, no harm to it, all the better perhaps, and then he asked if Emerson's surname could possibly be Callaghan, for if it were, he had a proposal to make. As there was no sign of the vegetables yet for the wagon, Emerson said yes, that was his name. The stranger then proceeded to say—in utmost confidence—that a price had been put on the Earl's head. A client wanted him murdered in Ireland, and the reward would be a year's wage for the five seconds it would take. Would Emerson Callaghan accept the job, admirably situated as he would be, riding at the Earl's side? Emerson was taken aback, needless to say, but then he remembered how we had risked our lives to the same end nineteen years before. He also remembered the Earl's hand pushing its way up my skirt.

Weighing the pros and cons, assessing his own personal risk as minimal, knowing I would more than approve, Emerson again said yes. And the man said they thought so, they thought so back in London, that was their thinking."

"Clovis," I said, "Unbelievable!" "And Emerson's reaction was so much more sensible than ours, Beulah, it was rational, far more likely to succeed." "Was he given other instructions?" "Only that he could choose his own moment in Ireland, that he should blame it on extremists, or a hunting accident." "Was he given money or is it to be a pure, hot-blooded, politically motivated vengeance killing?" Clovis laughed. "Beulah," she said, "we can afford new shoes for the children. We have tucked our portion of the payment underneath the kindling, by the stove, and your portion is here."

From a small pouch, taken from her pocket, she spilled a dozen gold coins across the table. "Good Lord," I said, "Clovis, I would feel shame receiving this, but for the good that will come of it."

JAIMIA, 17

The rumours haunted me for days, so I asked my uncle directly, passing by him near the river, whether the white man might be sent to the Puzzle. "Yes," he said, "he has a very good chance of ending there, and you, Jaimia, have yourself to blame, for your disobedience." I next went to the Headwoman and asked her the same question, and she said, "It's politics, Jaimia, you will find that politics are the bane of common sense. Your uncle is pushing for it, the Puzzle, relentlessly. My husband, although he does not wish to see it happen, might bend to his wishes. But my husband is also training the young man in highly focussed exercises, thinking that his size and strength might serve him well. The boars, after all, have been weakened by prolonged captivity."

Perhaps so, I thought, but they were still extraordinarily ferocious. To walk past them, to hear them spitting and grunting and hurling themselves against their cage, was a hair-raising experience. I found myself wondering if there were anything I could do to improve his odds, if worse came to worst. To that end I searched through my father's daggers, of which he had many—he was, before his injury, a formidable warrior—and I picked out one of his smaller ones, seven inches long from its handle of wrapped pandanus leaves to its iron-tipped blade.

At moonrise I hid it under my shift. I placed a bone needle in my hair. I walked by the carefree guards, and they waved me to the inner sanctum, saying, "Good evening, Jaimia." The shells of the curtain clattered. I lit the only taper and fixed it to the earth, and I was pleased to see that the nurses had provided him with a second pair of knee-pants, folded neatly by the mattress. By gestures, I asked how he was, and he must have understood me for he shrugged as though he were both good and bad, or both at the same time, so I thought our moods were similar.

Knowing how vulnerable he was, I bent to put my face beside his as a gesture of companionship. He did not move away but in fact held my cheek against his, with his hand, for a prolonged time. I could tell that he wanted me to stay where I was. In fact I was enjoying it too, and we must have shared that position for a full minute before we relaxed—it was awkward for me, physically, for I was half-bending—and then I sat down opposite him, the taper lending its circular glow to the space between. Rather than further delay my mission, I produced my father's knife and, picking up the new piece of clothing, I quickly wove, using my needle, a small hook at the inner seam of the right thigh, stretching its own material to do so. I then suspended the knife from it, and suggested he put the weaponized garment on, as a test. I turned away as he changed. He tapped my shoulder, and when I looked the dagger was fully hidden but its tip, he indicated, was a problem. Apparently it penetrated the weave when he moved his leg about, poking into his skin. I slipped out to the largest firepit, still warm with coals, and found several globules of congealed soap, formed from discards of coconut oil. I formed a ball the size of a berry. In the hut, I handed it to him, and he was able to place it upon the dagger's tip, and then he jumped about experimentally and smiled, and I thought the problem solved.

Then he affected a puzzled expression, asking me, I could see, why he might need such a knife, and why it should be hidden. Remembering how my uncle had drawn pictures for him, I searched the floor for a small stick and, sitting beside him with the taper before us, I did my best to explain.

QUERCUS ALBA, 251

From my shelf, I watched him gradually recover his strength. For decades I had been forced into total passivity, locked into myself. But once he began leaving for most of the day and returning exhausted, I found myself yearning for the same, for the out of doors. Little did I know how soon my wish would be granted, or what would bring it about.

The mood in our hut changed dramatically—at least it did for me—on the night the young girl presented him with a dagger and was secretive about it. They sequestered it in a new pair of dungarees. Danger was afoot, I concluded. They huddled by the light of a candle, and she began to draw on the earthen floor using the knife as etching tool. She was worried, I thought, and urgently wanted to communicate. From my vantage point I could clearly see her scratchings, and I did my best to interpret them. First she drew a cage-like structure containing three goats or pigs, and then she drew the same animals, only larger, running through childish depictions of trees, vines, and plants. Next the same creatures—somehow grown even larger—chased after a running stick-man figure. My sailor at that juncture pointed to himself, and to the stick-man, and raised his eyebrows as if to ask, Is that me? The girl nodded yes. Then she drew the stick-man assuming a defensive pose, holding a comically oversized knife in his hand. He was standing directly in front of one of the beasts, which by then had swelled to the size of a giant, with tusks curving over his lips. They laughed at her rendering, how ridiculous it was. Quickly she rubbed it out with her hand and drew a shakily-drawn stick-man lying flat on his back. She placed the beast on top of him, pressing down with both forefeet, crushing him. I wondered if the girl were crying, from the way her shoulders began to shake. If so, she quickly recovered and pointed to herself and said a word that sounded like "Jay-mi-a," with the emphasis on the second syllable, "Jay-MI-a." My sailor reciprocated, pointing to his chest, saying "AN-drew." At last I knew his given name. I watched as they pressed their faces closely together, as though they were kissing. Maybe so, maybe not, but either way they broke apart after a minute and curled up together, she behind him with her arm over his waist, lying partially on the earth, partially on the mattress. Judging from their breathing, they fell asleep and were motionless until the first glimmer of dawn. Then she stood to her feet abruptly, brushed remnants of the drawings away, straightened her shift, approached to within a foot of me, tapped me twice with her index finger, and left. Andrew was still motionless, dead, so to speak, to the world.

ANDREW GOLLIVER, 19

Having seen—if I understood her drawings properly—a frightening version of my future, I did not stint in the company of my guards. I lifted rocks on the mountainside as though possessed. I threw them tumbling to the scree below. At the beach I heaved a hundred coconuts into the air and caught them as they fell.

Then I dodged non-existent shadows and rolled on the ground and jumped to my feet as directed by the Headman. He was keeping a sharp but friendly eye on me, I noticed, but I was not reassured. I pushed myself harder, lest her frightening animal appear and I be unprepared. At times, especially in the open sunshine, by the lip of the volcano, I was conscious of the dagger within the looseness of my pants, how it twisted against my inner thigh. I worried it would be seen, confiscated, investigated, yet the guards were on such low alert that they noticed nothing. By a subtle adjustment of my hand or knee, I was able to keep it hidden.

My days of semi-freedom, it turned out, were down to three. But I was ignorant of that fact. Each dawn broke identically, with the same cooking fires, the same sun tracking heavenward through a sky devoid of clouds. The Headman would appear, yawning, stretching, casually giving orders. I would run, and lift and throw my stones, irregular chunks of pumice weighing fifty to eighty pounds each, carry them to the edge of the precipice, cast them to forgetfulness while the azure sea cascaded on the reef below. Then we would take a swim in the lagoon and race back to the village. In privacy, recovering from my day, back at the hut, I would look at my letter O and we would conclude, between the two of us, that our fates were as much in the air as one of my coconuts, reaching its apex, pausing, turning black against the sky.

In the evening, as the ambient air cooled, a single guard would escort me to dinner at the hut of the Headman and Headwoman. A rotating cast of dignitaries joined us, but always present was the man with the white feather. My personal Judas, I feared. Not that I was anything like Christ, far from it, but it served me well to think in Biblical terms, to keep an eye out for the man who might destroy me. He never smiled. Eventually, to keep up my spirits in his presence, I avoided his eye entirely, concentrating on my portion of breadfruit and silvery fish, the latter cooked in a wrap of leaves so that it fell apart in my fingers. There was always conversation, and much laughter and ease, and I noticed—how could I not—that all of their teeth were perfectly formed, with none of the rotten pegs of Englishmen. I also noticed the good nature of the leaders' governance, how the Headman deferred to his wife, and she to him, naturally and comfortably. How different that was, I thought, from the alternating silence and raging of Father, at our mealtimes.

When dinner was finished and bones cast to the dogs, I was dismissed. Dusk fell to darkness, to a soft beating of drums and the lighting of torches. My guard delivered me back to my chamber, to wait for Jaimia. She drew no more wild animals. Instead we learned to kiss, spending hours leaning towards each other until she made it clear that it was time to fall asleep, to be rested for morning. Then she tucked in behind me as she had done before, as though that position of innocence would bring me comfort and slumber rather than pitching my desire to its peak, so provocatively close she was. Blood coursed through me. I managed, however, not to turn to her despite bliss and torment in equal measure until I was rescued, finally, by the first birds of dawn, the barking of dogs. Then she would rise, remove her arm from my waist, leave me in a clattering of shells. I realized that I must have slept after all, for my energy was abundant. was ready for another day of mountain and beach, of racing, lifting, throwing, falling, jumping, wondering, waiting.

ADVISOR TO THE HEADMAN, 32

I visited the boars. Their food had been withheld for two days. We had given them only water, and one of them, a female, was sickly, lying on her side with a yellowish substance oozing from her nose. However the other two, the males, were in fine fettle. They tore at me as usual, growling, spitting, hurling themselves against the bamboo with such force that I felt compelled to back away. They would do well, I could see, on the jungle paths.

Next I went to the Headman. "It is time for the vote," I said, "please," and to my surprise he relented. "All right, Advisor," he said, "the people can choose, they have the right. But you must present each option without prejudice, without using inflammatory verbs or adverbs, and the third option—releasing him to the ocean on a seaworthy craft—cannot be glossed over." His wife was standing by his side. "Of course, Headman, and of course, Headwoman," I said, "and thank you." If satisfaction could ever be described as being fierce, that was how I felt.

I could have waited another day or two to consolidate my influence. But I was confident in the support of my warriors, so I pulled two of them from their morning chores and asked them to commandeer the drums, to begin the staccato rhythm we had not heard in years. Soon everyone was running to the centre of the village. I had the prisoner apprehended from his hut. I ordered that his arms be bound to his chest. I was pleased to see, as he stumbled forward, that his ingratiating smile had vanished, that his towering height was severely diminished when he was pushed to his knees. I asked the crowd to give us room. The Headman and Headwoman were standing well in the back, reduced to ordinary citizens for the vote, and briefly I reflected on the subtleties of power, for of course those two were absolved of any responsibility for the outcome, whereas I, by my foresight and daring, was on the hook, so to speak, like a fish, if something were to go awry.

But I did not hesitate. I hushed the assembly by raising my arms. Even the dogs fell silent. Touching my feather for emphasis, I said that it was time to decide the fate of the drifted sailor, who had been with us for so many weeks, that it was incumbent on all adult citizens to listen to the choices offered and to remember, once their vote was cast, that it could not be rescinded. I then stood by the prisoner's side, put my left hand on his right shoulder, and I intoned, as forcefully as I could without shouting, "Here stands a white man in our midst, and we have options three to vote upon."

"The first option," I said—returning to my normal speaking voice—"is to treat him as a threat and spear him through the chest as he kneels before us." Immediate shouts of disapproval rose from all quarters, reflecting a sentiment that did not surprise me. He had gained some popularity, after all, during his running about with his so-called guards in tow, young and unproven men provided for him by the Headman.

I moved on. I reminded myself to appear neutral. "The second option is to deliver him to the Puzzle." Fewer complaints were raised, also not a surprise to me for the Puzzle was, for many, a rare entertainment as well as a punitive exercise, a carnival as well as a murdering.

"The third option," I said, "is a very generous one, that we give him one of our better boats, tow him beyond the breakers, point him to the west, bid him goodbye."

A clamour of voices broke out, and many hands were raised, and for the next half-hour a lively discussion flowed back and forth, with some saying that surely there were other more humanitarian choices, such as keeping him as one of us, or enslaving him. A wag even said, "Make him advisor to the Advisor to the Headman!" My own niece asked, in apparent innocence, "What will happen if the Puzzle is chosen but he survives?" Laughter rippled through the ranks. But the Headwoman spoke up to say that should a person, man or woman, survive the Puzzle, he or she would be provided with the third option, safe passage. A small coterie of warriors—those who had accompanied him to the mountain and the beach—tapped their spears to the ground in approval, as though they thought that his survival was actually a possibility. Momentarily I paused, but

"Enough!" I cried, and I pointed to the sun at its zenith and said, "It is time for the show of hands. Should society seamlessly integrate this stranger, or should we guard against him? Vote, citizens! Those in favour of the third option—safe passage—raise your hands!" Forty-eight, I counted, a surprisingly high number, but a thrill ran through me for the numbers were not there, not for him, not for my niece, not for his other well-wishers. "Option two, the Puzzle," I said, and I counted sixty hands. "Option one," I said, and there were fifty votes, the vast majority coming from my cadre of warriors.

"Citizens," I shouted, clenching my fist, "the drifted sailor will be taken to meet the boars, our servants!" I gestured to have him lifted to his feet. I looked him in the eye and allowed myself a smile. Foolishly, he smiled back, for he was in ignorance and was taking my expression at face value. "There will be no delay in carrying out the sentence," I announced, and so began the ceremonial walk for all of us, every villager, every child, every adolescent including my niece—whom I ignored, for the time being, although I had plans for her—amidst an air more celebratory than funereal, to the swamp, to the boars' cage. With four warriors at my side I broke into a run, to check on the spirit of the animals, leaving behind the bound prisoner walking slowly. A very fine day, a cooler than average breeze welcoming us from the east. Ideal conditions, really, for what was to come.

ZEPHYRAX, 3

Judging from the stars at night, we had drifted a bit north since the island of glue sticks, as though instinctively seeking our traditional route. We were more or less following the artificial line of the equator, as drawn by human cartographers, dividing the northern from the southern hemisphere. By day, however, staring only at the burning sun and the curving sheen of the sea below, it was easy to wobble off course. We could have been anywhere. I said to my flight companions, "How ironic that we can, under usual circumstances, fly easily to a thimble-sized nest north of Lake Superior, yet today, expending maximum effort, we find only emptiness." "How true, Zephyrax," they said to me, "but let us play that little game of yours to cheer ourselves up!" So we recited, as in the old days, the words *flower, nectar, twig, milkweed, thistle, cattail, willow, fireweed, spiders, gnats, mosquitoes,* and so on, chanting in unison while our leaders surely were choking on their misplaced braggadocio. They had brought us to this extreme. Moreover, all of us could see that the worst was yet to come. As a flock, we had dropped our altitude slowly over the previous forty-eight hours, from one thousand feet to eight hundred to seven hundred, suggesting to any bird with a mathematical bent that in several days none of us would be airborne at all.

At that bleak hour, however, at high noon, we finally heard chirps of tempered joy from the vanguard. Word of possible landfall came back to us. There was, we were told, a speck upon the white-hot sea that appeared to be solid matter to our scouts, and although we had been led astray so many times, still we believed. We would have gone mad had we not.

An hour later we found ourselves descending to a rock outcropping that not even a wide-eyed optimist, a holy fool, could deem hospitable. It was a low reef heavily streaked with guano, upon which we had to hop, skip and jump individually from pointed rock to pointed rock to offset the burning of fecal chemicals at our feet. Although there were tidal pools—deceptively pretty ones—they harboured nothing but low ribbons of brown kelp waving back and forth sinuously and what looked like larvae, clusters of white ovals held together by a clear jelly, tempting to the near-starved but six inches or more underwater, inaccessible. Scattered reservoirs of fresh water existed on some of the flatter rocks, from rainfall, but those pools had become heated by the tropical sun and were ringed with crystals of salt, from evaporation, from sea-water contamination. They were unfit for any useful purpose except bathing, sipping, and gagging.

We had no choice, really, but to stay. Many of the flock were too tired to consider moving on. Many were suffering from a general malaise, from a form of depression or spiritual despair. Therefore we settled as best we could, pecking like tiny egrets into cracks for the odd windblown seed, for an ant or two, sipping at the brackish water until it was exhausted. Now and then, from a slight change in the wind, we heard our leaders chattering among themselves, pretending all was well, exclaiming that the profusion of white spiders that finally hatched on our seventh day, from those jellied eggs, were nutritious and tasty. The truth was, they stung our tongues and throats in protest as they were being swallowed.

Stasis set in upon us. There seemed to be no plan for escape. Then I, Zephyrax, took it upon myself to approach the leaders— they had by then separated themselves to a small peninsula of boulders jutting to the southwest—and I reminded them that we were still, despite all our troubles, the strongest of birds by body weight, that we had never been quitters, that our historical strength was founded in action, not in passivity. "We owe it to ourselves," I said, "to summon the courage to rise. We will die here from attrition if we stay." I then flew to the air and tumbled about with my best buzzing, to demonstrate vigour, and those birds who could see me snapped out of their lethargy. They fluttered their wings. "Zephyrax, how right you are!" they said—or words to that effect—and a minute or two later we rose as a flock from the Isle of Stinging Guano and resumed our westward course. But what a sad crew we were, as ragged as crows. We had forgotten what it meant to be rubythroats, we had lost our sizzle, our spark, we no longer cut through the sky like sheet lightning, energized.

FETU, 8

One of us was sick, our female. We knew she was dying. She lay on her side, hardly moving air. Her lips were pulled back from her incisors like dried strips of leather. The words she managed were always the same, "Curse them, curse them," and once she even said, "Fuck them all." Never had she sworn before. She barely drank from the wooden bowl of water slipped between the bars, looping her tongue to it, taking a few drops. Then one day our keeper, a reasonably kind woman, was replaced by a man who wore a feathered necklace, a coward who kept safe distance, taunting us with pieces of meat, with chicken necks and fish skins that he pretended to fumble, dropping them to the dirt beneath our cage. We charged at him, at that provocation, smashing our faces into the bamboo slats, showering him with flecks of blood and mucous, but his response was to poke at our female with his whip-like cane until she said to us, "Take vengeance on that son of a bitch, take vengeance." She could not see the four warriors he had poised at his back, the grey paste waiting for us on their spears. "Don't worry," we lied to her, "we will do it."

Then, for three days, he gave us nothing but water. Fury built up within us. A madness seeped into our reasoning. "Curse them, curse them," we said, forgetting that food deprivation had, in the past, meant that soon a victim would be forced up against our bars, that we would take his scent, run him down, gut and gore him. If in the process we lost our moral compass even further, if we were complicit with those we despised, if afterwards we were contrite, still we would snap up whatever leftovers would be tossed to us. In other words, we had already learned to wear our shame as a garment we could not toss aside.

Drums began to beat. An uncountable number of villagers rushed to surround us. Two of their so-called warriors leapt to the roof of our cage to unravel the vines, to lift our door. So impatient did the two of us become that we knocked against each other, our hooves slipping in filth. We fell against our female, scrambling up just in time to spit and snap at a face pressed up against the bars, to tongue his nose, smell him from a quarter-inch away, taste the fear that rose not only from him but from the guards who held him. Then we watched with anticipation as he was given a toy knife and pushed towards the jungle. Off he ran, and both of us pushed forward, needless to say, crying, "Me! Me!" hammering ourselves against the door until it was taken upward and both of us tumbled out, falling to our knees like penitents, not like the kings we once were.

I staggered up, anxious to establish primacy. I bolted, leaving behind the stink of rancid shit pooled beneath the cage. Fresh air coursed over my face. I took the path to the first corner, then the narrower trail to the hock-deep swamp, slipping, splashing through mud, euphorically. But even in the throes of that ecstasy I became aware that he, the present runner, had differentiated himself. He had taken to water immediately, purposefully, intending to sow confusion. I hesitated in my stride, wondering if he could be dangerous. Then I became distracted by the oncoming thumping of hooves, *dum-de-dum-de-dum-de-dum*, my cellmate's, Umar's. They had released us both, a novelty. Also, to me, an irritation, but he was slower, older. His extra months of incarceration had taken their toll. I slipped unnoticed into a bush of tangled thorns and watched as he ran by, wrong-headed, in the direction of the beach.

"Goodbye, Umar," I said, and next I tested the wind. Birds had fallen into silence. I raised my snout, recapturing the slender thread of the runner. I spun clear of my hiding place, leaving it in a flurry of superficial cuts, turning down the first path to even deeper swamp, and there I spied his first mistake, a carelessness, a foot-long skid in mud. My hackles rose of their own accord. I slowed to a trot as the pungency of his odour thickened from thread to rope. Frighten him, Fetu, flush him out, I thought, so

I took ten aggressive steps from shallow water to dry land, to a sun-dappled clearing, to ankle-deep leaves and jungle debris, to shock when the solid ground gave way and I was, unbelievably, chin to chin with a screaming white face covered with a skim of dirt, maggots, root-rot, under which he had been hidden. I was taken by such surprise that a cry escaped from me as well. I tried to jump away but found no purchase for my feet. I was body-to-body with him, unable to rise above, unable to hammer him down, and next I felt a hot liquid pouring down my chin and my breath faltered, the jungle's greenery spun three hundred and sixty degrees, I buried my tongue in loam.

ANDREW GOLLIVER, 19

I had one knife in hand, the secret one against my thigh. So I was not entirely without resources. I set out at a walking pace, cries of support and cries of derision following in equal measure. I reached the first corner, disappearing from their view. Immediately I broke into a sprint, leaving the main path, turning into a narrower track in the direction of the swamp, two hundred yards distant. There I entered into leech-laden, tepid warmth, into a thousand differing shades of green and black, through filtered sun and unfiltered shadow, ferns and bracken bending towards me, bending away. Maintaining full speed, I crossed a relatively bracing knee-deep estuarial finger of the sea and climbed up again to dry land. I stopped to consider my strategy. From the distance came a roar of excitement, announcing that the chase was fully on. I moved back into the jungle, and there I spied a natural concavity, a grave-sized depression six inches deep, just off the path. As good a place as any for a last stand, I thought, so I took Jaimia's knife from my dungarees, decapped its protective tip, lay face-upwards within the hollow, pulled everything within reach on top of me, sweeping armfuls of rotting leaves, tendrils of vines, slivers of bark, a hundred running and stinging ants over my bare chest, and there I waited, semi-smothered, motionless, listening to the jungle hold its breath. Finally came a rhythmic stepping close by, a set of hooves passing to my left only to return a minute later, slowly, snuffling, wheezing. I tensed, he fell directly upon me, as I had hoped. But fear overwhelmed me. In a frenzy of shouting I drove the tip of my knife upwards into his lily-soft throat, his four legs beat staccato on my chest, hot blood poured down my hand and wrist, bathing me in scarlet. He choked and died far more suddenly than I could ever have hoped. I threw him off, scrambled to my feet. Irrationally, sobbing, I severed his head from his body, cutting through gristle and bone until the knife blade snapped. Then I ran towards the sound of distant surf, two of my fingers stuffed into his nostrils, clots of dark crimson trailing from his chin.

THE ISLAND, 12,000

My islanders called their ultimate punishment the Puzzle, as though, by that gentle name, they could rob it of its horror. But to me it called into question their whole system of jurisprudence. All citizens, they claimed, were equal before the law, but in practice they bent the rules, allowing personal enmity to override process, with the result that, by my counting, seven villagers had been killed by boars in the past decade. At least two of those were neither murderers or deviants but were instead social misfits. They were harmless nonconformists who required, I thought, care and attention, not killing. But still they were sent to the Puzzle, barely aware, from their haphazard running, of what was going to happen.

Then the white man came on his raft. Having committed no crime—but for his accidental landing—he was condemned by, essentially, one powerful man. Not only was that official adept at whipping up public sentiment against the stranger, but he brazenly manipulated the voting mechanism. He required his warriors to vote en bloc and arranged for many of the village women, whom he thought to be antipathetic to his cause, to be at the river doing laundry, effectively denying them franchise. Then the sentence was carried out hastily and without appeal. Therefore, much as I understood the dilemma the boars were facing, much as I rued their sad history, I watched with sympathy for the young man as he killed the first of them, using guile, courage, and physical strength. Then he ran towards the beach and the second boar began to track him, with the result that the two of them were, at my last reckoning, five hundred yards apart and closing quickly.

Tangentially, I should like to mention that in the previous week, within the darkness of the new moon, I had witnessed another extraordinary shower of shooting stars. That made me think of our most clever warrior, employed as lookout on the mountain, who was, to the irritation of some, continually affirming that our world was round, rather than flat. I wished I could pick his brain on the shooting star phenomenon, for it occurred to me, just last week, that those transient flashes of light, as they moved across the heavens, were eerily similar in quality to the flash of flint on steel, which I had seen a thousand times over the firepits in the production of arrowheads. That observation led me to wonder if, somewhere above the round surface of our world, there might not be an invisible skin, a shield to protect us against flying objects, rocks thrown our way from the world of sun and planets, producing, when they met, sparks from the collision of materials.

Tangentially again, I should also like to mention that as humans claim ascendancy in the world, I am not hearing the same number of animal or vegetable or mineral voices. Increasingly shy? Numbers falling? Or are they rightfully afraid to raise their heads, lest the humans chop them off?

ANDREW GOLLIVER, 19

My first path after the boar's killing petered out to nothing. I had chosen poorly. I fought my way through forty yards of underbrush one-handed. I stumbled upon another trail that branched into three directions. Which to take, I wondered, but at least I had the sound of the surf to guide me. Or maybe not, maybe it was misguiding me, reflecting off the mountain, leading me astray. I might be running in circles, towards the swamp, away from the swamp, towards the volcano, away from it. But eventually there seemed to be a method to my madness for I caught a glimpse of emerald water several hundred yards distant, blue sieved through sun-mottled green. I took the next trail in that direction and the surf rewarded me by becoming louder. I could no longer hear my breathing, nor the vines brushing by, nor my footfalls. Certainly I did not hear the second boar until he burst at me from the undergrowth, waist-high. Black as a cannonball, he knocked me to the ground. Then he began to batter me to it, and but for the Headman's trick I would surely have been killed. Instead I was rolling, spinning back to my feet, up and running, and over the next hundred yards I evaded him three more times by throwing myself at the last instant, rising, spinning, running again as he slid past in a fury grown stronger by recurring frustration. Because of the proximity of the sea, the attacks took place soundlessly, as though we were waltzing together in a nightmare. Then we were out into blinding sunlight, sand underfoot robbing me of my quickness. I took partial shelter behind the trunk of a palm. I was overmatched and he knew it. He was pawing at the sand, ramping up his malice, trying to find me, raising his snout when, from desperation, I took the severed head from beneath my arm and with two hands, my back still to my tree, tossed it high to the air. It arced beyond him, thumping to the sand. He turned to it, squealing, running, attacking, his forefeet crushing it down.

Thank you, Headman, for your prescience, I thought. Then I broke for the water and was up to my knees before he turned, whistling maniacally, charging directly at me, leaping through the shallows. By then I was up to my chest, my neck, wooden knife in hand. I turned to face him, submerging, watching his hooves churn above me as he turned in a circle, searching. I pushed hard, feet against the rippled sand. I drove upwards at forty-five degrees, striking his unguarded throat just as I had struck the first. He spun full circle on my fist and blade, once, twice, a gush of blood heating the sea. Finally I rose to breathe and he was clearly dying, no longer a danger, but already the barracuda were there, flashing by. I abandoned him, leaving my knife where it was. I raced to the beach. I sat on the gentle incline stunned by the violence I had perpetrated. Twenty feet away was my old raft, angled to the surf, and just beyond was the boar's body, the predatory fish tearing and pulling at it, rolling it over like a toy. In five minutes the shallows turned a frothing pink. Then the fish were sated, and although the incoming tide brought the skeleton closer, I left it floating where it was. I picked up the first boar's head from the trampled sand and walked back towards the village, not knowing what else to do.

CLOVIS CALLAGHAN, 35

Miss Albertson asked me when I expected to hear from Ireland. Emerson was already gone two weeks. "I wonder," she said, "if perhaps we might hear of a certain man's demise, via urgent messenger."

I replied that my husband's intent was to act late in the journey, rather than early. By then, he hoped, he would have grasped the local situation, and so could shape the killing to context. He did not want suspicion to fall on anyone in Galway. He wanted the perfect crime, in other words—somewhat like ours, in fact—one that would leave nothing but bafflement in its wake. "Therefore," I said, "I expect to hear nothing until his homecoming. Then he will speak out, saying that he regrets what happened to the Earl but perhaps such a death will serve a higher purpose. It will shed light on the resentment that smoulders among those denied justice." "Oh, excellent, Clovis!" she said, "a powerful statement like that is well worth waiting for," and then she added, nervously, entirely switching focus— "if I might ask— as we are speaking of Emerson, your husband—could you tell me, you don't have to, but I want to know, forgive me, when you and Emerson are having sexual relations, is it pleasurable?"

It was characteristic of her, in conversation, to leap from one topic to the next, from a run-of-the-mill concern to something intensely personal, so I was not totally surprised. But I was unwilling to go into the details of the marital bed. All I said to her was, "Yes, yes, it is pleasurable, though in varying degrees," to which she said that her one experience was not, that it was painful, humiliating, and she would never forgive her father. "Not your father, surely!" I said. "No, not directly, but he stood outside the door, allowing it to happen." Oh dear God, I thought, and I said, "Beulah, poor Beulah, how fragile you must have been then, at thirteen." I kissed her on both cheeks, to comfort her. She sobbed, recovered, and for five minutes rested her head upon my lap.

ADVISOR TO THE HEADMAN, 32

In twenty-four hours, as per protocol, I would send out three search parties, each with ten warriors heavily armed, their purpose being to verify the death of the prisoner by his remains. Also to recapture the boars. I had already issued two spear-tips per party, coated in the paralyzing substance. If our luck held, another stranger might never drift our way.

From the boars' cage, I walked back to the village unaccompanied. But who was the first person I met upon returning? Jaimia, with her darkling brow, ducking back into her hut.

I thought to tease her a bit, as any uncle might do, so I followed her inside and, after saying hello to my brother, I placed my cane on Jaimia's left shoulder and said that her hair was very prettily done up. "But why the tears, Jaimia, why the long looks?" As she did not meet my eye, nor enter into the spirit of my game, I love-tapped her once to catch her attention, a quick snap, a corrective on her right arm. I said that she had much to be happy for on such a fine day, that I would cheer her up if she would let me, with abalone shells. "Come with me, Jaimia, to the river, where I have hidden some in the current." Dutifully she followed, though sullenly. As we walked I spoke to her of several disappointments I had suffered when I was her age, particularly when a girl I loved had passed me over for another, and when my brother—her father—had raced past me in the games.

"Oh, Uncle," she said, "too bad for you, that you have had such terrible times." I paused by a bed of flowers. With my cane I snapped the heads off a dozen or so white gardenias, and next I garlanded them for her, draping them around her neck. She still avoided looking at me, with the result that an irritability overwhelmed me. Despite my best intentions, I hit her twice more, once on each arm, and I said, "There, something to really cry about, Niece, rather than your white man."

She ran away, and not towards the river but to home. I could hardly chase after her without drawing undue attention, so instead I circled the boundary of the village and, at my own place, I banished thoughts of her and substituted a black feather for my usual white, to celebrate the eradication of evil.

Then came shouts from the distance and several villagers rushed by. Although it was too early for definitive news, I followed them only to find, standing on the path that led to the beach, either the prisoner or his spectre, standing tall, pants torn and stained blood-red, a ghoulish boar's head in his right hand. Before him stood two of my warriors with spears poised.

Had they thrown them, my problem would have been solved, but the Headman brushed by me and opened his arms widely and clasped the boy in his arms as though he were a triumphant protégé. They walked by me as though I did not exist. The fault of the talisman, I thought, his talisman, and although it had already proven its strength I rushed to his empty hut. There I struck six times with my dagger, at the north, south, east and west of it, and twice, more forcefully, centrally, chipping it to a whiteness, all the while listening to the celebratory shouting outside. Then I left the talisman as it was and joined the crowd at the firepit. There was my niece, still in my garland of flowers, wrapping her arms around his neck until, to respond to her, he dropped the boar's head and the dogs took to it, snarling and tearing and running every which way, even throwing it into the air.

The Headman finally acknowledged my presence. I was forced to announce full reprieve, that we welcomed our guest back from the Puzzle with respect, and then I walked alone down the empty path to see the last of the boars, the female. She was still lying on her side. She posed no threat, so I reached between the bars and struck her six times through the ribs with my dagger, to which she made no reaction but to tremble, and then her respirations ceased.

QUERCUS ALBA, 252

He could have jabbed at me a thousand times and chiselled out my heart—my letter O—and still I would have been overjoyed. Had tears been in my repertoire, I would have shed them, paradoxically, from pleasure. He was the first of his race to know that I was alive. Off he ran, however, ending our intense relationship but also—not coincidentally—heralding a change in the village wind. Our guards were withdrawn. Andrew was able to come and go as he pleased. That night the girl came to us smiling, rather than tiptoeing with concern. Once more they huddled over drawings, ones I could not see for their backs were to me. Smoke curled from the taper that sat between them, creating a dream-like haze similar to puffs of pollen riding on an afternoon's breeze, or to the mist that permeates a forest after autumn rainfall. Self-indulgent musings of mine, yes, but they turned out to be short-lived, for at daybreak it became apparent that Andrew and I, and possibly the girl, were to leave the island. Jaimia took me under her arm, as she had on our arrival. Andrew rolled up his mattress and as a party of three we stepped out into our last morning on the island. Already the villagers had formed a festive procession. The Headman and Headwoman, dressed in full regalia, led the parade, forming a line that snaked through the jungle to the beach, where a sailboat was pulled half-in and half-out of the water. Her dimensions were modest, approximately twelve feet long and four wide, deep-keeled for ocean travel, a red crescent sail to the single mast. The Headman waded out to his waist, and the vessel was pushed out to him. Holding the starboard gunwale steady, he motioned for Jaimia and then for Andrew. He boosted them aboard. I saw that Jaimia was bruised on both arms, as though she had been flogged and cut in the English manner, but the feathered man—my assailant and probably, by extension, hers—was nowhere to be seen. Nowhere until the same war canoe that had rescued us weeks earlier hove into view, rounding the promontory from the north, the same sixty paddlers in synchrony, and there he was at the bow.

Closing to us, two warriors at its stern fastened a long and sinuous line to the prow of our boat. Without further ceremony, they leaned to their paddles and spun us about and pulled us to the line of surf as it cascaded thunderously over the reef, crashing, falling. The canoe threw herself directly into the waves, bucking, plunging, yanking us back and forth on the tether, making her way towards open water, bursting through combers.

Then it was our turn to pitch and fall in her wake, skitter sideways as cold spray and water fell upon us. Jaimia cried out, reaching for Andrew with her free hand—I realized then that she had never been to sea—until we were past the danger, into the easy swells. Andrew began to bail with a hollowed gourd. Jaimia relaxed, they exchanged smiles of encouragement. Next the canoe retrieved its line, and my attacker, to whom I still felt grateful despite his shortcomings, leaned towards us from his forward position and shouted over the waves. He was obviously not pleased. The girl shouted back, as anyone might upon leaving home and receiving little love when doing so. The canoe shot away and returned through the breach in the reef. Andrew took the tiller in one hand, Jaimia's hand in the other, and we came about and headed west.

After weeks in darkness, I found my return to sea, to sea air, bracing. Thinking of our situation, I was reminded of the practice of coppicing, whereby a forester cuts a tree flush to the ground, and from that stump, that seemingly dead remnant, multiple green shoots rejuvenate, aiming skyward.

CATHERINE EGERTON, 19

Father had deemed me, before he left for Ireland, unfit to assume command of the estate. "You are a woman," he said, "and Gerald is a man. He will hold the reins." I knew every nook and cranny, every man, woman, child, every servant, far better than my husband did, but I decided not to rail against that particular injustice. Perhaps the assumption of responsibility will draw a greater seriousness from Gerald, I thought. In fact it did. Not once did he suggest he needed a breather in London. Daily he set out on horseback to survey the village and fields. He began to take stock of our buildings, remarking upon their condition, ranking them on a scale from one to ten, scoring them in a notebook he carried in his pocket. In the evenings he would tell me of a hayrick toppled over, a window broken, a well possibly tainted by manure, its stonework cracked. He had even noticed a fissure in the masonry of the chapel, its bell tower. "That will not do, Catherine," he said. On occasion he also investigated the local taverns—his breath betrayed him—but his interest in the estate was clearly genuine, focussed on maintaining its monetary value. In summary, his new authority was good for him, and I assumed the wifely role, patting him on the back.

As for Father's absence, he could have stayed away forever. Dinner became a relaxed affair. Mother still asked about Andrew five times before dessert and five times after, but I would answer that he was surely safe and sound. Gerald would amuse her, suggesting Andrew had absconded to Zululand, or Australia, or Canada. Mother grew overly merry at the thought of those wild colonies, her boy so brave! Then she might ask after Father, and Gerald would offer his Irish list of "Galway, Limerick, Cork or Tralee," and Mother would make steps with her feet as though dancing, and although it was painful to see her so reduced, at least she was no longer weeping as she did when Father slammed his fists to the table. So really, I thought, we were better off as a family, emotionally, with him away.

MISS ALBERTSON, 45

Finally, after weeks of waiting, I spotted Emerson at the front entrance of the manor. He was being greeted rather formally, I thought, by Lady Catherine and her husband. They ushered him out of sight to the drawing room. I took the opportunity to cross the carpeted floor and put my ear to the door, but their conversation was muffled, indistinct. My goodness, I thought, you must find Clovis! I had not seen her that morning. I ran upstairs and there she was in Lady Catherine's bedroom, pretending everything was normal, arranging the combs. "Quick," I said, "I have seen Emerson, come with me to the pantry!" I took her by the sleeve and nearly dragged her down the stairs. "Tell me, tell me!" I said. "Tell you?" she said, "Oh, about Ireland?" We laughed, we embraced, and she said, "Beulah, the deed is done, but not by Emerson!" I could not believe it, nor could I understand. I kissed her several times, attempting to calm my nerves, and she proceeded to explain how her husband had arrived past midnight, how he had regaled her with the strangest and most confidential story. He and Mr. Burke and the Earl had set out one morning west of Galway, intending to take inventory of the Amberley lands. They came upon an isolated hovel, which Mr. Burke quite sensibly suggested they pass by. There would be no prospect of money coming from there. But the Earl insisted on stopping. According to the map he carried, and the rental rolls, no payments had been made from that location for over a year. Scandalous, he said. They dismounted, stooped, and entered, and there they found two children, unclothed, bellies swollen from lack of food. Lying upon a ragged and filthy sheepskin was the mother, an emaciated woman of indeterminate age. The Earl became instantly irate. He began a search for coins, over-turning empty pots, spilling the contents of a small wooden chest, cursing. The children took fright and ran naked out of doors. Nonsensically, the Earl chased after them and was about to pounce when Mr. Burke, his agent of so many years, lifted his musket and discharged it, striking the Earl full square in the back, dropping him to the grass. Mr. Burke then whirled upon Emerson with a loaded pistol, saying that he had no quarrel with the oppressed servants of Englishmen. Emerson quickly said that he should have no quarrel with him then, for Emerson was on the verge of firing himself. Mr. Burke then shuffled the starving children back inside and asked Emerson to retrieve the tally of names and rents from the Earl's saddlebags. He wanted to know for certain the name of the poor woman lying before them. Emerson, realizing that he must be in the company of a hardened revolutionary, happily complied. He read out the surname, *Burke*, and whether there was a direct relationship between the agent and the children and their mother, Emerson never discovered. Mr. Burke was already busy tying ropes to the Earl's legs. Emerson joined him, and together on two horses they dragged the body five hundred yards over heather, rocks, stream, and gorse, finally down upon a windy strand where waves crested and roared and swept the sand. They continued into the wild Atlantic until the horses were chest-deep, and then they cut loose the ropes from their saddles and watched the riptide pull at the Earl, taking him parallel to the shore in the direction of a distant headland. They then surveyed the landscape in all directions, saw no witnesses, and the next day Emerson set out for home, his secret duty fulfilled, though not in the manner expected.

"Good Lord," I said to Clovis. We poured a glass of cooking wine to celebrate, despite the hour, but we had hardly taken a sip when we were summoned to the hallway. The entire staff was there, standing solemnly. Lady Catherine announced that her father had been murdered in Ireland, presumably by partisans. She was not entirely surprised, she said, and she would like to thank us all for our years of service to him, for the Earl was never an easy man.

At which point we applauded spontaneously, not for the dead Earl, whom we universally despised, but for her, whom we universally loved.

JAIMIA, 17

Extraordinary, I thought, that I should become so attached to a man I hardly knew, with whom I had not shared a sensible word. We spun over the froth of the waves, Andrew holding tight to the tiller when it was his turn, I the same when it was mine. In mid-afternoons, the sun at its most blistering, we adjusted our course just enough for the sail to cast a shadow over us, and, to compensate, we corrected our misdirection during the night, as best we could.

With sand that I had scooped from the beach before we left, with Andrew's letter O to draw upon, we took our first steps towards learning our languages. We matched a word with a drawing, then a phrase, then a sentence. It took weeks. Many of our etchings were, because of the pitching of the boat and our own clumsiness, quite ridiculous. As the waves frisked by we often found ourselves echoing their laughter. Soon we began, after making a phonetic breakthrough, to kiss each other more deeply, touching the tips of our tongues, breaking apart. I remembered what my mother had said to me before I left. "Jaimia, I am heartbroken but I understand." "Yes, Mother." "You will be with him for a long time, alone." "Yes, Mother." "Remember what you have been taught about sex." "Yes, Mother." "What are the various pairs, Jaimia, that can couple for pleasure?" "Woman and man, woman and woman, man and man." "Correct. You have learned well. Which of those pairings can produce a child?" "Woman and man." "Exactly, Jaimia, and that is why I give you this, some berryroot." She handed me a small rounded ball of pandanus leaves. Parting several of the fronds, I could see a red jelly-like substance within. "A fingertip a day, Jaimia, taken in the morning." "But Mother, everyone knows that there are berryroot babies everywhere, running about in the village." "For some it works, for others not. But please Jaimia, take it." She pushed it into my hand. We then walked all the way to the beach, remembering the happiest times of our lives. We cried, we hugged. "Jaimia, did your uncle ever force you to…" "No," I said, interrupting her, "but I never want to see him again."

Watching Andrew as he scanned the horizon, watching him as he slept, I waited for him to take the initiative. He was shy, I could tell, naive, embarrassed at first by bodily functions. We had breadfruit, dried fish, eight gourds of fresh water, fair weather, much to learn about each other. Mornings I took my fingertip of berryroot, melting it in my mouth. One day he noticed and asked, could he try it? "No, Andrew," I said, "it is only for girls." We kissed. Remembering another lesson of my education—pleasure delayed is pleasure doubled—I pulled myself away and pretended to scan the horizon for sails, for land.

ANDREW GOLLIVER, 19

It became our habit, after sunset, throughout the night, to huddle for warmth under a thin blanket. Her proximity tested my self-control. An embarrassing erection, mine, rose and fell of its own accord. From her kisses, she wanted me as much as I wanted her. But I had to keep one hand on the tiller and some of my thoughts on seamanship. Rather than become obsessed by desire, I tried to concentrate on the principles of navigation. Mr. Stevens, first officer of the *John Roberts*, had taught me the rudiments. In fact, the circumstances on the *John Roberts* were eerily similar to Jaimia's and mine. On both occasions the promise of sexual congress played itself out against the backdrop of celestial navigation.

One evening, some time after passing Tierra del Fuego, Mr. Stevens had put his hand on my shoulder. "Andrew," he said, "I will teach you the one infallible trick of sailing, how to find the equator. With that skill in your pocket, you will never be truly lost." "Thank you, Sir," I said, "I was hoping to learn that skill." He took me to the starboard rail. He explained, holding his arms out as though to grasp the sky, how the heavens rotated about Polaris, the North Star, in a giant pinwheel. "If you are in the Pacific Ocean, Andrew, as indeed we are, all you have to do is keep that brightness, that star, Polaris, do you see it? Yes, there. Keep it as close to the horizon as possible, neither too far above nor ever lose it below. The trade winds will then take you effortlessly, after a month or two, to a narrowing in the ocean called the Java Sea, shouldered on both sides by islands full of monkeys, leopards, and elephants. Ships of all nations ply those waves, English, Portuguese, Chinese, Indian, polyglot vessels with flags and bunting of all shapes and colours, designs that beggar the imagination, all heading, without exception to the same place, Singapore. Which is, my young friend, a Piccadilly Circus on water. English is the language spoken there, and much adventure can be found at little cost."

He then leaned against me. I felt his hardness press against my hip. Its presence called into question the purpose of his interest. He was my superior officer, a man whose demands must be met. I chose to pretend not to notice. I shifted my weight just enough to relieve direct contact. An awkward minute passed as we made a show of examining the heavens. I fixed the location of Polaris, its brightness, during that pause. Then, gracefully, he accepted my lack of response without condemnation. He finished his lesson by reiterating how easy the star was to recognize. "Once, my boy," he said, "I saw a blind man in Borneo catch a glimmer of it and cry out with joy, and I have seen Siberians warm their hands by its glow." Then he said, "Andrew Golliver, you are one handsome lad but quite innocent. Soon your seed will want a bursting forth." "Thank you, Mr. Stevens," I said, "for your kindness." Within a week came the shipwreck, and as Jaimia lay curled against me, her thigh against mine, Mr. Stevens' prediction for the bursting forth of my seed returned to me forcefully. Would that I were a Frenchman, I thought: I could confidently cup her breast in my hand and proceed from there.

QUERCUS ALBA, 252

She had brought aboard a supply of sand. They made drawings upon my overturned underside, where there was no damage. They practised words predominantly in English, in his language, not hers. Frequently they kissed. After the first week, they learned to tie the tiller to a seat post by using a pair of his dungarees as a makeshift rope. Thus their hands were freed. They lay flat in sunshine or shadow or in the pale wash of moonlight. I could sense their mutual attraction. They kissed for longer periods of time. Eventually, as I expected from watching the Haudenosaunee, those free hands began to explore each other further until by the fourth week they removed their clothes and pressed together face to face, staying like that for hours. One night she experimentally threw one leg over his and after much breathing and pushing, they melded together, as far as I could see. Then they fell apart and lay carelessly, not thinking of gusts of wind that might capsize us. They both fell asleep, in violation of all the rules of seamanship. I forgave them, remembering late June afternoons, pollen drifting, boughs sighing, bees in slow pleasure among stamen and pistil, the low-pitched crescendo and decrescendo cry of cicadas, the ground-pulsing fecundity of the Adirondacks.

But our oceanic world remained a dangerous place. By day thirty-one our water supply had dwindled to just one gourd. We turned in the direction of a distant island and ventured through its line of surf. Andrew and Jaimia went ashore with several of the gourds, leaving me where I was, alone. A pleasant enough beach, I thought, of black volcanic sand, but then I was startled by their sudden return, and they were saying "Pirates, pirates, one cove removed." They tossed aboard two full gourds. Quickly they dragged us back into the shallows and then we were into the teeth of the surf, pitching wildly on the incoming waves, and I spied three men running to the beach, in tricorn hats, roughly dressed, watching our escape, shading their eyes from the sun. Stereotypes, I knew, but none the less dangerous for it. "We are too small fry, I hope, for them to give chase," said Andrew, and indeed we were not followed after gaining open water. But my companions were both shaken, I could tell, as they discussed at length the rampant cruelty of the world. Jaimia surprised me.

I had thought of her as an innocent, yet clearly she was aware of the predations of the wealthy, how the underclass, she and Andrew—and the pirates too, for that matter—were forced by men of wealth and privilege to struggle for scraps falling from overladen tables. So she said, though not in those exact words. Tables? She had never seen one. Good for her, I thought, such a politically acute girl! Then she said that she knew they were heading for an English world, but did they have to study just his language all the time? "I am becoming a simpleton, Andrew, a parrot repeating only what you say to me."

I had hoped that conversation would continue, but our attention was drawn overboard, to the surrounding sea. "Look!" she said. Thousands of dead hummingbirds were floating upon the waves. "They must be the ones that visited my island," she said, "who were treated so harshly by my uncle." For the next twelve hours, eight or ten feathered bodies brushed up against us for every nautical mile. Andrew brought several aboard, placing them near me. "I too am familiar with them," he said. Their distinct colouration, which I remembered clearly from the debacle in the Doldrums, had not faded from their throats, and when Jaimia pried open their shuttered eyes, gently, sorrowfully, I fancied I could see fierce determination there, undiminished. Finally she reached overboard and placed their bodies back in their watery grave, wondering aloud if any of them, even a single one, might somewhere be alive.

ZEPHYRAX, 3

We entered—we did not know it—the last day of our migration. Dawn broke pearl-grey, and our spirits broke in concert with it. One bird after another plummeted to water until by late afternoon there were very few of us left. One hundred, two hundred. Then, overnight, despite the ceiling of stars, we entirely lost touch with each other. I realized near dawn that I was flying through silence, alone. The entire leadership had fallen away, and every companion from the ranks. Zephyrax, I thought, you are the last of the Valparaiso rubythroats.

I flew in a half-circle at five hundred feet. Behind me, a terrifying sight, a vast formation of a thousand whales forming a geometric V on the surface of the water, combing the sea with massive jaws agape, swallowing legions of us as though we were krill, vacuuming the surface. Sorrow overwhelmed me. I folded my wings and dropped precipitously and I might have continued in my descent—spiritual and physical—had I not spied, directly below me, a two-masted vessel. It flew no flag, and I wondered about its provenance. But I preferred to die on dry land rather than drown in water, so furiously I threw myself headfirst into her deck. But I failed in my suicide. It was not a skill I had practised or thought I would ever need. I delivered only a glancing blow, not even losing consciousness, and the next thing I knew a dark-skinned man with cutlass and beard was reaching down and picking me up, laughing, showing me to a dozen friends. He then walked to the starboard rail and was about to throw me overboard, I thought, when he changed his mind and his direction. He took me below deck. There, grasping me firmly, he rummaged about until he found a small, round cage made of gold wiring, with a wooden perch within. Placing me inside, he locked its tiny door, also made of gold. Then he took me back to the open air and gave me sugared water, dripping it to my beak slowly, drop by drop, using as conduit a narrow clay pipe reeking of smoke. I rested despairingly and finally I slept without dreaming, exhausted. The ship rocked back and forth. I expended no effort. But when I awoke to yellow-pink sunrise, I had somehow decided to fight, to live, to plan my escape as any hummingbird would, given a second chance.

With that end in mind, over the following days I sporadically rested at a strange angle on my perch, as though my neck were broken. I dulled my eyes, hoping that one of them would open the cage, if only from curiosity, and out I would go, buzzing with scorn. But my efforts came to naught. My captors looked at me only as children look at birds in a zoo, with curiosity and little else. I was an amusing piece of chaff, feather-fallen from the sky.

Therefore I languished in my golden-wire prison until one bright morning when, laughing among themselves, my sailors ran the flag of Portugal up the mast—they had many others to choose from, but Portugal seemed to please them the most—and half a day later we arrived in a large and busy port. We anchored well off from a line of finger wharves. Much hustling and bustling then ensued before I was transported, in a much smaller craft, along with other packages and trinkets, to what looked to be the largest warehouse on the waterfront. My cage and I were placed upon a trunk, money was exchanged, and I sat for two days without food or water, as though my new owner, or owners, were even more uncaring.

On a positive note, my cage protected me from the rats. Beady-eyed, huge and bristling, they snuffled at me after dark. "Zephyrax," I said, "look on the bright side," and so I did, darting at the rodents, watching them jump away.

CATHERINE EGERTON, 19

My husband always slept well, with or without drink. The news of Father's death had little effect upon him, that I could see. To be fair, it had little effect on me, other than to raise one very practical question, preventing my slumber on three successive nights. With Andrew absent, who was now in charge of the estate? On that third night, as though he were privy to my concern, Gerald sighed and stretched and turned my way, and I heard his voice, whispering, saying "Catherine? Catherine, are you awake?" It was the darkest hour, well past midnight. "Yes," I replied, "I have been obsessively thinking of Father, unable to close my eyes." "Remarkable, darling" he said, "for I have been doing much the same. In dream after dream I see him vanishing into mist, or fog." "Does he speak?" I asked. "No, but this I have realized, just now. Darling, he is truly dead. He is taken from us, and you and I are now the House of Amberley."

ANDREW GOLLIVER, 19

Nightly we kept Polaris tight to the horizon. Finally, just as Mr. Stevens had predicted, land appeared to port and to starboard at the same time, restricting us to an increasingly narrow strait. Dozens of Chinese junks materialized from nowhere, as though, I thought, a genie had sprung from the pages of a book and rubbed a lamp to produce them. They sailed every which way, with us, against us, criss-crossing. Next came a plethora of ampans and canoes bobbing here and there, braving the open water as though it were a child's pond. We saw, very close by, a warship flying the flag of England, possibly a sister ship to the *John Roberts*, a hundred cannon at her open ports. On we sailed, but more nervously, due to the crowding. Past midnight a dark ship of iron loomed over us, blocking the stars, forcing us to take evasive action. Had she struck us, no one would have noticed. Noxious smoke spilled from her single funnel. A stinking, acrid waterfall of soot cascaded down upon us, causing Jaimia to cough unabated for ten minutes. I clapped her on the back and squeezed her tightly with both arms, manoeuvring with my knee on the tiller until I found a fresher breeze. What would be the future of shipping, I wondered, if that dark and filthy colossus were an example, its single funnel capable of choking Jaimia. What if a thousand such ships circled the globe, blackening the sky?

Be that as it may, the next morning we saw, persisting on the horizon to the east, a yellow haze. "Singapore?" Jaimia asked, and I said, "quite possibly." Nervously, we intertwined our fingers. Our simplest days were over. More junks and brigantines appeared, and we became swept up with them, corks in a current, drawn straight into a large, protected harbour where a hundred such vessels moved about and a hundred more were anchored and a hundred more were tied to wharves. So many sails were being simultaneously eased or deployed that we were assaulted by a thunderclapping of canvas snapping, collapsing. We managed to weave our way through the madness and found, miraculously, an unused twenty feet of space at the end of a large wharf, to which we tied fast. Then, sharing glances of dismay but having no choice, we clambered up a ladder and found ourselves in even greater chaos, men rushing every which way with packages on wheelbarrows, rolling barrels up and down gangways, shouting, whistling, tap-tapping with whips on the flanks of bullocks, jumping from ship to shore or vice versa. Neither of us was able to take proper stock of Singapore itself, the town, except to see it as a blur of brown in the near distance. Jungle encroached at its farthest fringe, and they must have been burning it back, because a dozen pillars of smoke rose in frayed columns to the sky.

Jaimia was trembling. I had seen busy ports, she had not. All I could say to her were platitudes, for comfort. I loved her, I understood, we would be fine, she would become accustomed to it. Hand in hand we walked the length of the wharf, past intact and spilling packages of rice, gulls whirling in a tizzy, until we stood in relative calm before a cavernous building, its huge doors wide open, a sign above reading *McWhirter and Trenholm, Merchants, London and Calcutta.*

Steel yourself, step back into the Empire, I thought, you have no choice. And so we did, into a vast storage space, sunlight slanting down from a line of high slit windows. As our eyes became accustomed to the relative darkness, Jaimia whispered, "Look over there!" She pointed to an ornate trunk on which rested a small wire cage, ostentatiously painted in gold, and within the cage was a hummingbird, the iridescence of its throat feathers glowing even within that vaulted building, its subdued light. She went straight to it, bent and whistled. From my vantage point, I could not see the bird's reaction, and I was about to step towards her, to join Jaimia, when I was tapped on the shoulder by the first white man I had seen in Singapore.

HERBERT MCWHIRTER, 41

I arrived at six-thirty, the sun barely risen. Chao Tang stood up from his desk in the otherwise empty hall. We bowed to each other in our cheerful morning ritual, saying, "Good morning, Mr. McWhirter," and "Good morning, Chao Tang." He commented, as he always did, that it looked to be a lovely day for business. I agreed, and then I went to my usual walkabout, up and down the aisles of the warehouse, surveying the stock we intended to move within the next twenty-four hours. It was our practice to keep items bound for China close to the eastern wall— geographically closer to China—while those for India and beyond, to England, were kept to the west. All seemed in order. Mentally I ticked them off, first the spices, then the emollient oils, then gambier, pepper, tin, salt fish, shark fin, crates of muskets and gunpowder, flint, mother-of-pearl, rattan, porcelain, gold, silver, heavy rolls of cotton, lighter ones of silk, and, most profitable of course, several thousand tightly packaged balls of opium. At the far end, towards the entrance, were special goods of a more fragile and transient nature, plus items for sale to the general public including, I noticed, our little bird. And what do I see, lo and behold, but a native girl in a shift bending over the bird's cage, and—if I could believe my eyes—she was the companion of a young white man dressed as scruffily as she. I tapped him on the shoulder, half to startle him. "The bird," I said, "has languished here for days. It has no use. It cannot talk like a parrot, sing like a canary, chase after game, nor be fattened up for a meal. It is a throw-in with the ornamental cage." I had no expectation of making a sale with my patter, but to my surprise the young fellow said that the bird was of sentimental value, being familiar to them from a long voyage. Quite the plummy accent, I noticed, so it became clear to me that I was dealing with a well-born Englishman, concubine in tow. Well, this is Singapore, I thought, not so unusual, but how curious, his face was familiar. I assumed a more conciliatory tone, in case he were related to a friend or relative. I asked his name. "Andrew Golliver," he said. Then, as though all three of us were on equal footing, he introduced the girl to me, pronouncing her name as *Jay-mi-ah* with the accent on the second syllable. She made a slight bow, awkwardly. Undeniably pleasant to look at, so I pointed to the large sign above the door and confessed to being McWhirter, "in the flesh, at your service!" I invited them directly to my office. As we picked our way through the aisles, I wondered if my welcome had impressed the young man, and perhaps it had, for he mentioned that he had tied their craft overnight to my wharf, and perhaps there was a fee? "Nonsense," I said, "I have already waived the fee for a fellow countryman."

I led them directly to my desk, elevated on a dais overlooking the hustle of the office. Three or four of my salaried employees had already arrived for the day. I snapped my fingers—"Chao Tang!"—for two chairs to be brought. I urged my guests to make themselves comfortable, to sit, which the young man did quite naturally but the girl stayed on her feet until he motioned to her. She looked at him, hesitating. I realized that she had never seen a chair before. Nevertheless she did sit down, mimicking him, primly. Next I asked the young man his purpose in Singapore. "Jaimia and I," he said, "are embarking on life's journey together. Perhaps you could advise us on opportunities for employment. And accommodations. And, of course, we are interested in the bird."

Too many questions. They were testing my good humour. I waved my hand to summon Chao Tang. Where I found growing tedium, Chao Tang did not. I explained Mr. Golliver's concerns, passing the baton, so to speak, and without leaving my side Chao Tang gave a figure for the cage and bird, such a piddling total that it was, essentially, a gift.

The young man admitted, straightforwardly, that he and Jaimia were penniless. They had been so long at sea. "Perhaps a barter could be arranged," he asked, "whereby you keep our boat in exchange for the bird?" So he had a business head on his shoulders. I perked up and sent Chao Tang to inspect the craft and return with his opinion. As we waited, I shuffled through papers, racking my brain. Who is this young man? Take away his roughshod appearance, his questionable companion. "Dear boy," I finally asked, "who are the Gollivers, what is their history, where do they live in England? And, more importantly, what brings you here?" "Golliver," he replied "is nothing but a common surname from the west of England. There are many of us. And I am in Singapore as the lone survivor of the frigate *John Roberts*, shipwrecked months ago."

"Good God!" I said, "The *John Roberts*?" I pulled from my top drawer a notice I had received the previous week, from the Lloyd's representative in Singapore, from their office on Commercial Square. "A request for information concerning the frigate *John Roberts*, out of Bristol," I read aloud, "so long overdue that the insurer wishes news of her, in the hope that she is delayed rather than lost at sea." Attached to the notice, by a metal clip, was a detailed description of the *John Roberts* and a manifest of the crew. I traced my finger down the list and there, at the one-third mark, was Andrew Golliver, age 19, able seaman.

"You have risen from the dead!" I said, flabbergasted. He shrugged his shoulders. "I have been saved by Jaimia," he said, "and by a raft." "Extraordinary!" I said, whistling for pen and paper, apologizing for my haste, writing an immediate affidavit to the effect that I, Herbert McWhirter of Singapore, had personal knowledge of the total loss of the *John Roberts* with all men on board, save one. I signed it with a flourish and asked Mr. Golliver to do the same, his name under mine. He had no objection, signing with a practised hand. I will ask Chao Tang, I thought, to take it personally to Commercial Square. If there is a reward for the information, which there should be, he should claim it in cash.

I looked at the girl. I looked at the sailor. Good Lord! Good God! Of course! I snapped my fingers. What a small world, tiny England atop her vast colonies! Two years ago, the manor in Dorset, the brandied Earl, his faltering wife, the rundown maze, hounds, manure everywhere to step upon. Also a fortune past imagining. And—the real reason for my excitement—I remembered his two beautiful but passive children, one of whom was sitting before me.

"By all that is holy," I announced, "you are not Andrew Golliver, able seaman, you are the son and heir to the fortune of Lord Amberley of Dorset! Pull the wool over the eyes of McWhirter of Singapore? McWhirter, who has shot a brace of pheasants at your father's side? I think not!"

The boy did not at first react. Then, choosing his words carefully, he admitted I was correct as to his former name, but he had not deceived me. "Since Bristol, Sir, I have been Andrew Golliver. As Golliver I was shipwrecked, as Golliver I shall live the rest of my days. I am heir to no fortune. I have rejected it."

"Young man," I said, laughing with added gusto, as though we were actors in a comedy, "no one could give up such riches! I would have to set fire to my warehouse and my mansion on the Pearly Road, and still not approach such madness!" The boy must have suffered a head injury, I realized, or was overly besotted with the girl. He asked me to keep his presence in Singapore a secret.

He said that he and Jaimia would find employment and soon be on their feet. He might as well have said the moon was made of blue cheese. I humoured him. One day he would be the richest man in England, or close to it. "Son," I said, "your secret is safe with me. Down to business then, for I am a businessman. I accept your offer of barter, boat for bird. I also offer you employment in the warehouse. I also offer you and your mistress simple lodging in back of the office, two rooms on the second floor, with cooking stove and bed, free of charge." Despite my generosity, he corrected me, saying that Jaimia was his wife, not his mistress. Well, I thought, however did you get married on the high seas, young man? Outwardly, however, I apologized, admitting that I was too quick with assumptions, a behaviour that served well in negotiations but socially gave the impression of insensitivity. I became uncharacteristically flustered. Here was my dream investor, dropped into my lap. Since the death of Trenholm, we often struggled for capital. "Chao Tang," I called— he had just returned from the waterfront—"show them the rooms out back, please, for they are interested." By Singapore standards, the accommodation was palatial, with sash windows and potable water run in from the warehouse. They would be fools to pass it up. Off they went, quite happily, I thought, although they chose to head first for "the bird," those being the first words I heard the girl speak.

It was still not ten o'clock. But the mail packet was due to leave in an hour. I jumped for pen and paper. *Dear Earl*, I wrote, *I have fond memories of hunting pheasants at your estate. But that is not my purpose, to reminisce. Excuse my haste, but I have joyous news that would please any father. Your son and heir, Andrew, is alive. He is in Singapore, lone survivor of a cataclysm at sea. He appears to be physically healthy but I have concerns. First, he denies his heritage. Second, he is travelling under a pseudonym, Andrew Golliver. Third, his companion is a native girl, almost entirely mute. I have taken them under my wing nevertheless, providing a residence and paid employment for the young man. Already he has shown sharp interest in the business, asking pertinent questions and co-signing an affidavit to Lloyd's of London, bringing us both immediate financial benefit. Of course you will wish to correspond, and please do so care of the undersigned, yours, Herbert McWhirter.*

Chao Tang returned. "They are getting settled, and they are pleased," he said. I handed him the letter, to read and critique. "The grammar and style, Sir," he said, "are improving, but I distinctly heard the young man, Golliver, ask for confidentiality. With this letter, you are breaking an explicit trust." "Chao Tang," I said, "you are perfectly right, in a narrow sense, but this is a business letter. There are no rules in business. Remember, a doctor may judge success by the rosy cheeks of his patients, a lawyer by the gavel falling in favour of his clients, but a businessman answers to a harder, more cruel criterion, that of the bottom line. This gets our foot in the door of a very rich man. Now hurry, the packet for Calcutta is leaving on the tide, and our letter must be aboard. Quick-quick! Oh, and the affidavit! Thank you, Chao Tang!"

I clapped my hands, and off he went, briskly.

QUERCUS ALBA, 252

Harbour waves rocked me back and forth. Our boat bumped irregularly against pilings. A stranger—not a frightening one—clambered down and fingered the red crescent sail, moved the gourds around, looked at the worn clothing, wiggled the tiller back and forth, struck his heel down against the hull in several places. He picked me up and put me down, respectfully. Then he climbed up to the wharf and disappeared. Flocks of gulls screamed overhead. Someone was cleaning fish, throwing heads and tails in an arc to the water. Andrew and Jaimia would hardly abandon me here, I thought, and in fact the forest of pilings reminded me of home. Therefore I was not unhappy throughout the afternoon, nor at sunset when vanishing light turned the tiller and the transom a soft ochre-yellow, before fading to black.

JAIMIA, 17

We carried the bird and his cage up a flight of stairs, opened the window, placed the cage within the frame and let the window descend to it. "All of us can feel the breeze now," I said, "and all of us should be free." Andrew agreed. With his strong fingers, he bent two of the golden bars apart, creating a permanent second opening. "There, you are no longer a prisoner," he said. The little bird hesitated before buzzing through the opening. He zoomed twice around the room and zipped from the window, a blur. "Gone," Andrew said, "but the price was worth it." I imagined him perched on the lips of flowers, ecstatic. "I hope he comes back," I said, but then I started another of my coughing episodes. "Singapore's smoke, impossible," Andrew said. He clapped my back until I gained control. We kissed. We sat on the squeaky springs of the bed. We were about to do more when suddenly he said, "The boat, Jaimia, the boat!" Down we ran, rescuing the red crescent sail and the letter O, setting the gourds adrift ceremonially one by one into the harbour. Doing so, we openly broke with our past. "We are citizens of Singapore now," we said. And in fact it was only several weeks before we were at home in the neighbouring streets, brushing up without concern against the ponderous pack animals—bullocks, they were called—with their fearsome horns, tails whipping at flies. A hundred workers charging our way, rolling barrows and casks, shouting in as many languages. Easily we stepped aside.

Everything seemed possible then, in the early days of Singapore.

ZEPHYRAX, 3

They released me. They created an exit, prying apart two bars. Whoa, I thought, a trap, but all they did was smile at each other and pay no attention to me. I darted through the opening—thank you very much!—swooped twice in semicircles, buzzed out the window. In three seconds I achieved an elevation of two hundred feet, then three hundred, four hundred. Zephyrax, I thought, once again you know freedom. Looking back, they were shading their eyes to the sun, following my progress, but I must have been too small to see at that distance for soon they had pulled away from the window, leaving me on my own.

Immediately I felt a craving for something more substantial than sugar-water. The jungle was not far away, a thick tangle of brown and green. The cleared land of Singapore could not have been more than one or two square miles, a mere dot at the edge of wilderness. Wisps of smoke drifted in a thickening haze but, holding my breath, I was through the worst of it zip-zip and was rewarded with a cornucopia of riches, rivalling those of the Mississippi Valley. Albatross, I thought, perhaps you are not so stupid after all. The jungle's vegetation was chockablock with sluggish gnats, slow flies, defenseless aphids and beetles, overconfident spiders, sundry other bugs born without reflexes. None of them had seen a hummingbird. I went on a killing spree and drank my fill of nectars. Then I chose a twig to sit upon, oversated. Caution, Zephyrax, take your time, take your bearings. I staggered to the air and saw, hacking away at the jungle's edge with machetes, groups of men in servitude, dark-skinned, turbaned, festooned with chains tying them together at the waist. Their main function seemed to be to destroy habitat, mine included. The tang of kerosene and woodsmoke grew increasingly bitter on my tongue. Escaping, I moved inland to swamps lined by mangroves. No shortage of mosquitoes there, I thought, marking the position vis-à-vis the sun and the distant harbour. Then, for an overview, I flew back to the settlement, rising to eight hundred feet to see that Singapore was effectively divided in two by a sluggish river. East of the river rose a prominent hill upon which wide avenues had been cut through trees, bordered by substantial houses of brick or slate. West of the river, by contrast, thousands of rude huts were jammed together, edging towards the harbour in irregular waves of thatch. Unsavoury runnels of sewage flowed through these, forcing inhabitants to step and jump like grasshoppers. I hovered at one thousand feet. The population? I counted hats in approximately one-tenth of the alleys. I multiplied by ten. I concluded that the visible number was, roughly, forty thousand persons. Next I doubled that to account for those invisible, indoors or sitting in shadow. Eighty thousand, then, a tiny figure compared to our flock at Valparaiso. But I was the last of those so, almost certainly, the ratio of human beings to hummingbirds in Singapore was eighty thousand to one.

There was no point in railing against it. Fly on, Zephyrax, zoom at speed. I dropped to one hundred feet and entered what appeared to be the poorest quarter. A few citizens were leaning over the seawall, pouring fecal matter from wooden slop-buckets into the harbour. Babies cried, women cried, men cried or shouted. Enough, Zephyrax. I returned to the wider avenues. There, at intervals, box-like carriages on horizontal poles were being carried at a trot by quartets of dark-skinned men. White hands tap-tapped from curtained openings. We were in Asia, I understood, but racial privilege seemed unaltered, identical to that of Brazil or the Carolinas. Over the harbour itself I flew. Hundreds of ships were being choreographed by the prevailing wind. Dhows, junks, sampans—I had come to know them all— spun to the same master. Rowboats moved more deliberately to and fro. Shrill cries from the throats of too many gulls. Vultures lined up, blacker than cormorants on the peaks of warehouses.

And there was my cage, my former cage, pinned in the window not far away.

Would there be a better place, politically, to digest my insects? Stand not on ceremony, Zephyrax. I re-entered by the bent portal. The girl was resting on the bed, eyes to the ceiling, hands behind her head. If another rubythroat has survived, I thought, please let her be a female, and even if she is dowdy-plumed, bent of beak, a cast to her eye, I will love her instantly.

GERALD EGERTON, 22

I found Catherine in her bower, reading a novel. After kissing her on the cheek, I suggested that her mother be moved to a different wing of the building. "Why?" she asked, and I pointed out that Mother—she was not my mother but I was to call her that—could be better cared for if she were not constantly underfoot, if she were more protected from the agitations of daily life.

But no, Catherine was not keen. She objected to my use of the word *underfoot*. I did not insist. But several days later she came to me and apologized, saying that all marriages needed compromise, so yes, Mother could be moved. The east wing was, after all, but forty yards distant. "Thank you, darling," I said, adding that Mother might not even notice, given the state of Mother's mind, and what a kindness it was for Mother, for anyone Mother's age, to become oblivious to our imperfect world.

A week later, I broached an even more sensitive subject. It concerned the family solicitor. He had, I learned, within several hours of hearing of the Earl's demise, frozen the operating funds for the entire estate. "Does he have the right, Catherine?" I asked. To my surprise, it had been her idea. "Until the matter of our inheritance becomes crystal clear," she said. "But dearest," I explained to her, "by our marriage, you have revoked the right to make that decision, I believe." She quickly replied—to appease me—that it was a temporary measure, that she did not want riches to go to our head. But that temporary measure, overriding my legal rights, caused me to fly into a rage. I tore at the curtains in the bedroom and dashed them to the floor. "In London, I will be seen as a milquetoast," I shouted, "why should my hands be tied?" "Because," she answered, "all marriages require compromise, as we agreed to the other day, with Mother. And you have not always spent wisely, as you know, and Andrew is still alive."

Andrew! Christ! What were the odds of his returning? Zero, if it were up to me. She walked from the room. But I must have won her over with my performance. She arranged for me to have direct access to our London bank, saying there would only be limitations to the frequency of withdrawals. "It applies to both of us," she said. I felt I should not push any harder. Her virtuous brother was impossible to match. His shadow would loom over our future despite whatever he had said and done at his last supper. "Funny," I said, "I thought I saw Andrew spit the silver spoon from his mouth, and ride into the night." "He did," she said, "your memory is correct, but he signed nothing."

HUT CHINOIS, 7

Before I became a brothel in the settlement of Singapore, I was five separate and innocent huts, each containing a family unit. But as indentured slaves poured into the seaport, the ratio of male to female citizens increased to an intolerably high level, one hundred to one by most estimates, causing social unrest. A solution was sought and found. A middle-aged Chinese woman with business acumen purchased me and consolidated my five branches into a larger establishment. She set us apart from neighbours by a five-foot circular path, with crushed stone as a practical footing, restricting dampness during the monsoon season. Inside, a visitor would find himself in a waiting area,

Persian rugs spread upon the floor, scented candles at intervals for illumination. Next to that welcoming space were six smaller, private rooms, separated from each other by heavily brocaded curtains in red and gold. A dozen women from Shanghai were rotated through my doors, one month at a time. Pipes of opium were at hand for those who wished to enter a different world, one of requited dreams, I suspected, so addictive seemed the practice.

Why the bilingual name, *The Hut Chinois*? Laugh if you will, but English was the language of money and French the calling card, the sultry magnet, the language of love. There was no lack of customers, seven nights a week.

Was I a positive influence, socially? In the myriad parade of supplicants whose shadows darkened my door, I detected very little happiness, either before they entered or as they left. I was neutral, I thought. However, my owner certainly did well financially. She acquired, two years after opening her doors, a four-room house on the better side of the river and a punt that she rowed through the harbour on Saturdays, wearing a flowing white gown and headdress, garnering attention, a hundred sailors looking at her, asking "Who is she, who is she?" and someone surely answering, "She is The Hut Chinois."

ANDREW GOLLIVER, 19

Mr. McWhirter suggested that I start as a common labourer, in the warehouse. It would be the best situation from which to gain working knowledge of the business. There I could see the ebb and flow of inventory, how prices of commodities waxed and waned, how various ships of various capabilities were outfitted and scheduled for service, how personnel were managed, records kept, cash transported. And so on. He said that I might also be exposed to some of the seamier aspects of commerce. How bribes to foreign potentates can be disguised as payment for services rendered, how prices can be manipulated by withholding critical information, how local armed conflicts can be stoked or extinguished to our benefit. After three months, he added, I would be promoted to management.

Would such a generous offer be made to any simple sailor washed ashore? No. To accept, therefore, would be trading on my birth after all. But Jaimia and I needed food on our table. My father would be ecstatic to see me break so easily, to hear me say, as I did, "Yes, I am willing to learn the trade and all aspects of it and I can start working now, at this very moment." "No, no, not necessary, my good man," Mr. McWhirter said, "not necessary, later will suffice. Report to Chao Tang after the noon hour, and he will be your guide."

I stood up to shake his hand. But he stopped me, half-rising from his chair, motioning for me to sit again. He said that he had another proposition for me, a personal one, relating to his wife. Her name, he said, was Alma, and recently—"in confidence now, Andrew"—she had been stricken by a peculiar form of asthenia common to Englishwomen in the colonies, a malaise in which the initial flush of enthusiasm from the novelty of overseas service becomes replaced by fatigue and listlessness. The patient—she is almost always a woman—becomes incapable of doing anything but reading novels and gazing from windows. Perhaps, on a good day, she might pass her time creating imitation flowers from coloured silk. These patients, he added, lose interest in cooking or cleaning and, for that matter, they no longer function fully as wives. "To come directly to the point, could your Jaimia, for a steady wage, act as housekeeper and cook and companion to Alma? My household is becoming a sorry place for me, as presently it is."

I replied, measuring my words, that my wife was resourceful, energetic and positive in her disposition, and I would pass on his proposal to her as soon as I returned home. "Capital!" he said, and he waved me away and turned to papers on his desk before sitting upright, striking at his own forehead with his hand, calling me back, handing me a small purse. "The fruits of our affidavit," he said, "your half, go to the market, buy some fruit and vegetables, be careful with the monkey meat." And although I had vowed not to be an Amberley, responsibility drove me to walk away with the money, to wake Jaimia with the news.

For three months thereafter I reported to Chao Tang at eight each morning. Jaimia went to the Pearly Road. I priced and moved tons of ivory and gambier, tin and opium. Jaimia washed and scrubbed and dusted and cooked in the English manner. Jaimia also became pregnant. "I stopped our berryroot," she said. Our bird came and went on his own accord, but did not desert us. We furnished the apartment with two chairs, a table, a vase for flowers. We deemed ourselves to be the luckiest couple in Singapore until, at the height of that ridiculous, heartbreaking, loving time, calamity struck us down.

JAIMIA, 17

I learned to let myself into the house, to breeze into her bedroom and part the curtains for the day, to sing out in my most cheerful voice, "Good morning, Miss Alma." I prepared a breakfast tray and carried it upstairs, placing it over the bedspread, over her knees. Not that she ate much of it, but it was there for her. Then, for the rest of the day, I bustled about cleaning the kitchen, the dining room, the living room, dusting the piano keys, cleaning the stove, taking ashes to the garden, splitting wood, cleaning the windows so they were always spotless, killing flies, taking mice from the traps, cutting flowers from the garden—she had started it two years before but had lost interest—always following her spoken instructions to the letter. That said, some mornings she had nothing much for me to do, but still I kept busy by repetition, improving on the previous day. Afternoons, I prepared a dinner for her and her husband. The next morning, his portion was often untouched. "He stayed out very late last night," Alma would often say.

I wondered what was actually wrong with her. But I had been instructed by Mr. McWhirter not to ask. "She might break into tears," he said, "nor should you offer her sympathy, for that would be counterproductive. Just keep quiet and do your work." That advice proved impossible for me to follow. Mr. McWhirter was never home to see me, so I smiled at his wife as I dusted under the bed, and I sang songs from my childhood as I worked downstairs. One morning she said, "Jaimia, sing some more, don't stop." As my English improved, she took more interest in me, patting the bed, indicating I should sit beside her, asking me questions about my parents. "Do you miss them?" "Of course," I said. "Are there animals to fear, or snakes on your island?" to which I said "No." The last thing she needed was more frightening. I painted a picture of a paradise, where the only disruption was the sound of surf, rising and falling forever. "How beautiful that must be," she said.

One day, shortly after I realized I was pregnant, I had to rush outside from the kitchen to the garden. Morning sickness, I knew, usually presenting just as nausea for me, but on that occasion I vomited behind the flowerbeds, as quietly as I could. But when I looked up to her window, wiping my mouth on my sleeve, there she was watching. She called me up to her room. She ordered me to lie on the daybed. Then, totally out of character, she walked briskly downstairs to the kitchen and returned with a cool washcloth and laid it on my forehead. I admitted to her, as she obviously suspected, that I was two months' pregnant. She read to me then from a book of poems, many of which I did not understand. But I enjoyed the companionship as, I thought, did she.

After that she insisted that I become less of a whirlwind, as she called me, around the house. She said that she didn't like a young girl rushing about, heavy with child, while she lay abed for no reason. She also didn't like my coughing, she said, which was getting worse, and it could hardly help the baby for it must sound, to those little ears, like thunder or cannon-fire. "Lie on the daybed, Jaimia," she said, and she brought more of the cool washcloths. "Herbert will never know what we do, all he cares about is business and the Hut Chinois. He smokes opium there." I knew nothing about the Hut Chinois, and she did not elaborate. She began to join me in the afternoons, down in the kitchen, chopping vegetables so briskly that I ventured to say she was improving. She agreed, and she gave me credit for it. She said that I was an example of everything that she was not. How crazy, I wanted to say, how untrue! There I was coughing and holding my tummy and sweating while she was, as the English said, cool as a cucumber. "Lie down, Jaimia. Lie down, Jaimia." She brought me lemonade. "My goodness, sweetheart, look at us," she said, "our positions are reversed from when you came."

ALMA MCWHIRTER, 38

Herbert arranged for the doctor to make weekly visits. "Perhaps he can help you with your ennui," he said, "as God knows I can't." I didn't mind, to be honest, for it gave me something to look forward to, and one particular afternoon, when the doctor had finished his usual questioning and was folding his stethoscope, I asked if he would mind taking a look at my native girl, Jaimia, serving as my housekeeper. "Not only is she pregnant and vomiting in the garden," I said, "but she has a terrible cough, Doctor, deep and rattling, stealing breath from her. She breaks into drenching sweats, and for a pregnant woman she seems to be putting on very little weight." I added that I would pay him from my own pocket for the consultation. He waved me away, saying he would see her purely as a favour. "Has your servant girl ever spit up blood?" he asked. "I have no idea," I said, "but I certainly hope not."

I called Jaimia upstairs and explained to her who the doctor was. Shyly, she agreed to be checked. He sounded her chest and felt her abdomen and everted her lower eyelids. He placed his hands on her forehead and felt the tissues of her neck. Then he asked her, "How long have you been in Singapore, Jaimia, and when did you first have close contact with a white man?" She gave clear answers, saying that she had met her husband many months ago but they had been in Singapore twenty-two weeks. "Have you ever coughed up red-tinged sputum?" To my surprise she answered, "Yes, just yesterday, just once." "Are you feeling the baby kick?" "Not yet." "Thank you, Jaimia," the doctor said, "you appear to be doing well, but perhaps I can see you next week, to keep an eye on things." He patted her on the shoulder, and she returned downstairs.

The doctor turned to me and said that he might be telling her the truth, that she was fine. He hoped so. But there was also, he feared, a distinct chance that she had contracted consumption from her sailor. "Time will tell, there is nothing we can do, there is no treatment for it. Consumption burns like wildfire through the native population. Men, women, children alike." Selfishly, I asked him if she might be contagious to me. "Theoretically, yes," he said, "but you and I have little to fear for we are well-fed, healthy and white, we are not poor or half-starved or black or brown." "Thank you, Doctor, for seeing her," I said. He replied that he would, with my permission, reassess her at next week's visit as well, for by then the course of her illness should be more apparent. I was about to ask about Jaimia's baby, what would happen to the baby, but I did not, being too afraid of what I might hear.

DOCTOR GEOFFREY BATES, 38

Leaving the merchant's house, I had several thoughts. One, Alma was a remarkable woman who seemed to be recovering some of her zest. Two, if she were worried about contagious disease, she should look more to her husband than to the servant girl. Being healthy and white was no protection against venereal disease, and if there were one man dancing daringly close to syphilis in Singapore, surely it was her husband. He was an habitué of the Hut Chinois, and had come to me a half-dozen times with an embarrassed smile, saying, "Perhaps, Doctor, another shot of mercury?"

It was a predicament for me. He was paying the bills, after all, and expected confidentiality. But then I remembered how he had told me that he and his wife had ceased relations long ago, that her refusals were the root cause of his indiscretions. She had, he claimed, driven him straight to the Hut herself, just as I, a surgeon, might whip my horse on the way to the hospital. That metaphor, I thought, was nonsensical and self-serving, but I caught its drift. Therefore I realized that I need not worry about Alma. She had been celibate a year by my counting, and the merchant himself was still healthy despite his activities, remarkably free of the pox.

GERALD EGERTON, 22

I returned in late afternoon from property inspection to find Catherine rushing my way, throwing her arms in the air, whirling like a top, casting several pieces of paper flying in my direction. Well, I thought, whatever can this be? I bent to the floor to pick up the pages but she beat me to them, whisking them away, hiding them behind her back, saying "Two letters, Gerald, two letters in one day!" She continued, excitedly, saying that the first one, the blue one—she held it high in one hand—was from Ireland, concerning her father's death. "The investigation is closed, no culprit has been found, but there is a clipping included from the local newspaper. Very interesting, I'm sure, but I haven't read it because the second letter—Gerald, you will never guess!— is from Singapore, Singapore in Asia! Look at the state of the envelope, stained, torn by weeks of travel! Read it, Gerald, read it immediately!" Which I did, to find my knees almost buckling because it appeared that her brother Andrew was not dead in some foreign outpost after all, but alive and frolicking with a native girl in—I checked the envelope—yes, Singapore. "Well," I said, "and Andrew Golliver, he calls himself, how strange." "Hold me darling, lest I burst!" she cried out, and so I swung her about in a facsimile of joy until dizziness made us stagger. "What news," I repeated, "what extraordinary news! This calls for an immediate reply!" "Yes," she said, "help me, help me."

Together we wrote *Dear Mr. McWhirter, I write for my father, the Earl, recently deceased. I write for my brother, Andrew Amberley, recently found! I write for all of us in Dorset, grateful for your kindness. My love to Andrew and to his new friend, without reservation, and please extend my wish that they hurry home as soon as possible. Much has altered here. Tell Andrew, I am married now to Gerald. With this news we are happier than ever, yours, Catherine Egerton.*

As an afterthought, she slipped in the clipping from Ireland and sealed the envelope. "Oh, did you want to read it? From the newspaper?" she asked. "No, darling, I have heard Emerson's version, and I have no desire to relive it."

I left her to her happiness and strolled to the stables. Utter clarity came to me then, as I picked up a bridle in the tack room. Killing the Earl had been simple. Killing her brother could be the same. A week later I was in London, again in Southwark, sidling into the same dark corner of the same dark street. "Why, Mr. Smith," my intermediary said, "pleased to be of service. Who needs taking care of, and where, that I can consult with Mr. Figby." I pulled from my shirt a map of the Far East. We had just enough light to see. In the approximate middle of the map, I had pre-drawn the capital letter *S*. "Right here," I said, "Singapore. Do you know where that is? It's in Asia. And the target is a simple sailor, named Andrew Golliver." "My goodness," he said, "that is a way, isn't it." "Beyond your reach?" "Oh no," he said, "not at all, leave it to me." I passed a purse of gold coins, more than enough, I thought, to clinch the arrangement. "Yes," he said, peeking within, weighing it with his hand, "this should do it, Mr. Smith. Thank you, Mr. Smith. Oh, do you have, so to speak, a deadline in mind?" He laughed at his witticism, but I did not. "Now would not be too soon," I said, "and yesterday would be better."

HERBERT MCWHIRTER, 41

He took to the business as a natural. Within the first three weeks he had acquired an encyclopedic knowledge of the inventory, second only to Chao Tang's. For example, as a test, quite early in his employment, I asked him whether he had seen a porcelain teapot with a blue dragon motif, that I had misplaced or mispackaged. Immediately he was able to walk forty yards to the wharf and find, within a partially undone wooden crate, smothered by straw, the exact teapot of which I spoke. He was familiar not only with its origin, Jingdezhen, in China, but its intended recipient, a Mr. Franks at the British Museum. Really quite impressive, I thought, for a novice. I felt curiously proud of him, and proud of England too, that it could produce such a quick mind, subject it to God knows what adventures and terrors, and still have it function afterwards. Rule Britannia, I thought.

Nor was he physically meek. I saw him being swung by cranes deep into the holds of brigantines, to assess loading or unloading, and then, when swung up again, he jumped like a cat to the rigging. My plan to insinuate him into our business was bearing fruit, I thought. Chao Tang had nothing but praise for him too, so I was left in a pleasant mood at the end of each day. No urgency to rush home either, to the Pearly Road, for Alma was quite rejuvenated, risen from her bed. She no longer needed cossetting. Therefore I indulged myself most evenings, setting out as the moon turned through its phases, stepping across the footbridge to the Hut Chinois. There, my ledger sheets and profit margins were forgotten, first in slow ejaculation and then by the soft bubbling of the poppy, the pipe, the haze as gentle as fog. Eventually, still dizzied by my night's twin seductresses, I would walk homeward across the swaying bridge, and often I paused and stood motionless in the darkness behind my warehouse, feeling its pulsing monetary drive.

One night I heard the native girl coughing, coughing. A lantern was alight in their window. I saw the silhouette of the bird cage, and I thought how beautiful was the world for those in good health, how sad for those who were not. The opium seemed to bring out my natural kindness, not so obvious at other times. When I last saw the native girl, on the Pearly Road, returning from being with Alma, she looked quite wasted. She was sitting on a low rock to catch her breath, and she gave me a brave smile, pretending to be better than she was.

Where were the monsoon rains, I also wondered. Could it possibly be one of those rare years when they did not arrive at all? Better for commerce, if so. No clumps of dogs and rats drowned together in rivers of mud, backing up to the warehouse door, turning rancid in the sun.

QUERCUS ALBA, 252

Jaimia stopped going to the merchant's house. She was too weak to walk the distance. She did nothing at home but lie on the bed and cough and sweat, and now and then she sat up and wiped her face with a cloth. "I'm feeling better," she said to Andrew, and then, five minutes later, she did exactly the same thing, and said the same thing, as though she had forgotten the first time completely. Anyone could see the opposite was true. She was failing. He sat with her, or lay beside her, or crossed the room to sit against the wall. He offered her sips of water and thin soup, of which she took a teaspoon. He wanted to stay with her during working hours as well, but she refused him flatly, saying "No, leave me, Andrew, we need the money." *We*, she said, as though she thought they still had a future together.

As for the rest of us living there, the inappropriately cheerful bird who came and went, the red sail leaning morosely against the wall, it fell to me to be her second-best companion. It wasn't hard to do. Both of us were far from home, both of us were a fraction of our former selves. "Fight on, Jaimia," I wanted to say, and at times I felt myself shaking—heavy traffic outside may have contributed—in sympathy, as though the axe were once again coming for me. If worse came to worst, I thought, I would cast my lot with her. She was the one who had carried me from the beach, not Andrew. She and the feathered man, they both knew I was still alive.

ALMA MCWHIRTER, 38

On the third straight day that Jaimia failed to show up for work, I went to where she lived. I took the stairs to the apartment. For a moment I thought no one was there until the sheet on the bed coughed and twitched. She was under it, what was left of her, her hair and eyes, her arms, her legs like sticks. I touched her forehead and found it burning. "Jaimia, sweetheart, it is I, Alma, I have come to check on you," I said. Although she turned her face at the sound of my voice, God knows what she saw. She looked past me rather than at me, and she did not say my name. A bloodstained handkerchief fell from the bed. As there were coals in the little stove, I warmed enough water, stripped her down to nothing, washed the beaded sweat from her face, from her shrunken breasts, from the pathetic little mound of her pregnancy. She rattled and choked more than breathed. I could see, to my horror, that she was at her very end. I lost my courage then, being alone with her. I rushed to the warehouse and called out to her husband, "Mr. Golliver, go home! Go home!" and then I took flight to the doctor's surgery. I tapped at his door and described what I had seen at Jaimia's. "Doctor," I said, "please come and comfort her, comfort me too by your presence."

DOCTOR GEOFFREY BATES, 38

We made our way through the dust and swaying bullocks of late afternoon. At McWhirter and Trenholm we took the stairs to the second floor. I entered directly into a sparsely furnished room where the girl lay on a small bed, curled on her side, facing me. She was trying to cough but obviously had lost the tussive strength to do so. Kneeling beside her was her husband, a handsome and clean-shaven young man dressed in the clothes of a clerk, rising and introducing himself, shaking my hand. A birdcage was propped in the window, serving to keep the opening ajar, and within the cage was a tiny colourful bird of a sort I had never seen.

I wondered then if I had ever been called out to such a sad yet picturesque scene. I thought not, and then Alma, with tears streaming down her face, took my arm and gave me a gentle push towards the girl. To examine my patient properly, I knelt by the bedside. What I saw then would have stopped the heart of any caring person, for her hair was matted to her scalp and forehead, her eyes were sunken and dulled, her lips pale, and her chest moved only in quick and shallow draughts, advancing useless pockets of air. Essentially, she was smothering. Her abdomen was distended below the umbilicus in keeping with a pregnancy, but it was very clear, even without touching her, that she was in her death throes. Nevertheless I took my stethoscope to her chest for I knew, from experience, that it would be of comfort to her companion if I did so. I heard, as expected, near-silence and then distant rustlings and wheezings consistent with a terminal condition of the lungs.

Turning to the young man, I said that I had to be frank with him. His Jaimia was on death's door, and there were no treatments for her. She had a galloping form of consumption, or tuberculosis, the very worst kind, and, as he was obviously an educated man, he would understand the significance of my words. "Natives succumb quickly," I said, "they have no communal experience with the disease." Unfortunately, he then asked me how she could have contracted her illness, and I replied, in the interest of truth and science, that she must have received it from him, for they had spent so much time together. The contagion was transmitted by breath, by close living, by loved ones. "But it is not your fault," I added, "it is the way of the world as it is." "What about the baby?" he asked. I indicated, by dropping my hands, that the baby's case was equally hopeless. He then wept outright and sat on the edge of the bed. He repeated her name and looked so helpless that I asked him if he wanted me to stay with them to the end, however long it took. "I prefer to be alone," he said. Alma and I then took the stairs back to the slightly cooler evening, and I walked her home to the Pearly Road and said good night. The next day I learned that Jaimia had lasted only to midnight before breathing her last.

JAIMIA, 17

The merchant's wife had an hourglass which she turned once, twice, three times. Curtains of white cloth blew inward from the wind. Andrew was touching my face, telling me he loved me, that it was his fault, his fault, his fault. "No, no, no," I said each time. A flame was touched to the driest grass on the island. The fire swept towards us and the baby was playing happily at my feet and then we were hovering in the air over the lagoon, like those little green birds.

ANDREW GOLLIVER, 19

I washed her body and placed a clean shift upon her. I did my best with her hair. I covered her with a sheet from the neck down. Then I went to the bottom step and spent the night regretting the kisses I had given her, that had killed her. When dawn broke, Mr. McWhirter was standing before me, comforting me as best he could—empathy was not his strength—with a hand on my shoulder. Then he said that in Singapore's climate, we must bury her quickly. But, he continued, as she was a native, she could only be taken to the unmarked fields on the far side of the river. "Take her there by cart," he said, "to the western fringe, dig the grave yourself. Otherwise it might not be deep enough, against animals." As neither Jaimia nor I held ourselves to be better than others, I did not object. But then he snapped his fingers and said, "What am I thinking, Andrew. Surely I can arrange a proper burial for her, after all she has done for Alma. She should be interred in the cemetery by Fort Canning. Why not, I have done favours for them a hundred times over." He insisted on covering the costs for the plot, the gravediggers, a clergyman if one could be found. I was in such a state of emotional wreckage that I was grateful for the help, unsure that I could muster the strength for the cart, the bullock, the footbridge, the finality of burying her myself.

Later that afternoon, after a flurry of activity, four of us—Mr. McWhirter, his wife, the doctor and I—gathered overlooking he harbour, below Fort Canning. Her grave had already been dug to a depth of four feet, and her body was lying beside it, parallel to the opening, upon coarse grass. She was still wrapped in her sheet but for her face and hair, into which I had tucked an abalone shell.

No clergyman had offered to attend. We looked at each other, not knowing how to proceed. The doctor asked if I wished to say a prayer, and I said, "No, Jaimia needs none of those." "What is the custom on her island?" he asked. "I have no idea," I said, "I attended no funerals." Mr. McWhirter then said, "I have heard of wrapping bodies and leaving them in trees, but that does not seem right, not for Jaimia." Finally Mrs. McWhirter spoke up, more definitively, saying, "Jaimia has married Andrew, the grave is dug, we should bury her in the earth as though we were in England."

We placed two woven cords beneath her and lifted her and lowered her, ceremonially but wordlessly, to the bottom of the grave. I leaned down and opened the front of her shawl, above her breasts. There I placed my rectangle of wood, my O, tight to her chest. It would stay there forever. I stood and we took turns with the shovel, bending and lifting until she was covered and the hole was filled and the earth was flat. We tamped it down with our feet. Mr. McWhirter then placed a small wooden stick to mark the spot, assuring me that he would commission a permanent marker, one of cut stone, within the week.

QUERCUS ALBA, 252

He placed me in a leather satchel, cutting off light entirely. I felt his pace as he walked outside. I heard the hooves and the heavy breathing of bullocks and then we must have been at the grave-side, because movement ceased. I heard soft conversation. I recognized three of the voices. He took me from his satchel and touched me in my centre, at O, and wordlessly he bent to the open grave, in which she already lay four feet deep, in her white covering. He leaned down and tucked me inside her shift, close to her, against her breasts. Then he pulled the shroud over us both and I felt the first of many shovelfuls of earth cascade down upon us with a thump and a thump, and then many more thumps, and

I realized that I would never see the light of day again. I was being buried with her, with Jaimia, and I reflected that I had wanted this, hadn't I, to be with her. The earth was mine in the first place, earth had been mine from seedling to tree, so it was hardly a frightening place for *Quercus alba*. That said, the loam of Singapore was of a different texture and it possessed a different fragrance from that of the Adirondacks, trickling down to me. Yes, I would miss the sun, but there was much to be said for steadfastness, for being an oak to the end, to the end of the end.

HERBERT MCWHIRTER, 41

The girl's death, I hoped, would usher in phase two of our business relationship. With no personal distractions, I expected his dedication to *McWhirter and Trenholm* to leap to the next level. Also, his apprenticeship was set to expire, and I had promised him, or almost promised him, a managerial position. Such were my thoughts when, a week after the burial at Fort Canning, a reply finally came from England in the form of a thin envelope dropped upon my desk, its return address emblazoned upon it *The House of Amberley*. It was closed with wax and embossed by the Earl's private seal. To say my heart leaped would be an exaggeration, but quickly I slit the letter open and out tumbled a newspaper clipping, which I set aside. Also one page of handwriting, the author of which was Andrew's sister, Catherine. The Earl, she said, was recently deceased, she was married, she and her husband looked forward to Andrew's return. It was a spare letter, surprisingly so, considering the efforts I had taken. But it was positive, too, I realized, with no mention of the boy's abdication from the Amberley name.

All in all, things were looking up. He was two steps closer to riches. Father dead, Jaimia dead, both of them probably in hell if scripture could be believed, she a heathen, he a blustering tyrant. Move on, I thought. I tucked the clipping into the inside pocket of my jacket and asked Chao Tang to bring Andrew to me. "His father has died, I should break the news." Then I realized, "Wait! Stop! If I tell Andrew this, he will instantly know of our earlier letter. Treachery, he will think." I backtracked, I dismissed Chao Tang, I strode out to the end of the wharf to clear my mind, and there, in the sunshine, with wind whipping through my hair, I read the article from the Irish paper. It described, in typical leprechaun hyperbole, his father's death and the subsequent investigation, fruitless.

Well, there were times in business to ponder, there were times to act. I strode back through the warehouse, past the clerks, out to the courtyard, up the steps, and there was Andrew lying abed with no expression on his face. "I regret having to add to your woe," I said, "but I just received a newspaper from Dublin, handed to me by chance, from a passenger on the mail packet. You must read this, poor boy."

He took the article from me and held it towards the ceiling. He turned on his side for better light, and he might have been examining a bill of lading for all the effect it had on him. "If my father has died in Ireland," he finally said, "it is quite fitting, for he was a monster there." He dropped the clipping to the floor. I picked it up, somewhat shocked by his lack of caring. I was looking at a broken man, I realized, and not because of his father. "Andrew," I said, "take as many days as you wish, before returning to work. Your grief shall pass."

The fisherman must play the fish, not yank it to the creel.

ZEPHYRAX, 3

Personally, I was unaffected by the girl's death. Yes, she had been kind to me but she was from the island of glue-stickers. Enough said. Forgiveness had its limits. Andrew might lie near-moribund upon the silent bed but I had better things to do. The insects of Singapore had never seen a bird who could hover and advance and retreat while appearing motionless, who could glitter like jewellery in the sun, who could pose hidden in shadow. My beak, my dexterous tongue, both weapons of unimaginable destruction. The local flying ants, crawling roaches, fluttering moths had been poorly served by Mother Nature. Rather than jump at my approach, they sat stupefied. How long would it take them to adjust? A generation at least. In the Americas I had seen species-specific modifications much faster than that, but there our prey was familiar with our tactics. We had discussed it, my friends and I, during our failed migration. The ordinary tree snail, for example, whose shell from one year to the next developed a clever prolongation that denied our beaks' purchase on its flesh. By contrast, here in Singapore, target insects were so poorly constructed that I could raise my wings' clamour to a thundering just for the pleasure of seeing them panic. Then I would strike.

A life of ease, one might think, but it offered me too much time for self-reflection. I should be doing more. I should not be satisfied. The loneliness was killing me. A hummingbird should stretch the limits of possibility. Were the Americas, for example, within my range? To the west extended an unbroken vista of shrouded hills, swamp, rivers, jungle. Distant storms, retreating, advancing.

I stayed on, biding my time. I rested nights in the cage that had, incidentally, lost much of its golden patina. Multiple flakes of cheap paint peeled off in the humidity, leaving rusted iron behind. Andrew was equally at loose ends, lying in bed for days, letting his beard grow, not going to work. Now and then, more encouragingly, he walked to the end of the longest wharf, where he was joined by the merchant, and the two of them would sit with their legs dangling towards the water, and the merchant would talk, and Andrew might be listening or not. Money, and working for it, did not seem to be an issue.

Pull yourself together, young man, I wanted to say, you have more advantages than anyone I have ever seen on this sorry globe.

ALMA MCWHIRTER, 38

Herbert described, over one of our rare dinners together, how the young man had withdrawn from the enterprise, how frustrating it was. "It would be more prestigious for me to have an Englishman as first assistant, rather than a Chinese," he said. "How unkind of you, Herbert," I replied, "for Chao Tang has been loyal and hardworking and is raising four children on his salary." "True enough," he said, "but there are other reasons to want Andrew close to me, reasons you would not understand."

Rather patronizing of him, I thought, but I did not protest. Instead I ventured to say that Andrew's behaviour reminded me of how I was when I was at my lowest ebb, before Jaimia. "Perhaps he would respond to a more manly assignment, for example, as one of the guards against tigers," I said. Herbert put his utensils down. "Why, what an excellent idea, Alma, I should use you as a resource more often." He took his napkin, folded it, and, saying that he would do almost anything to rescue the young man from himself, off he went with dessert half-finished. "I shall speak to my friends, tap into contacts," he said. He almost ran from the house. Nor did he return until three in the morning when he slipped into bed and, saying how tired he was, he fell asleep.

He would be gone by sunrise, I knew, which he was. I did not miss him. I hurried about. The bedroom needed sweeping—a brief windstorm had blown leaves through the open window—and so I occupied myself until I heard the front door open and close and there were my doctor's footsteps on the stairs. "Alma," he said, "I have just popped by to make sure you are still doing well." "Yes, I am," I said, "although I certainly miss Jaimia and her company, how brave she was." He agreed and said, wryly, putting his black bag on the floor, "My education turned out to be useless. You might as well have asked a snake charmer to see her." He looked tired, and I told him so. "Dealing with tuberculosis can be dispiriting," he said, "for there actually is a cure. Not medical or surgical, but socioeconomic. If the lower classes could be raised up, by something as simple as a good diet, it might do the trick. We need a social revolution in the Empire, much like that of the French, but without the guillotine." I agreed, saying that I personally was not averse to social change if it were peaceful, that I had seen much cruelty wrought from greed and avarice.

We stood awkwardly about, with no other topic of conversation coming to mind. Then he suggested that he take a sounding of my chest, just to be on the safe side. He sat on the edge of the bed and patted where I should sit. How much kinder he was than Herbert, how compassionate. His eyes were as blue as Lake Windermere, I thought, on an October morning. "Yes," I said, "please do, doctor." Quickly I sat down and turned my back to him, giving access to my lungs. "Alma," he said, "allow me to lift up your blouse, just here, in the back, for silk can make a rustling sound through my instrument, and those sounds can be misleading." I turned cooperatively and raised my arms enough that he could pull the material free from the belt of my skirt. He did so and raised it almost to my shoulders, holding it there with one hand, and then I felt the touch of his stethoscope roaming my back, which was otherwise bare, for I had not completed my formal dressing. "Breathe in and breathe out," he said. I complied, and then he said, "With your permission I shall touch you with my hands, to sense for any chest rattles." I said, "Do whatever is necessary, Doctor, to pursue your goal." His stethoscope fell away and I felt his fingers tapping upon my ribs in three or four places, as though he were drumming upon me. I felt much attended to and cared for, and then he moved his warm hands forward and around to the front of my chest, accidentally brushing my nipples. He quickly pulled away, as though his fingertips had been burnt by fire, but just as quickly he returned them, cupping me amorously, unmistakably, pulling me to him, my back to his front, saying, "Oh Alma, forgive me, forgive me."

I turned and found him anguished, blushing. I said, "Forgiveness is not required, Doctor, be thorough in your examination, leave no stone unturned." I removed my blouse entirely then, pulling it up and over my head, letting it drop to the floor, and then my skirt followed, and my thin underclothing, so that I was naked. He stood up, breathing heavily. With a sweeping motion he flung the upper bedclothes to the floor. "Lie down on that plain white sheet," he said. I followed his instructions, holding my legs primly together, for surely, I thought, tuberculosis could not strike below the waist. But he said, "Alma, please, part your thighs." I did so. "Do I have carte blanche to continue?" he asked. "Yes," I said, "yes," and he said, "Oh God, such pale and wondrous flesh!" or words to that effect, words that made me feel beautiful. A thrill overcame me, so I was not ashamed of my nakedness. Nor did I shrink from him, nor from the brightness of the mid-morning sun pouring through the window down upon me.

I heard a few of the fallen leaves rustling on the floor, under his feet. "Remove those heavy shoes," I suggested, "and your suit and tie, so that we can be equalized." He responded with alacrity, shedding his clothing piece by piece until there we were, the two of us clearly seeking the same end. I opened my thighs more spaciously and he moved on top of me. I noticed he was rigid. He entered me then, and I did not cover my eyes as was my habit with Herbert. I felt him moving in me and on me and I listened to his whispered words of endearment, saying how much he wanted me, that I was desirable, beautiful, sweet compliments that brought adroit movements to my pelvis—long forgotten, I had thought—such that I brought a gasping from his lips and he hastened his stroke, uncontrolled. I hastened mine in concert until he shuddered and I shuddered, with such intensity that, as I lay breathing with him afterwards, I feared our futures were threatened. Surely, I thought, we would want this again and again.

Then he dressed in his suit and I dressed in a different outfit altogether, suitable for the out of doors. I wore a hat for the sun to cover my unruly hair. We went to the garden and had a lemon drink together, and he apologized for taking advantage of me, saying that he had never done anything like that before, but could he possibly come again on the morrow? I laughed. He kissed me on the mouth and our tongues touched, tasting of cool lemon and of each other. I said, "Yes, if Herbert can have his brothel, Doctor, it is only fair that I, his wife, can have whatever she wants, and whenever."

HERBERT MCWHIRTER, 41

"Andrew," I asked—we were sitting together at the end of the wharf—"do you have experience with muskets and pistols?" "Actually, yes," he said, "we trained extensively on the *John Roberts* to be battle-ready, God knows why." His sardonic answer did not discourage me. "I have news of a position as guard of prisoners, if you would take it. A break from the mercantile trade." "I have seen those unfortunates in their chains," he replied, "and to become one of their oppressors does not suit me." "No, no," I said, "you misunderstand, you would not guard against escape— none of them wish to run, there is nowhere to go—you would serve on their behalf, as protector against tigers. There have been so many attacks, productivity has declined." Hoping to overwhelm him by unrelenting positivity, I continued, saying that he would be the ideal candidate for the job for it required vigilance, discipline, a knowledge of arms, good judgment, and— I knew him well—love for the oppressed. To my pleasure, he asked for more detail. "You would carry four muskets looped to your shoulders, three pistols to your waist, several knives tucked to your boots. At sunrise, six days a week, you would lead a convoy of indentured workers and convicts—damned if I can tell the difference—to the edge of the wilderness. There you would watch over them as they cut vines and creepers, trickle kerosene, set fire to the cuttings." He asked why he needed to carry so many firearms. I explained that many of the crew were attached to each other by chains, and so could only defend themselves awkwardly. And the humidity of the rainforest played havoc with flintlocks, making a second and third weapon a wise investment. "As a general rule, Andrew," I said, "you will find, should you accept, that Singapore tigers are literally armed to the teeth. They are impervious to weather, their claws sink four inches deep into flesh. The man who guards against them must be courageous, selfless."

"Mr. McWhirter," he said, "I accept. If I am needed, I accept." "Capital!" I said. I took him by the arm before he could change his mind. We walked fifty paces to the main road. There we stood among bullocks and carts and bent-over men with yokes on their shoulders, water spilling from swaying buckets. Horses, carriages, large black birds picking at carrion. I pointed down the long avenue to where the street ended, to the wall of brown and green semi-obscured by smoke, a half-mile in the distance. "Be there at sunrise and meet Mr. Blackmore," I said, "he should be expecting you." Then I thought, to be sure of his fitness, "Have you ever killed a wild animal, by the way, other than a partridge or fox?" "Yes," he said, "but only under extraordinary circumstances, and I did not enjoy it." "No matter, my boy, if you encounter a tiger, you will be quick to pull the trigger out of fright alone."

I would write to his sister. I would recount how I helped her brother turn the corner on his melancholy. And, I thought, if he actually met one of those carnivores face to face, he might well say, "I have changed my mind, McWhirter! Quick, take me back to the warehouse, to the pepper, poppy and porcelain!" My next thought was how distinguished *McWhirter, Trenholm, and Amberley* would look on a sign. *McWhirter and Amberley* would look even better. I retired to the warehouse and drew several versions on a scrap of paper.

But I was getting ahead of myself. I put the drawings away and told Chao Tang I was leaving early. I set out for the Pearly Road, intending to thank my wife for her brilliant suggestion. A guard for tigers! But on the way I ran into the doctor with his medical kit, saying that he had just seen her. "She continues to improve, Herbert," he said, "and has just set out towards Fort Canning, to see the girl's grave, to place new flowers." So Alma was not at home. I returned to the warehouse. I would praise her later, surprise her with a few kindly words.

ANDREW GOLLIVER, 19

The earliest blush of dawn. Heavy dew lay on the road, causing clumps of dust to stick to my boots. But I was cheered by the novelty of my prospects, and soon entered a no man's land, jungle and mangrove falling back from the settlement, but not relinquishing domination. A million insects, a thousand birds cried out. From behind came the awakening sounds of the port, whistles and bells ringing, lower-pitched bells tolling from the necks of pack animals. I even heard the familiar buzz of our hummingbird as he flew by, bent on his own mission. Wood rubbed against wood, from the first stirrings of the wind. On I went to road's end, where vines and branches and bushes armed with thorns stood guard. Flowers spectacular in size and colouring burst forth. More to the point, for my own purpose, I came to a gathering of several dozen dark men crouched on the ground, smoking tobacco in pipes or in tight cylinders of rolled leaves. Many of them were chained together by filigreed iron wrapped to the waist, in groupings of five or six. An equal number were not chained, and to my surprise even those in restraints appeared cheerful. The atmosphere was not oppressive. They wore loincloths, tattered shirts, some were turbaned, most were not. Each had in his hand a machete, its wicked blade reflecting the sun. They tested edges against calluses on their palms, or made circular cutting motions in the air, slowly, in the fashion of snake-charmers, checking weight and balance. Several carts were close by, empty traces to the ground. Then there appeared from the jungle itself, stamping his feet, kicking at loose branches, a white man, presumably Mr. Blackmore. He was dressed exactly as I was, in loose brown cotton shirt and pants and a wide-brimmed hat for the sun, carrying one musket to his back, a pistol at his waist.

"Welcome to the front lines, Mr. Golliver," he said, and he explained that he had been scouting for the best avenue of attack for the morning's work. "We are now almost ready." Leading me to one of the carts, he removed its canvas covering with a snap and a flourish, and he presented four muskets and three pistols to me, and four knives in sheaths. "Any questions?" he asked. "I seem to be more heavily armed than you," I said. He laughed and explained that we would take turns shouldering the heavier load, but I, as his junior, would do mornings. It took a while for his back to loosen up.

"I should test the weapons," I said, and I lifted the first musket, inspected its firing mechanism, loaded it, aimed high into the jungle's canopy, and fired. I was not disappointed by the force of the discharge, the plume of flame. I repeated the same exercise six more times, with each musket and pistol, with the same positive result. Then I tucked the knives into my boots and declared myself, for the first time in weeks, ready for work.

"Good," said Mr. Blackmore, "it pays to be thorough." He then suggested that I position myself between the workmen and the fringe of jungle close at hand, to our left. "Show confidence at all times, Andrew, even if you lack it," he said, "and listen carefully for the sudden hushing of birds, the snap of twigs, the bolting of deer. Catch a glimpse of a paw, an eye, a stripe, the tip of a tail, fire away for God's sake. To wait is to be mauled or killed. As for cobras, avoid stepping on them. And keep a weather eye out for changes in the wind, or we will become fuel ourselves for the flames."

He patted me on the back and issued orders to the men. They began to gather fragments of wood and grass and larger branches, piling them against the retreating edge of the jungle, setting fire to them, backing away while others took machetes to the nearby underbrush. "Convicts," Mr. Blackmore said, "from Calcutta, working off sentences for crimes that in all likelihood they did not commit. I rule after my fashion, therefore, with a velvet glove."

I was pleased to hear my superior speak such words. My first day as a Protector was turning out to be more pleasant than I had anticipated. And no cobra or tiger materialized. Instead, we reduced ten acres of pristine greenery to ash and embers. By mid-afternoon the sun had devolved to a reddish disc, and each of us had taken on the appearance of a highwayman. My nose and lower face were covered with a dampened handkerchief, the brim of my hat pulled low against sweat, soot, grime.

CLOVIS CALLAGHAN, 36

I said to Miss Albertson that we seemed to be in a very quiet time at the manor. She said, "Do you mean emotionally quiet, Clovis, or quiet in respect to noise?" I said, "Both really, for the Earl and his furies are no more, and Lady Amberley has been sequestered to the east wing along with the pianoforte, thanks to Mr. Egerton. We can barely hear the afternoon concerts. And that is a bit sad, no more arpeggios in the drawing room, as in the old days. Catherine plays by herself now, with only her mother to watch."

"Their marriage," said Miss Albertson, "is not a strong one. Not only does he have his London sojourns, he has his brandy habit, his surly moods. It infuriates me. Toadies like Mr. Gerald are held in high esteem, yet highly accomplished women are treated as possessions, as lapdogs."

"I saw him yesterday," I said, "Mr. Poppycock himself, trying on some of the Earl's clothes before a mirror. Conventionally handsome, yes, we agree on that. They might fit him, I suppose, the overcoats. After all, the two are similar in height, or in lack of it, whereas—let us never forget—the solicitor is six feet tall and Catherine is five feet, nine inches. She towers over her husband. Oh, and Beulah, something else, why do you think he is suddenly so fascinated with the Far East? A dozen books and maps spread over the floor of his study! And he rattles on and on about Andrew, asking how long it takes a letter to travel from London to Singapore via the Cape of Good Hope, or via Suez, and how fatal are tropical diseases to travellers, and are there bloodthirsty pirates, and so on."

"Well," said Miss Albertson, "the last thing that man wants is to see Andrew walk through the door. Poor Catherine seems blind to this, which is no surprise to me. No parental love as a child. She is emotionally stunted, a condition I know too well." Her lower lip was trembling. I reached for her hand. "Their birthday is next week," she said, "let us hope that Andrew has more to celebrate."

ANDREW GOLLIVER, 20

My tiger attacked through a downpour at noon. The men were taking shelter beneath a sailcloth stretched between carts, smoking, chatting over the drumming of the rain. A yellow-orange blur sprang from the wilderness, seizing the nearest man by the shoulder, and with a terrible growling began to drag him backwards. I froze. I heard Mr. Stevens' voice, from the *John Roberts*, during weapon practice, "Fire, son, fire!" I whipped a musket from my shoulder, aimed and pulled the trigger. Nothing happened. Already the conjoined chain of men was rolling in a wild flurry of limbs, tiger stripes, guttural roars, useless machetes spinning to the mud. It was impossible to try another shot. Knife in hand, I threw myself at the animal's left shoulder, stabbing uselessly, falling to one side, watching his terrible face turn to me, snarling. An explosive report then tore past my ear and the cat fell dead, his huge face staring into mine. Mr. Blackmore, musket smoking, reached down and dragged me away and said, quite casually, "Usually it takes three to four balls to kill a tiger of that size, we are quite fortunate. Now let us see to our poor fellow." But we were too late, half the victim's neck was torn away, and he was lifeless. We freed the rest of our crew from their chains and joined them shivering under the sailcloth. Two bodies, tiger and man, lay side by side beside us. "Seven feet, I would estimate, in length, excluding the tail," Mr. Blackmore said, "and I have never seen a tiger of any size, for that matter, attacked with a knife."

He tipped his hat to me, for courage or stupidity or both.

RAZAK THE NAVIGATOR, 32

By our third week in Singapore harbour, my captain was in the grips of a terrible dysentery. He was lying in bed, drawing his knees to his chest, fouling the sheets. Next he vomited, and looked a pitiful sight. "Razak," he finally said, wiping his mouth with his hand, "you will be ashamed of me but I have accepted a commission to kill a man. I do not have the strength for it. Take my place, please, or we will lose our ship." I was taken aback, for we had sworn ourselves away from violence for the past seven years. "A man in London has a hold over a man in Calcutta, the man in Calcutta has a hold over me. I am sorry, Razak." Then he groaned for another five minutes while I thought of our ship being taken from us. I imagined walking the waterfront looking for another position. I remembered the various flags we had flown under. "Tell me, Captain," I said, "exactly what you mean." "Go to the jungle's edge and kill an Englishman, Andrew Golliver, a guard against tigers. I saw him a few days ago, wide hat, muskets, pistols." "Not defenseless, then?" I asked. "Against you, Razak, everyone is defenseless." A thin stream of feces, streaked with blood, spread out noiselessly from his buttocks, pooling briefly on the sheets. A cloud of even greater foulness filled the cabin. "They have already paid me," he said, "in gold coins. It must be done."

I went up to the deck, for fresh air. I weighed the importance of my captain and the importance of an anonymous Englishman. One was my friend, the other an oppressor. I went down below and asked him, "Where, exactly, by the jungle, does this Andrew Golliver work?" On a piece of paper torn from packaging, he drew, with a shaky and stained hand, a rough map of the settlement and its environs. He marked a spot with an X. I memorized it. I burnt it to ashes. I loaded my musket and set out towards the columns of smoke rising to the east. Avoiding thoroughfares, I struck into the far-more-difficult wetlands, clumps of mangrove, swamp-grass. I pressed on, often to my waist in water, rising to dry land now and then, allowing myself nostalgia for the similar flood plains of Kuala Lumpur, which I had explored a thousand times as a child. I kept the sun on my right shoulder. Woodsmoke grew thicker, I heard a chatter of voices, I parted enough foliage to see my captain's target, a white man with muskets and pistols. He was crouched, his back to me, playing cards with chained workers, some of whom must be my countrymen.

Leaving all considerations of fairness behind, I slipped from the jungle. I walked unobserved to his back, placed my pre-cocked musket a quarter-inch from his head, just under the brim of his hat. I pulled the trigger and the force of the explosion took some of his head away. He fell straight forward, his companions fell back, scattering their cards. I thought of shouting a political slogan, but that would have added hypocrisy to my sin. I slipped back into the undergrowth, retraced my steps through jungle, swamp, mangrove, back up into the crowded streets. I zigzagged through the shanties in case I had been followed.

Back at our ship, to my dismay, it appeared that my captain would not profit from my foray. He was dead, his mouth sucked into a tight circle over his gums, his eyes glazed. The jug of water was tipped to the floor. Gingerly, with two fingertips, I tugged the stained sheets from under him and pulled up a corner of the mattress. There it was, the purse of gold coins, soaked with ex-crement. I managed to grasp it—one corner was clean enough—and I carried it in that dainty manner to the railing. There I tied a fishing line to it and dipped it to the sea, swishing it back and forth, hauling it up, laying the individual coins out to dry in the sun. Then I took a blanket from my quarters, wrapped my captain's body in it, carried him up the steps, tipped him over the side. Many times he had told me that he preferred to die at sea. He drifted face-up into the watery shadows under the wharf. Had I delayed my murderous mission an hour or two, the Englishman would still be alive. I extended useless apologies to Andrew Golliver, whoever he was, for my efficiency.

ZEPHYRAX, 4

I had taken to flying daily, for exercise, over the settlement. If something unusual caught my eye, I would hover and observe. For the most part, I watched the human population in their social interactions, and I became particularly adept at picking up on dishonesty such as cheating at cards, or a hand tucking a vegetable under a gown at the market. I expected the worst of humankind, and so I saw it. But the most egregious criminal act I observed, and the only one disturbing to me personally, was Andrew's murder.

One moment there he was—I was at six hundred feet, well above the choking tendrils of smoke—and he was shuffling a deck of cards with his charges, all of them crouched in a tight circle, concentrating. Not particularly interesting, I thought, but then out of the jungle walked a singular-looking man, black hat thrown back from his forehead, a long feather attached to it. He had the dark skin and features of a mixed-race, so he was not at all remarkable for Singapore, far from it. But he had a musket held straight out before him, and he was approaching Andrew with nonchalance from behind. Without fair warning, he shot him in the back of the head. The convicts fell back in dismay but the assassin paid no attention. He turned and vanished back into the greenery, stepping first over the decomposing body of a tiger, scattering a pack of feral dogs darting at its flesh.

No doubt the murderer thought himself invisible, but he was not. I dropped down through vines and branches until I was ten feet off his shoulder, and in that position I followed him as he went deeper into the jungle, deeper to the mangroves, wading, never in a hurry, forging his way. Now and then he paused to remove his hat, to wipe his brow, to sight the sun. Finally he rose from the marsh into the poorest neighbourhood, where the huts were built so tightly together that somehow, perhaps by ducking into a hidden doorway, he lost me.

I was mortified by my incompetence. I spun through passageways, some dark, some blinding with light, to no avail. My respect for him increased a hundredfold, for it was not an easy feat to shake a hummingbird. I overflew five times, ten times, hoping to spot him on a wharf, a ship, only to see so many men dressed the same, or nearly so, that I discovered assassins everywhere. I had to perch at the top of an anonymous mast to regain my composure.

With no better alternative presenting itself, I flew back to the scene of the crime. There, to my astonishment, was Andrew, alive after all. He was stooping, lifting the body of the murdered man into a cart. A lone policeman, truncheoned, was standing by. The dogs were still tearing away at the tiger, snapping at each other to gain advantage.

A day later, I attended the funeral. It was a Mr. Blackmore who had fallen, and his grave was placed not far from the girl's. Little was said by the dark-frocked clergyman, and I was disappointed by his reticence. The killing, after all, had been senseless, brutal, and I expected to hear a clarion call for revenge. An eye for an eye, a tooth for a tooth. Instead I heard nothing but a pious homily or two, and we left the hillside, I thought, as a defeated party.

ALMA MCWHIRTER, 38

Two days after the murder of Andrew Golliver's supervisor, I found, on the bedroom floor, after Herbert had gone to work, several folded pieces of paper. They must, I thought, have fallen from his pocket. I picked them up, expecting an invoice or receipt, only to be surprised to find that it was a letter from England, from a Catherine Egerton. It concerned an Andrew Amberley, surely our Andrew, yet our Andrew was supposed to be a Golliver. How could that be, I wondered, but it soon dawned on me that Herbert was playing one of his double games. He was trading personal information for gain. He had discovered that our castaway was not a simple sailor, and had written to his family, wealthy and high-positioned. Currying favour, as I might expect. And here I was, holding the sister's reply. It gave me pause, because Jaimia had told me time and again that she and Andrew would live a simple life.

I refolded the pages and left them on the night table. Then I was pleasantly sidetracked by another visit from the doctor. We made a tempest upon the bed. Rolling from me, kissing me, he spied the papers and I encouraged him to read them. "Oh, summarize them for me, darling," he said, "I am far too languid." I did, and he replied that young Golliver might be the richest man in the world but he was not as lucky as Geoffrey Bates of Singapore. "Oh Geoffrey," I said, "apply your silver tongue to me again, directly," with the result that half the morning passed and he had to rush to his next appointment.

I was left alone, but in a state of happiness. Fond moments came hurtling back to me. How kind my parents had been, how I missed them, how my mother would take me shopping, how Father, a Manchester policeman, would share his mysteries from work with the two of us. "Let me pick your brains," he would say, lighting his pipe after dinner, and he would regale us with contradictory details in a case of homicide. We would pitch in with our theories, and sometimes he would say, "Yes, yes, I had not thought of that," and "Seek the motive, the motive." Were he consulted on Mr. Blackmore, he would surely say, "That man was targeted." But why, and by whom? Mr. Blackmore was universally liked and admired, and lived modestly. Then it struck me. Mr. Blackmore had been mistaken for Andrew. They were dressed the same, the shooter had approached from behind, and apparently Andrew was about to roll in riches. "Money or sex," Father had said, "money or sexual desire, there's the answer."

Well, female detective, you have already been unfaithful to your husband, be so again. Andrew must be told. I dressed and hurried to the curtains of smoke and fire and there he was, muskets and pistols hanging about him like the spikes of a Scotch thistle, handsome as ever but still visibly saddened by recent events.

"I have something you should see," I said. I took the letter from my sleeve and held it out to him. He asked me to walk with him, as he had to keep an eye on the crew. "Read it aloud for me, please," he said, and for the second time within an hour, I did so.

"Your husband has not been candid with me, then," he said. "No," I said, "he has made a serious blunder." Then, to explain my presence further, I related, with growing intensity, my theory related to the death of Mr. Blackmore. That he, Andrew, had been the intended victim. And why.

"Not only have I killed my wife then, but I have also killed Mr. Blackmore," he said. "No, Andrew, a hired killer has killed Mr. Blackmore." Not wanting to lose momentum in the solving of my case, I asked him directly, "Andrew, who could possibly want you dead?" After a long pause, he said, "Three persons. The first would be myself, for killing my wife and friend. The second, Jaimia's uncle from the island, but he does not have the means. The third, my sister's fiancé…well, her husband…for he is a man overly enamoured of money, and he dislikes me." I did not pull my punches. "Andrew," I said, "you should be alarmed. I am alarmed. When he discovers that you are still alive, he will send another hound from hell to track you down."

CHAO TANG, 34

My employer called me to his desk. He told me that his wife had discovered that "we" had written to England months ago, regarding Andrew. The cat was out of the bag, he said, but much good had actually come of it because Alma had developed a plausible theory: Andrew was the target for the assassination, not Mr. Blackmore. "Sit down, Chao Tang" he said, "and read this, my latest."

Dear Catherine, how terrible to read of your father's brutal end in Ireland. You and your mother have my deepest sympathy. I can only imagine how he will be missed by those with whom he interacted daily. But now I write for the future. Your brother seems to have fully recovered from his adventure on the high seas. He has moved on from our warehouse to become a highly-respected protector of prisoners, a position that suits his altruistic nature. His relationship with the native girl has come to a natural end. I have, and I know from your reply that you will approve, begun to encourage him to return to England. Often we sit informally at the end of a wharf, philosophizing and bantering. I point out how irresponsible it is for him to reject his patrimony. Money, I have said, is not in and of itself an evil. In fact a wise investment in London or Singapore is an investment in the future of England. Also, Lady Catherine, I don't wish to be an alarmist but a friend of his has just been killed by an unknown assailant, for no apparent reason, while working side by side with your brother. Singapore may not be the safest place.

I have a ship, 'The Rook'—named after the chess piece for its quickness—leaving in two months for Suez. I shall encourage Andrew to be aboard. From Egypt, he could repatriate himself through Marseille or Venice.

I must hurry. The packet weighs anchor. Should Andrew choose, despite my advice, to live in anonymity, I hope that you and your husband might consider extending your business interests to the South China Sea. Opium is proving profitable, and I expect, as a result of British policy, to double shipments to China in the next few months. Fondly, Herbert McWhirter.

"Well," he asked, "Chao Tang, your thoughts?" I suggested that he write more about the girl Jaimia, that if Andrew's sister were anything like Andrew, she would want to know how much they were in love. "Chao Tang," he said, "you do not know the English, how they treat inferior races. Rewrite the letter in your hand, please. Seal it, send it to the packet. Now, any other business?"

I broached the situation of the French nuns. "The Sisters of the Lamb Recumbent, I believe you have heard of them?" "Indeed I have," he said, "they are hooded witches who, on Friday nights, place themselves outside the Hut Chinois. They castigate the customers. The less I see of them the better." "It has come to my attention, Sir," I said, "that their time of service in Singapore has nearly ended, yet the funds for their return journey have failed to materialize." "Too bad, Chao Tang, as you can imagine, my heart goes out to them." "Bear with me for a moment, Sir, but my suggestion is to offer them passage on The Rook at no cost, as a gesture of goodwill to the Catholic Church." "Goodwill? Charity you mean," he said, "and why should I extend charity to three women whose appointed task is to bring guilt and gloom upon the settlement?" "Because," I answered, "with all due respect, there will be little cost to you for their passage, and if they were gone from Singapore, you might be a happier man." "Chao Tang!" my employer said, "I have underestimated you again! Yes, book them for Suez, book them today, but impress upon them to pray for my soul, demand that they widen the eye of their needle, that my camel darteth through when the time cometh."

I smiled to confirm my employer's wit. How contagious hypocrisy can be, I thought, for it had already entered me—and I was guarding against it!—like a worm.

MANON BEAUREGARD, 18

We were the Sisters of the Lamb Recumbent. A silly name, I thought, when I first heard it, but I was attracted, childishly perhaps, by its banner, showing a white sheep resplendent upon a field of green. My stepfather, dropping me at the side door of the steepled church in Montauban, said that I should have a go at the holy life. I was turning too many heads at home for my own good. The only head I was turning was his, but I could hardly turn to the streets for a living so I pushed open the heavy door that faced me. Two weeks later, I was accepted by the Sisters into their Order. The requirements were not severe—perhaps there were none—and within a month we were dispatched to Singapore. Singapore! I thought. And for two years! Well, if it turned out to be a mistake, it would be a relatively short-lived one, compared to my first sixteen years.

There were three of us. First there was our leader, Marceline, and second was her sister, Eulalie, and then I, Manon, by far the youngest. Although we were funded, apparently, by a Catholic organization—possibly, for this exile, by my stepfather?—we were not officially recognized by the Church. None of us had taken formal vows or undergone spiritual training. In fact we could best be described by the term *secular nurse*, but it was our mandate, nevertheless, to emphasize the role of Jesus Christ in everything we did. He, we were to say, could do miracles. Not the water-into-wine type of miracles, according to Marceline, for they were circus tricks, but practical everyday miracles relating to the healing of wounds, physical and spiritual. To be honest, I could not follow Marceline's theological reasoning much of the time, but in effect she demanded that we show abject humility in the care of others, that we lower ourselves lower than the low, as Christ would do. All right, I thought, for two years I could do it.

But even she, Marceline, agreed that we occupied an uncertain niche in the hierarchy of the settlement of Singapore. We were not nuns though we dressed as nuns—in coifs and long gowns— and we were not saints though we professed sanctity. Nor were we self-reliant, for as our funds from France petered out, we held out a small bowl after our ministrations, for payment, however meagre. Though I was naive at first, the horrors I saw on a daily basis soon opened my eyes. My own religious zeal fell far short of my companions'. Marceline was as ferocious as a nest of bees, Eulalie was unquestioning, a faithful servant to God, but I was constantly catching myself in doubt. For example, they could march through the poorest quarters of the settlement at a speed that taxed me in the heat, despite their being thirty years my senior. And although back in France I had not thought of myself as squeamish, they far outperformed me in nursing duties. They immersed their hands in streams of diarrhea without flinching, pulled tapeworms segment by segment from the bowels of babies, expressed blowflies from suppurating skin, kissed the foreheads of the leprous, drew crude crosses in ash and water with their fingertips upon the foreheads of women dying in childbirth. I thought that last rite, by the way, far exceeded our mandate, but they ploughed ahead anyway because, as Marceline said, "We should make as broad a furrow as we can in this field of heathen souls."

Once I found the courage—just once—to say to Marceline that I found our work a hardship, that our effort seemed far out of proportion to the result. She turned on me like a spitting mongoose, saying, "Manon! Hardship and suffering is the whole point. God commands us to pitch our tent among the poorest of the poor, where disease is rampant, where superstition reigns, where false idols are venerated. We must hold ourselves up as an example to nonbelievers. Otherwise, why should they believe the Bible any more than the Koran, or, for that matter, the *Thousand and One Nights* of Scheherazade, as a guiding principle?" As for our results, she pointed out, "Have we not converted twelve heathens to the Christian faith in the last calendar year?"

Well, perhaps so, I thought, but finding twelve Christians in Singapore could hardly compare to what I had read about in Africa, where missionaries handed white robes to their converts and walked them by the hundreds to the river, baptizing them en masse. But I could hardly say anything as traitorous as that to

Marceline. I kept my counsel and counted the months until a full year and a half had passed, and our return to France was on the horizon, only to discover that the funding for our voyage home had been stolen in the Strait of Malacca. Or so we heard. Perhaps it was never sent at all. Either way, Marceline seemed unaffected, and spoke of martyrdom. I did catch sight of her one day speaking to a Chinese clerk near the docks, and lo and behold, as it says in the Bible, a miracle was suddenly wrought. News came that we had passage aboard *The Rook*, leaving in eight weeks. The ship belonged to Herbert McWhirter, a sinner we knew from our vigils at the Hut Chinois, an addict, a fornicator. But we conferred and agreed that his offer, though self-serving, should be accepted.

Eulalie celebrated by twirling and singing a little tune, and I might have done the same had Marceline not instructed me to go straightaway to the McWhirter warehouse. "Write down the exact itinerary," she told me, and an hour later I was able to tell the others that The Rook would carry us first to Goa, on the west coast of India, then to Suez on the Red Sea. From there we would disembark and travel by foot through desert to Cairo, then to Alexandria, and then by sea again for Venice or Marseille.

"Oh Eulalie," said Marceline, "cease your tears of joy. Knuckle down, Sisters, we still have work to do in Singapore."

HERBERT MCWHIRTER, 41

From the sun angling through the upper windows, I could see that the working day was over. I walked to the massive iron doors and rolled them shut. I looked back to the office and there was Andrew, standing by my desk. I gathered myself to face him and strode his way with as much buoyancy as I could muster. I shook his hand. Even before he opened his mouth, I apologized for my letter to England, saying that when he first arrived I had been so startled that I had let my concern for his well-being override my principles. "Which I should never have done," I added, "though imagine the joy it brought to your sister." To my relief, he waved off my concern. "Water under the bridge," he said.

I lit a lamp. We sat in chairs on opposite sides of my desk. He said that my wife's analysis of recent events had radically changed his plans. His sister's welfare was now primary to him, and if her husband was actually hiring mercenary killers, as seemed possible, then he, Andrew, could hardly stay in Singapore. "Catherine and even my mother might be in danger," he said, "so I should leave at the next opportunity, however contrary that is to my previous intentions."

At last he was coming to his senses. Adjusting the wick on the lamp to brighten the atmosphere, I said that I was well prepared to help him. My brigantine, *The Rook*, was leaving in two months and he would be welcome aboard her. He could travel as passenger or armed guard, whichever he preferred, but the latter was a paid position. "Then that is what I choose," he said, "I still need to make a living, however modest." "Capital," I said, "but I give you fair warning, your duties will include keeping watch over three French nuns, the eldest of whom is a harridan. You shall serve as their Protector." "Do they have fewer claws than tigers?" he asked. I laughed. "Perhaps your sense of humour is returning," I said, "a good sign. Either way, *The Rook* will take you to Suez, Andrew, avoiding the storms of the Cape. It is the fastest, the most direct, the safest route. Now, would you prefer to spend the remaining eight weeks in the warehouse, or with your convicts?" To my disappointment, he opted for the jungle. He said that solitude suited him. We shook hands and I walked him to the stairs, and then I thought, is this a Friday? No, by heavens, a Wednesday. That trio of nuns would not be picking at my sleeve. I turned to the footbridge, thinking that my future charity on their behalf deserved an immediate, more earthly reward.

ZEPHYRAX, 4

The tiger shot by Mr. Blackmore had been dragged in circles by dogs. Its carcass was still visited by flies, but it appeared half-sized, like a worn and crumpled carpet. The teeth, however, were still fearsome. I zipped down to the left ear, by the hairy tuft, and there I perched at an angle that allowed me to examine the incisors of gleaming ivory, curved and pointed. I shivered. Had I a tooth remotely approaching that size, I could never fly. Wait, Zephyrax, you have no teeth at all. Birds do not have teeth. Birds are subtle, they are the opposite of tigers. Then I thought, remembering the sodden bodies of our flock, drowned at sea, we are really not much different from that poor beast lying before me, doing our best to get by in a world overwhelmed by malice.

RAZAK THE NAVIGATOR, 32

It became clear to me, from slowly deciphering the front page of the Singapore Free Press, that I had killed the wrong man. A Mr. Blackmore, not a Golliver. I regretted my mistake, but there was no need to correct it. Enough harm had been done. My obligation to my captain had expired along with him, and if someone else wanted to take a crack at Golliver, that was up to them. But the paymaster, I realized, might think differently, considering the gold coins he had spent. For prudence, I packed my sea-bag and struck out for the busier wharves of the harbour.

What next? I could continue in the cotton trade, if I had a vessel of my own. Impossible. I could sign on as navigator to any of a dozen ships. But I could also treat myself to a month of reading and contemplation. Ultimately I chose the latter, taking room and board with a family of sailmakers from whose residence it was an easy walk to the cemetery below Fort Canning. There I sat against a gravestone, weather permitting, and for self-improvement I studied the English language. I tripled my vocabulary within the first two weeks by fabricating special cards upon which I wrote difficult words, polysyllabic ones, in capital letters. Then, as I walked to and fro, I would pull one of those cards at random from my pocket and pronounce it as quickly and meticulously as I could. None of the cemetery's inhabitants questioned my sanity.

At last, three weeks into my studies, on a Friday night I sallied out to a sailors' bar, intending to practise my skills. A tricky process, I knew, with my dark skin, for no Englishman was likely to strike up a conversation. But as luck would have it, a bearded white man was drinking by himself, and he had a fine sextant on the table before him, turning it to and fro, ruminating. I summoned resolve. I approached him, pointed to the instrument and said, "Good Sir, I am Razak the Navigator, and I have observed that you have a fine-looking instrument of celestial navigation. Could I possibly examine it?"

I expected him to shoo me away, but he was welcoming. He pulled a chair over and suggested I sit beside him. "Razak," I repeated. Together we admired the design and workmanship of the sextant, an easy chore for me because it was a marvel of precision. It even had tiny etchings of whales upon it, blowing water into the air. After the instrument had been fully praised, I confessed that my main purpose of the night was to practise English. He was kind enough to buy me a draught. "I am Mr. Barker," he said, "navigator on the brigantine *The Rook*." Then he tested me, saying, "Razak, what is that?" and he pointed to objects in the room, asking me for their English names. I saw and identified a green bottle, a toppled cork, a mirror, a barman, a sailor with a torn coat, a chair in the corner, a rag for cleaning, various lamps and their wicks, a prostitute. "Good, and Razak, how does gin taste? Is it bitter or sweet? Do boots have shoelaces?" and so on, speaking to me as though we were equals. Which of course we were, but few Englishmen knew it.

Eventually it was past midnight and we both decided, after shaking hands, to retire to our respective quarters.

As we left the bar, however, within five steps we were set upon by thugs with knives. Mr. Barker, unprepared for battle, was stabbed two or three times before he could even grasp the course of events. I however, was never unprepared, and perhaps the contest lasted ten seconds longer than it should have, but it was soon resolved, with the result that poor kind Mr. Barker and three villains lay dead on the street. I picked up the sextant, of course, before realizing that I had not escaped injury. Blood coursed from my forehead, into my eyes. I sat down for a moment from unexpected dizziness. Perhaps I lost consciousness, for when I next looked up I saw three white women in long gowns peering down at me. Swans, I thought, but these were swans with hands instead of wings. They grasped me by my coat sleeves, lifted me up and escorted me at a brisk pace to a threadbare hut not far away. There they bathed my wound in warm, clean water and they applied a dressing, and one of the older ones spoke to me directly about Jesus Christ. I had heard of Jesus Christ before, of course, a Christian saint. She asked me to take to my knees and pray to him, to Jesus Christ, and also to his Father.

Well, I was not about to do that. However, I thanked them for their care, left one gold coin in their basket, and crept from the hut. I found my way back to my bed without further incident. In the morning, I thought, I would return Mr. Barker's instrument to *The Rook*. Then I realized, as *The Rook* would suddenly find herself short a navigator, perhaps the captain would take me on. My English had more than passed muster, after all, and it was time to leave Singapore. Those who had hired my captain would be much quicker on their feet than common alley thieves. And smarter too, in their planning. Discretion is the better part of valour, I had learned, an English phrase, an English sentiment.

ANDREW GOLLIVER, 20

Should I write back to my sister? No, for I would arrive in person as quickly as any letter. I would surprise her, knock casually on the manor door, materialize from nowhere and play a dramatic chord on her pianoforte. Or I would approach her as she sat in her bower reading, not far from the maze now gone to seed. "Oh, hello, Catherine," I would say, casually, as though I had never left. Then we would shout and spin in circles. As for her husband, I would have to treat him with respect. Alma's theory was conjecture, after all, our evidence circumstantial. Chao Tang had even cautioned me in that regard, on a different matter, saying, "Not every missing piece of cheese, Andrew, is taken by the first beady-eyed rat."

CAPTAIN WEDDERBURN, 57

Late in the year 1852 I came to the ship one morning to find carpenters building a small cabin just below deck, in the forward hold. McWhirter told me that I was to carry three nuns to Suez, a distance of five thousand nautical miles. He was having a private quarter roughed in for them. He apologized for the imposition, but it was being built with an eye to easy removal later, and so would not impinge on profits for long.

Fine, I thought. Let there be nuns. I was no longer a believer myself—observations of my own had changed my mind—but those who did believe far outnumbered me. Nuns deserved respect. "They are known officially," McWhirter said, "as the Sisters of the Lamb Recumbent, a name that causes me merriment. The first time I heard it, I wondered, is it the Lamb who is recumbent, or is it the Sisters?"

Grammatically, I could see his point. "I am being generous to them," he said, "but they have been a thorn in my side. The oldest carries a grim excess of Godliness with her at all times. She pounces on human weakness, imagined or real. The middle is light-headed and sings addled songs of nonsense. And the youngest, well, she is so comely in appearance that every man aboard will wish to tear off her robe and have at her." "Such will not happen on my ship," I said. And Mr. McWhirter said, "Of course not, of course not, but when you see her for yourself, you will not be displeased." He then absolved me of responsibility for their safety on board, saying that he had hired a young man for that purpose, an Andrew Golliver, and although Mr. Golliver was masquerading as a wild man with muskets and knives falling about him, he was in fact—"our secret, Captain, our secret!"— a wealthy English lord repatriating to Dorset. "I have a vested interest in him, Captain. Let me put it this way. If you should, hypothetically, need to make a sacrifice of weight to save *The Rook*, push the nuns overboard first, and Andrew Golliver last."

McWhirter was overstepping with his black humour. I replied that as captain of *The Rook* I would die myself before throwing any woman to the sea. "Joking, just joking," he said, "so good luck to you, Captain Wedderburn, and I will see you in several months' time, and both of us will be the richer for your travels."

Then came the morning to set sail. To my consternation Mr. Barker, my navigator, did not appear. In his place came a small, dark man with Mr. Barker's sextant in hand and a bandage of dried blood on his forehead. He wore piratical dress— the characteristic feathered hat—and, though soft-spoken, he recounted a violent story of street mayhem from the previous night. He had been able to save his own life from thugs, but not that of my navigator. That being the situation, he asked if I would consider him as applicant for the vacated position. "I am known far and wide as the Navigator, Sir, and I have extensive experience in the South China Sea and in the Indian Ocean." "Your name?" I asked. "Razak," he replied. "You are familiar with the currents to the west?" "Better than any man," he said. He did not appear to be boasting, merely stating a fact. The morning winds were picking up. The sun was breaking free of the hills. I thought to get underway as soon as possible, and if he failed me as navigator I could, after all, do it myself. "Razak," I said, "let me test you. Where are the shoals at the harbour's mouth?" He described them exactly, in detail, and pointed for emphasis. "You are hired," I said, "throw your sea-bag by the first cannon."

MANON BEAUREGARD, 18

Several days before departing on *The Rook*, we were helping to bury three babies in Pauper's Field. I wondered aloud if they might be accepted into heaven after all, despite not being Christian. Eulalie said, "They are hardly old enough to have sinned." Marceline looked up from shovelling to say, "Well, it might be nice for the two of you to look simplistically upon newborns as innocents, but these children, as they are heathens, will end up in hell regardless." Then she added, out of the blue, and quite caustically, I thought, that she wished to chastise me for my behaviour during the past two years. "Your constant questioning, your sullen streak, your insubordination has tested my generosity of spirit. I have placed a black mark by your name, Manon, on your permanent record, with detailed criticisms, and—one more thing, if you wish a word of advice—stop trading on what others perceive to be your uncommon beauty, a transient gift of no value on Judgment Day."

To calm the waters, Eulalie began to sing a sweet song under her breath. As for me, I had learned to say nothing in response except, "Yes, Marceline." I began to dig faster and deeper, thinking that the farther down I was able to go, the more protected the bodies would be from animals. Their mothers were standing close by, watching us, holding the wrapped ones in their arms. It was fortunate, I thought, that they could not understand what we were saying. Each of them had given me a tiny amulet to bury with her child, and I was able, when Marceline's attention was elsewhere, to tuck the simple treasures into their coverlets. Then Eulalie and I placed them gently, one atop the other, into the common grave.

Three mornings later we arose from our cots earlier than usual. Not a rooster had crowed. Having already packed our possessions, we needed only a few minutes to brush the floor and say goodbye to the hut. We walked towards the harbour, the odd lamp flickering through a doorway to guide us. I didn't know what Marceline and Eulalie were thinking, but I felt a surging happiness as I thought of my future, far from the Sisters of the Lamb. Then we were at the wharf, already bustling, lit by lanterns, the dark shape of *The Rook* two masts etched against the eastern sky. As the gangway was down and welcoming, we climbed to meet the captain, a courteous man named Wedderburn. He helped us navigate the open deck, past ropes strung at angles and bales of this and that for loading, to our quarters, which turned out to be a freshly carpentered, box-like room at the entrance to the forward hold. "Here," he said, "you will have access to both fresh air and privacy. You are the only women on board."

Dawn broke. More and more sailors appeared, running, throwing sea-bags to claim space. Many shouts were raised, winches lowered, packages swung to holds. A parrot flew to the rigging and talked to itself. Several cannon were rolled to their ports for greasing. I hoped they would never see use. To our surprise, the small dark man we had found in the street a few nights earlier was there too, our bandage still marking his forehead. He nodded to us in recognition. Then a young man no older than I rushed up the gangway, holding in his hand a half-gilded bird cage. He placed it upon an empty pallet and shook the captain's hand, and then he looked our way. Marceline said, "We should retire to our cabin for dawn prayer." "Please," I said, "Marceline, there is so much excitement at leaving, let us watch." The young man by then had moved to the starboard rail. "Just this once," said Marceline. As the winds of morning were to our advantage, a dozen sailors leapt to the rigging and *The Rook* began to slip creaking from the wharf, pushed out by several rowboats. I moved to the rail and stood beside the young man. We watched Singapore fall slowly away. Water birds whirled about us in great numbers, crying out with as much excitement as I felt myself. Then a tiny bird with vivid green feathering and a red throat buzzed by me and entered the cage. How wonderful, I thought, that he belonged there, yet he could come and go as he wished. The young man saw my interest. "Do you like the little fellow?" he asked. "Yes," I said, "I have never before seen such colours." He introduced himself, saying that he was Andrew, our Protector on the voyage, courtesy of the merchant. He asked me my name, and rather than being shy and diffident or even cold, as Marceline had instructed me to be with men, I pushed the hair from my eyes so I could see him better and I said, "My name is Manon."

ZEPHYRAX, 4

He carried my cage—I was still in it—and we were down the stairs, heading for the docks. Enough bouncing, I thought. I took off to the night sky, there to find a bustling at the wharf, demanding my attention. I perched on the warehouse roof, at its forward edge, and I saw several bullock drivers tapping the flanks of their beasts with sticks to keep them moving, men lifting bales and carrying them up the gangway of a brigantine, three women in grey frocks and white headdresses being ushered aboard. There was Andrew too, foregoing the gangway, climbing over the railing to the deck with my empty cage, placing it on a hatch cover.

So, I realized, we were on the move at last. I vocalized for a few seconds and then pendulumed back and forth to celebrate.

I flew to the ship and zipped through and about various parts of the rigging. Then I took to the tip of the mainmast. From there the stars above and the lanterns below were almost equal sources of light, the stars tiny and white as polished scrimshaw, the lanterns larger, more yellow, like goldenrod or buttercup. The lanterns moved and guttered as they were carried from ship to shore, or back and forth upon land. The outer harbour was still pitch-black. Next the sun peeked up, casting long shadows, and I realized that I was looking upon Singapore for the last time. At that hour, and only at that hour, did it look fresh and promising. Dew sparkled on thatched roofs, smoke from cooking fires was beginning to blow softly over empty streets. "Zephyrax," I said, "count your blessings." I was in much better shape than when I had arrived. I was no longer imprisoned. I was no longer hungry. Freedom, though mine might appear illusory to a cynic, had been granted me. "Oh Singapore, oh Singapore!" I whistled, "I shall always remember you, but I am not sad to say goodbye."

Finally, the ship was pushed and pulled away from the wharf. I entered my cage. Andrew was close by, talking to one of the women. She looked no more than a girl, much overdressed in a sack-like gown, wearing a ridiculous cloth helmet on her head, blonde hair escaping from the edges. She brushed some of those windblown strands from her eyes to look up at Andrew, a gesture I had seen Jaimia use many times. I wondered if it were not an affectation common to human females. If so, it was undeniably an attractive one, similar to the bending of the neck of a hummingbird to change the angle, to add a sparkle to the eye.

Then the two older women, similarly dressed, came to the young one and spoke to her, and all three went to the foremost hold, where they ducked their heads and disappeared below deck.

1853

GERALD EGERTON, 23

Catherine approached me in the library. "Another letter from Singapore," she said, visibly trembling. Oh joy! I thought, did they manage to kill him already? Is it possible? "Dearest, dearest," I said, and I composed myself to show sympathy. But she collapsed backwards on the sofa against a mound of pillows, splaying her legs out to the floor. She seemed incapable of words. I went to her side and took the letter from her while still she wept. I scanned it for the news I wanted to see, for confirmation.

Dear Catherine, it began, and my eyes jumped down the lines until I saw *your brother* and my heart dropped like a stone. The writer was speaking of him in the present tense! A fellow worker had been killed! Figby, I will cut you to a thousand pieces. I glanced down to Catherine's face and she was glowing, saying "I am so happy, Gerald, so happy, Andrew is coming home."

Home? I had not read that far. *Suez, Marseille, Venice*... Christ! Not only did they miss him but, as a result, he was scurrying back to us. A total cock-up, and I had paid for it.

I bent to Catherine and found a handkerchief in her sleeve. I gently wiped her eyes. "What news! What incredible news!" I said, in perfect honesty. Then Catherine was rising from the sofa and falling into my arms, hugging me with such force that I marvelled: how could she not sense my true feelings? I hugged her back as enthusiastically as I could. I danced her around the room. "Incredible news!" I repeated, and she said, "Yes, yes, and do you realize, from the timeline, that he must have left Singapore already, already he is on a ship with wings?"

I had much work to do. I took up a poker that lay close at hand and stirred the fire. Sparks took to the chimney with such a sudden roaring that "Christ!" I shouted, and I was forced to jump backwards as a considerable puff of smoke returned to the room. New and livelier sparks flew to the rug, smoldering there. I ordered one of the housemaids to stamp upon it, to put it out. Then Catherine said, "Gerald, let's read the entire letter together, aloud," and I had no choice but to agree, all the while thinking of the king's ransom paid for his death, to no avail.

CLOVIS CALLAGHAN, 37

I told Miss Albertson that I had been present in the library, dusting, and so observed at first hand the interaction between the lovebirds. "Lady Catherine was overjoyed, rendered speechless. But Mr. Gerald altered his features in the most hypocritical manner, wiping tears from her eyes while he composed his false face, twitching his lips and eyebrows in the most saccharine manner. Then he started a fire on the rug with his poker and made me jump upon it, to spare his silk stockings. Fortunately, I did not burn myself, my shoes were up to the task. Also my mounting fury."

"Do you remember, Clovis," Miss Albertson said, "I've been thinking, how you and I postulated that he would rather see Andrew dead than alive? How we wondered, too, about his obsession with the Far East? Do you think it is possible that he would stoop so low as to have Andrew killed?" My heart was racing. We interlocked fingers. "Yes, I do remember," I said, "and I have been thinking, he might well have been the mystery man behind the hiring of Emerson, for the murder of the Earl. That as well."

GERALD EGERTON, 23

I had to get to London without delay. Catherine ran across the lawn and grasped my horse's bridle. "Gerald, wait," she said. I calmed my steed. She looked up at me intently. "Gerald, does it matter to you whether or not Andrew has given up his inheritance? Whether he returns to claim it?" "No, darling," I said, "if Andrew has had a change in heart after an unsuccessful go in the world, so be it. It matters not to me." "An unsuccessful go? Why would you call it that? He was shipwrecked!" I could never alter her view of her brother. "Catherine, I am a happy man, as things are," I said, and off I galloped, resolving that someone would certainly pay for the Singapore folly and it would not be me. I would insist on a second pass at Andrew, cost-free. I would run roughshod over the low-lifes at the Duck and Spoon.

Miles fell away. So did my obsession, to a degree. I arrived at the city in a much better mood. Holding a perfumed handkerchief to my nose for the foulness of the river, I made my way directly to the Duck and Spoon. No more intermediaries for Gerald Egerton! Pushing open the door of the tavern, I found myself in a much smaller space than I had anticipated, as though an oppressive box had been built within an outer shell. And there was Mr. Figby, the only other customer, leaning on the bar. There was a barman too, skinny, tall and hairless. I ordered a glass of ale. "He is mute, and only listens to me," said Mr. Figby. He made a gesture with his hand and the drink was poured. "Thank you," I said, "and by way of introduction, I am Mr. Smith, provider of your purse for Singapore, for unsuccessful Singapore." I glared, as best I could. "You are not Mr. Smith," replied Mr. Figby, "you are Gerald Egerton, and as for Singapore, we have a bone to pick with you. You lied to us. You misrepresented our target. A simple sailor? He is an Earl in waiting, and Earls are twice the price."

Somehow, I had lost the upper hand already. I drank my glass to the lees. "Let me order a round for the three of us," I said. I was swimming with sharks. Drops of sweat ran down the middle of my back. The barman took his pint and swallowed it like a horse would drink, not even gulping. "Had I known the rascal's true colours," I said, "I would have been the first to tell you." "He is your brother-in-law. It took our researcher one hour to make the connection." "Mr. Figby," I said, "I apologize, mistakes have been made on both sides. Spilled milk! But now, take a second pass at him! He is bound for Venice or Marseille, kill him, kill him in both places!" "Gerald, I like you, your spirit is undaunted. Once the balance for Singapore is paid, we will accept your new commission."

I paid for a second round. I handed over my entire purse without counting and he promised to send his very best man to Venice, his second-best to Marseille. "Capital!" I said, and after several more tankards I asked him to provide proof of death upon completion. "Bring me a lock of Golliver's golden hair," I said, "or even better a death mask. Pour hot wax upon his face, peel it away." "The drink is getting the better of you," Mr. Figby said, "but if circumstances allow… at added charge." "Yes, yes," I said, "yes." The barman could drink and wipe the counter and pocket money simultaneously, so he was obviously not as mentally deficient as he appeared. "Extra coins for your trouble, good man," I said, spilling a few his way.

Eventually we left the tavern, not arm in arm, but companionably. It was dark by then, and I reflected, as we walked, that he was a fine man, a tall man, a respectable man in his way. Surprisingly serene. He strode beside me as calmly as a clergyman, as though he had not touched a drop. I on the other hand was reeling, and giddy too, for I was back in the game.

We parted, and my thoughts turned to the rest of the evening. I was into my sixth day of celibacy. Even a priest might explode from such imposed control. In that neighbourhood, it was a simple matter of asking, and I found her to be quite athletic, slender, even boyish, so it was almost like being back at school.

ANDREW GOLLIVER, 20

The Sisters of the Lamb Recumbent descended to their quarters after we left the harbour. But they did not stay below for long. It was too fine a morning, too much of an occasion. Thinking to introduce myself to the two I had not met, I approached them. "I am Andrew Golliver, your Protector for the journey home." The oldest, Marceline, was not impressed. "We already have a Protector, and his name is Jesus Christ," she said. But Eulalie, next in seniority, smiled at me bashfully and took me aside, confessing that she was pleased to have earthly protection as well. Manon then spoke up, saying, "Protector, tell us anything you can about the voyage, for we know so little." I invited them to sit with me on a hatch cover in the shade provided by the sails. There, with coloured pencils and a sheet of paper, I drew a rough map showing Singapore at the extreme right lower edge of my drawing. Then I drew the Strait of Malacca going west, adding rippling blue lines to denote water. I drew in green the twin land masses of Sumatra and Malaysia, left and right. "From there," I said, "we break out into the Andaman Sea"—more rippling lines of blue—and we were about to enter the Bay of Bengal when I became overly conscious of Manon's presence, close beside me. Momentarily, I lost track of my purpose. I recovered, saying, "Oh yes, let me see, next is the Bay of Bengal"—more blue, more ripples—"and then it will be open ocean to the south of Ceylon, then around the tip of India to Goa. After Goa, the Arabian Sea, westward, westward, always westward to here, the Gulf of Aden, and then the Red Sea, here, then northward to the port of Suez. After that, overland to Cairo, which is right about here, and after that, Europe by sea."

"My goodness," said Eulalie, "how various!" But the route was not as complicated as it appeared, I said, for although the bodies of water had different names, really they were one and the same, blending together. Manon said, "I am looking forward to Egypt, her antiquities." Eulalie said, "How long will our trip take, Protector?" "Four or five months," I replied, "depending on the winds."

Then Eulalie asked if she could see and hold the little bird. I said she could see him whenever she wished, if he were about, but no one yet had been able to hold him. "He values his independence," I said, "it's not easy to get close to him."

ZEPHYRAX, 4

I expected, for the voyage, to survive on sugared water. But Andrew had packed a dried-fruit-and-rendered-fat-and-dead-insect paste that retained its firmness even in sunshine. So I was well provided for. I pecked at it, in imitation of a woodpecker, whenever I wished. That put me in quite a good mood from the onset until, from one of my elevated locations, on a yardarm, I noticed that the man who killed Mr. Blackmore was on board. I recognized him not only from his dress, identical to the killer's, but also by his gait, which had a characteristic wobble to it. And, as I had picked up on the local scuttlebutt—the theory bandied about by the merchant's wife—I realized that he was potentially dangerous to Andrew. The malefactor was in our midst, so it was no leap for me to wonder if he might try to complete his mission. "Zephyrax," I said, "buzz in circles, chip-chatter in alarm!" I did, valiantly, non-stop for ten minutes, but all Andrew did was smile and wave me away. Forget it, I thought, life is cheap, disappointment is rife, sorrow expected. It is unwise to become attached to any one person.

On the positive side, *The Rook* was already racing towards India, so I was, in some way, getting closer to home. I pondered the coincidence that there were "Indians" in North America and "Indians" in India, yet they were culturally and linguistically worlds apart. Someone must have made a mistake, historically, anthropologically, to give them the same name. Or, alternatively—

more likely—white people made up the name for the North Americans. Looking at darker skin, they saw nothing worth differentiating. "Let's call them all Indians, whoever they are," they said, and so it came to pass.

MANON BEAUREGARD, 19

On our third day at sea, Marceline strode to the captain, plucked at his sleeve and said, "I have seen no crosses on board *The Rook*, Captain, not one. No depiction of Christ crucified. How do you expect to avoid the dangers of the open sea? By chance? If so, that is not good enough." Always she had the eyes of a zealot, piercing, silvery-grey, the same colour as the hair that poked out from her cowl. Before the captain could respond, she darted off to the gun deck, where the Malay sailors were at rest in their hammocks. There she picked up several small carvings— sculptural pieces in wood lined up on one of the closed gun ports—ostensibly to admire their artistry. But then she said, "Oh, how interesting, what idle hands can do," and she proceeded to throw them overboard, one by one, shouting about graven images. The captain caught her from behind and wrestled her to the deck—not an easy feat, for obviously he was trying to touch her as little as possible—and said to her, that all could hear, "Your Jesus is not master of *The Rook*, Madame, I am master of *The Rook*. Hang a cross in your own quarters if you like, but nowhere else, and apologize now to the men for their loss of property." He let her go, but she stomped off wordlessly, and only made amends a day later, after she was threatened with confinement for the rest of the voyage. "Let all bitterness and wrath and anger be taken from me," she said to the wronged sailors, "along with all malice." Did she actually believe that, or want that? I doubted it very much. But the Malays carved her a large cross as a gift, and she hung it in our quarters and never ranted again.

CAPTAIN WEDDERBURN, 57

I had come to think of the youngest nun as Cinderella. She was shabbily dressed and much put upon by her elderly sisters. She had no fancy-dress ball to look forward to, no glass slipper, but, when not praying below, she seemed to be forming a strong friendship with Andrew Golliver, her Protector. He might become her Prince, I thought, and so test the power of her vows. He certainly had some positive qualities. On the fourth day from harbour he approached me and said that guarding the Sisters of the Lamb was hardly enough for a man to do. "Are you familiar with cannons?" I asked, and he replied that he had served aboard a frigate so yes, he knew cannons. "Take command of firing exercises then," I said, "for it behooves us to keep both men and cannon in fighting trim. Aim at cloud shadows racing upon the sea." "Good," he said, "for on the *John Roberts* we were forced to shoot at whales." He then ran a prolonged exercise without a hitch, with Cinderella and her older Sisters watching, putting their fingers into their ears at the lighting of each fuse, jumping back in alarm, enjoying themselves until they rushed below, driven there by accumulated smoke and racket.

RAZAK THE NAVIGATOR, 32

Many a ship was lost for the simple lack of looking about. I took to the rigging at regular intervals to check for shoals, to check for sails. I also did it to enjoy myself, to remove my hat and let the wind blow through my hair. It also gave me a chance to consider the disturbing fact of the young white man's presence. As soon as I saw him vault over the rail, in Singapore, I realized that he was likely the man I should have killed. The right age, the right weaponry, and seen from behind he was indistinguishable from my original target. Well, I thought, it was good to see him alive. On our fifth day out of Singapore, he approached me—I was sitting on the deck not far from the captain's cabin—and he said,

"Hello, Navigator, my name is Andrew, Protector of the Sisters of the Lamb, with little else to do." "Razak the Navigator," I replied, shaking his proffered hand, "also with time on my hands." He sat beside me, companionably. We discussed *The Rook* and her captain, agreeing that we were impressed by both. I asked him how he had come to assume the position of Protector, a new rank in the hierarchy aboard ship. He laughed. "The merchant created it for me, a *sinecure*," he said. I asked the meaning of the word sinecure. "An unnecessary but paid service. He curries favour with me, with my family." How open he was, I thought. Then he said, "Tell me something about your life, Razak." Not wanting to be as forthcoming, I provided him with a highly edited version of my adventures upon the high seas. An hour passed in the telling. "How lucky you are," he said, "to have been so many places, done so many things. I have a long way to catch up." "Perhaps, perhaps," I said. Then we sat for quite a while in a silence before I asked him, "Andrew, why do you carry so many weapons? Have you ever had cause to use them?" "Not really," he said, "but once my muskets failed and I had to throw myself upon a tiger with a knife. Had it not been for the quick intervention of a friend, we would not be having this discussion." "Well," I replied, "that makes you more experienced than I, in hand-to-hand combat with tigers." "The man who saved my life, by the way," he said, "was killed later by an assassin, shot in the back of the head."

For a moment I thought that he had found me out. Was he accusing me? I shifted my weight to respond, if necessary, but no, he was simply describing a sorrow he wanted to share. "Terrible things happen," I said, "for inscrutable reasons. I extend my personal sympathy, Andrew." It was a confession of sorts, and it made me feel slightly better for what I had done, at my captain's request. I would have done it for no other.

ANDREW GOLLIVER, 20

After the first few weeks, I took to sitting with the Navigator in his usual spot by the port rail. He would light his pipe and I would listen to a story. He said that some of his tales were true, and some were made up, and some were repeated from friends. One afternoon I asked him about the four knives he had, tucked into his boots. "They seem to have no real handle-grip," I said. Taking one out to show me, he said they were throwing knives, "a half-pound in weight, eight inches in length, and delicately balanced." He had learned years ago to throw them, after observing how much safer it was to strike from a distance. "Razak, please, show me," I said. He rose to his feet, extracted two knives from his boot-tops, one for each hand, and with a motion that appeared casual but obviously was not, he turned and threw with both hands simultaneously, and to my surprise there were his knives, quivering, stuck in the starboard rail forty feet away. They were just two inches apart. Had he thrown them six inches higher or lower, they would have been lost to the sea.

"Good heavens," I said. He admitted that he would never have attempted such a trick had not the conditions been perfect. "Razak, can you teach me that skill?" I asked. "It is not an easy one," he said. I pointed out that we had many hours available, particularly in the afternoons. "I will be an eager student." He hesitated. "The sole purpose of throwing knives is to maim or kill another human being. It is not a talent to be encouraged." "Too late, Razak," I said, "too late for such a noble sentiment. I have seen you throw. I have been amazed. I wish to learn." "You flatter me," he said, but we spent the next few hours examining my relatively ungainly knives, stripping the leather handles from them until we were down to bare steel. As we worked he asked me, in passing, whether there were any leads in the police investigation of my friend's death. "No," I said, "for the only witnesses were convicts and they do not speak to authority figures. And Mr. Blackmore, though a white man, was without family or fortune. He was soon forgotten, though not by me." Razak then ventured, speculatively, that the assassin might be a poor man too, hired from a distance, that the paymasters were probably smoking cigars in Calcutta or London. "Most likely true," I said.

By then we were sharpening the tips and edges of my blades with various flints he carried in his pocket. He discussed, as we worked, the principles of flight through air of a pointed object, the effects of temperature and humidity on steel, the differing resistances of pine and oak and ironwood to penetration. Finally we could balance all of my blades easily upon a fingertip. "Today's lesson is over," he said. We rose from the deck and walked to the far rail. He removed the daggers he had thrown, and we agreed to meet daily, after the noon sighting.

I then repaired to the foredeck to check on the Sisters. Marceline had her chin on her folded arms and was looking out to sea. Eulalie was singing to herself in a thin but sweet refrain. Nonsense words, I thought, syllables of no meaning. "A pretty tune," I said to her. Manon, turning to me, said that it looked as though I was becoming quite a friend of the Navigator. "Yes, he is going to teach me how to throw knives. Perhaps, if you are not too busy, you would like to watch." I waited, expecting Marceline to forbid it, but she must have been lost in her own thoughts. She said nothing. Eulalie said, "I would like to watch, Protector. I was at a circus once, on the outskirts of Paris. A man in a top hat threw knives at tiny water balloons." "The more, the merrier," I said, "you are all welcome."

MANON BEAUREGARD, 19

We flew before the wind as though enchanted. We passed Ceylon on New Year's Day, and shortly after that we spent several nights in port, in Goa, to replenish supplies. The days passed seamlessly one into the next until our ship, I felt, was more home to me than the hut we had crawled about in Singapore for two full years.

But there was little for us to do. There was no call for nursing. Uncharacteristically, Marceline began to sit by herself and ignore her rosary. Once she even napped in the afternoon. She seemed gentler, somehow, which gave me the courage to approach her when I began to chafe at my garments. "Marceline," I said, "see how free and easy the sailors are, shirtless or in light cotton, while we are draped in wool and sweating underneath, even at night. May I shed my cowl, cut my sleeves, shorten my gown?" "Manon, child," she said, "we are surrounded by men." "True," I said, "but I have no fear of them, for we have the Protector and the captain, and the sailors have been nothing but respectful." Eulalie then said, surprising me, "We are racing through our allotment of fresh water, from sweating." "Yes," I said, "look at the bucket and ladle, that one scoopful is supposed to last us all day!" And I added, emboldened by Eulalie's support, that Marceline herself had told us, on torrid days in Singapore, that we must drink water to offset bodily losses. Marceline then laughed, not pleasantly. "Manon," she said, "your feigned concern fools me not. Should the two of you wish to flaunt yourselves before the crew, do what you wish."

I rushed to her and hugged her. I said that I had no wish to flaunt myself, only to be comfortable. She pushed me away. "Do what you wish," she repeated. Over the next two hours, in our quarters, Eulalie took up the scissors and cut my long hair so that it fell only to my shoulders. Then we removed the sleeves from our gowns and shortened the material so it hung just to our waists, keeping our white pantaloons—which usually did not see the light of day—as outer coverings for our legs. Then it was my turn to cut Eulalie's hair, improving her appearance immensely. Just as we were finishing, *mirabile dictu*, Marceline came in, shook off her cowl, and said I could not shorten her gown but "Manon, remove as much of my grey hair as you can, and shorten it to be like yours." Fifteen minutes later, the three of us stepped up to the deck and I was able to swing my arms in full circles for the first time since becoming a Lamb.

Later I whispered to Eulalie, "Whatever has happened to Marceline?" "Well," said Eulalie, "do you remember our twelve converts? In Singapore? Not one of them came to say goodbye at the wharf, and Marceline could not help but notice." Then she began to sing one of her lullabies. The sun set. A fingernail moon danced behind the mast. Without our cowls, we could see even more of the night stars.

ZEPHYRAX, 4

Any entertainment aboard *The Rook* drew a crowd. In the early afternoons, sea conditions permitting, Andrew and his new friend, the Navigator—who was also, I could not forget, his attempted homicidal killer—met on the foredeck for the purpose of throwing razor-sharp knives at a target. I sat on my favourite yardarm to observe.

They started with basic finger-strengthening exercises. The Navigator wound a rubber band about all five fingertips of Andrew's right hand, and then his left hand too, and asked him to stretch the bands as far as he could, repeatedly. Boring, I thought, but then the Navigator set up a board made from cork, six feet long by six high, setting it ten yards distant, supported there by stout barrels. He and Andrew stood against the rail and the Professor of Killing demonstrated, facing the target, the proper synchrony of the muscles of the lower back as they coordinate with the upper back, and then the shoulder extension, and the forward stride, arm and wrist following. This without a knife in hand. Andrew repeated the same movements several dozen times. By then I had been joined, in the audience, by quite a few of the sailors, many of whom imitated the pantomime.

The Sisters of the Lamb appeared as well, standing out of harm's way. Briefly they distracted me, for they had greatly changed their appearance. Their hair was visible, fluttering in the wind, and two of them had taken scissors to their heavy gowns, shortening them considerably. They leaned against the mast, all three of them, it being the most stable support. They watched as Andrew was finally given one of the throwing knives. He wobbled it uncertainly towards the cork, where it struck with its handle and fell to the deck. The Professor then re-demonstrated, for the fiftieth time, the proper sequence of movements, but throwing a knife himself for emphasis. It shivered a half-second later, buried to its hilt in the target. The sailors applauded. The Navigator bowed. Then he drew, using charcoal, a large circle on the board. He discussed, for the benefit of all, the number of rotations in the air required for a knife at that particular distance. Andrew then seemed to get the knack of it, burying blade after blade in the manner of his teacher, though not so deeply.

Over the next few weeks, the Navigator moved the target back a foot or two daily until it was jammed up against the starboard rail. By then Andrew was throwing quite well, harder and harder. "Penetrate bone," the Navigator kept saying, "penetrate bone."

Watching them, it was easy to forget the underlying, deadly purpose. But, as I had nothing else to do, really, except to fly about in semicircles and practise landings in various wind conditions, I made a point of never missing a session. Some of it was fully enjoyable. Pieces of cork flew hither and yon, blades drummed into the target. The board become so perforated that the setting sun shone through it like a sieve, or colander, creating spatter patterns of light upon the deck, a dappling. Then a new, solid board of pine was produced, and the Navigator and the Protector threw, and the Malay sailors threw, and the captain threw, and a scoring game was invented by adding circles and squares. The audience cheered, bets were laid, and although

Andrew now and then surged into the lead, the Navigator invariably struck back with a series of brilliancies at the end, never relinquishing his crown.

MISS ALBERTSON, 46

Mr. Egerton told Lady Catherine—he did not notice me, I was folding napkins—that if her brother were coming home via Venice, he would like to imagine, with her, the Italian landscape through which he would travel. She laughed merrily at the cascade of questions and observations that followed, such as what was the difference between a Venetian *piazza, piazzale, piazzeta*? And Venice must look lovely amidst the shadows of the full moon! And did Catherine know that Venice was not floating on the sea, as it appears, but is an island, with tides licking at her feet? Did she think that crowds would gather from curiosity at the docking of each and every foreign vessel? Catherine encouraged him in his Italian research, bending over his papers, saying that one of her acquaintance had taken the Grand Tour the year before and was most enchanted, in Venice, by the cheerful clapping of waves against the seawall. "And not at Piazza San Marco, as one might expect, but at the Chiesa di San Giorgio Maggiore, completely across the Grand Canal." "Really," her husband replied. "Yes," she said, "and how wonderful it would be to be there, to meet Andrew, under that full moon of yours." His back was turned to her but I observed his fleeting smile.

"Clovis," I said, "perhaps we should speak directly to her. She will listen because of our long time in service." But Clovis demurred, saying that we might open a Pandora's box, that it might even be discovered that Emerson had been hired to kill the older Earl. "Emerson did no crime," I said, "he did nothing. We are becoming more cowardly as we age." "Not so, Beulah," she replied, "more practical, I like to think. We are still, theoretically, at risk ourselves." We finished up with the laundry, dried our hands. "Let's agree on this, though," said Clovis, "if Andrew is killed in Venice, we will sharpen our pig knives and descend on Mr. Egerton as we did upon the Friar, and afterwards we will polish our blades and say to the investigator, 'Such a similarity in the killings! After all these years! Do you think a madman is on the loose, close by in Dorset?'"

HARTLAND FIGBY, 38

My barman was mute and hairless but he was far from stupid. When I took my business papers out from my coat to study them, he darted to the door and latched it against the unlikely event of customers. Then he wiped the bar with a cloth until it was dry. He stood across from me to nod or frown, to add his opinion to mine. We formed a quorum of two, as we had done half a hundred times. "We need to finalize our option for Venice," I said, and it was not long before we had settled upon our trusty ironmonger from Spitalfields, John Martin, thirty-eight, a prolific twenty-two for twenty-two in murdering. And zero repercussions. Yes, he had a fondness for wine. Yes, his wife was a moral firebrand who believed she had the same rights as a man, but he kept her in the dark when it came to his part-time vocation.

My barman furrowed his brow and made a *clip-clop* tapping sound on the bar with four of his fingertips, imitating the hoofbeats of a galloping horse. He was asking whether John Martin was capable of a journey to the south of Europe, on horseback. "More than capable," I said, "he served in the cavalry."

We shook hands. We drained our glasses. I asked him to make the arrangements. Supply the necessary weapons and powder. John Martin should leave from Dover within the week. "Does he speak the local languages?" he asked me in his fashion, pointing first to his tongue and then to a map he had pulled from beneath the bar. "No," I said, "not a word, but neither does a musket or its ball, and both are clearly understood across the breadth of Europe."

CAPTAIN WEDDERBURN, 57

A captain, even in retrospect, should never say a voyage was perfect. It would tempt the gods of storm and ill fortune. But in fact our passage from Singapore to the Red Sea was unblemished. My new navigator turned out to be so capable that at times I kept to my cabin and trusted the ship to him. At any rate, eventually we stood side by side at the helm as pincers of land began to narrow to us on both sides, presenting a rocky, desolate aspect despite the bright sunshine. Most inhospitable, with no life to be seen, animal or vegetable. As the winds were light, I excused myself and strolled to the rail, where I found myself close to the Englishman and the youngest nun, enjoying the same view. They were conversing in a mixture of languages, mostly French, and, as I had met my wife in Bordeaux and courted her there, I was able to clearly hear her address him by the intimate pronoun *tu*, rather than the more formal *vous*. And he was saying the same to her. He told her that when he was a child, his first governess had forced him and his sister—Catherine—to say *tu-tu-tu* many times over, before and after meals, until they had mastered the pursing of the lips and tongue convolutions that made it possible to pronounce that little word correctly, in the purest French manner. He then demonstrated what he meant by saying *tu-tu-tu* to her as they held to the rail. She said *tu-tu-tu* in return, a little more purely, I thought, than he could manage. Then she asked him how he could possibly have had a governess, for she thought that governesses worked only for the very wealthy. I had no wish to be an eavesdropper, but in light of what McWhirter had told me, that he was a lord of some kind in disguise, I waited long enough to hear him say that once upon a time he had lived in a fairy-tale setting, but it had not worked out for him. "A fairy tale!" she replied—I remembered then that she was, to me, Cinderella—but then she added that she would ask him no more, because Marceline had told her, "Be careful, Manon, curiosity is the first step to sinning."

Oh, I thought, where are we going now. He replied that one day he would tell her everything, but for now *tu-tu-tu* was all he could say. The end of his fairy tale had yet to be written. Well, where was this relationship heading, I wondered, with its back and forth *tu-tu-tus*, the gratuitous mention of sinning, their obvious attraction for each other, standing with elbows touching. The Protector, his Lamb. Well, I would never know, for soon we were parting.

I picked up my whistle to summon the crew, intending to make a formal announcement. But first I approached the Navigator at the helm, to say hello. He said, "Sir, stay a moment?" I therefore delayed with him, and to my surprise he said that, with my permission, he would leave *The Rook* to join the Protector and the nuns. "Razak," I said, "you signed for the return, to Singapore." "And I will honour that," he said, "but as you know, I have trained my replacement, and my new friends are facing quite a challenge. They know no Arabic, they must cross a hundred miles of desert by foot. Andrew has therefore asked for me to stay on, for my skills." It was true that he had been teaching one of the young Malays. It was also true that I could still do it myself. "Razak," I said, "you came to me as a surprise, you can leave as a surprise, but I shall miss you." I shook his hand. Then I asked him if he was being paid for his work, to carry on with the others through Egypt. "Money is not an issue," he said, "for the nuns have zero, the Protector very little, but I have a sack of gold coins from my previous employ." Was he serious? Not likely. "Well," I said, "the Arabs will be as poor as you, so you will not be out of place. Good luck to you all."

ZEPHYRAX, 4

Captain Wedderburn blew a low-pitched whistle, a signal that meant the entire crew, even those asleep, should gather on deck. All came running. "Our journey west is complete," he announced, "for we have dipped our toe into the southernmost waters of the Red Sea. A sparkling blue, as you can see, not red at all. The port of Suez is still five hundred miles north, but *The Rook* goes no farther. Passengers will be transferred to the Arab steamship whose smoke can already be seen on the northern horizon. There it is, curling like black licorice against the sky! Any questions?" "Captain," asked Marceline, "why can we not continue with you?" "Because the Red Sea, Marceline, despite its benevolent appearance today, is the nursery of blistering winds. Heated air pours down from shelves of rock—there they are, on either side of us—baking and cracking in the sun for millennia, churning up local currents, sweeping wooden ships, sailing ships, upon shoals. Witness the forest of naked spars and broken ribs cast upon the closer shore. Before steam and iron, only Moses could part these waters, only Moses could lead his people home with certainty."

Well spoken, Captain! I wanted to say, I could not have done better. "Lower the anchor!" he cried. There we waited in open water, and an hour later an iron ship, reeking of acrid smoke and coal dust, spilling foulness into the air, bumped softly against us in open water. The nuns stepped over to it one by one. Marceline had to lift her gown to do so but the other two, more scantily attired, leapt easily across the divide, their white pantaloons somewhat like, I thought, the slender legs of storks. Then the Protector crossed over with my cage—assuming I would follow him!—and the Navigator with two large sacks of powder and shot. So he was coming too? Zephyrax, you will have to maintain your vigilance.

Finally *The Rook* cut herself loose and slipped away, setting her sails. Goodbye, Captain and crew, goodbye to another bittersweet instalment of my life, over which I have no control. But wait, Zephyrax, be more generous. You are better off than in Chile, the Doldrums, Singapore. With that in mind, I flew four bold semicircles and three linear but angulated patterns to my perch on the Arab vessel, passing through coal-stink to do so, only to find myself, upon arrival, essentially imprisoned for the next three weeks by dozens of children. Each of them was accompanied by a personal goat, it seemed, and they all amused themselves by poking fingers, noses, and tongues between the bars of my cage. Now and then, frankly, I lost composure. In a surfeit of frustration, I would feint left and right and explode past their inquisitive faces into a downdraught of black particulate matter swirling from the ship's funnel, choking me, driving me to the windward side of the ship. There the air was pure but I was buffeted by the winds predicted by Captain Wedderburn, thrown against the corrugated iron hull, roughened to the consistency of sandpaper by constant exposure to salt. My aerial skills were sorely tested. Some of my feathers became bent out of shape from collisions. Little choice did I have but to return to my zoo-like enclosure, to the urchins with their pets, who ran to me with love and pleasure written on their faces. So the cycle would begin again—children, goats, mounting madness, escape, smoke, pyrotechnical feats of aviation—until Andrew or Manon would notice, and they would form a barricade about me for half an hour or so, allowing me to catnap, so to speak, to no longer con-template diving into the mouth of the funnel and immolating myself, bringing an end to my suffering.

Exaggerations, Zephyrax? Yes. But there were more indignities to bear. The shore rocks of the Red Sea were as barren as those of the guano islands. I was forced to scavenge for protein by picking bluebottle flies from the buttocks of the goats. The much-vaunted coal engine seized up in the cool of most mornings, leaving us adrift upon a limpid sea or at anchor on a wild one. Workmen in loincloths would then attack the engine from all sides, wrenches and hammers clanging, scraping on metal until I vibrated in consort with them. The engine would finally belch and sputter, turning the air to poison. Also, for the record, one hundred passengers were jammed together on a tiny open deck, Eulalie fainted twice from the heat, conflict raged between Marceline and an Arab leader over her defiant readings of the Lord's Prayer, and the Navigator deserted us for most of the trip as he pursued advanced lessons in Arabic. Our voyage of seven days devolved into a marathon of twenty-two: stop and go, stop and go, so much so that the iron vessel's inconsistency cost us the momentum of our fine sailing performance from Singapore. Such is progress in the modern world, I thought, never imagining that things could get worse.

Then came Suez. Six short jetties extended from a low con-glomeration of dull-brown huts clustered on the west bank of the shoreline. A dozen corniced tents as white as spindrift dotted the low hills. Much as I had in Singapore, I reconnoitred, counting one hundred and twenty-four camels, three hundred and eleven men, forty-two women, forty-five horses, one hang-dog donkey, all of whom were engaged full-time in idleness. It was a backwater of the first order, a way station. I expected that we would move on quickly. But no such luck, as it turned out, for the pulse of commerce in the Arab world was barely palpable. It took the Navigator eighteen days to purchase the only two items we actually needed, a wagon, and horses to pull it.

RAZAK THE NAVIGATOR, 32

My language teachers on board ship had been the Arab children who clambered over us, and their parents. None of them had ever been to Suez, so they were as much in the dark as we were as to the future. If I understood them correctly, they were fleeing tribal conflicts to the northeast and had hopes of settling in a more peaceful region. However, the complexities of their issues were beyond my comprehension. I said to the Protector, discussing their plight, that it was probably the same story we knew too well, the powerless being oppressed by the powerful, the unarmed being put to sword by the armed, the hungry starved by those sitting at full tables. That said, from their friendliness, I arrived in Suez with a positive outlook and in command, somewhat, of the language.

But there were tremendous gaps in my knowledge. For example, I presumed I would see sand dunes on arrival, but the landscape was like the imagined surface of the moon, treeless, with dirt and scattered rock, camels and hobbled horses with no grass to eat, men who said little to us but whose eyes did not let us go. A hot wind was blowing seaward when we disembarked, shaking the walls of the pitched tents of the Bedouin, as they were called. We thought it best to stay close to the families we knew, so we followed them beyond the perimeter of the cooking fires. They soon marked off a space for themselves by hobbling their goats, and in imitation we took up a much smaller area, on a patch of bare rock as sharp-edged as flint. The Protector picked up several pieces of charcoal, fallen from transport wagons. With those, we managed a fire. We heated scraps of meat until the fat and flames spat sparks at us. Night fell to a brilliancy of stars, sharp and clear, and we lay down side to side on a surface as hard as marble, but not as smooth. The older nuns groaned when they turned in their sleep. Looking up to the immobile sky, I thought that I could have been smoking my pipe in comfort aboard *The Rook*, or relaxing in my hammock, or both, but I was not discontent. I had known our lot in Egypt would not be easy.

In the morning, I headed down to the waterfront, carrying my former captain's purse. What could it buy, I wondered. Well, as it turned out, nothing. There was a scarcity of everything, I was told, no wagons, no horses, no water barrels, no dried fruits. A caravan was expected any day, or the caravan was late, or the caravan was waylaid by bandits, or the caravan was caught in a desert storm. After four hours I returned to our rock-table with just two jugs of water. "I would have done better with threats," I said to the Protector. I set out again in the afternoon to make a second attempt, to delve further into the ambience of the town, to find anything that might help us leave. Again I was rebuffed, again I heard about non-existent caravans. The goods on display were spoken for. Those wagons and horses? Resting after weeks of travel. No, they could not be hired or purchased. It dawned on me then that our hosts, if I could call them that, preferred us to stay.

And why should that be, I wondered, until I came upon, in the course of my fruitless wandering, a sorry group of a dozen dark men and women—in appearance they looked somewhat like me, I realized—chained by their ankles to iron rings driven into seaside rock. We had left Singapore, but we had not left slavery.

I felt a tap on my shoulder. I turned to find four bearded men in white robes offering to escort me to a nearby tent, smiling in a not-so-friendly way. They ushered me to a luxurious interior, with carpeted floors and pillows. A turbaned man rose to his feet and, with no preamble, offered me a large amount of money "for your youngest female, with light hair, with the figure she cannot hide beneath her robe." I put two and two together and realized that the Protector and I had been mistaken for slave traders, and that Manon was worth a king's ransom.

There was a time in my life that I would have accepted such an offer. That time was well past. Seeking the safest response, I said that the Englishman and I were not about to give up our prizes before Cairo, least of all the young one, but if the rich man were truly interested he could join in the bidding there. The Prince—let us call him that—waved away his messengers, and when we were alone he said that he was puzzled, for we did not have our women in chains. I said that fear was much stronger than iron, that at night we bound them together only by a silken cord. "A nice touch," he said, smiling, "but do you know how far it is to Cairo? There are bandits in the desert, they do not hesitate to kill." I shrugged. "The Englishman and I have resources," I said. "Fair enough," he said, and next he added, to my surprise, that he would personally guarantee our safety to Cairo in return for my word that he could buy her, that he could have exclusive rights. He would follow us step by step to the slave market. To that offer, I decided to agree. "You will pay in advance, the night before Cairo," I said. "It shall be done," he replied. We walked then into blinding sunlight and somehow a signal passed through the air because I was able to buy three small tents to carry uphill on my back, past the cooking fires and goats.

Before sunset we moved our threadbare camp another fifty yards higher, up the incline to a flat but pebbly area, to the side of the Cairo road. The wooden pegs supplied to us were useless against the stony terrain. We found rocks suitable for pinning down the twelve corners, and next we secured the three waist-high roofs by jury-rigging ropes to an outcropping of stone ten feet away on higher ground.

Set for the night, we thought, if only against dewfall. We set a small fire. We discussed our new roles as slaves and slave masters. Predictably, Marceline said she would be a slave only to God, and Eulalie sang one of her nervous airs. Manon suggested to Marceline that she should reconsider her position, for she would put us all at risk if she acted regally. I said there was one more element to my plan, and we should execute it before retiring. I unrolled our arsenal of muskets and, after demonstrating the proper loading with powder and ball to the Sisters, Andrew and I stood tall on the brow of the hill. There the sun silhouetted us to those below. Our three abject slaves—including Marceline, who proved to be highly efficient—then loaded the guns in sequence as Andrew and I fired dozens of shots into the ringing desert. When we finished our fusillade, fifty to a hundred men were watching from the settlement, looking our way. We slept well in our tiny enclosures after that, the three Sisters in theirs, Andrew and his bird in another, and I in mine.

In the morning, to better understand where we stood with the locals, I sought out one of our friends from the ship. He told me that Arabs are a proud people. Over the centuries they had given the world the most advanced techniques in engineering, in particular the quarrying and transport of massive stones. "Hence the raising of pyramids, statues, and obelisks," he said, "and we have also been in the forefront of medical and surgical advances, such as the suturing of skin, the cautery of wounds, forceps for the safe delivery of children, the trepanning of skulls for seizures. Plus our more commonly known contributions, barely worth mentioning. But I shall mention them anyway: hieroglyphics, papyrus, the plough, the sickle, sundials, water clocks, the solar calendar." Then, with a smile, he said, "Razak, I also have inventions of my own, in the developmental stage, such as the crocodile-slicer and the trained-ibis-seed-planter." He put his hand on my shoulder. "To be frank," he said, "as you can see, at the present time, all of us here are in thrall to the slavers. I am frightened myself. But we can both look forward to Cairo, the heart of the Arab world, a great city in which men of all faiths and races live in harmony." "Good," I said, "I look forward to it, once we have the means to travel."

JOHN MARTIN, 35

Mr. Figby called me by foot-messenger, asking me to report to his tavern. As he was the source of my employment in the killing trade, he must, I suspected, have chosen a new target. But I was conflicted. The chemistry of killing had become corrosive to me. Rather than becoming inured to murder, I had taken to watching my wife and three children asleep in their beds, marking their sweetness, their patent innocence, realizing that those I had killed were once the same. Shivers of self-revulsion coursed through me. But to walk away, to refuse an assignment? Impossible. I was connected to twenty-two capital offences, and only our mutual silence, Mr. Figby's and mine, stood between us and the hangman. We were a unit of two—three, actually, counting his hideous barman—locked together in a secret society of evildoers. Had I been able to confess to my wife, perhaps we could have run for the colonies. But more likely she would leave me. She was not one to accept ethical lapses. I had told her nothing, with the result that she developed an exalted view of the income of an ironmonger. So began a cascade of tiny lies to explain how I could purchase jewellery for her, mechanical toys for the children, boots and clothing beyond those of our neighbours. Cumulatively, those tiny lies added up to a mountain of regret. I became morose. I took comfort from flagons of wine, a habit she confronted me about, saying that her father was a teetotaller and I should imitate him if I wished to be a proper father to our children. To apologize, I took her to Regent Street for a necklace, a ring, a bracelet, whatever she wished. Had I bought her no presents at all, she would not have loved me less. Which tormented me even more, adding to my secret shame.

The Duck and Spoon. I entered, pretending cheer. There was Mr. Figby, in semi-darkness. A hard and clever man, no doubt of that, so I tipped my hat to him and leaned against the bar to his left. He asked, "A glass of wine, John Martin?" His barman poured me one. Mr. Figby asked after my wife and children. I replied as noncommittally as I could, knowing that he did not care. "I left them in charge of the store," I said, "so I should hurry back." "Of course," he said, "but first things first. We are in business, my friend. This time a young man, Andrew Golliver, a seaman. And guess where, guess where." I shrugged my shoulders, so little did it matter to me. "In Venice, in Italy," he said, "in eight weeks."

I immediately thought the task an imposition. "Venice?" I said, "that will take a month or more of travel each way. Whatever will I do in the meantime, with my business?" "I have arranged to replace you with a capable man. Tell your wife that your fame has spread across the Channel. Tell her that an Italian prince with a weakness for English wrought iron wishes to consult an expert. Some fiction like that."

Preposterous, I thought. He did not know my wife. But I could never fault him for his organization. He pulled from his great-coat papers that came, he said, from just such an Italian prince, featuring a most impressive wax seal, a return address in Venice, with handwriting more curlicued than a pig's tail. "Show her that," he said, "it is almost authentic, and she will love it." Still wishing to avoid the time away, I said that Golliver struck me as an English name, and if Golliver were travelling, why not meet him at Dover, or wait until London? Because, he said, our client was anxious for an out-of-country conclusion. I thought of the geography of Italy, its boot thrusting down to the sea, and I asked where Golliver was travelling from. "Egypt," he replied. "I would choose Marseille, myself, if I were travelling from Egypt," I said, "Marseille is more direct." He admitted it was a possibility, and because of that—"top secret, John"—he was arranging for a secondary man, not quite at my level, for Marseille. But I was not to worry because if young Golliver never arrived in Venice, and was killed elsewhere, I would still be paid in full. "Are there special risks?" I asked. "Not really," he said, "nothing you're not used to. We hear that he's well-armed and has travelled through inhospitable parts, but you will have the usual advantage. Surprise." "Does he know he is a target?" "No," Mr. Figby said.

I finished my wine. I motioned for another, feeling the need for it. "And why does Golliver need to die?" I asked. "Now John," he said, "none of that, we do as we are told." He handed me a piece of paper on which was written "Andrew Golliver, 20, blond, a head taller than most." We resumed drinking together, and after a while he confided in me, saying that many crazy things were asked of us in our profession, as I well knew, and our Golliver client, a nervous sort, a dandy, had asked that we take a lock of the victim's hair *post ipso facto*, as proof of the killing. Also, even more ridiculously, I was to take a death mask of the face, a warm-wax impression. I would find in my saddlebag a ball of sealing wax, twice the size of a goose's egg, for that purpose. "John," he added, "let me tell you, once upon a time, years ago, I was asked to do the same, to take a mask of a bearded man. The results were shoddy, the wax would not stick, I was crucially delayed at the scene and had to shoot my way out of a thicket of trees. Feel free to skip the mask if you wish. Clip a curl of blond hair from any passerby on the street, and our client will never know. But be gone from Dover, John Martin, by the end of the week." He dismissed me, passing me a heavy purse.

I left the Duck and Spoon. I would treat my wife to a silver locket and leather shoes. After Italy, I would persuade her that Australia would be a fine place for ironmongers, finer than Spitalfields. Our children would marvel at the kangaroos, the koala bears, at different birds shrieking in the night.

DEATHSTALKER, 18 MONTHS

I was a scorpion, four centimetres long, attractively coloured in several shades of lurid green. I lived in the Egyptian desert above the not-very-bustling town of Suez. My common name was Deathstalker, celebrating the strength of my poison. I had grown through seven uncomplicated moults before achieving my adult size, and, as I was required to feed only once every few weeks, I spent most of my time in what I called a cave. To be honest, however, my home lacked the capacity of a true cave. It was just a narrow fissure in an otherwise flat surface of rock, a crack into which I could tuck myself and disappear. But I could escape from it in a trice if needed, so really it was an ideal environment for me, neither spartan nor luxurious by scorpion standards, in neither too quiet nor too raucous a neighbourhood. When hunger struck it was a simple matter for me to zigzag down to the storage rooms by the docks, to the vicinity of burst sacks of grain. There obtuse mice and lizards sat licking their chops, so to speak, obtunded by greed and satiety, making them easy targets for my pincers to grasp, to squeeze. Then I would pacify them with my tail and have a full repast with essentially no danger to myself. The night premises were empty of footfall, and although the return journey required some care, I had become adept at it. I wove between rocks and crevices and the feces of camels and horses and men alike, bypassing the tents of the still-sleeping Bedouin, back to my fissure, my cave. I was confident but I was not naive. I had seen several of my brothers and sisters, Death-stalkers too, fall prey to birds—the ibis in particular, and the stork—when they had been unable to side-scuttle fast enough. But I was still alive, thriving in fact, because of my cardinal rule, which was never to venture out when the sun was in the heavens. I let only the moon be my guide, the glitter of stars, the smoky glow of fire embers, the snuffling and shuffling of horses fast asleep, the white on black of breaking waves.

My confidence was high, in other words. Or it was until one afternoon when several human voices approached more closely than usual and, to my consternation, I found a tight mantle of cloth being laid over me, smothering the roof of my cave. And me within it, trapping air to staleness. Then, for further discomfort, the humans shattered the evening silence by firing multiple musket or pistol shots into the air. Despite the racket, my instinct was to accept the situation and wait for it to pass. Theoretically I could live like that for months, and those transients would go where other transients had gone, down the Cairo road. Goodbye, I would say.

But after the second night of entrapment I became possessed by indignation, and then by rage. The close chatter of voices, the physical pressure upon me was too much. I lost perspective. I crept upwards, shouldering my impetuous way out of my fissure, finding by chance a tiny rent in the oppressive fabric, through which I was able to squeeze first my head, then my shoulders, my thorax, and lastly my poisoned tail. I was free, breathing fresher air although still trapped in the interior of what had to be a tent, overly filled with female oppressors, whispering together, chanting, praying. I counted three of them, each as large as a newborn camel.

I sought to wend my way past them, moving secretively, but suddenly I was covered by a cloth, a dropped garment. I panicked, I struggled with my footing. Then I was lifted into the air, within the bundle of clothing, and one of the females bared her shoulder to me. I fell against her skin. I lost all sense of caution and proportion. I swung my tail and struck her, and she screamed, and her blouse and robe, whatever they were, flew every which way as she collapsed to the floor. One of her knees almost crushed me. Then her companions were screaming too, and I was racing at double speed over the tent's floor to the entrance, out to the desert. Look, I thought, a shooting star. I was free and clear, or so I thought until I felt a sliver of pain, and somehow, though I had no wings, I was flying up into the sky, up and up, closer to the heavens than I thought possible.

What-what-what? I thought, and with horror I saw a thin spear, or needle, appear from under my chin, from inside me, and I realized that my own deathstalker had arrived in the form of a most unusual bird, buzzing like a maniac, no bigger than I but he had punctured me through.

ZEPHYRAX, 4

I heard a scream from Manon, from inside their tent. I looked over to the entrance and saw, scurrying from under the flap, an insect moving erratically, not in a straight line but darting here and there at angles, escaping. Although it appeared to be at the upper limit of my capabilities—its size equal to mine—nevertheless I determined to enter the fray because I felt, correctly as it turned out, that something reprehensible had taken place. With that determination, I assumed a flight position just off its right shoulder, hovering for a moment, then advancing, hovering, advancing, taking stock, recognizing that I was dealing with a scorpion, its body habitus identical to those I had caught and eaten in Peru. It was, undeniably, a charter member of the Deathstalker Clan, all of whom possessed a powerful toxin, sequestered in their tail.

"Zephyrax," I said, "let it run, let it go, back off, do not put yourself at risk." But as the women of our party had been almost certainly attacked while their Protector was sleeping, without full assessment I accelerated downwards at the requisite angle, sixty degrees, striking hard at mid-thorax with my outstretched beak, transecting its exoskeleton, passing easily into soft tissue. Effectively, I shish-kebabed it, just as the Arabs held their pieces of goat meat speared on wooden sticks. Keeping the angle of my beak to the sky so he could not slip away, and conscious of his barbed tail thrashing beneath, I rose with my cargo into starlight of such clarity that I could see my own shadow flitting below, slowed by the weight of my prey. A perfectly executed technique for the capture of scorpions, I thought, flattering myself.

The convulsive movements of my victim soon ceased. I landed on rocks at the sea's edge, dropping my prize at my feet, observing him or her—I could not tell the difference—for several minutes before picking the thorax apart and devouring it piecemeal. Its exterior colouration, I thought, was much different from that of the South Americans. More green, less mauve. Exercising the usual caution, I neared the tail, testing with my tongue for toxin, the seeping edge of it, discarding tainted meat before finishing the neck and head, pushing away the tail's glistening tip with my feet. It was a meal calorically challenging for a bird of my size, so I found myself digesting it for a full hour before attempting the trip back up the slope. I was hardly able to rise above fifty feet. I was happy then to perch on one of the three tent-cords that ran from roof to rock, resting, taking time to reflect upon what I had done, to realize that my unselfish, spontaneous, courageous, praiseworthy act was an example, surely, of inter-species altruism. I had risked my life for a girl that Andrew seemed to like, and for no personal gain. Well, it was true that I had eaten the scorpion, but only out of duty. Waste not, want not. Andrew and the Navigator were still awake, sitting together by the remnants of our fire, in ignorance of everything that I had done.

Then I recalled overflying the Americas, when we in the main flock would pass much of our time in philosophical discussion. On one occasion the concept of benevolence was raised, and we had agreed, unanimously, that every bird or animal lived only for itself. One of my closest acquaintances said, for example, that when she observed a human being feeding a dog, or ruffling its ears, those apparently loving gestures were a sham. They were meaningless, for the dog-ruffler was acting purely out of self-interest, to receive in return a tail-wagging.

If that philosophical bird were with me now—would she were, instead of rotting in the stomach of a whale—how we might laugh at our former certitude, in light of what I had just done.

MANON BEAUREGARD, 19

It was a lancinating pain, as though a hatpin had been thrust into my back, below my right shoulder, continuing through to my breast. I dropped my blouse. I saw a very large insect run past me. I screamed reflexively, and the next moment Eulalie was crying on my behalf and reaching out for me, while Marceline was looking at us with her coldest, least sympathetic eye. We were on our knees, as demanded by the low roof of the tent. Trembling, I managed to pick up my blouse, intending to hold it crumpled over my breasts. Then I turned towards the entrance, wishing to escape, watching for the insect, hoping not to see it. But Marceline reached over and grabbed me by the white material of my pantaloons, by my right leg, saying, "Manon, child, I forbid you to leave this tent in such a state of undress, snap out of it, clothe yourself."

But the pain had mounted to such an acute pitch that I wrestled myself out of her grasp. I crawled outside with no thought for consequences, meeting first the concerned gaze of the Navigator. Then the Protector came to me, leaping over the embers of the fire, putting his hands on my bare shoulders, asking me the cause of my distress. Eulalie was close behind, and she spoke for me, saying, "Manon has been stung by a monstrous bug, and I have seen it running away, a spider." Then Marceline came from the tent holding a taper, protecting it from the wind with her hand, saying, "All right, enough of this, Manon." I turned my back to show her the bite, as surely there must be evidence of one there. "Oh dear, dear," she said, "a Deathstalker, absolutely characteristic. See Eulalie, that raised circle of redness, with the central punctum?" Andrew said he did not like the sound of the name *Deathstalker*. Marceline agreed, saying she did not like it either, for she had seen far too many of their bites in the Vaucluse.

Eulalie then began a terrible wailing, asking, "Is Manon going to die?" "Yes," said Marceline, "most likely. She should confess her sins while able. And stop that blubbering, girl, blubbering will only spread the poison faster." Immediately the pain doubled. I might have fallen had the Protector not caught me in his arms and lowered me to the ground. I heard the Navigator then say that in Sumatra, years ago, he had sucked poison from a snakebite on a friend's ankle, with salutary results. Possibly the same treatment could be applied here. Marceline said, "No Sister of the Lamb will suck on another Sister of the Lamb, not on my watch, not for any reason, nor will I allow a man to touch Manon. That scorpion was a test from God."

The Protector then said that he had been hired to protect, that he had a job to do, that no proper God would set such a test. He crouched behind me and supported me in a sitting position. I felt his lips and tongue upon my shoulder, beginning a firm, rhythmic movement. Marceline pulled Eulalie back to our tent. "I have seen enough," she said. I was still shielding my breasts with my blouse but I wanted to cast it off, the better to breathe. But I could not, for the shame of it. Then the Navigator was standing over us with one of the Arabs from the ship, and they were conversing rapidly in Arabic. "Manon," he said, "I am told by our friend that the sting of a local Deathstalker, unlike that of a French Deathstalker, might kill a baby goat but never a healthy man or woman." They walked away to sit by his tent, and they lit pipes. Still the Protector continued with his therapy. Curiously, not only was I feeling better but a blissful tingling was coursing through me, as though the poison were actually a pleasant one.

RAZAK THE NAVIGATOR, 32

When it was clear that Manon would recover, we escorted her back to her tent. But the Protector was far too animated to sleep. We added charcoal to our fire and the three of us—Andrew and

I and the Arab, who spoke no English—sat together, appreciating its warmth. The little bird circled us once, twice, up well past his bedtime. Andrew then confessed, looking deeply into the quickening flames, that he was becoming attached to Manon, that although he often thought of his wife, Jaimia, with as much love and sorrow as ever, Manon, being so alive, was robbing him of reason. Had he not been in a position of authority over her, which complicated things, he might openly declare his love.

Tamping down my pipe, I said that our situation in Suez was so precarious that we could not break from our roles as slavers. Our women could be seen as nothing but chattels. A moment's tenderness could be fatal. I also pointed out, gesturing to the tents below, that the slavers had made a serious mistake when they declared their interest in Manon publicly. By entering into a bargain with us, they had played their cards too early, and would suffer for it.

Our genial Arab then drifted away, excusing himself, indicating the lateness of the hour. I changed the topic of conversation. I suggested to Andrew that I would alter my strategy as procurer of supplies. In the morning, rather than fruitlessly roaming the settlement, I would walk a mile or two down the Cairo road and wait for an incoming caravan. As they would know nothing of us, nothing of our circumstances, surely they would be more open to commerce.

We had nothing to lose, we agreed, so in the morning I set out with the sun at my back only to be disappointed by the emptiness of road, desert, and sky. On the sixth full day of waiting, however, a slow caravan of twenty-four camels came into view, stopping at my raised hand. An hour later we were the owners of a sturdy wagon, four horses, a map showing the location of springs and oases, five sacks of dried figs, spices, tea, and other odds and ends. I also learned, from their leader, a lively conversationalist, that on our proposed journey west we would see the same featureless desert for five days, but then we would come across a hundred small streams bursting from the banks of the River Nile, flooding the land, nourishing crops for as far as the eye could see. "Next," he said, "you will travel through grass growing to your waists, and bulrushes higher than a man, and you will see fish jumping through the open jaws of crocodiles, and herons flying through the air in the same pose they assume upon the pottery of the ancients. Then, after enjoying the marvels of Cairo, you will find all the liquid fingers of the Nile coalescing once more to the Mediterranean Sea." "Thank you," I said, "and do you have any more advice for strangers in a strange land?" Glancing at the purchases I had made, he suggested only that I add a donkey. "A donkey will carry enough weight to spare your horses, a donkey will not complain. Should your donkey die, his load can be transferred to the wagon and his personality will not be missed."

UBAID, 9

I was a working donkey named Ubaid, and my job was to carry bags of coal from Alexandria to Suez. "Ubaid!" the overseers would shout, and I would dutifully turn my head. Without having the social cachet or versatility of a camel or a horse, I often feared they might just put a pistol to my head and kick my body aside. But as more and more coal was needed—there were no local fuels for the steamer plying the Red Sea—I was kept in servitude. They threw burlap sacks across my back, filled them with raw chunks of anthracite or crumbling sticks of charcoal, and then they tapped me with a whip and added me to the very end of a train of elderly, arthritic camels.

I found no pleasure in it. Coal dust continually leaked from the sacks like water through a sieve, blackening our backs and legs as we walked towards the southern terminus. Our nostrils became ringed with sooty-black crustings. Our tongues became thickened with black mucous. The to-and-fro path we established over the desert darkened to a funereal ribbon. Black, black, black, a staining that could not be washed away, for no rain fell. So filthy and ragged were we, without fail, that we were shunted to the north side of the Cairo road by more fastidious travellers. Looking down, I could see my hoofprints from a month before. We were adding new black to old, and conditions were no better at the port in Suez where, often in the middle of the night, by the most easterly dock, we dropped what was left of our loads beside a mountain of coal, raising a choking fog from which we retreated as quickly as we could. Then we returned empty-handed, so to speak, to Alexandria, there to turn around and begin again. An endless grind, I thought, but, on the other hand, if I were not so employed, perhaps worse was in store—the pistol shot—so I lowered my head and trod on, back and forth for seven years while the camels became more and more irritated by my presence, baring their teeth at me if I approached or tried, out of loneliness, to listen to their conversations.

The truth was, I was eager for a different opportunity. But what were the chances of that, I thought, until early one evening in Suez when, after dropping off my latest consignment, I was approached by a waddling man much smaller than my usual keepers. He was dressed in dark clothes rather than in the flowing white of the Bedouin, so we made a good match visually. He wore a hat with a feather, ostrich or peacock, and pistols and knives hung about him like jewellery, their metal parts reflecting the sun. He checked my mouth and teeth. With a bucket of seawater, he dashed some of the coal dust from me, and he must have found me acceptable for the next thing I knew he had lifted several wicker baskets to my back and filled them with foodstuffs, with dried fruits and meats and tiny pellets of salt, and then he balanced the load and cinched my waist belt, pulling it a trifle tight. Perhaps he was not used to the care of animals, but even if not, his inexperience was a small price to pay to put an end to the tedium of coal trains.

In short, I could not believe my luck. I walked away jauntily with him to the start of the Cairo road. Dusk was falling by then, but we reached a small encampment—three meagre tents made of the cheapest sailcloth—with just enough daylight to spare. An inauspicious beginning, I thought, looking at his sparse possessions. He then removed my cinch and baskets and took the unnecessary step to hobble me, as though I might abscond to the desert or wander back to the Arabs, the last thing I would ever do. But how would he know, of course, not being privy to my inner thoughts. Then he whistled a tune and three unchained women came to look at me, and a man, and a small bird who lived in a cage that was not really a cage for it had a permanent opening in its structure, its bars bent far apart. A pet, I thought, who initially paid no attention to me.

Night fell, dawn came, and it became clear that we were breaking camp. My new employer appeared with quite a fine wagon, two horses to its traces, and two other horses saddled. The women dismantled the tents. All loose supplies were packed to the wagon, and the women climbed aboard. No coal dust, a miracle, I thought. My hobble was removed and my baskets were returned to me, and off we went on the actual Cairo road, not on the black-track. Already I was feeling chipper at my improved lot, though still disbelieving it. Then, even more miraculously, one of the women took a shine to me, jumping down from the wagon to half-walk and half-run beside me, telling me that her name was Marceline, asking me if could she touch my ears, and she did so in a soft and pleasant manner, speaking of a baby named Jesus who was born under a bright star while cattle lowed in a nearby stable. She asked me if I had ever carried a pregnant woman on my back. Was she light-headed, I wondered, but I did not care. Her hands were gentle. After a while the pace became too much for her so she returned to the wagon, but she continued to smile at me from her distance. I was so charmed by her friendship that it hardly bothered me at all when that little green bird, their pet, to whom I had been introduced the night before, decided to have fun by buzzing close to my ears. He even swooped back and forth between my legs, forcing me to jump from surprise, almost toppling me upon my baskets. The little devil, I thought, but his gymnastics were nothing compared to the nastiness of the camels of the coal road, nipping at me with their yellow teeth bigger than piano keys. So I was still one happy Ubaid, to be where I was.

ZEPHYRAX, 4

We left Suez behind. I took to the sky and watched our small party advance into the desert. We had two horses pulling the wagon, Manon tapping her stick from the driver's seat, Eulalie sorting various parcels. Marceline was walking beside, holding a rope, the other end of which was attached to the neck of a witless donkey. Andrew and the Navigator were on horseback, and before us stretched the Cairo road, tracking through a bleak landscape of rock and stone, pebbles and dust. Local windstorms spun here and there. Dried arroyos were cut into the landscape on both sides, much as in Mexico or Texas, and piles of dung from camels, pelleted like those of the northern moose, were every-where, scattered like acorns.

Looking back in the direction of the Red Sea from my early morning height of eighty feet, I saw first the flitting of my own shadow, elongated, and then several of the slaver tents being hurriedly pulled down, and a caravan of dozens of horses and camels and wagons being brought together. Their charges were quickly rounded up too, by the cracking of a whip, the women being forced into wagons, the men running alongside. I wondered if they were they in hot pursuit of us. But as it turned out they took up a position three or four miles to our rear and stayed there. Their horses, I could not help but notice, appeared superior to ours, prancing, holding their heads high, dashing about as though they could throw their riders into the air. They had panache. Andrew himself appeared to be very skilled at the reins, but the Navigator struggled for the first few hours. Eventually he gained a modicum of confidence. As for the horses pulling our wagon, they were blinkered, steadfast, putting one heavy foot before the next with absolute regularity, and it occurred to me—philosophizing again—that prancing and dashing were not necessarily superior to plodding. With that in mind, I decided to plod for a while myself. I took to my cage, on Eulalie's lap, and I watched as Marceline rubbed the donkey's forehead and ears, and I listened to her wistfully speak of Bethlehem and Nazareth, two towns, I gathered, that she thought we might pass on our journey.

The sun rose higher in the sky. We slowed our pace to preserve ourselves, as did our followers, their cloud of dust unchanging to the rear. We were lockstepped together, possibly by design. Now and then one of their riders would race up to us, lathered, and would speak only to the Navigator, and then rush away, swirling a sword in the air. They seemed as much bluster as substance, I thought, but they outnumbered us twenty to one and I could not help but wonder, having seen the Navigator's deceit as he walked from the jungle's edge in Singapore, if he had not hatched a similar plan. Then I would watch as he spoke to Andrew, and they would nod and smile to each other as true friends. I would feel vaguely guilty for my thoughts of treason. But I could not change my essential character. I was still a hummingbird, I would anticipate the worst.

On the fourth day of our passage, feeling a slight drop in the ambient temperature, I flew to a thousand feet. Far to the northwest I saw, shimmering in heat but surrounded by greenery, a large metropolis centred within a fertile valley of fields and crops, and a river as vast as the Mississippi flowing to it, through it and beyond, forming a delta where water interlaced intimately with land. Farther away was a pale blue flatness to the horizon, signalling, perhaps, another ocean to the north.

I returned to the wagon, wishing I could speak of what I had seen. But the Navigator and Andrew were a step ahead of me. They were folding their maps, and the next thing I knew Andrew said to Marceline that she should no longer walk with the donkey. "They are closing the gap," he said. With that news, Eulalie began to sing a medley of her nervous tunes, and Marceline boosted herself aboard the wagon, stepping up from the rear wheel, tying the donkey's rope to a wooden peg. Next Manon said something in French to the horses, galvanizing them. They even perked up their ears, and for the next six hours we increased our speed enough to keep the Navigator, looking over his shoulder, happy with our progress. We slept that night with a small fire, and the next morning, which I expected to be our last on the Cairo road, Marceline surprised us by foregoing her prayers. She rose before dawn and said, "Children, children, time to move, wake up," as though she were more anxious to leave than any of us.

ANDREW GOLLIVER, 20

Over a surprisingly short distance, no more than five miles, the desert vanished. Scattered patches of grass appeared in low hollows, and then wider swaths of reeds grew on dampened earth. We saw and heard clear water trickling beside us, and small ponds formed, coalescing into wetlands, fens and bogs. Bulrushes grew high enough to form walls of brown and green. We spoke to fishermen in shallow boats, and they said, "Yes, Cairo!" pointing to the west, and later we spoke to others who walked with fish in baskets, and they too said, "Yes, Cairo!" but whether it was my imagination or not, I could feel our margin of safety shrinking with every mile. Eulalie asked me directly, "Protector, whatever will happen to us now?" I did not have a good answer. "The Navigator and I have not finalized our plans," I said.

As if that uncertainty were not enough, there came a watery splashing from behind as a crocodile of monstrous girth and length lumbered out from the reeds to snap at our donkey, barely missing his leg. I managed a quick pistol shot to his open jaws, discouraging him. He submerged and slipped away with a trail of blood oozing to the water. "Protector, well done!" called out Manon, smiling as though she were fearless, but Marceline pulled her donkey's rope much tighter after that, and I did not feel more competent, far from it. The incident only emphasized that we were entering a world for which we were ill-prepared. Forge on, sailors, I thought, but with a strange city ahead and the slavers behind, and with no idea myself what next to do, I rode to Razak and again broached the plan for Cairo. "Eulalie is worried," I said, "and I am worried too."

And so was he, Razak admitted. But he thought that if we could find a small hill offering a view to the north and south, and if we camped there and built a fire, and if we gave our friends the impression we were settled for the night, they might lower their guard. With speed and daring, with our purse to pay for additional expenses, we should be able to blow through Cairo at midnight like a sirocco. "A sirocco?" I asked. "A desert wind strong enough to tear the hair off a camel," he said, "or so I am told."

RAZAK THE NAVIGATOR, 32

In the late afternoon we found an elevated quarter acre of grass and bushes with a stream running beside it. Although it was a very modest hill, it would do, I thought, for it offered a view back to our followers and a view forward to the city. "We shall pitch the tents here," I said. Then I cantered back in the direction of our pursuers and met one of their emissaries, as planned.

He handed me the agreed purse for my treachery, saying "Honour among thieves, Razak!" "In the morning," I replied, "the women will bathe themselves in the river and anoint themselves with oil." Off he galloped, and I tucked the money into my saddlebag and returned to the knoll.

We gathered by the wagon. "The finale is at hand," I said, "we have no time to waste." We collected dried twigs from the ground, larger branches from bushes, and piled them high at the hill's apex for a bonfire. Next we pitched our tents on the southern slope, visible to our followers, but on the northern slope, out of sight, we positioned our wagon, our donkey, our horses ready in the traces. We had a simple meal of dried figs and cool water and waited for the sun to set.

MANON BEAUREGARD, 19

Andrew asked Marceline if she would mind having her robe cut down, to match Eulalie's and mine. "Why?" she asked. "For greater freedom of movement," he said, "for soon you will have to ride an unsaddled horse, if you are able." Marceline said of course she was able, and so could Eulalie, for they had a rural upbringing and, from what she had seen, they were easily peers of Andrew's, on saddle or bareback. I then cut the arms from Marceline's gown, and much of the heavy skirt. She already had pantaloons to match ours, so next we demonstrated some non-Sisterly skills that had lain dormant for years. We leaped several times from the wagon to the backs of the stallions. The Navigator said that he was impressed, that we looked more like Wolves than Lambs to him, and just in time.

Then it was dark enough to light the bonfire. A shower of golden sparks rose straight into the still night air, announcing to anyone who watched that we were settled for the evening, that our tents were in order, that the slaves and their guardians were moving about as usual. And all of that was true, but also true was the fact that it would take only twenty seconds for us to cross over the brow of the hill to the wagon, to the horses, invisible to our followers.

RAZAK THE NAVIGATOR, 32

When the fire reached its maximum height, I dropped back into the darkness. I took the reins of our finest horse. We forded the stream and clambered up the far bank, I trusting the horse, urging him quickly to a gallop, barely holding on. In ten minutes we came to the first low buildings of Cairo. We slowed for directions. "The slave market, please? The slave market?" Soon we were well advanced into the heart of the metropolis, deep into its narrower passageways, to flickering lamps, to the permeating odours of sweat, charcoal, the urine of animals. Finally I was there, turning one last corner to the market square, empty at that hour but still redolent of sorrow, sorrow that could not be scrubbed away by moonlight.

I jumped from my horse, took bridle in hand and stepped into one of a dozen alleyways I could have chosen. Being in the poorest quarter, I expected to receive hospitality rather than suspicion, and I was right. The man who opened the first door upon which I knocked was friendly, and even friendlier when I showed him my coins. "I need five horses of the highest quality," I said, "for travel north of the city." He scribbled a note and sent me with his son—no more than ten years old—as guide. We walked past seven or eight abrupt corners and a hundred recessed doorways to a cul-de-sac. The boy knocked on another door, and a woman answered, peering from within, her husband looking over her shoulder.

SHANI, 36

We heard a tapping. From its secret tattoo, I knew it to be one of the family. I rushed to be first to answer, shouldering my husband aside. "Wait, woman," he said. "No, Masudah, it is my turn," I said, and there was Afonso's youngest boy standing outside. But he was not alone, for holding a horse by the bridle was a foreign-looking man with a fierce countenance, a musket to his shoulder and several knives and pistols stuck into his belt. At first I feared a robbery, but as Masudah was twice the fellow's height and more than capable of focussed violence, I showed no alarm. Moreover, at second glance I felt even more reassured, for our visitor seemed to be more a caricature of a warrior than a real one. A wizened child with a brooding eye, how interesting. I maintained my primary position at the doorway, pushing back against Masudah. I ruffled my nephew's hair. "What business do you have," I asked, "at this late hour?" He wished to trade a sturdy wagon, four horses, and a donkey for five rested Arabians. I laughed aloud, beating Masudah to it. "Your offer is ridiculous," I said, "for if your horses are anything like the one you are holding, then we can only give you half an Arabian, not five, even if your wagon is made of gold and your donkey of hand-beaten silver." "My wagon," he replied, "is of ordinary wood, but my donkey is extraordinary, for he will not bite or bray." He was playing games with me, attempting to break down my bargaining position with repartee. But our visitor then abruptly ceased his joking. He said that he needed five fine horses for Alexandria, that he needed them within the hour, that he would buy them on the spot and leave them in Alexandria, where they could be recovered. Money was no object. He took a purse from his belt and handed coin after glittering coin to me, counting "One-two-three, one-two-three, one-two-three," until he had far surpassed the cost of any five Arabians I had ever seen. Also I wanted the donkey, who did not bite or bray. "Accept, accept!" Masudah whispered. I imagined myself walking to market with that well-behaved donkey, and felt the weight of gold already in my hand. "Deal, if you include the donkey," I said, and then I let

Masudah brush past me, and he and the boy and the stranger left for the stables.

Ten minutes later, Masudah returned alone. He picked me up and swung me about in his arms, saying, "Shani, how much I love you, we have just doubled our income for the whole year!" "Yes," I said, "I know, but when will we have the donkey?" "Within the hour," he replied. "Did he ask for anything else, Masudah?" "Only that we send a dependable man, tonight, now, to the river north of the city, to arrange passage downstream before the moon sets. And Shani, I promised I would do that myself, in our ferry, as a gesture of solidarity with night travellers on the run from danger, whatever the source." "Excellent, Masudah, brave Masudah," I said, "a worthy cause indeed." My husband then raced away for the river, and I went outside to sit in the shadows, to contemplate our good fortune, to await the arrival of the wagon, the horses, the donkey who would not bite or bray.

RAZAK THE NAVIGATOR, 32

I pulled myself up to the far greater height of the Arabian, sleek and black. The boy jumped up behind, holding to my pistol-belt, and together we raced out of Cairo, back to our dying fire, to the Protector and the Sisters. Wisps of smoke ghosted about, shrouding us in mystery. There was no need to speak. Upon seeing us, Andrew had already given the signal. The wagon was churning axle-deep into the stream, climbing the bank, and we then became embodied as one in flight, four horses, two men, three women, one boy, one wagon, one donkey flailing behind. We clattered over bridges and cobbled avenues. The ten-year-old's hand pushed on my shoulder, pointing, "Turn, Razak! Turn!" and even had we been seen by the Suez contingent from afar, there was nothing they could have done. We were in full flight into the heart of Cairo.

UBAID, 9

The rope was so tight around my neck that I could hardly breathe. Rue the day, I thought, that I had left the coal road. I was running in a manner I had never deemed possible, the road a blur at my feet. I was cursing the shortness of my legs. I was being pushed beyond the limits of my capabilities. Collapse, fall and be dragged, I thought, but then Marceline shouted out, "Slow the wagon down, for God's sake, Manon, think of the poor donkey!" And she did slow down, almost to a walking pace. But then the man who had purchased me in Suez, who appeared to be our leader, came back and insisted that we run again. I sighed, I gathered myself to do my best. In a lung-bursting sprint we rushed into the old city, into its blind and half-blind alleys, and were it not for a herd of sheep that slowed us down—I heard their bleating—and had not Marceline reached over to loosen my knot a trifle, easing the pressure on my throat, I would have been throttled. As it was, we arrived at the city centre before midnight, only a few lanterns lit to the walls. We stopped just before my heart would have run out on its own.

Then we were surrounded by prancing horses. Arabians. How they despised me, I could tell, but I had learned not to be bullied. I did not dwell on my relative inadequacies. Instead I turned my thoughts to my friend, Marceline. A dire situation was obviously at hand, and I wondered if she might be taken away from me and put in chains. The slave market was but a trot away. Would some potentate pay a price for her, at her age? Then, selfishly, I wondered, if they did, would that same buyer take me.

But it was a fantasy. It was clear that my companions were leaving, and in a hurry. A stranger tore my wicker baskets from me and threw them over one of the spirited horses, dancing on his hind legs like a bipedal god, overly fascinated with himself. Marceline pulled herself up to the back of another of the superior ones. Then she reached down to touch my ears, a quick fondling before she was swept away, all of them gone in a trice, as though they never existed. I heard the hammering of hoofbeats recede to the distance. They were headed to the north, to the sea, to Alexandria, moving secretly and in haste. The women were not slaves but an integral part of a brotherhood or sisterhood, of which, obviously, I was no longer a member.

Was the rope too tight around my neck? No, it was sadness welling up, choking me. What next, I wondered. Was it back to the coal road? An Arab woman came to my side and looked me directly in the eye. I did not have the energy to bite or bray. She walked me to a stable, pulling me along as gently as Marceline had, and there she presented me with a small bale of hay.

ZEPHYRAX, 4

I had not flown at night since the death of the scorpion. I was not an owl with all-seeing eyes, with nocturnal pits of burning amber. But once again I had no choice. My cage was being rattled and slammed against the side walls of the wagon, throwing me about. To avoid injury, I flew from my perch and shot almost as high as the base of a three-quarter moon, orchid-shaped that night, or like a bowl of nectar precariously full, silvered, as crisp in outline as the stars themselves. Whichever resemblance it had, it was beautiful, and the ambient smoke from the streets of the city, from charcoal braziers and dung fires, did not penetrate to my height. I watched then in relative comfort as the Sisters of the Lamb Recumbent followed the galloping Navigator and the galloping Protector to the inner city, there to leap from the wagon and exchange their horses for better ones, larger ones, rested ones, horses of such quality that I could sense their magnificence, as though a wild trembling could be passed through the air between two species of such magnificence, theirs and mine.

Then, quickly, leaving the donkey—wise decision—they took flight, racing through empty streets, cutting diagonally across plazas and squares, recklessly, until they left the last of the city behind and were woven in a tight knot together, almost invisible but for the ghostly white of several of the horses, so that they appeared to me, from on high, as rapids might appear on a night river, the white of broken water coming and going, and reappearing again. Presumably, they had my cage with them.

They were headed to the north. Before us I saw, reflected in the still-ivoried moonlight, a vast wetland of rivers intertwined with more rivers and with floodplains, and fields of what appeared to be grain, some flooded, some not. Low trees cast shadows from the brightness of the heavens. The city's haze had cleared away. Before long, some of the waterways joined and widened, forming a greater river rushing to the north, and my riders came to a small wooden boat tied to trees at the shoreline. The trees were bent halfway to the water, providing a half-tunnel for hiding. The boat itself was painted white but for its funnel, blackened at the top. It was blowing smoke in the same manner as the one we had taken to in the Red Sea, the same tangy stink of seared coal clinging to it. I adjusted my flight to windward. I breathed more easily while they boarded. They filled the small deck, jumping from their horses, and immediately the lines were cut to shore and the vessel was swept into the current, spinning, catching itself by the slow starting of its paddlewheel. I followed them at a quick pace, keeping at five hundred feet to avoid obstacles, and so we proceeded throughout the entire night until the sun peeped up and the paddlewheeler slowed, reversing itself in a roil of water from its starboard side, sliding to a ramshackle wooden dock at the east end of a canal—or what wished to be a canal, I thought, for it was nothing but mud—where many slaves milled about with nothing to do but stretch and yawn, where water buffalo dozed in families, where two large barges were pulled partway to land, partway to the empty waterway.

The Protector and the Navigator and the Sisters disembarked. By my calculation they had been without sleep for twenty-four hours—as had I—so I was not surprised to see them walk no more than fifty yards, hobble their steeds, and lie down directly on the banks of the canal. The day's heat had not yet begun. I thought to join them. There was my cage, attached loosely to one of the horses' bridles, a horse who did not notice me. I silenced my buzzing as best I could—I was very close to his ear—and though my perch was tilted at a strange angle, I managed to sleep more deeply, I thought, than any owl could ever have done, in daytime.

Then I was roused to a jostling and a high sun. Andrew had taken my cage and was attaching it to his saddle by a leather strip. It must already be the noon hour, I thought. Curiosity seekers surrounded us, watching the Sisters in their new dress, or lack of it, as they fed and watered the horses. The Navigator spoke to the crowd and it disbanded. Within an hour we had set out for the west at a steady but not frenetic pace, much more relaxed than the night before. We were following the north bank of the canal. To learn more, I rose again to the sky, and before and behind us I saw the same vast fertile valley with water everywhere, intruding into the land like shining ribbons or tethers or fingers of silvery-blue. Not to my surprise—I had seen it earlier, before Cairo—in the far distance I saw the beginnings of another ocean, silvery water spreading from east to west, to the far horizon. As large as the Red Sea, I thought, reminding me of the Mississippi River as it swept into the Gulf of Mexico, and I wondered for the thousandth, pointless time if ever I would see those territories again.

GERALD EGERTON, 23

"Who is Mr. Figby?" Catherine asked, holding a sheaf of loose papers, "and why has he been given a significant sum of our money on three separate occasions?" Christ, had I slipped up? Perhaps so, I thought, for overconfidently I had written his name down in black and white not once but three times, for the killing of her father once, her brother twice. Not with those details, of course, just his name. "A colleague of mine in South-wark, dear. He advises me on investments." "For example?" she asked, and my reply was spontaneous and heaven-sent. "He is an expert on the Far East. He has advised me—well, advised us, Catherine—not to invest money into that McWhirter fellow's enterprise. Remember? In Singapore? Opium, Figby tells me, morally reprehensible. A business in which your brother was knee-deep, by the way, but it is not for you and me. Had I known your interest in day-to-day affairs to be so keen, I would have annotated my records more meticulously. I apologize." "Gerald, dear," she said, her tone conciliatory, "our expenditures need to be watched, that's all. Andrew will be home soon and he might have questions." "We can be proud, Catherine, for we have been provident managers," I said, "and there should be no more bills from Figby. And let's be realistic, Andrew still has dangers to face before he is home, safe and sound."

"I shall play some John Field," she said, "to Mother, to cheer myself up," and off she went. I had been to the east wing so seldom that I hardly knew the way. Nor did I wish to remember. "Give her my best," I said, "brava, brava."

JOHN MARTIN, 35

My wife's only caution to me, as I prepared for Italy, was not to drink wine. The Italians made the most addictive ambrosia, she had heard, and with my weakness in that regard I should not take the slightest sip. I promised her I would abstain. She was wearing a locket I had purchased for her on Regent Street, and she looked as fetching as ever.

Five days later I had achieved a Channel crossing. I was in France, and although I intended to make my entire journey by horse—I was accustomed to one for reliability, also for conversation—I heard of the presence of two modern trains, one of which ran south from Paris, the other east from Marseille. I managed to find a place on both of them, speeding our journey considerably, but each line eventually petered out in the middle of nowhere. Then we were back afoot, ahoof. Every morning, in my professional capacity, I checked my bags for pistols and dry powder, for the ball of wax I had been given. But the latter had hardened to the consistency of rock. I thought of my children, how I had practised making the death mask, warming the wax, massaging it to softness, pressing it to their smiling faces, how they said, "Again Father, again!"

Outside Nice I bought a musket of a most unusual sort. Its barrel was three feet long, allowing, they said, for greater accuracy. I took to the hill country to practise upon gourds and tomatoes and found remarkable certainty from thirty yards. I could even tear through a single grape, if conditions were windless. But those exploded fruits had a fragrance to them much like that of wine. In the afternoon I descended to Saint-Jean-Cap-Ferrat, where desolate white rock and low shrubbery met the sea. I was still in France, not Italy. At a farm, I purchased three litres of red wine. To be true to my wife, I would have to drink them before the border, but I found myself up to it. I perched on a clifftop and drank all three over a period of six hours, after which I tossed the bottles to the sea below. The tide was out, I realized, for I heard the shattering of glass. Then I reached into my saddlebag for the imbecilic ball of wax. I could no longer see or imagine my children's faces impressed into it, so I threw it as far as I could seaward, to follow the bottles, and heard nothing of its fall.

ANDREW GOLLIVER, 20

To the west I saw a wide canal dug into the earth, its slanted walls bordered by a line of palm trees running to the distance. But it was misnamed as a canal, for it had very little water in it, and much mud. Two barges lay high and dry on the far shore, and ten or fifteen workers sat beneath the palms, anticipating, it appeared, a day of leisure. We hobbled the horses within a reasonable patch of grass and lay down on the northern bank, as stunned by fatigue as we had ever been. There we lay side by side, touching shoulders, arm to arm, and inevitably we fell asleep until the sun rose to its zenith, blazing down upon us. I awoke to find Manon's arm thrown over me from a dream, and Eulalie singing to one of the horses, brushing his mane, rubbing his flanks, asking if we should not be on the move. "The slavers," she said, "might they not soon be upon us?" I reassured her, for they could hardly catch us by the ferry, and the overland route would be even more difficult. Marceline appeared from down the embankment. The Navigator was tapping his pipe against a rock, and within five minutes we had broken camp. A horde of stinging flies rose from the mud as though angered by our existence, causing us to gallop a short distance northward. I then suggested that we proceed at an easier pace, to spare the horses until we were closer to Alexandria. "And how long will that be?" asked Marceline, and the Navigator said, "Four or five days." We turned south to regain the side of the canal, cantering easily, and the noxious flies did not return. I watched as Marceline brushed several strands of hair from her face and tucked it behind her ears, and I wondered, not for the first time, how old she and Eulalie were, what their lives had been before they became Sisters of the Lamb. Marceline, it seemed, had lost much of her bitterness in the past few weeks, shedding it as she shed her cowl, as she cut her hair.

On the second and third mornings we increased our pace. By then we were stripped down to the barest essentials of food and water. Our horses were beyond compare, growing stronger beneath us, revelling in the exercise. There was no chance of going astray for the road was well marked by low white stones set at regular intervals, Arabic lettering cut within. Many travellers came our way, walking or in caravans. Our speed was matched only by our endurance, for we travelled twenty hours daily and slept for four. When Eulalie mentioned the slavers again, Razak said, "It is impossible for them to catch us, if we keep up our present pace. They have probably quit the chase already." A mood of quiet confidence had fallen upon us.

MANON BEAUREGARD, 19

I had taken to sleeping between Eulalie and the Protector. On the morning of our third night beside the muddy canal, Andrew rolled so close to me that my left elbow was pinned beneath him. I was reluctant to move, for he needed his sleep as much as I needed mine, and I found his proximity a comfort. Marceline was first up, and she noticed and said, "Manon, child, perhaps change places with Eulalie tomorrow." But we had become set in our ways. Without tents, the night chill fell hard upon us. We curled up like peas in the proverbial pod, and the next night we assumed the same order on the open ground—first Razak, then Marceline, Eulalie, me, Andrew—sharing a physical intimacy that brought us even closer together, figuratively as well as literally.

Some of us, under those conditions, became talkative before dropping off to sleep. Eulalie, for example, confessed that she and Marceline were not biological sisters but instead were cousins, raised on the same farm. I told how my stepfather had dropped me at the door of the church, leaving me, to say the least, in a state of uncertainty. The Navigator volunteered that he had started out life with a stroke of luck, picked out of a ditch by strangers, a throw-away baby no more than a week old. Andrew said—we were all on our backs, staring at the panoply of stars—that he had been holding back important information. The Sisters of the Lamb should know that he had been targeted for a killing in Singapore, that the assassin had missed, obviously, but might try again. That meant we were all at added risk. If he could, he would separate himself from us, but for his promise to the merchant, to be a Protector.

"Not necessary," said Marceline, "after what we have been through together, but tell us, why in the world would anyone want to kill you?" "Money," he said, and that curt, one-word answer brought laughter from Marceline, saying that only Razak had money, from what she had seen, and not much of it. "Unless," she added sardonically, "the Protector is a frog prince, awaiting a kiss." To which Andrew said that she was not far from the mark, but he was awaiting a killing rather than a kiss. Feathers of smoke dispersed overhead from the fire. By unspoken consent we all fell asleep, but in the morning, riding beside Andrew, I said, "Andrew, I would like to learn a useful skill, one that might help us in the event of another attack. I would like to throw knives." "Manon," he said, "we have the Navigator on our side. I am not unduly concerned." His response was rather cold, I thought, and I was about to flick at the reins and increase my speed when he reached out to my bridle and, holding it, said, "Manon, I would be pleased to teach you the throwing of knives, though I am barely qualified."

Three hours later, during a period of rest for the horses, he and I walked apart from the others, selected a palm tree as target—its diameter at most eighteen inches—and he handed me a blade. Without attempting a throw, I imitated the weight shift and shoulder-and-arm action I had seen so many times aboard *The Rook*. "Good," he said, "now go ahead," and although I lacked a man's strength, I did not lack for accuracy. I struck the tree ten times out of ten, and only seven of the blades wobbled to the ground. The last not only struck the tree but quivered, as it should if thrown with confidence. The little bird flew by, pirouetting, praising me for my skill.

ANDREW GOLLIVER, 20

The southern fringes of a city appeared. Knowing it to be Alexandria, we raced towards it for the singular pleasure of speed, to be slowed only by the sun-shadowed narrowing of the inner streets. There we were forced into single file through crooked turnings, through geometrically irregular plazas, past innumerable shops shaded by awnings. Finally we broke out to the fresh breeze of the harbour, well guarded by islands, filled by a forest of ships at anchor. As leaving was our primary goal, we went straight to the busiest of the wharves and, in keeping with our good fortune since Cairo, within two hours we were paid passengers aboard a Sicilian brigantine, *Temperanza*, fully loaded and leaving in one hour for Venice.

"The horses," said Eulalie, "are we really leaving them behind?" "No," said Razak, "We tripled our payment to the owner, we're keeping them." But getting such spirited animals up the gangway was not simple. They were skittish, reluctant to trust themselves to water, and it was only by bursting open a sack of carrots that we cajoled them to the deck. We then tethered them to the foremast, and soon the *Temperanza*, identical to *The Rook* in her dimensions but with tattered sails and a general appearance of disarray, cleared the shelter of the harbour.

Gone from Egypt, and not sorry for it, we sat with our backs to a line of barrels, out of the wind. Marceline asked, "Do you think, Razak, that the slavers, arriving in a lather at the central square, might have taken out their frustration on our donkey?" "No," he said, "no matter what they do to humans, they would never vent their fury on an animal." He then remarked, probably to change the subject, that there was a different feel to the lift and fall of the Mediterranean. "Do you feel it?" he asked, "the seabed? It cannot be as far beneath us as in the South China Sea." Farfetched, I thought, but how was I to know. Then he added that I would soon have circumnavigated the globe, matching the famous Magellan. "Magellan," I said, "was a real mariner. He set out with a purpose, whereas I have been buffeted about by circumstance." So we passed the time trading wry observations until the captain of the *Temperanza* came by with his regards. "Captain," Manon then asked, "may we spend an hour a day in weapon practice? Throwing knives?" "Signorina, of course!" He winked at me, patronizingly, but we gathered, Manon and Razak and I, at three each afternoon, our target the most beaten-up of the barrels. By our third day we were producing such a rhythmic thumping that several Sicilians joined in, and soon our multiple blades were flying, criss-crossing, drawing splinters and laughter in equal proportion. Bets were laid, coins were passed from hand to hand. Finally, Razak, as a grand finale, would, from thirty feet, slice several of the horses' carrots into pieces, which no one else could do with regularity.

On our fourth day a rocky landscape appeared to our port side, sparsely covered with bushes and trees. "The eastern aspect of Italia's boot," we were told, and it stayed with us as companion for more than three days, a low grey-green shouldering until we saw, arising from an afternoon's mist, phantom tips of spires and the curve of a dome, egg-shaped, suspended magically above the sea. "Venezia," sang out the captain, and in a following breeze *Temperanza* slid by a series of low islands, some inhabited, some not, to the main canal, to a myriad of vessels. A cacophony of bells rang out from steeples and campaniles. "For us," said Eulalie, "they ring for us!"

Temperanza pulled expertly to a wharf. We disembarked and led our Arabians to solid ground, to columns, to statuary, to a crowded plaza. The horses stamped their feet upon the cobble-stones, feeling the solidity of earth. Magellan would have stopped here forever, I thought, had he seen it.

CLOVIS CALLAGHAN, 37

I was braiding Lady Catherine's hair. "Clovis, tell me about your children, how they are doing." "They are polite to adults, Lady Catherine, attentive to their lessons, and active in the out of doors. They can also be ruffians, fighting over nothing." "How sweet," she said, "perhaps I will have children someday." "Of course you will," I said, "you are young. Why, I was childless at your age." Then she asked about Emerson, what kind of man he was. "A loving man, a fine father and, as you know, a dutiful footman. We have always been very happy together." Then I thought, how insensitive you are, Clovis! Portraying yourself so positively while she seems disconsolate much of the time. "Of course," I added, "you have asked me about my family on a very good day, when my spirits are high, but if you asked me tomorrow, you might get a very different answer." "I do not think so," she said, "for I have watched you for years and your good humour is always evident, in contrast to mine." When she said the words *in contrast to mine* she was, I perceived, offering me a direct invitation to ask her about her own life. It was the last thing I would ordinarily do. But under the circumstances, I decided to go ahead, take the bull by the horns, ask her directly about Mr. Egerton. We were speaking in such soft voices that even the chair upon which she sat could not have overheard us. "Lady Catherine," I asked, "how is Mr. Egerton, as husband?" She answered that he was far too often in London, that he seemed more interested in the manor than in her as a person, that she was having second thoughts, third thoughts even, about her marriage. "But there is nothing I can do, the die is cast," she said, "which makes me fear, when Andrew comes home, that he will find me quite the pathetic creature." To that extraordinary confession, I responded by telling the absolute truth, saying, "My Lady, dear Catherine, you will never be a pathetic creature. You are beautiful, talented, and above all you possess an open heart, the most commendable of traits. But, to be honest, several of us, among your servants, have observed in the course of their duties that Mr. Egerton is, forgive me, something of a schemer. And a hypocrite."

For a moment I thought I had gone too far, too fast. In fact my hands were shaking. But it turned out that my instincts were correct. She turned to me and asked me to stop tending to her hair, to sit across from her, to look her in the eye and tell her my innermost thoughts about her husband, his character. And so I did. I said, "Miss Albertson and I have grown close over the years, as you know. We hold nothing back from each other. We are convinced, Lady Catherine, that Mr. Egerton paid for the murder of your father in Ireland. He also paid for an unsuccessful strike against your brother in Singapore. And why would he do that? To gain control of your fortune. Admittedly we have no proof. Perhaps—forgive me—you should comb through your financial records, follow on his heels to London, identify his accomplices. We feel you should not wait. If you find wrongdoing, and if the justice system fails to provide satisfaction—you are a woman, after all, and he is a man—then you should take a page from your husband's book of betrayal. Arrange to have him killed, extrajudicially."

I had been so frank with her that I nearly rushed from the room. She said, calmly, "Thank you, now please finish my braid." And so I did, holding the mirror for her, moving it from right to left, left to right, thinking what a chance I had taken, also how sensitive and beautiful she was, but how naive and how hideous was the man she married.

RAZAK THE NAVIGATOR, 32

I disembarked from *Temperanza* holding two of the horses by the reins, remembering how once they had intimidated me but now they were, astoundingly, under my deft control. I suggested to Andrew that we find a private spot and take stock of ourselves, all of us, before we moved on.

With that in mind, we walked a few steps to the nearest plaza, and there we tethered the Arabians to an iron post in the shade of an arcade. The Sisters were anxious to visit the nearest Campanile. "Perhaps," Eulalie said, "they would let us ring the bell!" Off they went while Andrew and I chose to lean against one of the open arches of what he called a *portico*—an Italian word, I gathered, taken over by the English—scalloped into the masonry of the plaza's wall. Nearby, close to the water, two separate pillars rose to the sky, one adorned by a lion with wings, the other by a swordsman standing triumphantly upon either a crocodile or a dragon. "Which animal is that?" I asked. It was hard to be sure, we agreed, for neither of us had ever seen a dragon. We were interrupted in our discourse then by two Italians in uniform, rattling away in their mellifluous tongue. They made shooing motions with their hands, meaning "move along, move along." I opened our purse and invited them to receive payment for our lodging, such as it was. After a hesitation, they did so, taking several coins each, and then they walked away. So, we thought, settled for the evening. The Sisters then returned, saying they had climbed the entire height of the Campanile and were ravenous. "There is a restaurant in the plaza," said Marceline, "and nothing but dried figs in our saddlebags."

Leaving the Arabians, we walked into the square. Men in aprons were dashing about, setting up tables with white linen and folded napkins. "We must look like wild animals," said Andrew, "so perhaps we should sit at one of the outermost tables. We have much to celebrate." Within a minute, a courteous waiter placed a menu before us. Then he returned with silver cutlery and wine glasses free of fingerprints, and he adjusted each of the women's chairs as though they were dressed in finery, addressing Manon as *Signorina*, bowing as though we were kings and queens rather than the dusty creatures we were, refugees from the desert.

JOHN MARTIN, 35

I had been frugal travelling. I slept in the rough, I bought day-old bread from farmers, various sticky jams and marmalades. I bought hay and shrunken apples for my horse. Now and then a stray goose fell to my musket. After my weakness at Saint-Jean-Cap-Ferrat, I crossed into Italy. There I had promised my wife to abstain, and I held to that promise through Turin, Milan, Verona, Padua, and all the countryside between, breathing in and out for relaxation, now and then taking my long musket from my saddle and firing a ball at a rabbit, hitting at least an ear or a tail, if not the whole creature himself, for a stew.

When I reached Venice, however, the psychological pressures on me mounted. I was to kill a Golliver—I had forgotten his first name—yet the Italian authorities refused to allow me to sleep outside, close to the waterfront, where I could keep a direct eye on arrivals. On my first night, wrapped in my blanket in an alleyway, they moved me along, poking at me with a stick, forcing me to find room at an inn. They also looked askance at the pigeon I had caught by the neck, confiscating its half-defeathered body. To survive, I had to purchase bread and cheese every day as I waited for Golliver. But Golliver did not come. My expenditures were such that I began to experience one of my heavy torpors, brought on by an excess of polar opposites, anxiety and bore-dom. For which there was but one cure, no matter what I had promised my wife.

I found a small tavern not far from the waterfront. I fortified myself there every day at its noon opening, returning whenever necessary, late afternoon or evening or sunset, after my labours had proven fruitless. What else did I do? I walked the waterfront back and forth repeatedly, from the Giardini to the Palazzo Ducale, observing and scanning the new ships, watching passengers descend and scatter to the canals, and, to tell the truth, the longer I stayed, the more despondent I became. I had little hope that my target would arrive. I was no fool, I could read a map. No one in his right mind would travel from Egypt to England via Venice. They would go through Marseille or south of Gibraltar by sea. Knowing that Mr. Figby had sent another killer to Marseille, I felt that he might have downgraded me, that I was his second choice. If that were the case, perhaps I had not been paid as well as Monsieur Marseille either, despite my exemplary record.

Foolishly, I allowed those negative thoughts to become a burden. I persevered however, inspecting the incoming vessels with reasonable care. Twice daily I even circled the entire island lest his ship had docked inconspicuously. Yet very few vessels came from Egypt, and those that did were chockablock with short, muscular men with dark hair, or their hair was covered. None of them was blond. I began to wonder how long I was to stay in Venice, and would I indeed be paid my fee if nothing happened, and how long would it be before my money ran out, and how was my wife, and how were our children. On some of those occasions one carafe of red wine turned to two, and I even learned how to drink in Italian, saying *Eduardo! Mezzo litro di vino rosso!*—and how to feel cheerful again by sipping at the *vino rosso* until the call of duty dragged me back into the frying pan of the sun. The dancing waters of the Grand Canal near blinded me. Never did I see a blond Englishman. Nor could I make inquiries, for the obvious reason that if I asked for him and he died five minutes later, the authorities would pounce and I would be decapitated in their most prominent plaza. Already I had witnessed one such execution. Some abject criminal, led up to a French-style guillotine built with no decorative flair, just solid wood and an unpolished blade. The head rolled six feet before it was gathered in a sack. And what would happen to my family, if that were me? Debtor's prison.

Mezzo litro. Another carafe. I drank it all. I was sick by then of scuttling priests and nuns and flocks of pigeons and a thousand ships. I ordered a third carafe and finished it easily. Then I wandered by duty and habit back to the docks and found myself standing in the shadow of a tall brigantine arrived from God knows where. There, almost disembarked, was a young man holding tight to an excited horse, and his hair was as blond as a sheaf of wheat. Close beside him stood a young woman of exceptional beauty, rivalling my wife, and a small dark man, and several other women dressed in white trousers. He spoke to the girl in English and she called him by name, Andrew. Andrew! The first name I had forgotten. Andrew Golliver! Yes! He was here! Mr. Figby had not done me an injustice after all.

But I was befuddled by wine. I cursed myself. I had over-indulged to the extreme. My weapons were at the inn, five minutes away at a run. Had I been better prepared I might have shot him before he even put his second foot to solid ground. But I was not prepared. By then they were down the gangway, so I sidled close and followed them to the plaza. They stood together in the shade, looking up at the buildings that had once impressed me, when I had first arrived. Then I thought, what if they jumped to their horses and left?

I ran to the inn. I took my pistols and hid them in a bag and tucked my long musket under my coat. It was invisible, or nearly so. My hands were tremulous. I stopped at the tavern for one final glass. "Steady, steady, be steady," I said, "think of an escape route." There were a thousand alleys and canals, any one of which would do. I left to shouts of *"Ciao, Giovanni, ciao!"* and, as soberly as I could, I headed for the plaza.

ZEPHYRAX, 4

As soon as we were safely ashore, I zipped away to have a bird's-eye view of my surroundings. I reached a height of one thousand feet. The city of Venice, I realized, was set within a semicircle of tidal flats and marshlands. There were at least a hundred other islands north and south, some built upon extensively, others untouched, untrammelled, adorned only by windblown grasses and estuarial flowers. And, no doubt, insects. But already it was late afternoon, shadows were lengthening, conditions were not the best for surveillance. I dropped to just above ground level, into a warren of narrow canals and alleyways pinched for space. There I noticed—but I did not stop to sample—multiple floral displays cascading from window boxes, profusions of vines climbing walls without trellises, rising from water's edge to rooflines, spilling up and over into horizontal gardens greener even than the heart of the jungle. Disoriented by the profusion of such beauty, I briefly became lost. The same little bridge kept appearing to me three times, four. Frustrated, I headed for the highest perch I could find, a golden-winged statue atop a pyramidal steeple atop a rectangular tower. "Excellent, Zephyrax!" I said, for it was a glorious vantage point from which I could look down directly into the main square, from which I had flown thirty minutes before. There were the five swishing tails of our horses. There were Andrew and the Navigator and the Sisters, sitting at a table with a white cloth covering, light dancing from glassware placed before them.

TULIO QUERINI, 40

I was a waiter in a bar ristorante in the Piazza San Marco, in Venice. We were renowned for our traditional atmosphere, for our congeniality, for the quality of our food and drink. Also for our extensive patio, spreading into the square itself. Tourists flocked to us from all of Europe, aristocrats for the most part—

so they thought of themselves—wealthy young men and women embarked on a rite of passage they called the Grand Tour. They travelled with trains of servants and carriages and horses and footmen. Always they came to us first when they arrived in Venice, to the Piazza San Marco for the Campanile, the Basilica, for the view across the Grand Canal. All of Venice, of course, was a highlight for them, for we were a singular city, beautiful to the extreme, well-known for our maritime history and our ecclesiastical splendour, and above all for the pellucid light that intermingled with the shimmering blue of the Adriatic so that it appeared to the uninitiated as if two separate sources of light were reflecting back and forth upon each other, a phenomenon captured well in the paintings of Canaletto.

What I thought of the rich foreigners, I kept to myself. But in truth I had no respect for their lives of inherited ease. They snapped their fingers at me to catch my attention. They shared food with their dogs. But I came to realize, for my own sanity and self-respect, that I could be one of their servants for an hour or two without losing my dignity. I was pleased, after all, to be employed on land, not on the water for my living, to have a home and a family to return to nightly. So I went about my duties in good cheer and was considered a valued member of the staff.

One afternoon, nearing the supper hour, there came to our establishment an extraordinary troupe of characters. Three women escorted by just two men, the women dressed in dusty and torn outfits unwashed for days, with grey skirts down only to their thighs, and blouses with sleeves rolled to the elbows. Loose trouser-legs of what once was white in colour, I suspected, cut to a style I had never seen before. Their hair was short and unkempt, loose and free to the wind. They were speaking French to each other but were unlike any other French women I had seen, for their clothing was so ragged and poor. And the men were not much different in their shabbiness. One of them was tall and blond and well-mannered, the other short and dark and with a feathered hat. But I thought them, as a group, to be a refreshing change from my usual perfumes and giddy laughter, chaperones with faces caked with whitening. When they sat at one of my tables, I was pleased to serve them, pleased to take their order for two carafes of wine, pleased to point out items on the menu at the lower range of expense. They quickly accepted my suggestion for baccalà mantecato and fegato alla Veneziana, to be served in three dishes to share. Thus they saved me the need to stand and smile and explain what was meant by *primo* and *secundo*, to take back several drinks to the bar which did not please them, to fetch a bowl of water for the little dog defecating at my feet, my usual experience with tourists.

JOHN MARTIN, 35

Golliver and his party were sitting by themselves. But I was not quite ready. My glass of wine needed to pass more fully to my blood, my brain, my spirit. I walked past them as though they were tourists and I a harmless professor of architecture, gazing at the Gothic wonders of the Palazzo. Under that guise I made my way to the Campanile, the tower that stood at the inner end of the courtyard. There I leaned against its red-brick wall and felt the late afternoon sun beating down upon me for ten full minutes, tingling my face. Then, for self-assessment, I held my hand up to blot out the sun. It was not shaking. Under cover of my cloak, I checked my two pistols, primed and loaded. Finally I exhaled, intending, as usual, to turn my blood to ice for my performance. I only partially succeeded, sweating as I was from the heat beating down, the heat also beating up, reflecting from the paving stones. Plus the weight of my heavy coat. But the moment should no longer be delayed, I knew, so I extracted my long musket and, holding it tight to my side, as though to imitate a crutch, I steeled myself and began to walk the hundred yards or so back to the restaurant.

No one noticed me, no one fell from me in alarm. I passed through the crowd as sinuously as a river might pass through a series of stones. I found myself at thirty yards from their table, close enough to be sure of my aim yet far enough away to make escape a near certainty. They were pouring wine for each other, as I had poured wine for myself. I found myself musing on that coincidence as I dropped to my knee and raised my musket in their direction. A body or two scattered from my sightlines. I had the Englishman's head well situated. I pulled the trigger confidently, routinely, and next came the familiar blast and roar and recoil and somehow, when the smoke cleared from my view, his head was undamaged. In fact he was looking back at me, and instead I had killed one of the women at his side, by the wavering of my aim. I drew one of my pistols and sighted him and fired but my hand did not obey me fully, wobbling in the singularity of the moment. I saw the hat of his male companion float away, thrown to the air as in some farcical play at the Haymarket. A giddiness overcame me. The Haymarket! How we had laughed at their antics! I ignored my other pistol. With my useless musket to the fore, I approached nearer and nearer to them, the table empty now but for wine and blood spilled to the linen. Where was the Englishman? He had rolled away, I guessed. I was utterly without a plan. I wondered in fact if I were not walking through the streets of London, or poaching for deer. I was deaf from the close explosions of my weapons. Many people were running from me when I felt, to the right side of my neck, a sharpness and a blow like a heavy stick, or from forged iron, from a blacksmith's anvil, or perhaps a sword. My strength left me entirely.

I was on my back. I was on London Bridge. I was looking up at a bright sun, but I was unable to move. The blond Englishman appeared, looking down at me, lips moving senselessly, hands touching my cloak, running over my chest. I saw the dark man's face too, his head bare, peering down, and finally, though I did not deserve it, an angel came. The sun haloed her head in gold. She put her hand tenderly to my neck, where I must have been wounded, and painlessly she gave me a benediction. I had come to heaven despite the number of my sins, and I felt a great peace come over me.

MANON BEAUREGARD, 19

While waiting for dinner, I noticed pigeons prancing not far away, picking crumbs from under chairs. I took a heel of the bread given to us by our waiter and walked in their direction. I crouched down before them, and with my throwing knife I cut tiny chunks from the crust and scattered pieces in their direction. To say they were interested was an understatement. They rushed at me, clucking and cooing and bobbing their heads, and I said, "Hello, I am Manon, out of Egypt with an offering."

Then I was startled by a shot. I looked up to see a man upon one knee, in a martial stance, smoke pouring from his shouldered musket, thirty feet to my left. I saw where he was aiming and there was poor Eulalie at our table, already murdered, I thought, for a great red patch was growing on the middle of her chest. She was looking down at it, and then she toppled forward, striking her head on the table's edge before falling from her chair. By then the musket man was on his feet and moving confidently forward, aiming a pistol with his left hand at either Andrew or the Navigator, at which I could not tell. My pigeons flew into the air, forming a curtain before me. He shot his pistol and then raised his musket as though he could fire it again, despite not loading it. I stood from my crouched position, took two steps in his direction and threw my knife with all the strength I could muster, aiming at nothing in particular but his body, hoping to distract him. But my aim was high, from excitement. The blade struck him directly in the side of the neck. Immediately he paused and tried to look back in my direction, but instead he rotated stiffly and fell to his back. Then he began an involuntary dance of shaking and convulsions, so that I thought, as I ran towards him, that I had severed his spine. Andrew was first to the man's side, bending down to him, his hands probing into the pockets of the long and heavy coat. The Navigator too, pushing with the toe of his foot, trying to adjust the awkward angle formed by the head and neck, to straighten it. I reached between them and wrenched my knife free. From the resistance it offered, it had been stuck in bone. Next I was wiping the blade on my skirt and the Navigator was saying to me, his hand on my shoulder, "Manon, drop it right now to the ground, do not claim it as yours." I did as I was told. Then I ran to Eulalie, lifeless in Marceline's lap, her open eyes staring skyward. Marceline was weeping. I rushed back to the man who had shot Eulalie and bent down to look closely at his face. "Why have you done this," I shouted in French, and then in English. Vapours of alcohol rose to me, repellant. I thought he understood, for he tried to answer, moving his lips. But nothing intelligible came forth. Fine tremors overtook his arms and legs. He passed urine through his trousers, a thin trickling to the bricks.

ZEPHYRAX, 4

I was still perched high above the square when the shots exploded. I controlled myself. I maintained my posture. I observed the madness unfolding below, dozens of people running every which way, shouting, crying, children held awkwardly in the arms of desperate sprinters, old men and women hobbling ludicrously, as though they feared death even at their advanced age. Accept your fate, I wished to say. More to the point, however, I saw Marceline holding Eulalie, and I saw the monstrous bloodstain blooming on Eulalie's chest. Had I not seen so much mayhem since Chile, I would have been surprised. But still, I thought, Eulalie? She should be the last to suffer, if there were justice in the world. "Go, Zephyrax," I said, "go," and I let myself fall, almost gliding. I landed on Eulalie's shoulder. Only Marceline was still with her, and only Marceline noticed me. "Oh, little bird," she said, "little bird."

TULIO QUERINI, 40

The tall man was kneeling to the body. He ran his hands inside the heavy coat and pulled out a sheaf of papers, which he pocketed. Then, as I was expecting, and fearing, the two soldiers who patrolled the area came running. One policeman said to the other, "Mauro, a double murder! Just our luck to be on duty!" The other replied, "Raffaelo, a trick I learned in Rome: arrest a foreigner, clap him in jail, blame him for everything."

So, I realized, my interesting customers would be scapegoated, doubly victimized. That did not go down well with me. There was a vile murderer on the ground. I turned to the small dark man and said, in English, "I will take responsibility for the death of this man. It will simplify matters. It will also be an honour. Otherwise an injustice is about to occur." Before he could answer, I turned to the first officer and said, "I, Tulio Querini, veteran of the battle for the Chiesa di San Geremia, have witnessed the first killing, that of this poor woman"—I pointed to her, where she lay—"and in response, fearing for the safety of others, I rushed with my decorative sword in hand, taken from behind the bar. I approached the killer from his right side and struck him there, in the side of the neck!" Of course my statement would hardly be believed had I not actually taken the sword and rushed out to the plaza at the time of the shooting. But I had, on a soldier's reflex.

The policemen looked at me with profound respect. Mauro said, "A military man in the right place at the right time! Excellent! The case is solved. A deranged man has attacked and killed a tourist, but a local waiter has avenged her, showing the same courage as he had in the insurrection of 1848."

"Yes!" I said, "I confess to that!" By then, many of the scattered diners and tourists were returning, gathering around the fallen woman, stepping carefully over broken glass. Some were crying, some were enraged, some were struck dumb with grief, but all agreed that they had seen, or thought they had seen, or might have seen, through the flock of startled pigeons, my act of heroism. The officers were even more satisfied as they listened to those unsolicited fantasies. To assert themselves, however, they asked me to inform the visitors that they had twelve hours to leave Venice. "They have brought violence to a place of peace. They are no longer welcome."

Unfair, I thought, but I translated for the sake of my customers and they did not object. Next I offered to find a coffin and a cart and a horse to carry away the body of their friend. I recommended a pack animal from the Arsenale and sent a runner for that purpose. In the meantime, I suggested that they stay at the restaurant, as they were now the sole customers. I brought their food to them but it was cold. They picked away at it. Flies began to circle the woman's body, and the tall man finally said that the situation was intolerable, they would return to the portico and rest, and await the night, and leave at dawn. "Slaughtered for no reason. Her name was Eulalie," he said to me, in a private, touching memoriam.

ANDREW GOLLIVER, 20

A haze began to form on the water, from differing temperatures. A more solid fog then began to creep towards land. A wagon with a coffin appeared through the mist, pulled by a small but muscular horse. Together we lifted Eulalie in her pantaloons and grey tunic and set her within the plain box. Manon said that she would miss her singing and her kindness. Marceline said, "Adieu." The waiter then nailed down the coffin's lid and said good night to us, and we were left alone in our reduced state, one flickering taper to dispel the darkness, and a great deal of uncertainty as to our future.

We crowded together in the wagon for warmth, our backs against the casket. "I apologize for having failed as Protector," I said. Razak said, "I was too slow to react." Manon said, "It was a bolt from the blue, you are both forgiven. Now Andrew, read to us from the papers you took from his coat." She turned the taper upside down and dripped wax upon the coffin's lid and fixed the candle firmly to it, shedding an uncertain but passable light into our laps.

I took the pages from my pocket but they required peeling from each other. Many were stuck together by overlapping circles of red, by spilled wine, I thought, as though a glass had stood upon them and been repetitively jarred or spilled, or carelessly moved. Eventually I imposed a semblance of order on them, however, and began to read aloud, and it became clear that they were unsent letters written in a wayward hand. Each was two or three pages in length, each was addressed to a Mr. Figby at the Duck and Spoon—a tavern, I guessed—in Southwark, in London.

I read the first aloud, and then the second and third. Really, they were much the same, identical in tone and purpose. Each declared that the writer was unhappy with his lot, that he intended to retire from the killing trade, that he no longer had the heart—or lack of heart—for it. He missed his wife and family. He could muster no ill will for the Golliver person. He had walked the waterfront too long. He knew every bollard by name. Golliver was already dead in Marseille. And so on, and so on. He repeated himself often, and each of the three letters was signed with a shaky flourish *your faithful servant, John Martin*. I shuffled through the other seven letters and there was nothing different in them but for the very last signature, on the very last page, *Giovanni Martini*. He was becoming Italian from the fruitless length of his stay. "So," I said, "there we have it, a litany of complaints ten times written, ten times addressed, ten times stained with wine, ten times unposted."

Marceline then asked, quite reasonably, "How in the world would he know your name, how would he know to look for a Golliver in Venice?" Abashed, for I had kept the Sisters in the dark, I said, "I have suspected for months that my brother-in-law, in England, is pursuing a personal vendetta against me." "You should have told us," said Marceline. "Yes, but I could hardly believe it myself, so I said nothing." Marceline then spoke vehemently, saying, "Innocent blood has been shed. But let there be no self-recriminations, Protector. We have to move on, and we have just discovered a treasure trove of information, the name and address of the man responsible for Eulalie. Remember Leviticus, chapter 24, verse 20! An eye for an eye, a tooth for a tooth. It is time for us to balance the ledger, and if I were not leaving you in France, I would travel to this Duck and Spoon, find this Figby man, and without giving him a chance to respond, I would kill him with one pistol shot."

We sat in silence, hearing only the snuffling of our horses. Then Razak said, "Harsh theology, Marceline, but you are not alone in your zeal. And we should not forget that another killer, and not a drunken one, could already be lying in wait."

A chance gust of wind blew out the taper. The thickening fog began to roll over the sea wall from the Grand Canal, drifting past us with an accompanying chill. We pulled our clothing tighter, and although Marceline and the Navigator soon drifted off to sleep, Manon and I found ourselves leaning against each other, quite awake. "Perhaps," I whispered, "We could cross the square and visit the Basilica, our last chance." We detached ourselves carefully from the others, climbed from the wagon, and walked out into the Piazza San Marco, the mist all-enshrouding, the church invisible. Lest we became separated, I reached for her hand. She took mine equally, and together we walked into our future, the distant lapping of water on stone— from the canal behind us—our only guide.

ZEPHYRAX, 4

I had no wish to be a prurient observer but there I was, inadvertently, when they consummated their relationship. They slipped away from beneath the portico, holding hands—a new development, suggesting a ratcheting-up of intimacy—and felt their way into the all-encompassing mist. Perhaps they were about to tour the large church, I thought, and, as my plans for a morning overflight and detailed examination of Venice had just been quashed by the authorities, I chose to follow them on the off chance that they might find entrance to it, even at that hour. If so, I would tag along. I would assess the interior functionality and design of what had appeared, from outside, to be an ecclesiastical wonder. Not once did either of them, Andrew or Manon, turn to look in my direction as they breached the fog. I assumed that the sound of my wings, my buzzing, had been softened by the elements, and was inaudible. Proof of that came quickly, for in a minute they bumped up against one of the stone supporting pillars of the church, and, surely confident they were not being watched, they turned to each other and kissed as though they were starved for affection, wildly, passionately, deeply, abandoning all reserve. Next their united bodies turned in a half-circle and fell against a small door cut within a larger one, of heavy wood overlaid by copper. To their surprise, probably— certainly to mine—it opened from their weight. They stumbled within. I followed without hesitation and found myself in a cavernous space lit by several distant rows of votive candles guttering in the church's ambient currents of air. Above me rose a vaulted ceiling of the purest gold, shimmering in its own light as though embedded with sparkled glass. Below were intricate mosaics, unreadable in the shadows. Not a soul was about, and although the interior of the Basilica was quite stirring, emotionally, for me, from its high and gilded domes to its distant mysteries, Andrew and Manon seemed more interested in each other. In fact they were shedding their clothes hurriedly and laying them smoothly on the chill of the floor, as a covering. Manon then lay down on her back and spread her legs apart, and quickly he was on top of her, beginning the same rhythmic pushing that he had done a hundred times with Jaimia. But he was too hurried, thoughtless at the speed of his movements. If women were anything like female hummingbirds, I thought, then go slower, Andrew, go slower, bury your head in her neck, and whisper, whisper to her.

At that juncture, however, I turned away. I was in a roil of emotions, too jealous, too shy, too judgmental to watch. I set out instead to explore the nooks and crannies of the interior, the various naves and passageways, galleries, and several chapels too dark to enter. A sanctuary, a bronze door, a polished cross upon a table, perpendicular walls of gold, the golden domes of the roof. I was much impressed, particularly when I caught a glimpse of my own feathers reflected in a smoky mirror not far from the choir stalls. Then I returned to the lovers, hoping they were finished, and in fact they were, they were redressing, handing each other pieces of clothing. They heard me and looked up. I somersaulted in the air, pretending to have just arrived, changing direction to save them embarrassment, and as a trio we ghosted back across the plaza.

Back on my perch, I could not help but reflect how much the two of them had changed. Once Andrew had been helpless upon a raft, once Manon had been, I assumed, a caring nurse. Now both of them were coldly competent with death, and sexually charged with each other. Zephyrax, I thought, all of us have changed, and perhaps in England, if there are hummingbirds there, you will be equally fulfilled.

RAZAK THE NAVIGATOR, 32

Early in the morning, when only Manon's pigeons were on the square, the two policemen arrived to supervise our departure. "An iron barge has been provided just for you," they said, and indeed two Venetians were already tying it briskly to a short wharf at the foot of the two columns. Eulalie's horse and cart were ushered to it, and then the rest of us followed. By smoke and steam we traversed a narrow body of water to the mainland. We disembarked, and then we trooped slowly, funereally, in a westward direction through marsh and wetland. Cultivated fields eventually bordered the road. When the sun was high, Andrew held up his hand and we stopped by the edge of an orchard. There he and I took shovels from the cart and dug down through loose stone and loam to a depth of six feet. Then we lowered the coffin and covered it and stamped upon the earth for permanence. Marceline and Manon planted a makeshift cross made of wood from the wagon's siding, on which they had burnt, using the sun and a cast-off pair of spectacles, the name *Eulalie*.

Afterwards, we did not delay. We left the cart and its stubby horse by the side of the road with a note to return intact, please, to Tulio Querini, waiter, Piazza San Marco. After that we made much faster time, propelled by an urgency to reach England as soon as possible. We spent our first night in Padua, a town almost as beautiful as Venice, making me wonder if all of Italy were so pleasantly built. Then I wondered, by extension, whether architectural splendour brings contentment to those who live there, or whether sorrow lurks in every corniced brick and crevice. "The latter," said Marceline, when I asked her opinion, "contentment is for Heaven."

I agreed with her privately, but as we progressed through Italy and then another country, Switzerland, there were times that I felt content. I had never seen such high mountains, green rivers tumbling from snow-packed peaks, meadows bursting with colourful flowers. Rain showers came and went, and our Arabians, unhobbled, took to walking out from under the trees at night, letting torrents dash down upon their bodies, holding their heads high.

We descended to foothills, to rocky plains, to farmland. Marceline and Manon shouted, "We are in France!" They rode in circles to express their happiness, and it was then that I learned even more about the strangeness of the human heart. Outside the town of Dijon, amidst fields of mustard and groves of trees, we had to say goodbye to Marceline. "I live not far from here," she said, "on my parents' farm." She rode away at a half-gallop without another word, leaving us to remark on her abruptness. "She has always been unhappy," said Manon.

But then, a few hours later, we heard galloping from behind and there she was, racing past us, dismounting, standing in the middle of our dusty road, saying that she had not been forthright. "I have no family, no farm, no home. I have nowhere to go, please may I cast my lot with you?" "Marceline," I said, "as a fly-covered baby picked up from a watery ditch and kept out of pity, I welcome you back." And Andrew said, less emotionally, "Many children are unloved from the first instance." Manon reached for Marceline's horse, took him by the bridle, turned him to face in the direction of our travel.

So we were reunited, moving steadily westward, steadily northward, and with everyone we met, Andrew and I held our muskets casually across our laps, fingers to the trigger. We smiled and said, "Bonjour," but we did not turn our backs to carry on until a good distance had opened between us.

CATHERINE EGERTON, 20

Every afternoon, I marked my brother's imagined progress on his journey home. I allowed fifty miles per day by land and fifty by sea. I sat with the merchant McWhirter's second letter on my desk, a world atlas on my lap. I calculated distances first between Singapore and Suez, and then between Suez and Cairo, and then between Cairo and Alexandria. I saw sandstorms and camels and green oases, olives, tangerines, the wavering notes of Arabs at prayer, the muezzin call. I heard the creaking of masts, the fluttering of sails as my brother plied his way to Marseille or Venice. Then there were fields of lavender and hilltop towns as he advanced through France. Calais. Dover.

Many of those routes were convoluted, unpredictable. I developed a technique, stretching a thread upon the atlas's pages from one seaport to the next—forming a scoop, for example, around Ceylon and India—thus approximating the voyage's actual path. Then, by comparing the length of my thread to the scale provided on the page, I could roughly estimate the distance. But the variants of wind and current were unknown to me. I had sent to London for old newspaper accounts of those who had made similar journeys, and I pored over those for clues until I came to the conclusion that if Andrew were not already in England, then surely he was close. A few days, a week, at most a month or two, and he would be here.

"Why," my husband asked, looking over my shoulder, "have you used a red thread rather than a white one, when you have so many of the latter?" I explained how Clovis, while doing my hair, had reminisced about a number of things, including our birth, Andrew's and mine. "She reminded me that our ankles were encircled in coloured threads, and Andrew's was red. So I thought it fitting that the travelling thread would be the same colour, welcoming him to the manor a second time."

"Catherine," he said, as though impressed, "how thoughtful." Also I detected no irony in his voice when he bent to my map of France and said, "He is probably at Arras by now, if he has been able to leave Venice." "If?" I asked, "whatever do you mean?" He mumbled something about the authorities, about passengers from Egypt being quarantined for tropical diseases. "Nonsense," I said, "I have never heard of such a thing, and I have read widely on Egypt." "Italy, Italy, I was referring to Italy," he said.

One morning he announced plans to visit the city once more. He would leave the next day. "Fine, darling," I said, not objecting because it opened an opportunity for me to take Clovis's advice: *follow on his heels to London*. As soon as his horse disappeared to the east, I called for Emerson. "A carriage please. And would you accompany me? We are off to London to spy on my husband, and I will need your skills and local knowledge." "Certainly," he said, and he did not look surprised in the slightest.

EMERSON CALLAGHAN, 35

Lady Catherine and I reached London on our fourth day. We went directly to the Cavendish Hotel, on Jermyn Street. Upon asking at the desk for her husband, she was told that Mr. Egerton had not stayed with them since the spring. But they had—"A delicate matter, Madame"—prepared an envelope for his attention and sent word of it to his home in Dorset. "Are they unpaid bills?" she asked. "In fact, yes," the clerk admitted, pulling from his desk a package wrapped in string. "I shall take care of it," she said. Putting it in her purse, she was then escorted to her room on the second floor and I escorted to mine, on the third. Looking about at my accommodation, I thought that a footman had never been treated so luxuriously. There was a four-poster bed with red velvet curtains, a chesterfield adorned by brocaded peacocks, a wardrobe with three woollen blankets, and, from the window, a distant view of St. Paul's, other rooftops in between, a hodgepodge of shapes and angles. Thank you Clovis, I thought, for surely her candour with Lady Catherine had brought me to such splendour. However, I had barely time to bounce upon the bed experimentally before Lady Catherine knocked and entered. "Set out for Southwark, please, Emerson," she said, "wherever that is, and make enquiries there for a Mr. Figby, an advisor in investments, I understand, with a specialty in the Far East. And then ask also for Mr. Egerton."

As there were still five hours before sunset, I set out on foot past St. Paul's and took Blackfriars Bridge into Southwark. The market was closing down for the day, but there were dozens of vendors about and it was simple for me to discover, within five minutes, that Mr. Figby was a well-known local fixture. But he was a far cry from a financier. Instead he was, according to the most colourful fishmonger I had ever spoken to, the conductor of a symphony orchestra of crime. Violins, trumpets, kettledrums all played to Figby's tune. "Really," I said. "Yes," said the fishmonger, "for example, if I wanted the baker—that fellow there—killed for his impertinence, all I would have to do is mention him to Mr. Figby, pay the fee, and soon he would lie dead, his mouth stuffed with crumpets. Not a bad idea, actually. Should you wish, you can find the conductor of the orchestra downriver at the Duck and Spoon, drinking blood from an ale glass."

I thanked him for his frankness. "I had no idea," I said, "of Mr. Figby's character." I then asked about Mr. Egerton, but the fishmonger had never heard of him. After walking the entire district and asking a hundred others, it seemed Gerald Egerton did not exist in the consciousness of the city. By then shadows were lengthening considerably. I returned to the Cavendish and reported to Lady Catherine that her Mr. Figby was not a specialist in the Far East but a much-feared master criminal who hired others to do his will. Her husband, on the other hand, was unknown, which was, in Southwark, probably a commendation.

"Perhaps, perhaps," she said. She handed me a workingman's outfit, a loose one-piece garment in drab brown, saying that she had purchased it around the corner and I should wear it over my distinctive livery. "If you are to be a London spy," she said, "you will need a proper London disguise. In the morning put it on,

Emerson, return to the streets, search methodically for Mr. Egerton. He is in London, and he is not an inconspicuous man. Our strategy will be to follow him from a distance, the better to know his habits."

I then retired for the night, thinking how fortunate I was to be in the city of my birth, witnessing first-hand the subtle wash of moonlight on the dome of St. Paul's. How fortunate that I could write a letter to my wife on a desk of mahogany and lie down upon a four-poster bed, a pillow of down. I resisted drifting off to sleep, the better to appreciate life as a nobleman. I also had time to contemplate the custom of marriage, how good and bad variations could be found within it. Happiness and sorrow, fidelity and deceit, good and bad fortune. I was thankful that Clovis and I did not have to send spies after each other to know where we stood.

Church bells continued to ring until eleven, but eventually I slept. In the morning I donned my loose disguise and stepped out to Jermyn Street. I shaded my eyes from bright sunshine only to see our quarry himself, Mr. Egerton, rushing to the hotel entrance. I could scarce believe it. I had not walked fifteen feet. His eyes passed over me as though I were invisible, so I carried on down Jermyn Street as though nothing had happened. But after three or four steps I doubled back and watched from a corner of the lobby as he spoke to the clerk. Then he raced up the stairs to see Lady Catherine, I assumed. Uncertain what to do next, I went to the narrow alleyway on the east side of the hotel and positioned myself there, leaning against the wall. But within twenty seconds there he was again, rushing from a side door, brushing past me, turning to the east before I could even register his facial expression. So, I realized, he had not seen his wife at all.

As a spy, what should I do? Report to her? No, follow him, I decided, for otherwise my morning's easy gift would be lost.

GERALD EGERTON, 23

I should have hired a carriage, or taken a horse. My right heel was hurting from the cobbles. But there I was on Duke of York Street and it was just one more turn to the Cavendish. On I strode. I took the front steps as jauntily as I could at that hour, a trace of perfume, source uncertain, wafting from my sleeve.

"Good morning, good fellow," I said to the clerk at the desk, but Christ! he upturned my day by arching his brow and rubbing his chin and saying, "Mr. Egerton! Your wife is here, she has taken your envelope to her room." "Impossible!" I cried out, but he turned the ledger to me and there was her signature and room number, registered the previous evening. I feigned delight. I bounded up the stairs as though starved for affection, but instead I walked straight past her door as silently as a soft-footed rabbit would creep past a sleeping fox. Once I had done so, and gained the back staircase, down I went thumpety-thump in double time, out the door to the laneway. I had no time to spend mollifying her. I had allotted all of ten seconds to the Cavendish, not three hours. "Dearest, I shall return," I announced to no one, and off I went to my next appointment, on Fenchurch Street. To the gunsmith's, his advertised array of pocket pistols.

I hired a carriage, thinking it would hasten me along. But there were so many other top-hatted conveyances blocking the road, or travelling at counter purposes, that I might as well have crawled on my knees. Eventually I arrived, but I did not apologize for being late, nor did he expect me to. He was pleased with my custom. "This, Sir, is a very fine piece, very fine, but be careful, it is loaded." I turned it in my hand, admiring its craftsmanship. "A little Queen Anne," he said, "ideal for street robbers. Usually a lady's gun sequestered in bosom or purse, but occasionally a man will carry it, for utmost discretion." He took it back and surprised me by spinning on his heel and firing the pistol straight into a solid block of wood leaning against the back wall.

"Nine cubic feet of the finest Spanish cork," he shouted as the explosion rang in our ears. Lo and behold the pistol had certainly worked, for there was a smoking hole in, I thought, the heart of Madrid. I then tried it out myself, with his guidance, loading it and pulling the trigger no less than a dozen times until I felt, quite quickly, that I was expert at it. As proof, there was the entire province of Castile a smoking ruin before me, motes of Spanish cork dust intermingled with gunpowder drifting about in a haze, settling on our shoulders.

"What power," I exclaimed, "to be held in a secret hand!" "Indeed Sir, it does have its merits." "Would this gun," I asked, "kill a man as large as a bear?" "The Queen Anne pistol," he answered, "is accurate only at close range, so I would not recommend it for a bear unless the bear were a foot away and charging." I remembered how close I had been to Mr. Figby, shoulder to shoulder, his coat sleeve touching mine.

"I will buy it!" I said. I handed over the sum demanded. I put the pistol inside my right shirt sleeve and practised letting it fall to my hand ten times, twenty times. Finally, to close our transaction, holding my loaded pistol pointed casually in his direction, I asked him to forget that I had ever been there. "Confidentiality, Sir, is the bedrock of my business. I have already forgotten you." "Capital!" I said, and I set out for the Duck and Spoon, thinking myself a very busy man. Next I would hear of her brother's death in Venice, and if Mr. Figby failed a second time, I had in my possession an answer he should understand.

But as chance would have it, my plans changed. I found myself, after crossing London Bridge, under a familiar window. Although ten in the morning was not, for many, the most popular time for sexual release, my nerves were on edge. A few minutes later I was taking off my shirt before a nervous girl, alarmed by the sight of my gun. "Miss," I said, thinking to allay her anxiety, "do not bump up against this in the throes of your passion, lest you experience a second manly discharge!" I was not sure if she understood the humour, but it was not for me to educate her.

EMERSON CALLAGHAN, 35

Mr. Egerton never looked behind. At Trafalgar Square he hired a carriage, and I thought I would do the same, but the streets proved to be so congested that sauntering on my part did the trick. His conveyance stopped and started and crawled along the Strand to Fleet Street, to Ludgate Hill, past St. Paul's to Cannon Street, Queen Victoria, Mansion House, Lombard Street. Finally to Fenchurch, with which I was familiar from childhood. He disappeared into a shop with crossed muskets over the door, and next I heard a series of shots from within, and I would have been alarmed had not a rag-and-bones man with his cart and pony passed by. He assured me that explosions came from there regularly. "A gunsmith, no harm to it," he said. Sure enough, twenty minutes later my quarry reappeared with, I thought, a cockier attitude than he had shown on Jermyn Street. His head was up. He was striding more briskly. I assumed that he had purchased something small and dangerous, to boost his confidence.

Foregoing a carriage—having learned his lesson—he headed south on foot, crossing London Bridge, turning to the right, staying close to the river. Heading for the Duck and Spoon, I thought, but suddenly he stopped mid-stride and craned his neck to a nearby window. He entered an unmarked door at street level. "Be patient," I said. I settled in to wait, but when he had not reappeared in half an hour I went to the same door and pushed it open to a set of unpainted and creaking stairs. I took them to the second floor. There I opened another unmarked door to a very different atmosphere, to a large room with a fireplace roaring for warmth, three or four lanterns of Persian design casting a low red light, several armchairs covered by silken material. Two well-dressed gentlemen were standing together in conversation, and a woman turned to look at me, her lips and fingernails painted a blazing scarlet. I was not born yesterday. I had entered into a brothel, and not a cheap one. I apologized, I excused myself, saying that I had chosen the wrong building, the wrong door. I returned to the street and waited at a distance of forty yards, pondering what I would say to Lady Catherine, whether what I had just seen should be a portion of the day best forgotten.

Two hours passed—more time than I would ever spend with Clovis, I thought, no matter the occasion—and still no sign of Mr. Egerton. Finally, at one o'clock in the afternoon, he stepped out into the street more languidly than he had entered. He turned and made his way to a small wooden building set apart from all others, backing directly to the River Thames. Over its door were the words The Duck and Spoon, flat upon a wooden board. So I had been right. Ramshackle to say the least, it was a box-like structure perched directly over the water, supported by crossed timbers disappearing into tidal surge. It must have secure footings, I thought, or already it would be on its way to France.

Mr. Egerton entered, and the door closed behind him. I had been advised to be discreet. I should go no further, I thought. I turned back to the Cavendish Hotel with plenty of time for contemplation, to decide upon the substance of my report.

CATHERINE EGERTON, 20

I met Emerson in the tea room. He asked if I wished a full telling, or one edited to spare feelings. "The former," I said. He proceeded to take me through my husband's day, from his astonishing arrival at the Cavendish in the early morning, his firing exercises at a gunsmith's, his three hours at a Turkish salon, his entering the lair of Mr. Figby. I should have felt embarrassed, sitting with my footman, a man twice my age, my failings as a wife painfully apparent. But he was quiet and respectful, and he was, after all, Clovis's husband.

"Well," I said, "I asked for this, and now I know what my husband truly is." I reached for a teaspoon without shaking. "Nothing will be easy now. By marriage I have passed all of my possessions into his hands. He could throw me under his carriage, run over me with impunity." "I doubt that he would go to such extremes," replied Emerson. "Your wife and Miss Albertson," I said, "have already concluded that he has tried to kill my father and brother. Why should he stop at them?" My footman did not bat an eye. He advised me to visit my London solicitor, to ascertain my rights. I had already thought of that of course, and I would do so. "We're not leaving London, Emerson," I said, "you never know, we might even run into Andrew on the street. It happens in novels, it might happen to us."

RAZAK THE NAVIGATOR, 32

The Arabians were our strength. They moved under us through France, past farmers tilling fields, cattle grazing, flocks of geese loose to the side of the road. Navigation was simple. It was of no concern to me if the stars were out or not, or how high the sun was at noon. The roads were well marked, and Marceline knew many of the towns from her previous postings as a Sister of the Lamb—Troyes, Reims, Saint-Quentin, Arras, Bruay-la-Buissière—names which did not come easily to my tongue. She laughed at my pronunciations, as did the others. I rode by her side to practise those impossible words, even offering to show her the throwing of knives in return. She refused, saying we had more than enough of those skills already. So our idyll through France continued carefree, until one night near Saint-Omer, north of Paris, when we gathered with more serious intent around our campfire. It was time to solidify our thinking, to consider our plan for London, for Mr. Figby and the Duck and Spoon. The Venice letters had afforded us a glimpse of our adversary, and we would be wise to be fully prepared.

Two hours later, with the unspoken approval of our five Arabians, and possibly our hummingbird's as well—his opinions were more difficult to assess—we concluded that I, Razak, would enter the Duck and Spoon alone. Our reasoning was threefold. In the first place, I was unknown in England, whereas Andrew might be recognized. Secondly, I had shown an aptitude, in Suez, for the subtleties of intrigue. Thirdly, I openly acknowledged that I had been violent in my past, and my familiarity with decision making under stress might be a valuable resource.

I accepted the responsibility of meeting our adversary, therefore, but, poking at the embers of our fire, stirring them to flame, brightening our faces briefly, I added that I wished to politicize our action. "We have not only Andrew to defend," I said, "but a principle. Members of the underclass—John Martin was a good example—they are pawns, endlessly replaceable, yoked into poverty since birth, sent to kill by cowards. Therefore we strike not only for ourselves, my friends, but for them as well." After a moment's silence, Marceline clapped her hands vigorously and said, "Oh Razak, little did we know, when we bandaged your head in Singapore, that such radical ideas would pour from it later!" Laughter ended the discussion, yet my point was made and taken, and our London plan was decided upon and not mentioned again.

Two days later we reached the port of Calais. The Channel, as Andrew called it, was being thrashed by high winds, appearing as a grey tumult of waves and currents colliding, provoking none of the romantic pangs that struck the heart—my heart—at first sight of the South China Sea. However, its formidable presence did prompt me to say what a fortunate country England was, to have such a barrier to the rest of the world. No armed force could approach her except by sea. Throughout France, by contrast, we had seen hilltop fortifications fallen to ruin, derelict castles, crumbling stone walls, moats ankle-deep in brackish water, as though the resident population had feared invasion for centuries by virtue of geography alone. They had tried, un-successfully, to defend themselves. Marceline said my observations were correct, that armies had swept back and forth across France countless times. "And," she added, "not all of those armies were foreign. The French themselves are as ravenous as the rest, and do not mind feeding off their own kind." Manon said, "You too, Marceline, are becoming radical, the longer we travel."

We set up camp on the beach, a wide semi-lunar expanse of sand. After nightfall, bats swooped for insects, silently, efficiently. Then came a silhouette moving west to east above the white line of surf, a two-masted vessel with ghostly lanterns swaying, making her way into the harbour to the north. A gibbous moon began to slip down and away. I, so long on horseback, felt the sea wind ruffle my hair. At sunrise, those same winds had moderated, but their lessening had no effect on the ocean, which continued to toss jaggedly. Moderate incoming waves curled to a sandbar fifty yards from high tide. Restless for progress, we left the beach for the inner harbour of Calais, and there we found the two-master from the night before, looking much less mysterious in the light of dawn. Her captain said that they were turning about quickly for Dover, as soon as they had loaded. "Yes," he said, "you are welcome aboard."

By ten we were underway, winds moderating. At mid-afternoon white cliffs hove into view. "Dover!" Andrew shouted, but the tempest was now offshore and grown to such a fury, from the warm presence of land, that we might have been blown all the way back to France had not the captain ordered the anchor to be dropped, the sails furled. We stood off at a distance of a half-mile from England's shore, at an impasse. Around us, the sea's surface was white with spindrift, the waves paradoxically calmed in the lee of the cliffs. "If you wish to go ashore," the captain said, "before the winds abate, it will have to be by row-boat. Little danger to it, we do it all the time."

We did not hesitate. Eight oarsmen were appointed to us, and two rowboats were lowered over the side in a complex feat of seamanship, ropes and pulleys coordinated fore and aft. Next the most difficult of manoeuvres was undertaken, the loading of the horses. The first and largest Arabian was picked up into the air by a wide strapping under his belly, and the crane-like device to which he was attached swung him up and over the froth-strewn sea. He was about to be lowered to the first rowboat when he decided to have no part of it. Eyes bulging, hooves pummelling the air, he twisted free of the strapping and plunged headfirst to the sea. A heroic action, I thought, a shout for liberty, and it certainly struck a chord with the other four horses because as one they laid back their ears, bared their teeth, snapped their tethers and hurled themselves over the rail in a mad clattering. They disappeared beneath the surface but rose just as quickly, and then, most sensibly, began to swim in tandem towards shore.

"Bravo," the captain shouted, "there's spirit for you! See if you can match them!" I thought we did, though less spectacularly. Marceline and Manon climbed down the side of the mother ship on a rope netting, settling into one of the boats without incident. Andrew and I followed, landing like cats, and after that it was just fifteen minutes to the beach, to the cold shadows of the cliffs. The Arabians were waiting for us, shaking with excitement at their daring, visibly proud to be the first of our party to reach England.

We built a bonfire to warm ourselves. We settled for the night. "How far is it," I asked, "to London?" "Two full days at an easy pace," said Andrew, "so we should be well rested for the Duck and Spoon."

GERALD EGERTON, 23

Upon entering the tavern with my Queen Anne tucked into my right sleeve, I was surprised to find the place empty but for the barman. A great frustration welled up in me. I would hear nothing of Venice or Marseille from a deaf-mute. Well, I thought, for sanity's sake, Gerald, vent a portion of your fury. I clapped my unencumbered hand down on the bar and demanded to know where Mr. Figby was. To my surprise the fellow pulled out several smooth pieces of paper, a quill pen, and an inkwell. With a rag he wiped clean a sodden patch on the bar. Fastidiously he dipped pen to ink and wrote, in a script marvellous for style and clarity, *We apologize for the inconvenience but Mr. F. has been called away on urgent business. He will return in two days' time, at three in the afternoon, and he will be pleased to speak to you then.* Well, I thought, never judge a book by its cover. I moderated my displeasure. "Has word come your way," I asked, "from Venice or Marseille?" With another dip of the pen he wrote, *I cannot reveal details of any business transactions, but I can offer you several options for drinking.* Disappointed but not wishing to leave, I said, "Yes, two pints of ale." I drank them down quickly to dispel a vague and growing unease. I had expected already to be confirmed as Dorset's richest man. Oh well, patience, I thought. To be realistic, there were more immediate concerns. Catherine was at the Cavendish! Oh Christ, what cunning I would need to approach her. I could not just pick her up and take her to bed, I was fully spent from the girl. I ordered a third pint. I looked about and thought, what a dispiriting place. The river was a blur through the one filthy window, and I could feel the tidal surge sucking at her timbers, at my feet. "Catherine," I said aloud. "The simple solution is, I shall avoid you."

I settled my bill. I left for my most recent accommodation, a set of rooms in the shadow of the Tower. My Queen Anne still warmed my wrist. Men lurked in the shadows at the next corner, so I dropped the pistol from my sleeve to my hand and I whispered, "Come on, blackguards, rob me now." But no one did. I was dangerous, and they could sense it.

MISS ALBERTSON, 46

Clovis said, in the kitchen, after the midday meal, "Beulah dear, when the cat is away the mice can play." My heart double-thumped in my chest. I thought she was referring to Emerson's absence in London, that he was the cat and we, Clovis and I, would be the mice. We could play together, free from constraint. But in fact her thoughts were more innocent than mine. "We can build a fire in the drawing room," she said, "and sit with our feet up on the leather footrests and sip from brandy. There are several bottles in the breakfront. We can pretend we are toffs."

I smothered my disappointment by clattering dishes into the sink. There would be no physical intimacies today. Nor did I wish to hear her say, one more time, that a married woman accrues loyalty, over the years, to her husband. Of that I had heard enough. "An excellent proposal," I quickly said, "yes, let us sip our drinks before the open fire."

The heat from the fireplace was languorous, seductive. She and I shared the same footrest. Now and then our ankles touched, one of us leaning forward with the poker, adjusting the logs. The flames licked more hungrily before settling back, as though they were excited, then contrite. Foolish Beulah, I thought, for allowing your feelings to surface. I escaped moroseness by saying, wittily, "Isn't it too bad, Lady Callaghan, that we have no servant girl to call upon to adjust the fire, that we have to make the effort to sit up entirely on our own and lean forward, and move our arms in a circle, with the poker?" "Why yes, Lady Albertson," she replied, "but good servants, as you know, are hard to find." We refilled our glasses. "Clovis," I said, "what different personalities we have." "Oh, not entirely, Beulah, we have shared so much over the years." "And why are we different," I continued, "because—this bears repeating, Clovis—our upbringings were like night and day. My parents were uncaring, yours were kind. From an early age we diverged emotionally." "Beulah," she said, sitting up, placing her drink on the side table, turning to face me, "the twins' childhood, my God, Andrew and Catherine in the maze, your early years paraded before men as a virgin bride, those are unspeakable traumas, they are memories buried alive in the soul, in the very soul, yet the burying turns out to be imperfect, grass and earth crack and crumble, the soul crawls out from the smothering grave prone to bouts of melancholy, to acts of violence, heaven knows, to addictions, self-crippling behaviours. The most recent example, of course, is Lady Catherine, her marriage."

Oh Clovis, I thought, there you go again with your heated analysis of the human heart. I wanted to say out loud that I loved her, but I lost my courage. I poured another quarter-inch of cognac into my glass and sipped from it. I was a coward, afraid to bare my soul. Next, she would probably remind me of how my mother had gripped my chin in her fingers, how she had applied blush to my cheeks while farmers waited in the parlour. "Beulah," she would say, "that is why you are what you are today."

Still the fire roared. By chance the butler came by and was surprised to see us sitting and drinking. Clovis invited him to join us, and eventually we had quite a subversive party forming. The coachman and gardener and gatekeeper told stories of their own from olden days. Several of the chambermaids, becoming tipsy, pretended to be able to play the pianoforte. They thumped upon it ferociously. "No, no," we said, but then we thought, what harm can they do? "Oh, go ahead," I said. Even the dour cook entertained us by singing a ballad in which a young girl, wandering in a meadow, returned the kisses of a passing soldier. Unfortunately for her, and for him, her father the King was watching from horseback, from within a copse of trees.

ZEPHYRAX, 4

We were not in England more than an hour when it became clear to me that there were no hummingbirds. The roadside and nearby woods were blooming with wild rose and honeysuckle, dog violet, red campion, wood sorrel, yellow archangel, orchids, bluebell, bramble, nightshade, foxglove, cowslip. Yet no rubythroat hovered before them. Many of those blooms, intricate, delicate, were being nuzzled by honeybees as I watched, but otherwise it was a feast gone to waste. Pearls before swine, I thought. Geese and ducks and grebes flew by, none of whom had interest in nectar. Similarly obtuse were the many swifts and egrets and herons that appeared, and plovers and godwits, gulls and quail. A partridge pecked at a forest path. A swan floated like a frigate on a pond. Mergansers beat their wingtips on water. I saw a flock of pigeons as stupid as those we had seen in Venice. A cuckoo. A nightjar. A crane frozen over her own reflection, pleased with herself. Snipes and whimbrels in their own worlds. Nearing London, there were profusions of woodpeckers banging their heads against trees. Kingfishers, vireos, siskins, and so many different warblers that to distinguish one from the other required a bird more interested in ornithology than I.

But there were no hummingbirds, as though England lacked the imagination of the Americas and could not match it in creativity. "More to the point, Zephyrax," I said, "do not ever raise your hopes again. Only a fool would do so, to dream of impossibilities, to have those dreams repeatedly crushed."

RAZAK THE NAVIGATOR, 33

The environment in the South China Sea had been salubrious. The sea air was bracing, beaches were of pristine white sand and tidal wrack. Fresh water cascaded from the hills. Although the larger settlements were not tidy, they were unpretentious and managed a rough civility. Rural England—once the Channel was crossed—was more or less as I expected, with well-tended fields, immaculate hedgerows, woodlots and pleasant watercourses. But the city of London was, to say the least, a disappointment. Not only were the buildings and statuary blackened by deposits of soot from the excessive burning of coal, but the quality of the ambient air was, in one word, repugnant. The River Thames had been gradually transformed over the centuries from a windswept tidal marsh, alive with waterbirds, to a stew of fecal matter. A million bowel movements slipped into it daily from open sewers, overwhelming the river's capacity to refresh itself. A dreadfully thick odour rose from it, a sulphurous wafting that pervaded streets half a mile inland, cloying to the nostrils. Already I had seen citizens vomiting from disgust, kneeling on the embankment, then running away. "Andrew," I said, "if flies could land on water, they would do so as thickly upon the Thames as caramel on crème brûlée." Andrew laughed at the analogy but apologized, as though he were personally responsible. "Dorset, where we are headed, if all goes well— will you stay with me, Razak, when this is over?—it is an entirely different place. You will find it spotless. Or almost spotless." Whether or not that was true, privately I questioned the greatness of the British Empire, that her populace could foul their own nest so thoroughly while marching about the world as gods, naming the rest of mankind as their servants.

CATHERINE EGERTON, 20

Emerson and I spent our next day rushing about uselessly. My solicitor was *hors de combat*, as it turned out. He had fallen the previous weekend from a tree in his orchard, fracturing his leg. Emerson tracked him down at his home on Chalk Farm Road, where we found him laid up in bed with a large wood-and-plaster contraption attached from hip to ankle. The visible foot, poking out from under the blanket, was a sickly blue colour, approaching purple. Although it must have been a painful condition, he was taking far too much laudanum for it, we thought, for he was unable to tell us whether the fracture was above the knee or below it. Nor did he know the prognosis. Nor did he seem to care. Now and then he would chuckle for no reason and reach for his bedside medicine. It was clear to us that we had come to Mr. Grandy in vain, that he was incapable of giving us complex legal advice. I pointed out to Emerson, as we stood over him, that under the word *laudanum*, on the medicine bottle, was the word *poison*, and the ingredients were listed as alcohol, 65 per cent, and opium, 45 and ½ grains per fluid ounce. There was also an appalling dosage schedule, in smaller print, suggesting that children could be given it by the drop, one for each month of age, for cough, colic, toothache or tantrum.

"Can you imagine," I said, and Emerson replied, "No, I cannot. Clovis has been campaigning, for several years, to have laudanum banished entirely from the village." "She is a far-seeing woman in so many ways," I said, "and if she could witness Mr. Grandy in his present state, she would have more than enough ammunition for her crusade."

The solicitor then reached for his medicine. We moved it out of reach, bade him farewell, and returned to the streets none the wiser for our visit. Back at the Cavendish, there was no sign of my truant husband. "Emerson," I said, "My days as a shrinking violet are over. I will disguise myself and join you in the streets."

The next morning, in identical coveralls, but with a hood to cover my hair—we looked like mendicants from the time of Chaucer—we walked all the way to Waterloo Bridge Station. We then crossed over into Southwark, and after several turns and twists Emerson pointed out the Duck and Spoon. "Unprepossessing, to say the least," I said, "but you gave me fair warning." We could hear the pilings creak and groan against the outward rush of the river. Rotting boards at the roofline bent inwardly. We sat down directly across from its door, across from its faded sign portraying a wide-eyed duck balancing on the handle of a spoon. "Does that have a legendary meaning of some sort?" he asked. "None that I know of," I said. For support, we set our backs against the wall of a much more substantial building, of fieldstone, and there was even a patch of sunlight resting there to warm us. The earlier rain had passed. Traffic on the street was minimal, so I took advantage of the next several hours to fall into reverie, to review the course of my life, how it had come to such a sorry pass that I was sitting incognito, dressed in rags, waiting to pounce on my own husband for his perfidy. I was not proud. I mentioned these feelings to Emerson and he said that I was only twenty years old, that I should be generous to myself.

Time passed. We stood and stretched and sat back down again and shared a package of bread and cheese. Not a soul approached the tavern until three hours had gone by. Then a tall man in an outsized greatcoat suddenly turned to its doorway and entered, and fifteen minutes later the man I once loved—for reasons I could not remember—clean-shaven, whistling, stretching out his arms, checking the length of his sleeves, oblivious to roadside idlers, walked directly past us to the same door, paused for a moment, and went within.

What should we do, we wondered. It was three o'clock, and to tell the truth I had no idea how to proceed. It might be dangerous to approach the tavern, we agreed, or premature, or both. But then the marvellous coincidence I had been hoping for actually occurred. There appeared on that narrow and dirty street, just forty yards away, to our left, a most remarkable troupe of characters. There were four riders and five horses, horses of the highest quality. And although the riders were strangely dressed, exotically, and two of them were women riding freely, without saddles or hats, hair to the wind, and although the men were covered with a profusion of muskets and pistols as though they had jumped from the pages of *The Three Musketeers*, it took me no more than a second to recognize my brother. Despite the wildness of his hair, his carriage on horseback was unmistakable. I leapt to my feet, disbelieving yet believing, and ran towards him with Emerson but a step behind, saying, "Lady Catherine, wait, be careful, wait for me."

ANDREW GOLLIVER, 20

The two beggars were upon us so fast that my hand went to my pistol. But the first of them was crying out my name so fervently that I paused. And fortunately so, for when he tore off his head-dress there was my sister in such an extraordinary disguise that I was doubly shocked. I sat unmoving in the saddle for another moment while she grasped at my knee, and then I came to my wits. I leaped down beside her. "Catherine!" I said. We held onto each other. She was crying, I was ecstatic. We turned circles while the others watched. I then recognized her companion as one of our footmen from the manor. "Emerson!" I said. I grasped his hand as my sister clung to me, Razak looking down upon us, bemused. By then Marceline and Manon had dismounted, and I introduced them. We effectively blocked the thoroughfare with our celebration, but those who stopped seemed unperturbed, content to watch what must have looked like a circus performance. And so it seemed to me as well until Razak, relatively unmoved, nodded to a sign above a tavern door, across the street. The Duck and Spoon. We had arrived at our goal. I explained to Catherine that we had business to transact there, and it could not wait. "Gerald just went in there," she said, "and I warn you, be careful, he is trying to kill you."

Marceline was already tying the horses to grillwork on a nearby window, and Razak was taking his first steps across the street.

GERALD EGERTON, 23

There was my deaf-mute acquaintance behind the counter and, yes, Mr. Figby, turning his head my way. My time had come. Unfortunately—Christ, Gerald, pull yourself together!—my nonchalance and confidence deserted me, as a sponge might lose water. Was my pistol still there? Yes it was. "Oh Gerald, Gerald," Mr. Figby was saying, beckoning to me with his finger, shifting his bulk to allow me room beside him, saying, "A glass of ale?" I had lost the power of speech but I was given a moment's grace when he tipped his head back to drink from his own, half-empty glass.

The barman placed an overspilling portion before me, a complimentary one, I assumed. But no, he held his hand out for payment. With my Queen Anne lurking where it was, it was no simple matter to comply. Crossing my unencumbered left hand to the right pocket of my jacket, I managed to spill a half-dozen coins to the counter. He picked through them till satisfied. Gerald, I thought, drink deeply and quickly from that glass! I took a huge draught and felt my heart slow reflexively. Within a minute I became myself again. "Cheers!" I cried. Mr. Figby was by then motioning for his own refill, and although his gaze seemed fixed upon the mirrored line of bottles on the far wall, he began to speak to me, saying, "Gerald, I suppose you mean to ask about Venice?"

"Yes!" I was about to say when the tavern door burst open behind us to a shaft of sunlight thrown across the boards. In walked a short, dark-skinned man wearing a wide-brimmed hat. Jesus, I thought, a highwayman, Dick Turpin shrivelled to three-quarter-size. But it was, after all, a public drinking establishment, so what could I do but wait as he ordered, from beside my shoulder, a "tankard." "I am very, very thirsty," he announced, as though any of us might care. I tried to share a glance of frustration with the barman, but he was pleased, obviously, by the influx of custom. He smiled hospitably. He filled a glass for the intruder and pointed to the only table, ten feet away, under the window. Then I forgot about the stranger because Mr. Figby had resumed speaking, without lowering his voice, saying, "Yes, Venice, difficult news, Gerald, difficult news. Our man there, though superbly qualified, was outfoxed, outshot, outrightly murdered on the bricks of the Piazza San Marco."

"Outfoxed," I said, "outshot?" "Yes, Gerald, although I use the word *outshot* metaphorically. He was not shot, actually, but rendered paralytic by a sword blow to the neck. And where was he? Just a stone's throw from the Byzantine cathedral, in the Piazza San Marco. Perhaps you have seen it, the church, the bell tower? Magnificent."

ZEPHYRAX, 4

At first I thought it pleasing that an English business had honoured a bird by using her common name upon a sign. Even though that chosen bird was the dumbest of all avians, a duck, a creature with no flamboyance, a plodding gait, awkward flight, useless for anything but diving underwater. Humming-birds, by contrast, are quick and radiant and clever and capable of feats of great courage—scorpion, you may speak from the underworld!—but we remained, as far as I knew, unrecognized by public signage.

To remain in good humour, I decided not to dwell on the better fortune of ducks. I chose instead to perch upon the fore-head of my favourite horse, our proudest and tallest Arabian. For several months he had been allowing me to stand boldly between his eyes, attaching myself to the loose forelock of his jet-black mane. Allowing me? Well, he had no choice, really, for once I had established my position, his ears lacked the necessary rotatory movements to brush me away. I could remain as long as

I wished, facing forward atop his elongated skull. There I served as a rubied jewel in his crown, so to speak, just as he served as plinth, or support, for me. We were a majestic pairing. If painted on a sign, we would be *The Horse and Hummingbird*, or, better, *The Hummingbird and Horse*. I imagined such an establishment on a far different river, where raccoons washed crayfish by moonlight, turning their prey in their paws, where deer drank their fill of water untouched by human waste.

I landed on him perfectly, midline. He shuffled his feet. The woman we had just met? She bore an uncanny resemblance to Andrew. How passionately, but asexually, he had hugged her! To tell the truth, I was a bit alarmed, fearing that he had found his mirror image and fallen in love with her, as I might do, should my female counterpart appear. What about Manon? I was about to plumb that concern more fully when, uncharacteristically, my perch shook his head so violently that I lost my grip. I was thrown upwards just as the Navigator entered the Duck and Spoon. Mid-air, I was struck by a foreboding, a fear that something momentous was about to happen, that the interdependencies we had forged would be shaken or realigned.

I did not like it. I flew to the tavern's fly-encrusted window, but could see nothing but dim shadows and vague movements. I cursed my physical limitations. If I were the same size as my stallion, I could smash through the filthy glass, wreak havoc. I pendulumed about the building. I sought out Andrew and perched on his shoulder, hoping that his friend would notice me and be impressed. And she did see me, smiling and saying, "How marvellous!" But his mind was elsewhere. He paid me no attention. To hide in my cage would be a defeat, I knew, so I returned to my stallion, being careful to land more softly, to perch exactly in the midline, to keep my claws, such as they were, well away from his glossy hide.

A small pleasure, some might think, to stand upon a horse's head. To those doubters I would say, "Imagine yourself to be the last hummingbird west of Chile, caged and uncaged at the whim of others, powerless, blown about like a feather, and then tell me what is a small pleasure and what is not."

RAZAK THE NAVIGATOR, 33

I sat with my tankard by the only window, populated by flies both dead and alive. But it shed enough light for me to see, more clearly, the trio of conspirators hunched by the bar. The oldest— surely Mr. Figby—was heavily clothed. He had his back to me, but I heard him speak distinctly of Venice, of Piazza San Marco. Razak, I thought, you are already hearing an open acknowledge-ment of guilt. No need for restraint. I took one of my pistols from my belt and placed it on the table, to be better prepared.

GERALD EGERTON, 23

"Tease me not about Venice, Sir!" I cried, "another muck-up! By Christ, here's an answer for your swindling!"

My pistol fell easily to my hand. I cocked it, I thrust it into the folds of his overcoat and pulled the trigger. In the confines of the bar, the resulting explosion, though not massive, was enough to rob me of my hearing, substituting for it a high persistent ringing. A smoking hole appeared in the fabric of his garment, marking passage of the pistol ball on its journey to heart, lung and liver. But Christ! He neither grimaced nor clutched at his side, nor did he fall. In fact, in defiance of all the laws of physics and biology, he continued to speak normally, turning to me, saying—I could read his lips—"Oh Gerald what have you done, what have you done."

Then he stood to his full height, removed the damaged coat— he was, to my dismay, not a monstrous man at all but as fine-boned as an eel within that greasy carapace—and, holding it up against the feeble light from the window, he put his index finger through the hole by which I had shot him. Then he put the same finger through a second hole, by which the ball had exited. He was demonstrating, for my benefit, that I had missed him entirely.

Christ. I placed my little pistol on the counter. "Forgive me, Mr. Figby," I said, "a shocking misfire, just a little toy, harmless, as you can see!" But he was already nodding to the barman, and the barman was reaching beneath the counter. His hand reappeared with a much larger pistol in it than mine. He pointed it directly at my face, and smoke and fire belched from its muzzle. At that range I could guess the result only too well. I had, after all, seen Madrid ablaze from just my lady's gun.

Duck, Gerald! was my first thought, duck at the Duck and Spoon! But so many regrets were colliding with each other inside my head that I did not move. I found myself thinking kind and gracious thoughts, uncharacteristic thoughts, particularly for my wife, Catherine. I should have been a better man to her, and to her family for that matter. Too late, Gerald. Even the high ringing noise in my head disappeared.

RAZAK, 33

The circle of thieves fell out, spectacularly. The young man to Mr. Figby's left—by his age, our Mr. Egerton—raised his voice in volume and pitch and without fair warning discharged a shot from a hidden pistol, directly into his companion's chest, from extremely close quarters. But the ball, pea-sized from the modest sound of its firing, somehow missed its target. I was then privileged to witness a phenomenon I had seen just once before. White smoke rose up from within the confines of Mr. Figby's coat, curling up from the inside of his collar, enveloping the back of his head in a visible haze. Remarkable. But the haziness dissipated as Mr. Figby began to play with the young man, as a cat might with a mouse, performing a pantomime with his coat,with the new holes blown within it.

Silently, I cocked my pistol. The barman then, without altering his facial expression, pulled a short musket from beneath the counter and, equally without warning, shot Andrew's brother-in-law directly in the face, propelling him up and off his feet and down to the floor. There he lay upon his back, a pudding of bright red bubbling up upon his features.

I would be next, I knew, as inconvenient witness. I therefore shot the barman before he or Mr. Figby could turn fully in my direction. I aimed past Mr. Figby's ear and struck my target exactly where I wished, in the left temple. He dropped out of sight, Mr. Figby's back still to me. Impressively, he made no effort to turn. Holding my second pistol upon him, I walked to the tavern door, locked it, dropped its iron bar into place. At its clatter, he swivelled his head and said, "I am unarmed. I can use you in my business, I can use your talents. Your name?" "Razak," I said, "from Singapore, from my captain's ship." I took direct aim at his head. "Razak," he said, "stay your hand, Razak, come, share a drink. On the house, it's fair to say." He stood and redressed himself in his coat. "Do you feel the chill in the air? Regardless, it's time to seek common ground, explore mutual interest. Whatever you are being paid, Razak, I shall double it."

I circled to the far side of the bar. I tapped the counter with the handle of one of my knives. "Mr. Figby, please, place your right hand here, palm down." He complied. I drove my blade down through the bones not of the hand but of the wrist, fixing him to the counter. Instinctively he grasped for it with his left hand. I had my second dagger ready and, using it just as efficiently, I transfixed that wrist as well. He was then as fully secured as a man could be, as a rare moth might be to a specimen board. Sweat poured from his face, but he did not utter a sound.

An urgent knocking then came to the tavern's door. "Razak," he said, "if those are compatriots of yours, they too can be accommodated." I offered to pour him a drink. I filled a glass from the tap and held it to his lips, encouraging him to sip from it, tipping it slowly back so he would not choke, holding it higher and higher until he had swallowed the whole measure. His eyes were on the ceiling, therefore, when I shot him in the centre of his chest, and again I was treated to an unusual sight. The woollen strands of his sweater caught fire from the proximity of the discharge, flames bursting from the material as he collapsed to the bar. Then came a sizzling as the fire drowned itself in a pool of malt and liquor, rendering a sweetness to the air between us, somewhat like burnt sugar. "With my captain's compliments," I said.

MANON BEAUREGARD, 19

We heard three shots. The first was a tiny *pop*, the second a louder *boom*, but the third, following instantaneously upon the second, was the reassuring *crack* of one of the Navigator's pistols, a familiar sound from the desert. Upon hearing the triple salvo, Emerson and Catherine appeared alarmed, but I was able to reassure them by pointing out that the Navigator had fired his weapon last—I was sure of it—so he was almost certainly the victor.

Andrew strolled casually across the street. Catherine turned to me and said, "My brother seems to have developed, during his travels, an enviable *sangfroid*," her accent in French exactly the same as his. "Hard-earned *sangfroid*," I said, "and on this occasion it reflects our confidence in the Navigator." Then came a fourth *crack*! She gripped my arm. "Surely the authorities will soon be upon us," she said. But pedestrians were still weaving their way up and down the thoroughfare, unconcerned. "No one has noticed a thing," I said, "no one cares." By then Andrew had opened the door and was waving for us to enter.

We were quick to do so, into a murky haze, to drifting specks of powder, two dead bodies on the floor, another suspended by knives, impaled on the bar. Razak was fine, conferring with Andrew. Catherine stared down at her husband, recognizing him not by his face—it had been shot away—but by his curly hair, his lace sleeves. Her demeanour, horrified a moment, turned cold. "It's done then," she said. "Yes," I replied, "we have only the physical mess to clean up."

Emerson relocked the door against a chance customer. "The ebb tide is with us for an hour," the Navigator said, "and there's a staircase from the back door, built for urinating. Ideal also for our purpose, for we will only be seen from the river." Catherine and I took her husband by the heels of his boots and dragged his dead weight over the floorboards. We bumped him down the stairs until our own feet were ankle-deep, feeling the pull of the tide. "One, two three," we counted, and we tumbled him to the Thames. A funeral cortège of gulls cried out wildly, picking at his hair until he disappeared. Then we stood aside for Marceline and the Navigator with Mr. Figby, Andrew and Emerson with the barman. "Were this Paris," I said, "the Seine being a millpond, gendarmes would be reaching for those bodies with grappling hooks already." Marceline then suggested that we burn down the Duck and Spoon to destroy any evidence that might be used against us. "The building is a safe distance from others," she said, "and I see two barrels of lamp oil, there by the bar." Razak and Emerson sprinkled the accelerant widely until Razak said, "Enough." He removed the iron bar from the door and, as we stepped outside, he tossed a match within.

Unhurriedly, we crossed the street. We mounted our horses. It wasn't until we were almost to the corner that we heard the first inhalation of the inferno. Then an explosive roar. Turning, we saw the Duck and Spoon as a giant fireball, crumbling almost instantly, falling as ashes to the river. Next we saw, as though Mr. Figby and his compatriots were reborn, a squadron of confused rats scrambling up the bank, scrambling in the street, looking for a new home.

ZEPHYRAX, 4

I found the antics at the tavern much in keeping with everything I had seen since the Doldrums. Human beings gave each other no quarter. They preferred annihilation to compromise. Then I thought, be fair, Zephyrax, for you are hardly perfect either. There I was, puffing out my chest, overly proud of being a bauble upon my stallion's mane as we pushed through lines of stalled carriages towards, I soon learned, the Cavendish Hotel. And there, in the lobby, did I not preen my feathers in an excess of vanity, before a mirror? I did. But next, as so often happens to those with a mercurial bent, my surfeit of self-satisfaction reversed itself. I fell into despair. My cage had been assigned to Marceline's room, and her wallpaper was covered by highly realistic drawings of monkshood, foxglove, and bog orchid, multiple images of each cascading from floor to ceiling. On all four walls. It was impossible for me not to awaken every half-hour, impossible not to shuffle miserably on my perch. I half-dreamed of nectars and then of females, erotically. Finally I became obsessed by the upcoming sunrise, knowing I would be exhausted from insomnia.

But in fact, when dawn broke, my sleeplessness left me untouched. I felt fully rested. I shared in the general excitement as we departed with tack jingling to the west, to open country-side. Hoping to catch a glimpse of my future, I flew to nine hundred feet, and from that height I saw our roadway stretching before us, narrowing into the blur of distance, into wilder, less cultivated land. But even there, in sight of untamed moors, I saw flocks of sheep and goats grazing in pastures, and isolated fields of brown grain shimmering, and hedgerow after hedgerow forming formidable barriers. I tried to pass through one of those, experimentally, but I was stopped by thorns, by a dense weave of branches. Nevertheless I heard cheerful voices of those who thrived in such tight quarters, sparrows, warblers, wrens, robins, a thrush, a blackbird. Even a partridge, doddering out to take flight with a thump of his wings. But there were no rubythroats, and, despite my vow to be stoic, my isolation pressed hard upon me. Then I remembered the thousands of us drowned at sea and I said, "Zephyrax, buck up, if not for your sake, then for theirs, in memoriam. Practise your blazing eye, straighten your spine."

I returned to my cage. Its golden patina had long since been chipped away to base metal. On still nights, it gave off a distinct vapour of rust and dryness. But I took to it nightly for its familiarity, and in the afternoons for a rest on my perch. On those latter occasions, starting on the first day of our journey, Andrew's sister placed me beside her in her carriage. The roadway by then had been reduced to baked mud, with ruts and stones galore, causing irregular jouncings. But she bolstered the cage on all four sides by piling soft and accommodating pillows around it, and I imagined myself as one of those mindless albatrosses, bouncing from puffy cloud to puffy cloud, far removed from terrestrial concerns.

We were three days out of London when Andrew joined us in the carriage, choosing to sit with his sister—and thus with me—rather than ride in his usual position, by Manon. It was an unusually hot day, but a breeze came through the window. He said that he wanted to speak to Catherine of his past, his present, and his future. That last certainly piqued my interest. I cocked my head to one side and listened carefully as he said to her that he hoped to stay just a month in Dorset, if she agreed, reacquainting himself with what they called the manor. Then, also if she agreed, he would travel to Ireland and transfer ownership of their estate to those who had survived the famine. By doing so, he said, he would come full circle. I had no idea what he was talking about. His sister replied that she was pleased to see that his essential goodness had not changed while he was away. He answered ruefully, saying that in fact he was much altered, that he had suffered significant hardship. He had lost a wife and unborn child in Singapore and had never been quite the same. He had even, he confessed, been forced by circumstance to kill in order to survive, and had he not met Manon, God knows what would have come of him, so dispirited he was.

He reached for his sister's hand. Neither of them spoke for a full five minutes. He was betraying an excess of sentimentality, I thought, and I might have fallen asleep from the tedium had he not then looked directly at me, for the first time in days. He asked his sister to look at me too, take a very close look. He picked up my cage into the air. He called me his prize, his rubythroat, and then he said, remarkably, that I was his oldest friend.

I recoiled instinctively. I had no friends. But he continued to speak to his sister, saying that he had learned that I was native only to the Americas. Therefore I would find no companions in England or Ireland, and he thought it only fair to take me to Bristol—a seaport, I presumed—where he would arrange passage for me across the Atlantic, to Boston or New York.

At that my heart jumped, but the carriage simultaneously hit a rut and jumped too, making it hard to distinguish one jolt from the other. He put my cage back down between the pillows. Then he went on, describing our entire history together to his sister. How first he had seen thousands of us in the Doldrums, clustered upon a floating derelict of a ship. How wondrous we had appeared, drifting from the fog. How his captain had callously unleashed a cannonade. Next he described the storm, the shipwreck, the raft, his rescue at sea, the island, Jaimia, Singapore, *The Rook*, Suez, Cairo, Venice. Listening to that unravelling of our life together, I was much taken by its depth and breadth, how we had shared life and death, sorrow and happiness, loyalty and deceit, greed and sacrifice.

I was even more astounded, embarrassed even, by how highly he spoke of me, telling his sister—ludicrously!—that I had saved his life by merely flying in and out of the window of the rooms behind the McWhirter warehouse, in Singapore. "Jaimia was dying," he said, "but my hummingbird saved me just by being there." I had never given those days and nights another thought. Catherine said she understood, that a life force, however small, instilled hope. "Perhaps, Andrew, one day you will write down all of your adventures in a storybook, so that I and others can live them vicariously." "No," he said, "I don't think so. There are too many heartbreaks."

Zephyrax, I thought, admit it, not only are you friends with him but you are friends with Manon and Marceline and the Navigator. And with several of the horses. Had I the tongue, I would then have described, to his sister, my version of the storybook she wished him to write. How our hummingbird leaders had failed us off the coast at Valparaiso, how we had flown across the Pacific against all common sense, how we descended, after the shipwreck, vindictively, upon Andrew on his raft, thinking to drill holes in his head. We had not done so only because of the lateness of the hour. Then I would have told her more, how we were glue-sticked at Jaimia's island, how we carpeted the sea with our bodies, how we tried to force ourselves through a pitiless sky. How we were scooped up by the baleen of whales. More positively however, I would have told her how he, Andrew, had pried open the bars of my cage on the very first day we met. He had offered me freedom, and surely that was one of the kindest gestures ever made by man to bird. I could have gone on in that appreciative vein for quite a long time, I realized, had I the tongue for it. Well, actually, I did have the tongue for it, but they did not have the ears to hear.

He kissed his sister on the forehead. I could tell that he was preparing to leave the carriage, and I wondered—it hit me like the proverbial thunderbolt—if I might miss him more than he would miss me, when I was gone from Bristol. He was a human being and was forgetful, I was a bird and was not.

Wait, wait, wait, I wanted to say. His hand was on the door latch, pressing it down. "Wait," Catherine said, as though her voice were mine for that moment, and she went on to sing my praises too, saying that she had never seen anything like me, that my beak was so pointed, my wings so transparent, my skills at hovering unsurpassed, my neck feathers a collection of rubies. "I love your little hummingbird too," she said. And he laughed and said he was hardly surprised, for everybody did. Next the carriage came to a halt and he stepped down. I buzzed out of my cage, I flew semicircles around all five of the Arabians, I buzzed the Navigator and the two Sisters of the Lamb Recumbent. Then I flew as high as I could until the air was so thin that my breath was short, yet still I could not see the town of Bristol. ★

ACKNOWLEDGEMENTS

Hummingbirds fly solo, authors do not. Thank you to my wife, Cheryl Ruddock, for reading multiple manifestations of this novel and for drawing various lines in the sand. To Nora Ruddock and Martha Webb, for their advice. Thank you at Breakwater to Rebecca Rose, Jocelyne Thomas, Samantha Fitzpatrick, Nicole Haldoupis, and Claire Wilkshire for their skill and devotion to the cause. They are almost as brave as Zephyrax. Thank you, Rhonda Molloy, for the design. Thank you to the writer Jessica Grant, surely the best editor ever chosen for a book like this. She has the heart of a lion, the eye of an eagle, and experience with talking tortoises. Thank you to James Langer for giving this novel its start towards a life in print. Thank you to Padma Viswanathan and Barry Callaghan for appearing unbidden from the sky, with commendations. Thanks as well to the unlocked vaults and displays of the British Museum, the National Museums of Singapore and Suez, and the Naval Historical Museum of Venice. Thank you finally to the rubythroated hummingbird whose beak caught in our porch screen one summer afternoon, who upon release (a finger touch) showed no gratitude at all, buzzing us furiously for an hour afterwards.

NICHOLAS RUDDOCK is a Canadian physician and writer. His first novel, *The Parabolist* (2010), was shortlisted for a Toronto Book Award and an Arthur Ellis Award. His second novel, *Night Ambulance* (2016), was a Next Generation Indie Book Awards finalist. He has won numerous international prizes for his short fiction, including the Bridport Prize (UK) twice, the Sheldon Currie Fiction Prize, and the Carter V. Cooper Prize. He was shortlisted for the Moth International Poetry Award (Ireland) in 2020 and the *Sunday Times* EFG Short Story Award (UK) in 2016. One of his stories ("How Eunice Got Her Baby") has been filmed by the Canadian Film Centre, directed by Ana Valine and narrated by Gordon Pinsent.

He lives in Guelph, Ontario.